Recipe for Second Chances

"As a reader and a writer, I am always over the moon when I find a new author with a refreshing, wonderful new voice. Such is the case with *Recipe for Second Chances*—I couldn't turn the pages fast enough. When I got to the last page, I felt sad that the story was over. I wanted more. To me that is the mark of a really good writer."

—Fern Michaels, author of 153 (and counting) *New York Times* bestselling novels

"*Recipe for Second Chances* is the ultimate 'one who got away' romance—especially for lovers of lusty chemistry, glamorous locales, and decadent cuisine. A heartwarming, escapist treat!"

—Tia Williams, *New York Times* bestselling author of *Seven Days in June*

"*Recipe for Second Chances* is a sweet, utterly charming romance that swept me away to the Italian countryside, and I never wanted to return! Full of lush settings and mouth-watering food, I absolutely loved every delicious morsel of this book."

—Lynn Painter, *New York Times* bestselling author of *Better Than the Movies*

"This tender, sun-drenched tale of second chances and emotional growth unfolds as richly as ricotta—livened by the lemon tang of the past. *Recipe for Second Chances* will sweep readers away against a vivid backdrop of luscious food and heartwarming friendships."

—Jen Comfort, author of *Midnight Duet*

"Great banter, a sexy good-guy hero, and the kind of strong female friendships we all love to lean on—plus Italian truffles and chocolate cake. I'm in!"

—Elizabeth Bard, bestselling author of *Lunch in Paris* and *Picnic in Provence*

Ali's Cookbooks

"Ali Rosen is saving our dinner parties one dish at a time."

—Carla Hall, chef and television host

"It's a necessary and delicious addition to any collection!"

—Kwame Onwuachi, James Beard Award–winning chef, *Top Chef* judge, and executive producer of *Food & Wine* magazine

"Ali's got us, and I'm so glad that she does."

—Dorie Greenspan, author of *Baking with Dorie* and *Everyday Dorie*

"I want to give Ali Rosen a big high five for writing this book."

—Pati Jinich, James Beard Award–winning and Emmy-nominated host of *Pati's Mexican Table*

Alternate Endings

OTHER TITLES BY
ALI ROSEN

Recipe for Second Chances

COOKBOOKS

Modern Freezer Meals
Bring It!
15 Minute Meals

Alternate Endings

ALI ROSEN

Text copyright © 2024 by Ali Rosen
All rights reserved.

Published by Montlake, Seattle

www.apub.com

Amazon, the Amazon logo, and Montlake are trademarks of Amazon.com, Inc., or its affiliates.

ISBN-13: 9781662513725 (paperback)
ISBN-13: 9781662513718 (digital)

Cover design and illustration by Sarah Horgan

Printed in the United States of America

To Alana:
The most realistic thing in this book is that supportive friendships can survive the distance from Ireland to New York. Love you and always rooting for your rom-com.

I like things that look like mistakes.
—Frances Ha

I love that you can't help but be yourself around me.
—Beyoncé

Chapter One

January 2

I always feel his toenails before anything else. It's like they were designed in a lab to be as sharp as humanly possible. The way I wake up every morning encapsulates motherhood—my son climbing into bed, sweetly wrapping me tight in his arms while also unintentionally drawing blood with his feet.

"Mommy, Mommy, Mommy. It's six thirty. I can wake you up now."

"Just because you *can* doesn't mean you have to," I mumble, pulling my son's warm, bony body closer to me and burrowing my face into his neck for that particular scent of sleepy body and little-kid freshness.

Maybe I hold him tight a little longer than normal. I hate that I'm going to be leaving him tonight, even if it's just for two days. And besides, the Monday morning after New Year's is always going to require a little leeway in my ability to wake up. Especially since this year Bash made me stay up until midnight for his first time ever.

I hate to say I'm feeling a night of Uno and sparkling cider on the second day, but I'm clearly not capable of staying up late anymore. *Is midnight still considered late? Who the hell knows at this point.*

"Can we get out of bed?" Bash murmurs absentmindedly, like his whole heart isn't quite in his request yet.

"How am I supposed to get out of bed when you're wrapped around me like a koala?"

He giggles and clings even tighter in response. "Yeah, but I'm *your* koala. So you can just pick me up with you."

I shake my head at him, but I can't help smiling.

"I don't know if anyone's mentioned this to you, Sebastian Richardson, but you're not the center of the universe. Some of us are allowed to decide when we get out of bed."

"Actually, no one could be the center of the universe," he says earnestly. "The universe has been expanding since the big bang. So there could never be an actual center, since it's always moving. And even if the earth *was* the center of the universe, molten lava in the core would be the center. Not me."

"Enlightening," I deadpan.

I never know whether to be impressed by Bash's spongelike ability to retain information or terrified at how many questions this inevitably prompts in my direction from him. At least he's too preoccupied with asking me about the melting point of marshmallows or the mechanics of the Wonder Wheel to realize that most kids his age would be asking for siblings or wondering why Mommy and Daddy don't live together anymore.

I stumble my way to stand, and Bash jumps on my back. At least I smell the killer combo of coffee and pancakes wafting in from the kitchen.

"Bash!" I hear a voice from the same direction as the coffee. "I think I actually managed to not fuck it up this time!"

I sigh deeply. "Language, Mona!"

"Sorry, but this one actually required serious emphasis."

I roll my eyes through my sleepy fog and try not to fall over as Bash nimbly slides off me and grabs the plate Mona's holding out to him while beaming.

I shouldn't be surprised that they're both ignoring me now. Living with Mona and Bash is like having two cheerleaders going back and forth to pump each other up at every moment of the day. They both live their lives with brazen enthusiasm and no apologies. She's the robust, wild-haired, late-thirties doppelgänger to a lanky, know-it-all six-year-old.

I guess it's fitting that he would be more like his aunt than either of his parents. He got his dad's irrepressible intellect and my can-do attitude, but his entire personality is essentially Mona 2.0. I've inadvertently cloned my best friend by having a kid with her brother.

Mona moved in when Lucas moved out well over a year ago. We all co-own this East Village brownstone together (an investment idea that made *perfect* sense when Lucas and I were, ya know, planning to stay married), so as a temporary fix, Lucas moved into Mona's ground-floor apartment, and she moved upstairs with us.

Except it fit so well we've yet to change the arrangement. And I'm especially grateful for it this morning, when I have to get into the office early, and Mona's going to take Bash to the bus.

I grab a plate and shovel pancakes and coffee into my mouth as quickly as I can before pulling on some clothes, attempting to brush my hair, and haphazardly throwing some items into a suitcase for a trip that I have no idea what to pack for.

I saunter back out into the living room and catch the tail end of Mona and Bash's debate about who's going to misbehave on the bus this morning.

"Ten bucks says Ella makes a fourth grader cry before you even get to school," Mona says, her mouth full of pancakes.

"No *betting* about the behavior of other children," I say to her pointedly, while Bash giggles so hard he snorts into his food. I kiss him on the head. "See you Wednesday night, okay? I promise I won't let this new work travel become a big thing."

"It's okay, Mommy, love you," he says, giving me a squeeze. He's so good. It makes me almost able to ignore the syrup he's just wiped on my pants, and I squeeze him back even harder.

I pull the suitcase out the door and make my way into the cold, bundling up for the walk westward, away from my little pocket of the East Village and up and over toward Flatiron, where my office is.

My phone buzzes in my pocket, and I know I can't ignore it any longer. My perfect Mona and Bash pancake bubble is gone, and in its place is a wall of texts from my ex and my boss—my most frustrating pain in my ass and my most beloved pain in my ass.

Might as well look at the more annoying set first.

Lucas: Bash's chess club is meeting on Tuesdays now instead of Wednesdays.

Lucas: I sent them the payment for the new semester since they said you hadn't done it yet.

Lucas: And I scheduled the parent-teacher conference and put it on your calendar since you didn't respond to my text about it. If the time I picked doesn't work for you I'll just do it by myself.

Lucas: And I'm getting him a haircut since he's with me tonight and it looked too long this weekend.

I feel irritation and relief in equal measure. At least this slew of messages is just his standard run-of-the-mill passive-aggressive non-sense, and he hasn't instead continued the previous week's irritation over tonight's work trip. These texts I can ignore. There's never any point to me responding when Lucas gets into one of these multilayered trains of thought where he has to point out every little thing he does, always with a tone of disapproval.

As though any mother has ever texted her kid's father to share all the things that she does. The piles of sign-up sheets and doctors' appointments and playdates and holiday planning and school supply purchasing and clothes choosing and shoe measuring and stain removal and nail cutting and game setup and every other possible thing that somehow encompasses motherly responsibilities are not shared with Lucas. It's as automatic as Bash wanting me to kiss his boo-boos when he falls down.

But that's not a thought for today. I'll have bigger issues to deal with once he realizes this one-off trip probably isn't going to be so one-off. He gave me so much grief about switching one day of our schedule that I shudder to imagine what that'll turn into if I can't stop it from becoming more than that.

I sigh and swipe into Brigid's messages. Ever since she's been in Ireland, I've been waking up to all her thoughts because of the time difference.

Brigid: Can you get those projections for Q2 organized today so they're ready before you arrive tomorrow?

Brigid: And we can skip over the new year pleasantries, correct? I did not celebrate with a plastic hat. I do not have any resolutions. I assume you are the same.

I snort at her blunt message. Brigid is brilliant and has worked her ass off to build an impressive company from the ground up. No matter how long I work for her, I'll never quite get used to her dry frankness, but she's always liked the way I work efficiently and continually praises me for having, as she says, "No drama that you actually tell me about, thank god." Anyone in our office who ever played games or tried to suck up got the boot so fast their heads must've spun. Brigid has no time or energy for anything other than unfeeling analysis and rigor.

As much as her style might be jarring, I like working for a CEO who's all about the work. The office politics so many of my friends have to deal with don't exist for me. So I appreciate Brigid for who she is. I need more known quantities in my life.

Bea: Roger that, Brigid. Heading in now.

Brigid: Well if you're walking then I imagine you'll be there soon. How someone with such tiny legs can move so rapidly is beyond me.

I laugh and put my phone away.

By the time I make it to the office, I'm ready to tackle the day. A brisk walk in the cold frosts over the external noise from my headspace; if I can keep moving, I'm always okay. I peel off all the many layers that January in New York requires and sit down at my desk.

It's strange seeing Brigid's corner suite empty next to mine. She placed a lot of value (and paid a premium) for Breck Data to have the highest floor in the building and the best views.

She'd spent years working her way up as a data scientist in companies where she was typically the only woman in the room, until she realized there was a gap for marketplace data focused on consumers with children. It wasn't an area viewed as cool or sexy, and as such (and with most things concerning adult women), there was an opening.

Breck Data was started to close that underserved gap, and it has grown exponentially in the ten years since we launched. I find it mildly hilarious that a woman who wanted nothing to do with children has built her own mini data empire from empowering parents. But it works.

And it's always worked for me too. I *love* my job here as the VP of business development. I'm the translator; I'm the harnesser of complexity; I take the abstract work of data scientists and package it into an enticing and understandable metric that everyone needs. I'm good at it.

But looking at Brigid's empty office, I know it's the first time in a decade that maybe I need to push for more—ever since Brigid pushed *me* for more and potentially upended the fragile balancing act I have with my personal and professional lives.

A week before Christmas, she summoned me into her office the moment I came in. Even with a quiet week before the holidays, she still looked impeccable. Her dark-brown hair was styled in her same sleek bob; as always, she wore a statement necklace, and her consistent maroon-red lipstick was paired perfectly with her flawlessly tailored blazer. Brigid was consistently herself, no matter that the engineering team had taken to wearing sweatpants for the week.

"Standing up while I'm sitting isn't giving you quite the height advantage you might hope it would," she said when I walked in.

It's impossible not to enjoy her barbs, since they're undercut by the fact that she secretly loves everyone who works for her far more than she'll ever let on. But I sat down and waited for her to speak. I should've been tipped off to something strange when she momentarily hesitated before getting started.

"Right," she finally said, sitting up even taller in her lithe frame. "So I'm getting divorced and moving back to Ireland."

I did a double take. Thank goodness I wasn't drinking another coffee yet, or I might've spit it out. *What the actual hell?*

"Okay . . . ," I finally said, not quite sure how to react with so many things running through my mind, not the least of which was what the hell was about to happen to my job.

"It's not going to affect you in the slightest," she continued with her typical nonchalance. "The company will still be headquartered here, and we already have the team in Galway anyway, so we're used to doing some things on Irish time. I've already hired that new CTO, and he's starting right after the holidays. All this will do is perhaps accelerate our plans to expand into the European market. I know you don't really have extra bandwidth right now, but I want you to take over managing this office—"

"But I—"

I could think of a million reasons why I didn't want to suddenly be everyone's de facto boss. I'd barely had a moment to digest that Brigid would no longer be in the office every day, let alone adding in additional responsibilities.

"Don't argue. If you say yes, I can convince the board to make your title fancier. And in exchange, you won't have to actually do anything differently, just be the person who has to deal with people when they need a tiebreaker in the office." *So essentially my job already*, I conceded to myself, realizing that arguing was probably futile.

"You don't really want my opinion, right?" I finally said.

"Not really at all, no," she replied.

"All righty then. Apologies for your divorce—"

"None needed."

"—and let me know if you need anything else from me at this particular moment."

"Right. I'm going to plan for you and the rest of the executive team to come out to Ireland in January so we can make plans for moving forward."

At that she'd opened up her laptop again to signal that she was done with the conversation.

Later that day, her assistant forwarded me plane tickets to Ireland and blocked off two days in my calendar for the first week of January. Brigid and I didn't speak about any of it for the rest of the week.

The lack of discussion about her personal life wasn't surprising. Hell, it's one of the things I like most about my work-life. When I was drowning in personal crises, this was the one place I could come where no one knew, no one asked, and I was only being judged on the merits of my work. I brought in clients and money, the two things that made the entire business worthwhile. As long as I did that well—and I most certainly did—no one ever bothered me about anything else. I could give Brigid the same courtesy of not prying.

But with our mandated time off for Christmas and New Year's, I had more time to think than I usually allow myself. And the only conclusion I came to was that if Brigid was going to change the rules of our finely tuned operation—at the worst possible time for me—then I needed to set my own terms too. Maybe we don't talk about our personal lives, but my life is too fragile right now to not play my cards, when she's playing hers.

Things with Lucas have felt like a tentative tightrope walk above a viper pit for the past year. We'd preliminarily agreed to the house swap and that Bash would stay with him every other weekend, since we both wanted Bash to sleep in the same place during the school week. Bash has dinner with his father two nights on the weeks when he doesn't have the weekend, but I know Lucas is itching for more.

And now, the actual divorce and custody negotiations are looming later this year. If Brigid is going to ask me to travel to her constantly, then that'll be Lucas's perfect ammo to change everything. I need more than just a fake title boost. I need a raise and a promise that the travel won't last forever so I can buy Lucas out of the house but still have negotiating leverage for custody.

So maybe Brigid and I won't talk about my reasons, but tomorrow, when I land in Ireland, we're sure as hell going to talk about it. Talking frankly about business has *always* been something we've been able to do.

But in the meantime, there's not a damn thing I can do about it today. Today I need to pull everything together and get to the airport in time for my flight so I can kick ass when I arrive.

I'm going to keep walking forward as quickly as I can and play by the rules that are already set for me.

CHAPTER TWO

JANUARY 3

The gray overcast sky only makes driving up to Brigid's new house—mansion? castle? lair?—seem more dramatic. A five-hour overnight flight and an hour-long drive through misty, vibrantly green County Clare has made me too sleep deprived to prepare for this level of total Brigidness.

When Brigid explained that we would all be meeting at her new estate, I hadn't really given it much thought. But of course when she sold her over-the-top apartment in New York, I should've assumed she would purchase something equally absurd in Ireland.

I knew she'd grown up here, but since we blessedly never discuss anything personal in detail, I sort of just expected we'd be in Dublin or some other city-adjacent area. But apparently when Brigid starts over, she really starts over.

As my cab drives up to the entrance of what is clearly a historic behemoth, I gawk at my surroundings. Solid gray stone is covered in patches by curling vines creeping their way northward. Small turrets at the top give an air of grandiosity that's impossible to ignore.

"Welcome to Callaghan Castle, Miss Leal," a portly middle-aged man says with a flourish as he opens my door and I practically tumble out, startled by the gesture.

So, I guess castle *it is, then.*

I straighten up and try to compose myself, then reach out my hand to shake his, which he returns with fervor.

"I'm Des Cronin, and I manage the house for Miss Breck."

"Nice to meet you, Des," I say, trying to give him back a smile that matches his own enthusiasm.

It's a bitterly cold January day, but Des seems content in a scratchy-looking mustard-yellow sweater and a beat-up pair of corduroys. His weathered look is a perfect match for the imposing limestone masonry and massive wooden door that stand behind him. He follows my curious gaze up the castle.

"It's so lovely havin' Miss Breck living here now. Parts of this castle were built over seven hundred years ago, an' the most recent owners were hoping to sell it to someone who wouldn't turn it into an Airbnb." I snort at the modern conundrum, and I see Des's eyes crinkle in amusement. "Don't think it's too batty; Ireland has over thirty thousand castles and castle ruins, ya know. We went a bit mad for 'em when the Normans invaded an' everyone was fighting, so they all needed fortification."

"That's just about the most succinct history lesson I've ever received," I reply. I love the chortle that trickles out of him, like he can't help but release it.

"Miss Breck said yeh'd be my favorite." He winks as he grabs my bag from the back of the car and starts heading inside. "Come on then, everyone else is already gathered in the drawing room having a cup o' tea."

I cringe at the thought of seeing all my work colleagues when I look bedraggled coming off a plane. If I can be anything, it's put together externally.

But then again, nothing about this morning is normal. Instead of meeting up with Brigid and our team in a typical New York office setting, I feel as though I've bumped my head and slipped through a portal to a cozy but monumental Irish castle, complete with—apparently—chandeliers, worn burgundy carpets, and wooden banisters so ornate it's hard to stop myself from running my hands along them.

The drawing room is in the same vein—light-turquoise carpet melds into elaborate butter yellow drapes, and another chandelier highlights the carved wooden ceiling. A green toile wallpaper covers the walls, and I would've fully questioned whether I was in the right place if it hadn't been for Brigid and two of our other colleagues, Lane and Greg, lounging on the worn sky blue couch and talking animatedly while holding teacups with excessively floral patterns.

"Oh good, Bea's finally arrived," Brigid says, beckoning me to come sit down, with no explanation whatsoever for how we've all ended up in this strange new home of hers. Even in a more casual setting, she still has her signature maroon lips and a necklace that probably weighs five pounds. "Let's wait for Jack to come down, and then we can get started."

I look over to Lane, and she whispers, *"The new CTO."*

"Ah." I nod back. I forgot Brigid was having our new chief technology officer start with this trip.

"Do you want to go up to your room or anything first?" Lane asks, her eyes still on me. Bless our CFO. She might spend her days staring at numbers and spreadsheets, but she's an intuitive people person who can always read the room.

But I also know Brigid well enough to know that the shower I'm so desperately aching for is not in the cards for me at this moment.

"Thanks, Lane, I appreciate that, but I'm okay."

I shoot her a grateful look, and the small smile she gives me lets me know she understands completely. I wish I could pull her aside and ask whether she knows more about the castle and what on earth Brigid is thinking with this move. Are we really going to just roll up to this place and have countryside brainstorming with a side of fishing and horseback riding (or whatever else goes on at a castle? How the hell would I know?)?

I plop down on the sofa and try to smooth out all the wrinkles from my shirt.

I hear Brigid trill from across the couch, "Good, Jack's here; let's start."

I look up, and the view is like a sledgehammer to my chest.

This castle really *is* some kind of messed-up *Alice in Wonderland* fever hallucination.

You know when you see someone completely out of context, and it's so startling because they just do not fit in the place where you are? That is what's happening to me as I see that Jack, our new CTO, is also Jack Sander, high school ex-boyfriend (*sort of?*), claimer of my decades-lost virginity, and confusing contrarian, whom I haven't seen in twenty years.

And the only man before Lucas who I'd wanted to strangle.

I'm so startled that I actually move one hand slowly over to the other one and lightly pinch myself just to be extra sure I'm not dreaming/nightmaring/hallucinating.

Nope. Still in reality.

And based on the subtle raised eyebrows when he sees me, I'm also definitely not mistaking him for someone else.

"Long time, Beatrice," he says, and I'm momentarily unable to respond.

It's like seeing a ghost. A very tall, very solid, ice-blue-eyed ghost with the same damn floppy hair and just a few more crinkles at the sides of his eyes.

Long time? As though the last time I saw him hadn't ended with me crying and him never saying another word to me again. *Not long enough to forget you're an asshole, buddy.*

He's watching me, and I can't tell what the man is thinking. He was always like a goddamn sphinx, unreadable and unknowable, and the recall of it all zaps through me like a static shock.

With everything I'm worried about with Lucas and custody and unexpected work travel . . . now I have *this* to contend with too?

"Ah, you already know each other," Brigid says, blissfully unaware of the roil of rage I'm trying to contain. "Good. So let's get to it."

I exhale the breath I didn't even know I was holding and silently give thanks for Brigid's total encompassing work focus, so I can get a grip.

Jack sits down on the only chair left available, which happens to be right next to me, but he shifts his gaze over to whatever Brigid is now talking about.

It's infuriating that he's sitting close enough where I catch his post-shower smell. It hits me like a sensory déjà vu. The man has not upgraded his soap in twenty years. He's like the basic boy starter pack of Old Spice lilting off him. Half of me wants to slap him across the face in revenge for my teenage self, but the other half is paralyzed by memories of a different kind. I'm a sixteen-year-old sneaking into his room in the middle of the afternoon again, snickering in a shower, that soap lingering in the steam.

I take a deep breath, cross my legs, and try to shove that image out of my mind.

It's also just dawned on me that I'm decidedly *not* smelling like a freshly showered person, and I cringe as I look down at my leggings. I may have come far enough in my life to no longer care about what Jack Sander thinks of me, but I am *always* put together, if nothing else. A messy bun, no makeup, and stale crumbs lingering on my shirt is not the ideal way to see anyone you haven't seen in twenty years.

Twenty years.

Shit. And now I just feel old. *Thirty-six cannot be old.* Have I really been having sex for twenty years? Have I now been having sex significantly longer than I wasn't? Does it still count if a few of those years went by the wayside because I was in a bad marriage and basically stopped having sex?

"Bea?" I swivel my gaze over to Brigid and realize everyone is looking at me. "Did you sleep on the plane at all?"

"Oh, sorry," I say, snapping myself back into focus. "I missed what you said?"

"I was asking about the second quarter projections."

"Oh sure, let me pull those right up."

I scramble into my bag for my laptop and fumble it out, then open it up to the PowerPoint deck I created for this meeting.

"Sorry, yeah, just a little jet-lagged; don't worry, I'll get over it."

I launch into my bullet points, letting the muscle memory of everything I've been working on take over.

This has always been my superpower, and I'm relieved it isn't failing me now. The last few years I've been especially grateful to have honed the ability to block out whatever is buzzing around my personal life when I need to work. I'm the master of it.

And apparently I'm able to get off a flight with practically no sleep, rock up to a charmingly lavish house with no explanation, learn that the junk food in man form from my teenage years is now working with me, and still give a presentation that my boss will love.

We all go back and forth over the next hour, bouncing ideas off each other; I have to admit that being outside the office and focused like this is remarkably productive. I've always been impressed by the talent that Brigid assembles. She hires the best people and then, like a well-dressed conductor, keeps us all moving forward in harmony.

And it feels like battery acid in my stomach to admit that that also probably means Jack isn't going anywhere soon.

It's been easy to ignore him for most of the conversation, since he's apparently still the kind of man who absorbs rather than shares. Granted, he's new, but I would've expected a recently appointed CTO to try to mark his territory a bit more. But that never was Jack's style, even when I knew him at an age when most teenage boys are at the peak of insecurity.

Today he's pulled together and neat, with a fancy pen and pristine notebook at the ready. Infuriating.

"Let's take a break for now," Brigid says, standing with that flair of finality she always has when she's done with a conversation. "We can all meet in the dining room in half an hour, since, Bea, you really should probably shower and change."

I close my eyes and take in another deep breath, trying to ignore the (*definitely correct*) comment. While I slowly stand up, Lane and Greg walk out behind Brigid, chatting about their flights in.

I realize Jack is watching me, and I'm jolted.

"How've you been, Beatrice?" he finally says.

Ugh, of course. With him it was always "Beatrice." I used to find it charming and grown up, but in this moment it's exceptionally annoying and way too familiar.

"Fine," I say, sharper than I intend.

I can't help it, though—I'm exhausted and already annoyed at another series of passive-aggressive texts from Lucas, so adding Jack into my day is like a blast-from-the-past lighter fluid designed to make me want to burn all men to the ground. *Seriously? This guy?*

He raises an eyebrow, but I raise one right back. It should've been obvious that even twenty years later we wouldn't be capable of small talk.

We never were.

And so for a moment we just stand silently, staring. It feels unfair—I'm struck by the familiarity of being dwarfed by his stature, but now that swimmer's frame he always carried so smoothly has broadened to make him even more arresting in person than he was as an eighteen-year-old kid. His white tee and jeans sit on him like they're confident to be there.

He breaks eye contact first, and some immature part of me wants to feel smug about it. He reaches into his bag to get something, and the smugness is replaced by confusion when I see he's pulled out a scone and is holding it out to me.

"Do you need a snack?" he says simply.

"Why?" I ask, eyes narrowing, waiting for the catch.

"I seem to recall a fondness for snacks and a not fondness for being hungry," he replies.

We're somehow both swimming in unmistakable familiarity that's as obvious as daylight. But it has to be mockery I'm seeing and not sincerity. After all, he still has the same small smirk of a smile.

So I take the scone. Because, yeah, once I saw the damn thing, it was pretty clear I was obviously hungry.

I take a bite, and he's still watching. "Don't act like you know me," I finally say, and it makes him snort a laugh. I narrow my eyes. "What?"

"I like that you still get flustered when you're hangry."

I gasp. "You can't say that to a colleague!" I admonish, like the goody-two-shoes sixteen-year-old I was when he last knew me.

He holds up his hands in surrender. "Sorry. I'll just . . . leave you to your scone."

He gives me a sheepish smile, and the way my body instantly reacts to that look wallops me. But neither of us moves to leave; I guess we're both stuck in sensory overload.

He's disarming, this ghost, this memory, this intangible person whose retention in my pores I'd been able to write off in subsequent years as teenage infatuation. But being in front of Jack, traitorous skin pulsing at the sight of him, it's clear that that assumption was me giving myself the easy way out. I spent so many years being angry for how we'd ended that I forgot that a lot of my anger was rooted in losing the one person who'd somehow made me feel exposed and protected, all at the same time.

I should be immune to him at this point, and it's infuriating to realize I'm not.

But I'm sure as hell going to make myself be. Between Lucas's texts burning a hole in my pocket and Jack standing in front of me, I've already had enough for today of this memory lane stroll between the first man who made me feel like I wasn't enough and the last. At least they both strengthened me into building my walls so high that no one can get to me now.

"Well," I say, standing up straighter—and trying to ignore the fact that I have crumbs falling off me and strands of hair stuck to my face—"I imagine we'll have time to catch up, now that we're going to be working together. Nice to have you on the team."

I walk out before he can say anything else, so pleased with myself for my maturity and tact. Jack Sander is not going to goad me, ever again. I'm not goadable anymore. I'm a grown woman, immune to reticent men who subconsciously make it their goal to somehow be both my tormenter and my fantasy.

So why is it that when I get back up to my room, all I can think of is the memories that have suddenly been rereleased, buried treasure accidentally rediscovered and unearthed?

And while I *want* to be indignant and *want* to stew in the last time I saw him, I can't stop a different day from battling its way to the front of my memory. All I can picture is the first time he kissed me.

CHAPTER THREE
TWENTY YEARS AGO

My heart squeezed at the sight I had all to myself.

It's not just that Jack was hot—anyone would see that instantly; looking at his frame directly felt a little bit like staring into the sun—but that fact had become a given in the last few months of knowing him.

The heart squeezing came later, though. That came from chipping below the bust's exterior slowly and delicately over time. For the most part he *was* as silent as a stone. We were two determined worker bees seated side by side in art class.

But we had the same deadpan sense of humor, and I found myself making quips just to see the shape of his lips when they pressed together, quietly trying to avoid giving me the smile I knew he was keeping from me.

The heart squeezing today, however, came from the way he'd already carefully set out my half-assed canvas and lowered the easel to my pint-size height; the way he'd meticulously lined up all my brushes in the order he knew I used them; how he'd gotten me two cups of water for light and dark paints, even though he'd taunted me a thousand times by reminding me that it didn't matter.

"Standing and watching me work isn't going to magically help finish your project, Beatrice," he griped without turning around.

I smirked, even though he couldn't see me. His ice-blue eyes were fixed on the painting he was working on. There was no indication that he even noticed me except for the commentary. I imagined that in his mind, I was like an annoying little sister he begrudgingly found amusing.

It would've been mortifying if he could've seen the role he played in my mind.

"It's not my fault that your work is so bad it stops me in my tracks," I countered.

"Charming."

All I could see was his sandy hair and the back of his head, although I was desperate to see his attempts to hide his grin. Jack had this young Harrison Ford sort of look that *maybe* made me go back and watch Indiana Jones a few times just to see that swoopy side grin they have in common.

I sat down and stared at my own half-finished work. I was already distracted.

When we sat together like this, I relished the stillness around us. It was Saturday night, so no one else was even breathing near the campus art building of our high school. The hazy streetlamps beamed in through the floor-to-ceiling windows, and we sat inside our glass box and painted.

I couldn't remember how these evenings started, but by this point they felt as essential to me as air. No whirring schedule, no obligations, no socializing. Just a paintbrush and a quiet friend. A safe space to be ourselves outside the normal school weekday hours.

"How was your meet?" I asked, delicately retiring the banter. Every Wednesday and every Saturday he competed in the pool, and then at night he came here.

"We won," he said without looking over, the phrase tinny and hollow.

"Your enthusiasm is deafening."

From this angle I could see his face out of the corner of my eye, and I caught the small twitch at the edge of his lips. Even his fraction of a smile was enough to make my heart pound.

"My dad was there today; he brought some recruiters," he sighed.

I waited, giving him the silent space to decide how much to say. My words were always casually thrown out, splattering across the room, but his were measured. His counted. When he shared something, it was on purpose.

"It was fine because I knew I got to be here tonight," he said finally.

A nonanswer, but one that spoke volumes.

I wish I wasn't equally as enamored with melancholy Jack as I was with just plain hot Jack, but again, I couldn't help it. *He laid out my brushes for me.*

He didn't say anything else, and I didn't ask him more. We both zoned into the projects we were working on, the mood calm.

I knew his older brothers all played sports at the same college where his dad had gone. It went without saying that that's what was expected of him too. Yet if I could bet everything I owned, I would bet it was not what Jack wanted. I was an only child with mild, straightforward parents, and my family ran easily, like a car with a well-oiled engine; Jack's seemed to be a bit rusted from within.

Although how the hell would I really know? All I got were these snippets, these guesses, these fractions of intimacy that I was probably reading too much into.

But sometimes I was so sure I knew him that I could practically taste it. Sometimes I couldn't help but believe that this wholly new, all-consuming urge I felt standing next to him was indisputable chemistry. That it was two sided. An electric current needs something to bounce off of to exist. And for me, it *existed*, deep in my marrow, with pining-level chemistry.

He started rustling around in his bag, and I soaked in the chance to watch him, his worn-out jeans hugging close as he leaned over to find whatever he was missing.

He pulled out a chocolate bar and two hamburger buns from his bag, and I couldn't stop my grin.

"Can I help you?" he asked, evidently noticing the glee written all over my face.

"That's just . . ." I was trying to stop myself from laughing.

"What?"

"What's your plan there?" I finally said.

He turned toward me, a full-body readjustment, and it was a little bit like adding a burst of air to a fire, fanning all the flames I could tamp down when I wasn't looking at him so directly.

But he didn't seem to notice that my grin was replaced by wide-eyed admiration. I doubted he ever noticed me noticing him. "I was going to offer you some," he said, "but not if you're going to mock it."

You know when you only want something because someone says you can't have it? That is now how I instantly felt about hamburger buns.

"Oh no, I'm not mocking," I said sincerely.

"Yes, you were," he teased, still with only that crinkle of a smile, his face not betraying him nearly as swiftly as mine always does.

"Jaaaack," I said, trying to temper the whininess that wanted to escape. "I wasn't, I swear. It just wasn't . . . what I was expecting."

"They had snacks after the meet. I didn't think an actual burger would hold. But this can be like a . . . like a chocolate croissant or sandwich or something."

"I love it," I replied sincerely without even considering, and I moved to take it out of his hands. But he lifted both items up high and far out of my reach. His arms were so damn long. Another way to make me feel like an annoying little kid around him.

"You only want it now because you're competitive," he replied, and my mouth dropped. Damn it. He saw everything.

"I am not! Anyone would want a . . . chocolate burger?" I was trying not to laugh again, I swear I was, but the idea that you could just stick a chocolate bar inside a bun and turn it into a snack was both endearing and ridiculous.

"See! You think it's a dumb idea."

"It's a great idea."

"You only want it now because I'm saying you can't have it."

"I would never do that," I lied.

"You only played Trivial Pursuit with me because I said I was really good at it, and you insisted you were, too, even though you'd clearly never played."

"I absolutely love Trivial Pursuit."

"You didn't know how to put the pieces in the pie," he pointed out.

"Doesn't mean I can't grow to love it."

Ugh, did that come out as breathily as it sounded in my head? I couldn't unhear it once I said it, and it instantly made me look at him with that longing I always got when I remembered that he wasn't really mine.

But he didn't seem to notice; he rolled his eyes at me, acquiescing, and he wordlessly snapped the chocolate bar in half, slid a piece into the bun, and handed the concoction over. Our fingers brushed, and I wondered how the chocolate didn't melt from the contact. But instead of ruminating on *that* embarrassing thought, I took a bite.

And my grin came back. Because actually, it was, admittedly, extremely delicious. And for the first time all night, he grinned at me too. The full force of finally getting a real smile out of him was a warm, glowing spotlight.

Then, without saying what I would have said (*I told you so*), he turned back to his painting. The grin dimmed a bit and settled into a self-satisfied contentment as we both refocused on the task at hand.

Sometimes I wanted to shake him and just say, *Hey, isn't this easy? Don't we have fun together? Don't you feel this too?* That ease, that support, that sense of a trust fall come to life? Like a person who'd catch me if I stumbled but also would probably be the one doing the pushing, making me go out on every limb for my own betterment.

But I couldn't say it. Because I'd ruin whatever this safe space was that we were for each other.

So for another hour we sat quietly painting. He never ate a snack for himself, but I certainly finished mine. And we focused on the task at hand, together but lost in our own little worlds.

"Do you have more of that burnt orange color?" he finally asked, breaking the silence.

He swiveled his chair so he was facing me, and I turned, smug that he needed something.

"The one you're looking at that you clearly know I've been hoarding?"

"I just need a tiny dollop," he said with a sigh.

I couldn't help myself, incapable of not poking and prodding at him, like a toddler who wants attention. I lightly dragged my paintbrush through the color and dotted it on his nose.

"All yours," I singsonged gleefully, enjoying the perplexity on his face as he decided whether to laugh or shout.

He stood up and took a step toward me. I was sitting on a stool that'd been pumped up as far as it could go, but he was still towering over me. Looking up at him from this angle so closely put every inch of my body on high alert, as involuntary as breathing.

He watched me, clearly still deciding, and I hated that he was always able to be so neutral, without giving off any hint of what lay beneath.

He took a single finger to the paint fleck on his nose, removed most of the paint, and then slowly, nimbly, placed it on mine. And then his whole face lit up into the sweetest mischievous smile I'd ever seen.

Was I dying right now? Because I couldn't breathe anymore. I don't think I'd ever seen my stoic, sarcastic, sort-of-friend look at me with so much *joy* before. And I couldn't explain what was happening to my heart rate.

"Why'd you do that?" I whispered, batting away at his fingers.

But he caught my wrist in his hand, and everything shifted.

It was too deliberate. This wasn't one of his shoulder nudges or accidental brushes against my arm that previously would have set my entire body on fire. He was holding me, and he could surely feel my pulse raging.

My mind was racing too. *Is this what being turned on feels like? Is it always this amazing? Because if it is, I can see why people are obsessed with sex.*

He'd barely touched me, and that electrical current felt so loaded that it could've exploded, and I'd turn into a pile of dust right in front of him.

"Just for once I wanted to do what I wanted," he murmured, his thumb grazing my wrist.

We both stared at each other for a few moments, unsure, magnetized. And then he pulled me toward him, his lips hungry on mine, and suddenly every new sensation I'd been feeling ever since the day we met was engulfed by something stronger than I knew was possible.

CHAPTER FOUR

Okay, so maybe it was premature to think I could be immune to Jack.

I am not immune.

But I'm also taking too much satisfaction in watching Jack's clipped response to me goading him into taking a hard-line position on whether tech companies need more regulation. *Maybe* I suspected that he would hate that.

I will say that a shower and fresh clothes have hardened my resolve to be a better person and live in the present and ignore Jack regarding anything but work.

But now we're all sitting down for lunch, and Brigid's been talking about some article she read this morning about new regulations. I see him twitching, and I just *know* he's going to have something to say about it.

The temptation to find out how much has changed is too great. So I've solidly championed something I don't really care about.

And yup, nothing has changed. Not one iota.

"From an engineer's perspective, there's a lot of potential downsides both to creativity and consumer growth," he says, his fork in midair, clearly punctuating his point. I want to stab back.

"Thank you for mansplaining tech companies to a bunch of executives at a tech company," I reply dryly.

Lane and Greg try to stifle their laughs, but I adore that Brigid just snorts loudly in amusement.

"I'm not . . ." He pauses, and I watch the flicker of realization in his eyes. He knows I don't really care.

And maybe he also knows I'm messing with him. I can visibly see him toning himself down, like a gas flame being intentionally reduced from a roar to a low flicker once the pot is already boiling. He was always good at putting up a mask when he wanted to be inscrutable, and I can see now he's adapted that talent for his professional life as well.

"We'll just have to agree to disagree, Beatrice," he finally responds cordially, instantly taking back the upper hand.

I viscerally blanch. The teenager inside me is still swinging wildly, trained to poke at this man until I win whatever we're arguing about. It's muscle memory; it's second skin that's slipped back on without me even noticing.

Except he's shed his at a moment's notice and replaced it with a sleek, professional, adult veneer. And I need to bottle my petulance up and quickly wrap my extra twenty years' worth of maturity back around me like a trench coat.

I grab a piece of Irish soda bread from the wicker basket at the center of the table and focus on sloshing it with a heavy coating of the rich whipped butter next to it.

"Did you two used to work together?" Greg asks, trying to find the light between the cracks of whatever is unreadable about this situation.

"Nope," Jack says succinctly, grabbing his own piece of bread and dipping it casually into the lamb stew steaming in the bowl in front of him.

The question is lingering, like a balloon that's a few days old and starting to wilt.

And I, unfortunately, have never met an awkward silence I didn't feel compelled to fill. "We went to high school together, but we were in different grades." Greg and Lane are nodding along but haven't said anything else, and Brigid looks bored, so naturally I keep going. "We took an art class at the same time. We were paired up together for this one project. I mean, just one semester, obviously. But that's when we met, because otherwise we were in different grades, but then we . . . stayed friends."

I'm babbling. *Why am I so nervous?*

Jack is watching me again but saying nothing to bail me out. I bet he barely remembers any of this anyway.

"So where've you been between high school and here?" Greg jokes to Jack, missing all my blustering and amusing himself by getting back to what clearly was his original question.

"I did my bachelor's and master's in computer science; then I worked at Microsoft for a few years, then for two smaller companies, got promoted to CTO at the last one, and now I'm here."

Greg nods, obviously happy to be back on a solid, boring, job-focused topic. But Lane, ever the people person, has to interject: "And what about outside of work? Hobbies? Family?"

I'm annoyed with myself at how much I lean in to hear the answer to this one. I'm not *not* curious about what Jack's been up to for the last twenty years.

"Oh no, I mostly just work," he says with a shrug.

"I can see why Brigid loved you," Lane says with a laugh, and Brigid swats her good naturedly.

"How so?" Jack asks sincerely.

"Oh," Lane says, clearly taken aback at even the thought of trying to explain Brigid to anyone, especially in front of her face. Brigid has arched an eyebrow in Lane's direction, so I can see she's thinking the same thing. "I guess . . . 'mostly just work' sounds like it should be her motto, I suppose," Lane says diplomatically.

"Isolation as a virtue," Greg chuckles, waving his arms at our surroundings.

But Jack doesn't seem to be laughing. "Sounds ideal," he says.

"Really?" Lane isn't buying what he's selling.

"If this is Brigid's dream life, then I get it. I love my work. I love living by myself. No one tells you what to do, and there's always problems to tease out to keep you busy and entertained." Lane is still staring at him, clearly unconvinced, so he seems to try to relent a little. "Come on, I'm a coder at heart. Don't you expect us to like sitting in a dark, quiet room alone with headphones on?"

I can see his answer placates Lane and Greg. He's forced himself into an understandable archetype that they can paint over. But I'm watching his eyes. They've always been the giveaways on his otherwise stoic face. I can see the *more*. I can see the boy who used to do everything he was told, and I can see that he's somehow managed to burn that all down. I wonder how. The succinct single-sentence career answer didn't answer *that* part.

He must notice me watching, since he crosses his arms (in a way that . . . doesn't make me *not* notice how good his arms look), and I get the sense that for whatever I see in his eyes, he's catching what's behind mine too. He sees into me like I'm a code he's hacked and can flip through easily without warning. There's that déjà vu again, only now the only thing I know is how much about him I currently *don't* know.

It's unsettling.

I *hate* that those eyes still somehow snake right through me and into my gut. The air feels charged, and I resent it; I resent my adult self—my successful executive and mother adult self—for somehow trip-wiring back to adolescent attraction with a man who crushed me like a bug.

But if the tension feels like a high wire for me, Brigid clearly doesn't notice or doesn't care and has already mentally moved on. "Were you able to get the design team's notes for the updates, Jack? I'd like to see them after lunch."

"Yup, I have them at the ready for you to look at whenever you want," he replies, seemingly unruffled.

His eyes flick back over to me, and I wonder if he can see the unease that's surely written all over my face. But he's rearranged himself and now seems as serene as the glassy lake outside the castle.

I want to say something. I have so many questions on the tip of my tongue. I want to still be angry, the way I felt toward him for *decades* after we stopped speaking, but seeing him in person, the anger is mixing with everything else he always made me feel. With only a few words, looks, and scones (?!) exchanged between us today, somehow that convoluted internal web extending through my veins is already the same that it always was with him—attraction, fondness, intrigue, and exasperation.

Damn it.

My reverie is broken by Bash's ringtone (his very on-the-nose choice of Bill Withers's "Just the Two of Us"), and I almost drop my phone in surprise from the interruption. I mouth *sorry* to Brigid and abruptly stand up, answering the FaceTime as I walk to the other side of the room.

"Are we Sebastian the crabby this morning or Bashful the happy?" I whisper, unable to contain my smile at his sleepy face crowding into my screen.

"Crabby, because Daddy's apartment doesn't have pancakes." He makes a pouty face, but I can tell his heart's not really in it, and a hint of a smile is lurking behind it.

"Mona's literally upstairs, Bash, and considering she's the only one who makes the perfect pancakes, you don't need me to be there for this equation to work."

"Daddy says we don't need to bother Mona."

"Well, he's being nice and giving her a morning off," I say sincerely, with just a petty dash of hope that Lucas is listening to my compliment so I'll get credit somewhere in his mind for being nice. "I'll be home tomorrow night anyway, so you'll have a regular school night."

"I know, it's okay."

It's the first time he's slept out of his normal bed on a night before school. I feel so much guilt that I've disrupted his already uprooted life of schedules and parent shuffling, even if I know he doesn't ever mind being at Lucas's.

"Thanks, kid. I hope you're being good for Daddy."

"I'm always good!"

"The rubber ants and cockroaches I found in my bed the other day might disagree with that."

He tries to giggle without me noticing, and I love the way the phone shakes from his silent laughter. "I have no idea who put those there."

"Me neither. I'd better call the exterminator."

"You should!"

"And you should go get dressed so you aren't late for the bus. Thanks for calling me before school—I appreciate seeing your face."

"I love your face, Mommy."

"Love yours too, Bash."

After a quick kiss, the call ends, and I'm left looking back at a blank screen mirroring the goofy smile on my face.

I turn around and realize everyone at the table is watching me, all of them having gone respectfully quiet so I wouldn't be bothered on my phone call. But now that it's over, I'm self-conscious that a little piece of my personal life was so openly exposed. Everyone at Breck Data knows I have a kid, but I suppose they've never actually seen me in mom mode.

"Sorry, everyone," I say breezily, slipping back into my chair as I grasp for something to say into the silence to make everyone stop focusing on me.

"Don't say sorry for that," Jack replies quietly.

I whip my head around, ready to pounce at being told what to do. Maybe I shouldn't be so jumpy at work, but with Jack, I never could help giving him my unvarnished self, and apparently, nothing's changed after twenty years.

Only, when I really look at him, the expression on his face is not the mansplaining version I've become used to seeing lately with Lucas. It's sincerity and encouragement. It's shades of that safe space that always nudged me not to give others too much of myself.

I'm so shocked to see that again that I'm momentarily lost for words.

Thankfully, Brigid being Brigid, she doesn't notice or let the moment linger. "Right, well, the other thing I wanted to discuss with everyone is the schedule going forward." That has my attention. My churning confusion over Jack is going to have to get compartmentalized. "I'm going to need all of you—the whole executive team, really—to come to Ireland bimonthly so we can meet together in person like this. I think this'll work really well, and I want to make sure we get it regularly on the books. So we'll start planning for that."

She snaps her attention over to Jack, as if to indicate that the conversation now is truly over. "We can go over those notes here, if you want to," she says to him, and he dutifully pulls his laptop out, already back in work mode without another thought to what she's just said.

But even though she's wordlessly dismissed the rest of us, I can't stop staring at Brigid, unable to move even if I wanted to. There's nothing shittier for a single mom to hear than an offhand comment that's going to mean having to be in another country twice a month, every single month. This is worse than I thought.

I'm trying to imagine whose reaction is going to be more extreme—Bash, once he realizes how often I'll be gone, or Lucas, once I try to adjust our schedule even the slightest amount.

Definitely Lucas. Always Lucas.

I've got to get in front of this.

"Brigid, can we chat for a minute when you're done here?" I ask, trying to keep the shakiness I'm feeling out of my voice.

"Sure, come find me in an hour or so," she says, her eyes already on Jack's computer, completely unaware that she's dropped an even larger bomb on my life than I was already expecting.

I pace around my room for an hour, unable to get anything done other than try to psych myself up for the conversation I know I need to have.

Today has been a one-two punch of all my insecurities piling on me. First, a reminder that I'm never enough for anyone—I'm already painfully aware that I wasn't for Lucas, but then this morning I got to relive the memory that I *also* wasn't enough for Jack twenty years ago either.

And on top of that, I've got the ultimate stone weighing down the pit of my stomach: imagining standing in front of a judge and explaining how, right when my son's life has been upended by his parents' separation, I've decided to jaunt off to Ireland every two weeks. It doesn't matter that I'm great at my job. It doesn't matter that it gives me financial stability. It doesn't matter that Lucas also travels for work. All it'll look like is that I'm the mother who left her kid in his time of need.

But damn it, too much is at stake to have a pity party for myself and let the opinions of men affect me. I'm going to fight to save the two good things in my life. I'm not going to be forced to choose between the job that makes me happy and the kid who makes my world go round.

If I really can't talk Brigid out of this destabilizing idea, then I need to insist on a raise. And a real title bump. It's the only way I'll be able to stave off Lucas's accusations that I'm not prioritizing. At least if I can contain his frustrations and attach my plans to a promotion, then I'll be able to control the narrative. And maybe make the difficult parts seem more temporary.

By the time I walk back downstairs to see Brigid, I'm ready.

Except all that psyching myself up apparently wasn't necessary, because Brigid stands up the minute she sees me and starts talking.

"Oh good, Bea. Listen, I know you and I talked in December about changes that will come with my move. So I'm temporarily making you the chief revenue officer, and I've got something in the works that will convince the board to give you an even better title bump that comes with an actual raise. Just give me a few months, and you'll see—this is going to be great for you."

I'm momentarily rooted, chewing gum stuck to a desk, the fight I was preparing for halted by her words.

"That, um . . . that sounds good, Brigid."

"Is that what you wanted to talk about?" she asks.

"Well . . . yes," I say lamely.

"What did you think, I was going to make you fly out here constantly and not have a plan to make it worth your while?"

I want to say *Uh, yeah*, but I refrain. Surely she can still see it written all over my face, though.

She tsks at me, like I'm a schoolgirl who's disappointed the teacher, pats me on the shoulder, and walks out of the room.

I should've known that in a world of disappointing men I still need to fight, Brigid wouldn't let me go into any battles without having her as a gladiator in my arena.

Chapter Five

"I'm sorry, I don't understand what I'm looking at right now."

To anyone else, the question Rika has posed would probably be related to the three grown women sitting in their respective bathtubs joined together on a video call. But that particular activity is a ritual none of us questions after years of bath-time catch-ups, after a period with kids and jobs that made our schedules too hectic to always find time to meet up in real life. Tonight, when I couldn't sleep due to jet lag, Rika knew just the solution.

Rika, our other friend Clem, and I all met in middle school, so we have that kind of chemistry you can only get with people who watched your awkward ascent into adulthood and know it lurks at the back of every grown-up interaction. There's something undeniable about the way the three of us balance each other out, like the way a restaurant can have mismatched vintage plates and silverware and somehow, all together, it looks perfect.

The deep-green tasseled drapery and ornate wooden canopy bed behind me is, admittedly, an unusual addition to the proceedings. The comical abandonment of the contents of my suitcase onto the bed adds another layer.

"You're looking at one of six ornately decorated guest rooms in Brigid's midlife crisis postdivorce Irish castle purchase."

Rika leans in closer to her screen with her usual comic abandon, as though that'll give her some clarity. "Is that a stage we all have to look forward to in the coming years? Because I'm already stretched pretty thin with work and the kids, so I'm not sure I can add that in."

"I think we can all safely assume that anything Brigid does is a uniquely Brigid occurrence, and none of us have to replicate it," I reply.

"So what exactly is she doing?" Clem chimes in softly, her calm demeanor trying to get us back on track of answering the question.

"I honestly have no idea. Obviously she's just gotten divorced and wanted to move back to Ireland, but I'm not sure why she's suddenly upended her entire urban lifestyle for a countryside existence, complete with a home out of a *Masterpiece Theatre* show."

"Is the wall covered in the same fabric as the curtains?" Clearly Rika hasn't gotten over my room yet.

"And the lampshades on the little sconces?" Clem adds, finally letting Rika distract her, the devil on my shoulder persuading the angel for once.

I sigh. "Yes and yes. Everything in this house seems to be antique and elaborate, and I have no idea whether she purchased it like this or if she's secretly been planning this for months, and this is the result of a yearslong renovation that none of us knew about."

"And knowing her, she'll probably never tell you," Rika says with a laugh.

"No, definitely not."

I take a sip of the Irish whiskey I've poured for myself into one of the crystal tumblers I found in the room.

All day I haven't been able to shake how over the top it is, even for Brigid, that she's just summoned us all here and now apparently expects us to do this so often. It's like stepping into an alternate universe of blazing-green grass, raw and frigid stone walls, an impossibly still lake, and elaborate tapestries.

"Well, maybe a new intricately designed setting will bring out the creativity in all of you?" Clem says. She always tries to find the optimism.

"Who is 'all of you,' by the way?" Rika asks. "How many people is she going to keep flying in and out?"

"Well, she has a number of people already on the team in Galway, so they can easily drive less than an hour here whenever we're in town. And I think you guys have met Greg, our head of operations, and Lane, the CFO."

I pause, not knowing how to possibly throw the massive torpedo of Jack into the conversation. But there's really no way around it.

"And actually, funny thing. Remember Jack Sander? From high school? Well, he's apparently now our new CTO. Small world, right?"

For a second I think the screen has frozen because no one moves. It wouldn't be the strangest thing for the Wi-Fi to be a little spotty when we're so far out in the country. But it's pretty clear from the expressions being beamed back to me that it's not the Wi-Fi that's reacting right now.

"What?" I ask, bracing.

"Oh, I was just wondering if you think *we're* dumb or if you're actually that dumb yourself," Rika says with a roll of her eyes.

"Of course we remember Jack," Clem translates kindly.

"She means we remember *you* around Jack," Rika retorts.

After a day of having the past whack me in the sternum, I've reached a tipping point where I need to put my big-girl pants on and remind myself that history is just that. "You mean I was a typical dramatic teenage girl? That was twenty years ago, Ri," I say, trying to convince myself as much as her. "I hardly think seeing some boy I used to hook up with when I was sixteen is particularly interesting. I'm mostly just glad we got a new CTO that Brigid is excited about."

"'Some boy,' right. Your self-control around that man was as strong as an eggshell," Rika snorts, like the version of my id who's been dying to break free all day. "And now you're acting all blasé about it, which probably means you've already cracked."

"Okay, I'm a mother and executive and have dated all sorts of *delightful* people in the meantime, and he's living his own life with his own people, I'm sure very happily. So I'm not sure what 'cracked' is supposed to mean in this context."

"Oh, does he have a family now?" Clem asks earnestly.

"No, I mean . . . no." I purse my lips, hating that my determination to bottle up my anger and replace it with indifference is being dismantled by Clem without her even trying (unlike Rika). I'm definitely not going to get into the grumpily content lonely island that Jack Sander has apparently turned into in the intervening years.

"I can understand why you'd want to pretend like it doesn't matter," Clem says, shifting back to the original point with a tentative note, "but it must have been awfully jarring to see the first person you really loved in such an unexpected way after so long."

"I didn't *love* him," I snap back like a rubber band.

"Well, whatever you want to call it," she says, ignoring my semantics outright. "You shared a lot with him at a very young age."

"Water under the bridge," I respond quietly.

"Okay then," she says with a nod.

We're all silent for a moment, and I take another long sip of my whiskey.

"I'm sorry," Rika says finally. "Or actually, I'm not sorry. We're all just going to smile and nod and pretend like this is not outrageously annoying for you? Jack Sander is a prick. People don't simply stop being pricks because they age. He toyed with your feelings and had the emotional depth of a goldfish."

I can't stop myself from laughing at Rika's rant, and my laughter seems to give everyone else the leeway to respond in kind. There's relief on Clem's face, and I have to imagine it's from not having to state the glaringly obvious.

"Yes, fine," I murmur. "I definitely agree that the main emotion is pure annoyance that I have to even think about Jack Sander again. He would not be my top choice for someone to deal with on a day-to-day work basis. Although I will say—"

"Nope," Rika says, pointing a finger right into the screen. "See, this is what he does to you."

"I didn't even say anything!"

"You didn't have to. You were going to give us some nonsense about how we can't judge people based on who they were in high school, and how we all grow, and maybe he's really good at his job, and you're going to pretend like he didn't jerk you around for months and then refuse to take you to prom and leave you crying in a driveway, only to literally never talk to you again."

My jaw drops at the meticulous arrow she's shot straight into the center of the bull's-eye.

"Okay, I'm thirty-six years old, and I'm not going to have a conversation about *prom*."

"Oh, I think we're gonna," Rika says, fiery and ready for battle.

"I'm not pretending anything," I flare. "I can't still be mad about a teenage boy's actions."

"But aren't you?"

My mind flashes to that day. To the last time I saw him. To the only time we ever had a fight. To the only time I ever came close to telling him how I felt. And he'd looked at the ground and said, *I can't.*

"I think it was easier to be angry at him," I admit. "So yeah, when I saw him, my first instinct just trip-wired back to being angry. But he's prepared and professional, and . . . he gave me a scone?"

I don't even know why I said that. Rika's eyes almost pop out of her head. "So the anger immediately dissipated, and now we're back to finding him unbearably sexy?" She laughs.

I nervously nibble at my bottom lip. "I wouldn't say that."

"Alexa, play 'Some Things Never Change' from *Frozen II*."

The trilling opening chords of Disney music starts playing from a speaker in Rika's bathroom.

"Should I know what that is?" I say.

Clem jumps in. "It's a Disney movie song. I hate to admit it, but it's probably my fault it's on her mind, since Max has been playing it to Ben every time we go to Rika's house—"

"Alexa, shut up!" I say, pleased to see that my voice stops the song.

But Rika is already grinning because her point has clearly been made.

"I mean, yes, he's still attractive," I huff. "But so what? I'm older and wiser and more mature, and I'm much more capable of controlling myself than when I was essentially a horny teenager."

Rika smiles. "Well, at least we've reached the honest portion of this conversation."

"I think . . ." I'm trying to find the words. Everything roiling around my brain reminds me of a bunch of ingredients poured into a single bowl, that need mixing and kneading to form something coherent. "I don't know—the issue isn't *him* specifically. I don't even know him anymore. It's me, you know? Seeing him when everything is so awful with Lucas is like a giant rubber stamp reminder that I have horrible taste and choose unavailable, difficult people."

"That's a lot of decades of life to condense into one sentence, my dear," Clem says. "Cut yourself some slack; you've dated some nice people."

"Eh," Rika says, cocking her head to the side, seemingly dubious of being able to remember anyone worthy.

"At least Rika can be honest," I say, and she chuckles. "Yes, I was young, but Jack was a total disaster. College was just a series of non-entities who are so trivial they don't even count on the radar. Then, after that, Gillian was cheating on me for the better part of three years before I figured that out. And until Lucas, no one else really stuck. And we know how that turned out. Ideal would've been learning my lesson the *first* time I believed I had a connection with someone, only to have them drop me like a too-complicated hot potato—always gotta find an opposite to attract and apparently obliterate me, right? So now on top of everything with Lucas, I get the additional bonus of seeing a daily reminder of my abject failure in getting other humans to think I'm worth being with."

I see Clem shift, and I'm not sure why. I know she's gotten the brunt of my meltdowns lately, since Rika is up to her knees in newborn. But she almost looks angry, and Clem never gets angry.

"That's enough of that, Bea," she says firmly, and I can see from the expression on Rika's face that neither of us was expecting that. "It is not 'abject failure' to have relationships with flawed people and learn and grow from them."

"But I—"

"Stop it. You've gained every time, not lost. Yes, you and Jack were like two deranged magnets, crashing into each other over and over again. At the time, I kind of loved watching you run headfirst fearlessly, even if I didn't love the heartbreak in the end. But him being closed off as a teenager and hurting you is hardly an unusual outcome for a high school boyfriend. Dating around in your twenties is normal. And Lucas gave you Bash, so that could hardly ever be a failure."

"Thank you, but I think divorce can't just be glossed over—"

"No one is glossing over anything. But I'm not going to let you stew in a bathtub drinking whiskey and obsess over Jack Sander like we're sixteen again because you're all roiled up about Lucas being rude to you over a career that you're *kicking ass at*."

Rika snorts and is failing to contain a grin. Clem never curses, so I must be in major need of a pump-up. And it does make me feel a little cherished to watch her getting so worked up over my internal battles.

"Thank you, Clem," I say, and she nods at the acknowledgment. "I need you to handle everything in my life, please," I joke, trying to lighten the mood.

Rika tuts. "Bea, none of us can handle our own lives without each other. That's why we need to take bubble baths over video calls with our friends."

We all wrap up and shout our goodbyes, sending kisses to various kids and significant others virtually before turning off our devices.

A wave of exhaustion envelops me, and I try to stave it off by wrapping myself in the waiting cream-colored robe. I'm hopeful that maybe between jet lag, my friends, and the effects of soaking like a prune in warm water, at least maybe I'll be able to sleep tonight without staring at the ceiling for hours.

But it's impossible to fall asleep when the knot in my stomach is still wide awake and pulling me in every direction. I miss hearing Bash breathe from the room next to mine. I brood over wondering how Lucas is going to react to me traveling more for work. I actively try to extinguish the jealousy I feel over the thought of Bash maybe loving Lucas a little bit more after getting more time with him.

But humming below all of that, a long-dormant simmering volcano, is Jack. Stupid Jack Sander, placidly emanating strength and disquiet. Jack with his apparently unchanged penchant for irking me with a simultaneous ability to understand me.

Shades of today's conversation (*"I seem to recall . . ."*) hum along and entangle with vaporous memories. Pads of fingers delicately touching a painted portrait. Worn-in gray jersey sheets tangled. Joni Mitchell's "Case of You" brimming from his speakers. And yes, that awful moment where we stopped speaking because he wouldn't agree to something public with me after so much time in private.

So many taunting nostalgias, far enough away that they don't retain the same power over me that they used to, but now they're mixing with today's immediacy.

I swirl Clem's words around my brain like whiskey in a highball glass. *Two deranged magnets.* I read once that magnets are a rare element in nature because they're able to exert control over other objects without actually needing to touch them. Is it inherent then? Two magnets that are drawn together will always be drawn together, no matter how much time has passed? Or does time weaken the pull and allow them to be strong enough to stand next to each other without crashing?

I've always sort of assumed that my inability to stay away from Jack—my need to poke at him, turn him over in my hands, see him from every angle, even if he was too sharp for me to handle—was because of my age.

I had a much easier time pushing every other subsequent relationship away. Breaking up with Lucas hurt because of what it did to Bash, but no one could ever accuse us of being magnets, just shades of the same color that matched but could exist easily without the other.

I can shake it all off, though. I've worked with plenty of men I also found attractive, and even more men I found annoying—so what? I can handle Jack Sander. His perspective on me never included enough interest or respect anyway. Of course I was surprised to see him, so it was natural that I might be thrown off. But I've grown and matured, and his opinions don't matter to me anymore. Some things can change.

CHAPTER SIX

My face is practically frozen by the time I turn the key in the lock to our house. Just the walk from the cab to the apartment at night is enough to numb me all over, but maybe that's a good thing after the two days I've had in Ireland and a flight home to think everything over.

A gin and tonic is the next stage in my line of defense.

I throw my coat and keys down and immediately make a beeline for the freezer as Mona comes out of her room, dressed up for going out.

"Want a drink with me before you go wherever you're going?" I ask, hopefully.

"Always," Mona says. She grabs two glasses and places them right in front of me as I gingerly pour gin into the glasses, like a boozy dance we could perform elegantly with our eyes closed.

A splash of tonic and a cheers give way to easy silence as we both sip on our drinks and stand, neither of us caring enough to move away from the fridge toward a more comfortable locale.

"You want to hear the terrible joke Bash told me today?" she finally asks, blessedly circumventing any questions about why I look so exhausted.

"Do I?" I laugh.

"Why don't scientists trust atoms?" she says with a sly smile. I don't even say, "Why?" There's no point. "Because they make up everything."

I groan.

"And on that note . . . ," she says, then finishes off what's left in her glass in one fell swoop. She places the empty vessel in the sink, gives my cheek a kiss, and grabs her purse, clearly ready to get back to her evening. "Bash and Anna are playing cards in his room. He already had dinner. I'll catch you later."

I squeeze her shoulder on her way out. For someone who lives her life so out loud, she can be startlingly observant about the moments I need to talk about nothing.

With the house quiet, I finally pull out my phone to do the one thing I've been dreading all day.

Bea: Do you mind coming upstairs tonight for a minute? I need to chat with you about something.

Lucas: Want to give me any hints or should I just be at your beck and call?

I purse my lips and try to breathe. This is *exactly* why I've had a knot in my stomach all day. Lucas can't help himself.

Bea: It's about my work schedule.

There, I'm not responding to his taunting. Maybe this means I'm growing. A few months ago I would have called him out for being an asshole. But maybe it's also because I need all the goodwill I can muster from him today.

Lucas: Can I come up before Bash goes to bed?

Bea: Sure.

I put my phone down and go into Bash's room. He jumps into my arms and starts rattling off everything he and his friends did at recess, and I try to listen as much as I can, when my mind is already whirling from the dread of what's coming next.

The front door opens, and I hear our nanny, Anna, intercept Lucas. Their chat is muffled from the other room, but I catch the animated way he's engaged—he always drinks in stories about Bash like the proud father he is, and his laughter loops through me like a pinch of pleasure and pain all at once. Anna eventually leaves, and Lucas's head pops in the door.

"Hey, kiddo—how was your day?" Bash leaps from me to his dad (I swear that kid's agility is going to lead to a career in acrobatics someday), and his stories continue to go a mile a minute.

I quietly let myself out of the room and into the kitchen, where I tidy up and try not to listen in while they're chatting.

"Mooooommy," I finally hear from the other room.

I walk back into his bedroom, dark except for the globe night-light and glow-in-the-dark stars that speckle his ceiling. I give him a snuggle and a kiss—Lucas has seemingly already completed his round of good nights—and walk out. I close the door behind me.

Lucas is looking at me expectantly, and the dread that's been held at bay by Bash's sassy smile suddenly comes roaring back to the front.

"Drink?" I ask before pouring myself another gin and tonic.

"I guess that depends on whether you think I'll need it," he says suspiciously.

He can smell it on me. He knows I'm nervous and can't suss out yet what that's going to mean for him.

I pour him a drink and slide it across the table. He sits down and doesn't look at me at first, only taking in the drink, the glass, the table—all items he picked out for our home when this home was *ours*. Now he's the interloper drinking out of glasses he prefers, sitting in the chair with a straight back that he wanted.

"So I know I mentioned that Brigid moved to Ireland . . . but for the next few months, I'm going to have to go every two weeks," I finally say, with a directness that I muster past all my fidgety internal roadblocks.

"Why?"

He's finally looking at me, and the expression is as unreadable as ever.

"The whole executive team has to. You know how Brigid is—there's no arguing with her once she's made up her mind."

"So maybe it's time to look for a new job."

I can feel the heat emanating from my pores at this comment, like he's fanned slowly simmering embers and turned them into flames.

"You know that's not a possibility," I finally reply, my jaw tight, aching against the pressure to unleash every thought that's been building up in my mind.

"Why not? You have a kid—that's not a responsibility you can just hand off."

"You travel for work," I say, ignoring the implications brewing beneath that statement.

"Not every other week forever."

"It's not forever. And this isn't up for debate," I retort. "This is my job, my income, and the company I've been with for over a decade. I'm doing this. So I was *hoping* we could talk about reorganizing our schedule a bit to figure it out."

I'm breathing heavily, letting my anger mask the terror that's lurking in my body, all the way to my fingertips. This job is my unmovable anchor. For seven years, my life has tipped on its own axis one giant event at a time—pregnancy; marriage; a new baby; miscarriages; IVF; separation; lawyering up for our impending divorce. The moments play in front of my eyes in a flash, and the only life raft I can cling to is the stability of my job. The company I *love* working for. The company where I'm good at what I do. The company I believe in that also gives me the financial independence to not have to fight with my ex. The company where I can transform into my badass work self when my personal life is overwhelming or excessively joyous or throbbing with pain.

I'm terrified because Lucas doesn't even realize that he's casually thrown out my worst nightmare as a suggestion. And I'm even more terrified that he'll double down later this year, when we have to actually formalize this thing in court, if he knows how much the idea could hurt me.

I have to make this conversation less aggressive.

"Look, I know it's not ideal"—he snorts, as though the attempt at mollifying him is as absurd as I feel—"but my work is important to me. And Brigid says she's going to promote me and give me a raise, so this will be worth it in the long run. And besides, this wouldn't be reducing your time with Bash but just adjusting some days *and* getting him to sleep over on those nights, which I know you want."

"I'll do it," he says quietly, and I almost let the sunshine back in until I realize quite suddenly that a very distinct "but" is coming. "But then I get more time."

My mouth falls open in shock. I can't *believe* he's using a routine scheduling conversation to try to screw me out of time with my son. Even he isn't usually that heartless.

"Right now I only get five out of fourteen days, and two of those days he doesn't even sleep in my home," he says, continuing on like we're discussing something as innocuous as the weather. "If my every-other-week weekdays have to now revolve around your boss's inane schedule, then I want him sleeping over extra nights. If I have to adjust constantly for you, then something has to be in it for me. We were only *not* having him sleep over on weekdays in the first place because you decreed it would be disruptive to him. But obviously that wasn't true if you're so willing to change it for your boss. You said you don't want to fight through lawyers when it comes to it, then fine, but I want more custody. I'd *get* more custody if we actually contested the divorce."

I breathe in, trying to contain my anger before responding. Of course he wants to use this against me to *get something*. Nothing is ever enough for Lucas. It's all a negotiation.

"Angling for more custody by threatening my job is really unfair," I say finally.

The understatement of the fucking century.

"Oh yeah, I'm unfair?" he replies, his voice rising an octave, the way it does when he starts to get indignant. He pushes his dark hair that's clearly in need of a haircut out of his eyes, and the movement is sharp, like he's trying to contain himself. But instead he stands up, letting the full force of him tower over me. "You're the reason I don't get to *live* with my son anymore. It's your way or the highway, and I'm supposed to just take it—"

"It takes two people to split up," I spit back, unable to stop myself from rising so he's back at eye level, and now I'm gripping the opposite edge of the table as we face off against each other—this table that he excitedly picked out in an antique furniture store that feels like it was in another world from the one we're living in.

"Well, it only takes one person to give up."

"Oh, *I* gave up," I scoff. "Let's ask the doctor performing surgery on me for the fourth time whether women in happy marriages usually have to show up *alone* to a D and C."

He visibly flinches at the comment, and triumph and regret simultaneously tangle together in the pit of my stomach.

"Damn it, Bea," he finally says, leaning over the table, his knuckles turning white from the pressure he's clearly holding up. "Glad you can be so flippant over something that was hard for *both of us*."

My eyes widen, and if looks could kill, he would probably collapse on the floor in an instant. This man has the audacity to stand in front of me and try to claim that after four miscarriages, five rounds of IVF, and more shots of hormones than I could ever count, his pain is somehow equal to mine. That he could even *fathom* the hell my body went through for him. That once he realized the IVF was only *for him* at a certain point, he never chose me over the theoretical family he believed he needed to have.

I'm burning, every inch of me a mixture of simmering rage and resentment. How do we always get here? How does everything loop back into this unsolvable knot at the center of our destruction? We've burned down every shred of love and admiration we once had for each other at the altar of our immovable stances on having more kids. We didn't have a foundation that could hold under the weight of years of loss and heightened emotions and exhaustion pushing us to the brink.

And underneath everything was the cruel fact that the crux of any marriage, our sex life, was always a bludgeon against us. Our first few fumbling times landed us a baby (a great one, but an unexpected one nonetheless) and then became tainted by the cruelty of our failure to have another kid. Can love ever flourish when sex causes so much heartache? Our marriage never would've worked. Sometimes I'm glad we were so hastily forced into seeing that.

"I am not or have ever been flippant," I finally breathe, daring him to contradict me.

"I can't argue with you anymore, Bea," he whispers, the fight drained out of his face. He finishes his drink and stands up straighter, like he's made a decision. "If you want me to cover for you traveling, then you have to give me an extra day. You don't get to summon me, ask me a favor, berate me, and then expect me to just make your life easier. That's my offer. Take it or leave it up to court to decide in a few months."

CHAPTER SEVEN

Half an hour later, the doorbell rings, and when I open the door, Clem swoops in instantly. She throws a bag of baked goods onto the counter and immediately pours herself a drink to match the one I'm holding. I sit down at the table, waiting as she gathers a few plates and sets out an array of cookies, rugelach, and doughnuts.

When she sits, she softly holds my hand, and I realize I'm still shaking a little.

"What can I do?" she says quietly.

I love this about her. Of our threesome, Clem has always been the rooted center that we can all hang on to. When I want analysis and advice, I call Rika. But when I need to be steadied, I only want Clem.

Sometimes I'm envious of her husband and two kids, that they get to be wrapped up in her competency and kindness at the end of every day, while I'm struggling not to trip on top of Bash and bring him tumbling down with me. But then I feel grateful that in a moment's notice, she'll give the three of them a kiss good night and redirect herself toward enveloping me.

Me, with my perfect kid but upended, messy schedule. Me, with my stable income but instability oozing from every pore of my personal life. Me, with my cherished friendships and wrecking ball of romantic entanglements. My walking contradiction of happiness and sorrow. My modern midthirties life in all its glory, laid bare on a table piled with gin and baked goods. It's exhausting. But there's strength in having someone holding your hand.

"I got in a fight with Lucas," I finally reply, stating the obvious.

She squeezes my hand and waits for me to continue, no verdict lining her beautiful face, no hair out of place in her sleek low bun. Just a sounding board at the ready. I take a deep breath and tell her all the ugly details.

When they finish pouring out of me, she finally whispers, "I'm so sorry," and leans in to gently wipe the tears off my face.

"Why does it have to be like this?" I say, defeated by reliving the conversation.

"I think . . ." She stops, clearly unsure of whether it's appropriate to say whatever she's thinking.

"Don't hold back on me now! I need advice, even if it's not what I want to hear."

She nods, considering me.

"Okay." She bites on her lip a moment, summoning the words. "Then I think you should just give him the extra day."

When she sees my stunned expression—*We're agreeing with Lucas now!?*—she holds up a hand to quiet me.

"Just hear me out. The last few years have been hell for you. You've done the absolute best you can, and I'm so proud of you for making some really hard choices. You were stuck in a loop of loss and waiting, and you're finally free from that. So be *free*. You have Bash—he's worth everything that came after. You have a career that you love. Focus on that. Put your head down and work and be a great mom. Let the lawyers mediate among themselves. Don't get distracted by Lucas or emotionally draining ex-boyfriends showing up. Just give yourself some time to heal."

I give her words a moment to absorb, sponging them up until I feel full of them. I take a few deep breaths and pick at my nails in the meantime. Healing. What would that look like? It's been a year since Lucas moved out, and I don't know if I'm anywhere near whatever normal is supposed to look like for me at this stage.

"He's just so . . . angry with me," I say quietly. "And he makes me angry too. We're both like the worst versions of ourselves when we're around each other now."

"I know, sweetie, I know." Her thumb is circling mine, the motion repetitive and soothing, as though she's trying to calm me all the way down to the center of my nervous system. "But that part is going to take time as well. I don't know when or if that subsides, but either way it needs time. I hope the temperature reduces eventually, but you can't solve it right now. The good news is, for all your crap with Lucas, he's a good dad. Bash loves you both. It won't hurt *him* to spend an extra night with Lucas. And that's all that matters here. You can still be a present, excellent mom *and* take on this new work phase, even with all the strings Lucas is attaching to it, okay?"

"I'm so drained from fighting with him," I say, feeling resigned. "I hate it. I *hate* it."

"So take the scenario you have in front of you."

"Okay," I say, quietly concurring. I know she's right. I can do this.

I sit up a little straighter, feeling more determined and steady now that Clem's gotten me to see a path forward.

"Well," I finally say, trying to lighten the mood, "at least this makes Jack's zombie reappearance in my life seem like a much less significant car crash."

"Whoa, whoa, whoa. Don't conflate any of this with Jack. The only commonality in both is that it's just bad timing," Clem says gently, obviously not buying my unearned levity.

"I'm the queen of bad timing, apparently."

"So let the timing be what it is. You have no idea what things will be like with Lucas in a few years—this is where you are now, so give him what he wants, and let it get to better timing. And as for Jack . . . you're not sixteen anymore. Let's assume everyone's grown up a bit."

"Even me?" I tease.

"Jury's out on you." She smirks, planting a kiss on my forehead.

"At least the double whammy of exes this week is a perfect reminder that I should never be allowed out to date again. The thought of emotionally involving myself with another human ever seems too exhausting to fathom."

There's a flash of sadness in Clem's eyes that I wish I hadn't caught. But it's replaced so quickly by a smile that I can almost believe it wasn't there in the first place.

"Timing, remember? Let's just take it all one step at a time, right?"

"Right," I reply, hoping that all those steps will eventually get me somewhere with more solid ground.

CHAPTER EIGHT
FEBRUARY

The rifle is heavy on my shoulder, and I feel perfectly ridiculous with these large safety glasses sitting gingerly on my nose, nipped red by the February air. But I have to give it one more go because I *hate* how truly terrible I am at this.

"When the clay is thrown, you want to imagine the trajectory and shoot to where it *will* be, not necessarily where you see it," Des says, for what feels like the hundredth time this morning. "Okay, Bill, release it!"

Another clay pigeon goes flinging up into the air. The misty grayness against the vivid green of the expansive open field somehow makes it harder to see straight. Once again I shoot and completely miss the target.

By our third trip, I guess Brigid's decided we're not being Irish enough for her. After a productive day yesterday ensconced in our strange castle bubble, today Brigid *insisted* on chucking us into nature and having Des show everyone how to shoot, reminding us of how very not normal our biweekly situation is—this slightly off-kilter version of reality where our chic urban boss has instead transformed into chic mistress of a country estate, outdoor sporting garb and all. I thought I might need to have my ears cleaned when she said it.

Thankfully she isn't making us shoot anything real. Instead she's having us shoot clay pigeons, a remarkably boring activity where you point a gun at inanimate objects hurled into the air and don't even get something to eat if you succeed.

We're standing in a wide-open field we all trudged out to so early that there's still a layer of hazy dew seeping into my skin, despite the borrowed boots and Barbour jacket. Next to us is a thrower trap, which looks like a stationary, bright-orange leaf blower. But Des assured us it can throw the clays up in the air twenty meters, as though that distance means anything to anyone.

"Oh well, can't say I didn't try!" I chirp, hoping that this will end my continued humiliation.

"The word 'try' is carrying a lot of weight in that sentence," Jack chuckles behind me.

I turn around, not quite able to carry off haughtiness as strongly as I'd like when I'm fumbling clumsily in the giant Wellies that Des lent me.

Of course, unfortunately, Jack looks amazing in Des's borrowed shooting gear. His boots look distinguished, unlike mine. His jacket is zipped up, and the collar looks refined. His tall frame makes him look like he belongs among the vivid scenery, rolling hills a perfect backdrop to an attractive man.

But I'm ignoring all of that.

With the shock of Jack's presence worn off, we've fully slipped back into the observant linguistic dueling of our teenage years. It makes me weirdly giddy, the overt honesty I automatically have with him. He's always seen right through me, so I can't fake professionalism when I find him annoying or frustrating the way I would with anyone else in my life.

"We can't all be raised in a barn," I retort.

"I don't think people typically shoot things in barns," he says with an air of seriousness, even though I can see the side of his lips twitch up ever so slightly.

"Maybe they do . . . for target practice?" I spurt back, wishing I hadn't inflected my brilliant answer into a question.

He snorts, obviously aware of my taunting fail.

Damn it.

I turn to Lane, somehow actually looking kind of adorable in a flat cap, and hand her my gun. "Your turn, Lane!" I gesture her forward, praying that she'll take the hint and release me from this humiliation.

I watch as Lane gleefully misses every single clay and still appears to be having a blast. It's hard not to smile at her willingness to make a fool of herself in front of her coworkers.

I can feel eyes on me, and I turn to see Jack looking at me curiously.

"What?" I finally say.

"I'm surprised."

"Is that an unusual occurrence for you?" I smirk, happy to be lobbing whatever is coming my way back at him.

"I'm surprised by *you.*"

"Why?" I hate that I'm curious, but I am. I hate that he's repositioned me from snarky to nosy in three seconds flat without even having to try.

"You gave up so quickly."

I'm prickly with defensiveness immediately, and I wish I didn't notice how much my heart is drumming against my chest, a loud clock ticking away the seconds. "I didn't *give up.* I had my turn, and it was time to move on."

"Seems unlike you."

"To do what?"

"Not be competitive."

My skin is searing from his acumen. I close my eyes to take a deep breath, but I have to instantly open them again after getting a flashback to a flipped-over Monopoly board in his former room.

"This isn't a competition," I say, trying to muster up the ability to convince myself along with him. "No one is *winning* at shooting. This is supposed to be a fun outing to bond coworkers and make us all forget that Brigid is dragging us here every other week. It doesn't matter who actually shoots the most clay things."

His face remains passive, but I hear the small huffy snort, like a horse impatiently nudging a human along. He isn't buying what I'm selling.

"*What?*"

"Played any Trivial Pursuit lately?"

His voice is low and still has that slight rasp of morning grogginess. Anyone else would think he's changing subjects, but I know what he's doing. He's leaning toward me but looking down on me—which I know isn't exactly in his control, based on the differences in our stature—but the teasing expression is not unintentional.

An electric current shivers through me, and I see his eyes clock the slight movement. I'm silently cursing myself, even as I try to stand up straighter and shake off the twinge happening below.

"I have not. Less free time now than when you last knew me."

He nods. He's practicing his most effective trick on me now, the one I was never able to maneuver around. His ability to stay silent, maintain eye contact, and *wait* for me to speak is unnerving.

I want to be mature, like I'm able to with every single other human on the planet.

I want to let it go.

But with Jack, I just *can't*.

"I could probably beat you now, though," I finally say, inevitably, unable to stop myself.

I get that half smile from him. "Good," he finally says. "She's still here."

"Who?"

"Competitive Beatrice."

"You're trying to *make* me competitive by badgering me."

I don't know whether to smile or pout.

"Ah, I didn't realize that the mere mention of a board game made you incapable of remaining even keeled."

"Listen, when you last played me, you'd been alive like twenty percent more time than I had, so of course you always won." The bark of laughter that peels out of him at that gives me a twist of satisfaction. "And besides, if I'm so disappointing to you in my shooting abilities, this isn't much of a pep talk."

He nods, taking the point in, fiddling with a lock of hair that's curled from the mist, and I hate myself a little for noticing.

"Focus more next time," he says.

I watch him, wondering if that's really all he's got. It's easier to study him in this cloudy gray daylight. His face is more angular than it was when we were younger, but his eyes still are impossible not to follow. I see them flit down to my mouth, and I feel rooted against the muddy ground, a tar pit slowly pulling me down.

My body is always so aware of his.

"Has anyone ever mentioned to you that you should be a motivational speaker?" I finally say dryly, ignoring the heat radiating through me.

"No," he says, looking amused. "Has anyone ever mentioned to *you* that being a smart-ass doesn't come with a corner office and a 401k?"

"If only I'd known that sooner, I'd have tried to swipe Brigid's office once she moved here," I retort.

"You certainly move fast enough."

"What do you mean, I 'move fast enough'?" Once again I can't hide my curiosity, my pulse tripping over his remark.

"You walk quicker than any person I've ever seen. I used to be able to spot you all the way across the quad just from your gait."

I've never been able to tell with him when he's sincere or mocking me. Is it an insult or just an observation?

"Not in these oversize boots," I say, bringing the conversation back to the present day.

"Even in those oversize boots," he replies with a chuckle. "You ran out here like the clay pigeons were going to fly away."

I have a response on the tip of my tongue, I swear I do, but Des beats me to it (or maybe saves me from myself).

"All right, ludders, this day has moved from fuzzy to true drizzly, so I think it's time ta pack it in."

He starts loading up the gear, and Jack instinctually moves in to help. Greg, Lane, and I follow the lead and start gathering as well, although when Des looks around satisfied, I notice I'm carrying about one-tenth of what Jack has.

We all trudge back up to the house like a few lost puppies, soggy from being left in the rain for too long. Des and Jack are slowly meandering, chatting, but I scurry back to try to avoid the rain that has become decidedly more than simply mist.

There's a canopied seating area across a porch of stone pavers that looks out onto the field we've just come from. Someone has already set out teapots and biscuits, and it feels foolish not to sit down on the sofa and dig in. Greg drops his gear down, passes on the tea, and heads inside. But Lane plops into a chair next to me and pours herself a cup.

"How do things just *appear* at this house?" I ask.

Lane is holding the mug up, steam curling in front of her face. "It's a bit magical, isn't it? Even if it doesn't seem at all like a place I would picture Brigid."

"No," I reply, happy that Lane has provided an opening to what I've been thinking for the last few weeks. "I thought Brigid was one of those city creatures who considered walking around Central Park a hike."

Lane laughs, and I can see the mischievous glint even behind her rain-dotted round glasses. But then she softens. "I guess her divorce affected her much more than she's expressed to any of us."

I feel a pit form in the bottom of my stomach, and I divert my eyes into my mug, as though I'm going to find something fascinating in there. I wonder if most of my colleagues even know *I'm* getting divorced.

But even if they did, there's certainly no way they'd know I've been hollowed from the inside out because of it. My carefully constructed persona has enveloped the heartache and hasn't allowed any cracks to give them a glimpse of what's inside. I've always assumed Brigid's no-nonsense demeanor is her base personality, but if someone knew only the work side of me, would they think any differently?

The thought is broken by Des and Jack joining us, Des throwing down all his gear while Jack neatly lines his up. They pour their own cups of tea, both looking content. Des parks himself in a chair and immediately puts his boots up on the white wicker coffee table—an action I'm hoping Brigid *never* sees—and Jack casually sits on the other side of my sofa. I want to bottle up his nonchalance and rub it all over myself, because his proximity makes me nervous, and I need the feeling to go away.

"So how's your kid?" Jack asks, not looking at me while he pours himself a cup of tea.

"Pardon?" I say, not even sure if he's talking to me.

But he looks up, and those almost translucent blue eyes are boring right into me now.

"Your kid? Isn't that who calls you whenever we're here?"

I have to blink a few times to take in the question. We've regressively poked at each other, but neither of us has actually tried to start a real conversation in the few weeks we've been back in each other's orbit. Sincerity seems like shakier ground. I don't know what to do with it, so, of course, I babble to fill the air.

"Um, yes, Sebastian, my son. He's six." Jack says nothing, once again waiting for me to fill the silence he's happy to endure. "He's staying with his dad while I do these trips, but he always used to sleep in my apartment on weeknights, even when he had dinner with his dad. So now that that's changing, I feel like I need to answer when he calls. Especially with the time difference. I don't want him to think he can't reach me."

What am I *saying*? Why am I oozing personal information out of every crevice right now? Why do I care if Jack knows anything about my life?

"That's good," he says, nodding slowly.

Does he do this intentionally? Maybe when I was younger, I never noticed how aggressive it feels for someone to be so inadvertently pithy. I wish I wasn't physically incapable of stopping myself from painting over conversational gaps.

"Yeah, it's been fine. I mean, so far, I guess. This is only the third trip."

I chew on my lip, unable to stop myself from letting all my fears about Bash and these biweekly meetings seep in from every angle.

"I'm afraid the longer it goes on, the more he'll get upset about me being gone. And he's getting an extra day with his dad, so I'm hoping he likes that rather than feeling like I'm there for him less. He's an easy kid, but you just never know; he's at an age where he takes things personally now—"

Jack puts his hand on mine, and his touch is both so familiar and sudden that it makes me jump and pull my hand back. A lick of heat shoots up my spine; my babbling instantly stops. I stare at him, mortified by my reaction, wondering if he's even noticed but also unable to stop the pounding that's taken over the inside of my chest. I don't understand how he can still have this physical effect on me, like every inch of my body is on high alert when he's in the vicinity. It's unnerving.

He finally speaks, quietly: "I'm sure he's okay."

That knocks me back to my senses.

"Ah, because you're an expert in child-rearing and the psychology of divorced children and their feelings of abandonment?"

I'm being rude, but I feel safer behind that pinch of anger. Although the rudeness is getting harder to muster the nicer he is to me.

"No," he says slowly. "I just figured a loved kid would be okay. You jumped to psychology all on your own." He takes a sip of his tea, as though we were discussing something as casual as the weather.

"It doesn't matter," I mumble, embarrassed that he's probably right.

"If you say so."

He takes another long swallow of tea without ever moving his eyes from mine.

I spent so much time wishing I could root around inside his brain; he was always such a fascinating, quiet mystery to me. In this moment, I want the opposite—wishing I could get away from the unknowable scrutiny. Wishing I didn't have an extra layer of confusion thrown in as a wrench for me to focus on when my life already feels confusing enough.

"It's nice of you to ask about my kid, but you don't have to. We don't know each other anymore, and it's fine if we just talk about work and like . . . the weather."

"Whatever you want, Beatrice," he says softly.

If only I could do what I wanted. But that concept is from such a long time ago.

CHAPTER NINE

Later that evening, the wheels touch down with a thud on the tarmac, and I immediately pull out my phone.

Bea: Landed. Tell Bash I'll be there in less than an hour hopefully.

Mona: Oh don't worry, he's becoming exceptionally skilled at stalking the flight pattern of your plane. Did you know that wind speed can affect how long a flight takes?

I laugh and stand up to get my carry-on out of the overhead bin. Not even two days away from that kid and I'm itching to have him prattle on to me about some esoteric topic.

While we're waiting for the flight attendants to open the door, my phone beeps again.

Mona: Also, I hit on this guy at the gym today who politely reminded me that I slept with him and then ghosted him a few years ago. Oops.

Mona: BUT after I apologized profusely we got to talking and he asked if I had any friends I could set him up on a date with. He's hot—want me to introduce you?

There's a feeling that burns right in my center at this casual offer. Nerves? Not quite. Regrets? I have a few (ha). Exhaustion? Certainly plays into it. I haven't been on a real date since Lucas and I broke up. I have, admittedly, had some drinks and gone home with people a few times, but there wasn't a lot of talking involved.

The idea of actually going on a proper date with someone who might be emotionally available is both thrilling and terrifying. Like I said to Clem a few weeks ago, I'm not sure *I'm* emotionally available.

I'm gonna need a quorum on this one.

But the line starts moving, and I find myself exiting the plane and making my way swiftly toward a taxi.

I hop in and ignore Mona's text, instead pulling up my group text with Rika and Clem that's aptly named *Kid Pics and Better Jobs*, which really cuts to the essence of what most of our communication centers on.

Bea: Am I ready to go on a date?

The answers come back simultaneously, in the brutal honesty only your oldest friends can give you.

Clem: I think only you can answer that, sweetie.

Rika: Hell no.

Clem: But if you think you are, I say go for it!

I roll my eyes at the decidedly unhelpful duo on my phone.

Bea: Super helpful guys. So glad we're on the same page.

Clem: Who would the date be with?

Rika: Please don't say Jack Sander.

Bea: Seriously Rika?! NO.

Rika: You're right, you wouldn't ask before being a moron about that.

Clem: Stop trolling her.

Rika: Impossible not to.

Bea: Try and make it possible.

Clem: ANYWAY. So who, Bea?

Bea: A guy Mona knows asked if she had any single friends she could set him up with, so she asked me.

Rika: What am I missing?

Bea: What do you mean?

Rika: Is Mona not single anymore? Is this what happens to me when I'm entrenched in kid land?

Bea: Mona is single.

Rika: Ah ok. So she probably already slept with him or something.

Bea: Bingo

Rika: I'm sorry but, no, you don't need a Mona sloppy second.

Bea: To be fair, I'm her brother's sloppy second.

Clem: How dare you talk about my friend as SLOPPY or SECOND.

Rika: I wonder how Lucas would feel about you describing yourself that way.

Bea: Mona would find it hilarious because she was always desperate to get me to embarrass Lucas in front of him.

Bea: She tried to get me to rank him in bed while we were all having dinner one night. While he and I were engaged.

I can't help but chuckle at the memory. It warms the part of my heart that's feeling icy toward Lucas.

We started out so frothy and light, a whipped-cream-topped-sorbet kind of relationship. I can picture that moment of sitting around at dinner, hand intertwined with Lucas's, a few bottles of wine between the siblings (and me pregnant and stone-cold sober), with Mona trying to pry something out of us both. And looking at him and anticipating the little life we were growing together. We didn't even have to say it.

I remember the contented feeling from that night, and it pangs a little.

The warmth goes back to ice as I think of everything that came after.

Clem: We're getting off the plot here. Do you WANT to go on a date?

Bea: I don't . . . know?

Rika: Then that's a no.

Bea: How can you be sure?

Rika: Because taking someone home from a bar is different than having to sit through first date questions.

Rika: "So, tell me about your last relationship."

Clem: Omg please don't even make me think about sitting through something like that again.

Bea: Gee thanks, Clem.

Clem: I'm just saying . . .

Bea: But maybe that's just it. No one actually WANTS to go on dates.

Bea: . . . But don't I have to go on dates to "get back out there" at some point?

Clem: Some point can be any point.

Clem: There's no right time to decide you're ready to let another person in.

Rika: You can let people in (your vagina) without letting them in (your heart).

Bea: Thanks for that clarification

Rika: You're very welcome.

Clem: I think if you have to ask the question maybe the answer is not yet.

Bea: No advantage to just ripping off the Band-Aid?

Clem: Not with a blind date. That might be a little more pressure for a first date back post divorce.

Clem: You've done the first sex thing. You're already doing great.

Rika: GREAT! We're so proud.

Clem: So don't feel pressure to rush yourself.

I can feel myself tearing up. Today has been so long, and not just because of my jet lag. Even though I showered after clay pigeon shooting, I still feel like I smell of mud and an elongated day. But my friends have my back. They make me laugh, they make me secure, and they make me feel like everything will be okay as long as I keep putting one foot in front of the other.

Bea: Have I told you both today how much I love you?

Rika: I have a tiny human spitting up on me as we speak. I don't think sappy is available in my bingo card today

Clem: Love you too

The cab makes good time, and when we reach the house, I bolt out and up my stairs toward Bash. At this time of night, every minute counts.

But upon entry, I notice not everything is as I left it.

"Why is there a large pumpkin here?" I yell, setting my keys on the side table and then hanging up my coat. "And a cake?"

It feels so impossible that just this morning I was shooting at airborne objects, and now I'm back in my apartment, albeit with a time change that's making this particular day hold extra hours. But I'm not so tired that I've imagined this strange confluence of items sitting on my kitchen counter.

"Oh, it was on sale!" Mona shouts from her room.

I grab a bottle of wine, and Mona walks in, like a moth to a flame. I hand her the bottle.

"You know it's February, right?" I say as she screws the top off and starts pouring wine into glasses.

"I do know that, yes," she says.

"Okay, because I legitimately didn't even know you *could* buy a pumpkin this time of year. Let alone why you would want to."

I sit down at the dining room table and reach for the glass of wine she's sliding toward me.

"Well, you can. I saw it and thought to myself, 'Why do we restrict all our pumpkin-related fun to the fall?' So I bought it."

"And what are we going to do with it now?"

"I didn't get that far," she says, just as I hear the thump of Bash's footsteps.

A tiny ball of energy crashes into me, and I lean down to smell my son as he squeezes every ounce of air out of my lungs. He hops into my lap, and Mona heads over to the kitchen counter.

"You didn't respond to my text," Mona finally says, nonchalantly, clearly being as nonspecific as possible in front of Bash.

"Yeah, I know," I respond, taking a moment to rumple Bash's hair while he grins up at me and then grabs a comic book off the table. "I don't think so yet, Mon."

I'm sort of grateful that with Bash in my lap, there's no way this can turn into a longer conversation. But Mona doesn't look like she was going to push anyway.

"Whatever you need," she says as she comes back over to the table, balancing the cake along with some plates and cutlery. When she sets it down, I snort at the sight of it. On top of the vanilla icing, it says, *Congrats on Not Murdering Your Coworkers or Ex-Husband (Yet).*

"That's a highly specific cake," I say, appreciating that Bash is now fully engrossed in the comic and not paying attention to his aunt's murder-related humor. Mona is also ignoring me as she gingerly slices into the cake and doles out pieces onto the plates.

"They told me it was bad luck to buy a grocery store cake and not put a message on it. So I thought I'd get something jaunty and adorable for you."

"Why, thank you."

At least the wine is hitting the spot.

"I *am* correct that you're back in one piece from this Ireland trip, and no one's been thrown off a seaside cliff or anything, right?"

"Fortunately or unfortunately, Brigid still is alive and well in her castle." I haven't mentioned Jack to Mona. Unlike my high school friends, she's never heard those stories, and I'm too tired to explain the context or hear whatever her inevitable hot takes would be. "Do we have anything to eat other than cake and raw pumpkin?"

"Nope," she says. She passes me a fork and digs into her own piece. "I got distracted at the store. Although I did buy the wine, too, so that's useful—"

"We might have different definitions of 'useful.'"

"I'll do a grocery order tonight to get actual food delivered. Relax. How was the trip?"

I relay the basics to Mona, and it's nice slotting back into routine life. It's like the two days in Ireland are an exhausting fever dream, but once I'm back in my home, I can power back up to normal.

"So what did you learn while I was away?" I ask Bash, eager to catch up on whatever I've missed.

He puts his comic away and sits up straighter, then grabs a piece of cake.

"I've decided I want to be a teenager."

I try to keep my face from looking dubious. "You'll get there eventually," I reply, as seriously as possible.

"Teenagers smell," Mona points out, mouth stuffed full of cake.

71

"Yeah, but when I'm a teenager, I won't have to pay any bills yet, but I *will* be allowed to drink wine."

"Who says you can drink wine as a teenager?"

"The sixth graders at school say that the high school students drink," he replies with more authority than I would've been able to muster at his age. "Ella and I talk to them on the bus."

"Oh, great," I say, looking over at Mona, who seems to mostly be trying and failing to cover up snorting laughter.

"It's fine, though. Daddy says I don't have to pay bills until I'm eighteen. So that means I'll have a few years to drink wine but *not* pay bills. So it's really the ideal time."

I smile a bit as I imagine what conversation Lucas was lulled into that necessitated talking about bill paying.

"Well, I'm sorry to break it to you, kid, but the drinking age in the US is twenty-one. And maybe you'll be allowed to have a sip of wine at dinner before that, but I'm not really sure that's the kind of drinking the sixth graders are talking about. You're still pretty far from both drinking wine and paying bills."

I wait for the argument or follow-up, but he already seems to be ten steps ahead of me, as always.

"Daddy already told me that, too, and he said you would agree with him because you two always have the same opinions about being parents."

"He did?"

My heart twinges a little bit, and it's hard to admit how much of a salve it is to hear that.

I know rationally Lucas and I are lucky to have the same relative values when it comes to raising a kid. And I know that no matter how much we argue, neither of us wants our poor relationship to affect Bash. But I always worry that the digs Lucas lobs at me are the same ones he offhandedly mentions to Bash.

It's hard not to ache from thinking about all the teachable moments I miss, all the questions I never get to weigh in on because I'm not in the room. My parents have always been pretty uncomplicated for me; I *hate* that it's not the same for Bash.

And it's hard not to worry about how high the stakes are for me to make these trips work without them becoming something Lucas can use against me.

But I have to get better at letting those types of things go and try to hope that maybe Lucas isn't constantly trying to sabotage me. After all, I hate his guts most of the time, but I still would never whisper a bad word about him to Bash. Maybe, *maybe*, it'll all be okay. Maybe I can manage this tightrope and not piss Lucas off and somehow get through this year with both a raise and my custody.

And with cake. It's not bad to have cake in there too.

But in the meantime, I force Bash into a tighter squeeze. Two days of distance is still a lot, after all.

Chapter Ten

Early March

It's strange how the deep-green trappings of my room and the gray weather outside have already started to feel ordinary.

After a few months, by this trip, I have my routine down: melatonin-infused evening flight; nap in the taxi on the way to the house; shower on arrival; coffee and emails before Brigid summons us all. If I push through the day, I'm tired enough at night to fall asleep. Then the next day I can get through more meetings before taking a late-afternoon flight to land back in New York before Bash's bedtime. It's working. I can do this.

Truthfully, as I sit at the desk in my room, wearing one of Brigid's fluffy robes and enjoying the silence while I finish up some notes on my laptop, I *almost* feel relaxed.

It's not that my day-to-day life is so stressful, but there's something freeing about extricating myself from my environment every few weeks. I can ignore all my mundane home repairs, Bash admin, and to-do lists.

The thought is interrupted by a knock on my door.

"What's up?" I say, eyes still glued to my computer while I keep typing.

"Do you have a travel printer?"

My head whips around at a voice that automatically pours heat into my chest like a marshmallow over a crackling fire.

Jack is standing in my doorway, leaning casually to the side, his sandy hair swept back and damp. It makes me instantly grumpy how quickly my mind goes to the gutter of trying to picture *his* shower. *Sleep deprivation is a hell of a drug, apparently.* I feel like I've gotten better at ignoring whatever tension clearly still lives between Jack and me, but come on—I'm only human.

"Yes," I say automatically before my brain sparks back to life. "I mean . . . not really."

"What?"

His eyes narrow at me, and his gaze makes my fluffy giant robe feel as sheer as a curtain.

"Well, I *have* a printer, but it ran out of ink."

"Then you don't have a printer," he says, raising his eyebrows and trying not to smile, although I can tell it's taking some effort.

"Not functionally, no."

"So just say no."

He's watching me, and even though I know he hasn't moved from the doorway, it's as though there's some gravitational pull collapsing the room in on itself.

"Yeah, but if I said that, and then you somehow saw the printer, you'd say I was a liar."

"Yeah, but you *are* a liar because you said you have a printer, and you don't."

"Okay, sure, but I came by the lie honestly."

I raise my eyebrows right back at him, and he fails this time at not letting his face react. I love seeing the smallest of smiles finally quirk onto his otherwise serious face.

For a moment we're trapped in a staring contest, an unspoken humidity between us that neither of us can seem to break. But then he shakes his head at me, turns silently out of my room, and shuts my door behind him.

The gentle thrum of power from having the last word is satisfying, and I revel in it. I have to admit I enjoy this verbal game of tennis we've slipped so easily back into. And somehow that's made the anger I've had at the memory of Jack start to dissipate a little bit in the presence of the real-life, quietly playful Jack in front of me.

Frankly, he's distracting.

Okay, maybe I'm not as good at ignoring him as I want to pretend I am.

But on the other hand, maybe I need distracting. I need to look forward to being here.

I thought coming to Ireland would mean a biweekly albatross of Brigid around my neck, but instead it's started to feel like a weight being removed. Maybe a change of scenery on a constant basis is actually a jolt I need.

If Lucas wasn't so irritated constantly, it might feel downright palatable.

But Lucas *is* irritated.

When I called last night before I got on my flight, I said good night to Bash and then attempted to make small talk with Lucas, as though that could ever be possible.

"What's happening in the big apartment tonight?" I asked, having noticed they were all upstairs.

"Yes, please rub in that you get to live in the better apartment with my son and my sister, while I have to live practically in a basement," he shot back, all pretense of politeness gone now that Bash was out of the room.

"I wasn't . . ." I paused, trying to remind myself to take in a deep breath before saying anything I'd regret. "I was just making conversation."

"Well, *my* sister Mona is cooking dinner, and since you guys live in the *big apartment*, even though you're gallivanting across the ocean, we figured it would be better to do it here."

"I'm not gallivanting," I said, finally letting the irritation get the better of me and show in my voice.

"See, this is what you do. You just get mad. You decide you're angry so you won't have to actually feel bad. You don't have to consider whether this is hard for me or whether you're actually doing the right thing. You can simply decide you're mad at me and I'm horrible so you won't have to consider your own actions."

"Well, that's a wildly speculative psychoanalysis for a Monday, isn't it?" I shot back, not even bothering to temper my anger just to make a point.

"If you say so."

I sighed. Lucas was intractable, an electric fence whose switch I'd long since misplaced. And even though I'd hoped his additional day with Bash might soften him—he was getting the extra time he wanted, after all—all it'd done was give him a biweekly reminder that I irritate him. Every thought toward Lucas was like a prick to my skin, and lately the pricks were adding up and starting to bruise.

"Sorry for not wanting to get attacked on a phone call. On that note, I'll talk to you tomorrow. Give Bash another kiss for me."

And then I hung up before he could throw me another retort.

So yeah, I need every distraction I can get.

Unfortunately, clay pigeon shooting is *not* the distraction I meant.

"Are you sure we have to do this *again*?" I moan.

This time Brigid has come with us and seems to be delighting in our misery. Somehow, she's managed to wear flattering army green riding pants and a tailored tweed coat that make her look like she's on the cover of a home magazine. Being out in the country has not diminished her need for perfectly applied lipstick or statement hats.

But adding to the country Brigid mystique is the fact that she, apparently, is an excellent shot. I shouldn't be surprised, but it's still pretty badass to watch. Unfortunately, it seems I'm here to be her polar opposite—unkempt and unable to hit a single clay bird of any kind.

"*We* don't have to do anything. But I'd like you to stay out here and do it again because you, sincerely, need to practice," Brigid replies after my latest failed attempt, waving me away with her hand.

"Do I, though? Is this a skill I need in Manhattan?"

"Get Jack to help you—he's good," Brigid says, ignoring my question. She starts to walk back inside, taking Lane and a few of the other team members who joined the morning activity with her.

"Yeah, but he's soooo smug about it," I shout after her as she walks away from me.

"I can hear you!" he says (*smugly*) from the camping chair he's lounging on.

I turn toward him and have to fight the urge to stick out my tongue. My inability to people-please with him is oddly freeing.

"Yes, that was the intention!" I shout.

But this time, instead of ignoring me, as usual, he's already getting up.

"All right, I can't watch this sad state of affairs anymore. We're going to practice, and you're going to actually hit something for once. You can't sit down later for a brainstorming session with the team if you've been utterly humiliated on the field here."

"To be humiliated, I would have to care."

"You care," he says quietly, and I hate that he knows the parts of me that haven't changed. I hate that when I look at him, I can see the challenge in his eyes, the one that he already knows I'm still unable to ignore.

"All right, fine. But *not* because I care about actually getting better. You're wrong about that. I will only admit to caring about getting Brigid off my back."

I grab hold of one of the rifles, ready to go.

"Okay then," he says, and I'm surprised he lets it go as quickly as that. But then he's standing behind me, and the closeness of him is so jarring that it makes me jump. "What?"

"'What' yourself!" I retort. "What are you doing?"

"I'm going to show you how to stand properly when you hold the rifle so you don't look like a cartoon character waving a loaded weapon around."

Oh. Shit.

My heart is beating faster, and I'm a bit irritated by the way he's physically got me on guard. Maybe it's the way he looks at me with the comfort of someone who already knows what you look like naked.

But it's frustrating me that I can't stop my body from reacting to him. He's got his jacket zipped all the way up again, and he looks perfectly pouty and extremely hot. It's impossible not to notice him even when he's far away, but at this distance it's like being a dog wearing a shock collar every time I get too close.

I have to shake it off, though. This is ridiculous. I'm a grown woman, and I've seen plenty of attractive men.

"Okay, fine, what do I need to do?" I say, rolling my shoulders as I get into position. I look up to the sky through the rifle's scope.

"Slow your roll for a minute," he says, then takes the rifle out of my hand and sets it down. "Start by just bending your knees."

I try to mimic what he's doing, but I can see the effect it's having is one that requires him to hold back a laugh.

"Am I *bending my knees wrong*, Jack?"

"Not so much 'wrong' as 'not correct for this activity.'"

"How diplomatic."

"Here," he says, putting the rifle back in my hand and then coming behind me again.

He puts one hand on my waist and one on my elbow, and I hold my breath to try to prevent whatever his nearness is doing to me. It's embarrassing that simply having him stand behind me makes me sizzle like an egg on a hot summer sidewalk.

Thankfully he's oblivious to whatever he's doing to me because at this point he's all business. "Okay, so you need your body to be firm but loose."

"That's what she said," I mumble and turn my head to see his reaction.

He rolls his eyes, and I'm a bit giddy with getting a rise out of him. "Take this seriously."

I bite my tongue because I am, definitively, *not* taking this seriously. But since he's trying to be helpful, I can stop being such a smart-ass. He takes a deep breath, clearly trying to will himself to ignore me.

"Your elbow shouldn't be so rigid. You want to aim and have confidence in that aim, but you need to be able to move with the shot. If you're nervous and clench up, you'll never have that fluidity."

This is the most words I've heard him string together since we've been working with each other, so that alone should surprise me. But I'm barely listening to him because all I can feel is the firmness of his body behind me as he gently uses his hands to get me into the right position.

I'm powerless against the memories it unleashes. Hands on hips, fingers skimming elbows, but in very different contexts. That voice ringing in my ear. The way my small frame fits like a puzzle piece into his large one.

It reminds me of other ways we fit together.

"Do you have it?" he says, and I'm pulled out of the trance.

"What?"

"Do you get the movement now?"

"Oh, sure, sure," I say, hoping he won't notice my sharp intake of breath. What is *wrong with me* today?

Maybe my lack of a consistent sex life in the last few years is really making my mind invent things that aren't there. Or maybe all it's had to get off on lately are memories, so it's delving back into the vintage pile. While my coworker is kindly trying to teach me something, I'm here practically ogling him.

I mentally shake it off. "Yes, that's super helpful, thanks, Jack. I bet I can do it now."

His eyes narrow at my enthusiasm, and I feel a little guilty that he's already so used to my snark that genuine goodwill is suspicious. But he lets it go and walks over to the thrower trap.

"Ready?" he says.

"Yup," I reply, unable to stop looking at him.

"Beatrice, for god's sake, look up instead of at the thrower."

Oops. At least that's what he thinks I'm looking at.

I turn myself toward the sky and try to maintain the stance he taught me. The first few throws are just as bad as all my other ones. But after every round he walks back over, adjusts me a little bit, and says we'll try again. By the fifth or sixth round, I'm wondering whether I'm just mortally incapable.

But that's until I hit one.

The sound is incredible. It's a firecracker that's all mine. Instead of the single shot I'm used to hearing, I get two, and the second sounds like a victory lap. It's a crackle in the sky that makes me leap off my feet and grin as wide as the Cheshire cat.

"I did it!" I shout, running to Jack, as though I'm a kid on a sports team who needs validation from her coach to make sure he saw her success.

But as I make my way over to him, the morning dew catches me, and I slip and fall. Hard. And right into the mud.

Figures.

I can see Jack's eyes widen as he comes toward me, his expression somewhere between worry and amusement. But I'm still beaming when he stands above me, my jeans wet from the muddy ground and my hands covered in dirt.

"I know I fell, and I should be embarrassed about that, but I'm still so excited that I actually shot the thing that I don't care."

He's so stoic usually that the small smile he gives me now feels like the elusive sun has come out.

He resists teasing me and instead reaches out a hand to help pull me up. I grip it before I realize I've now got his hand covered in mud.

He pulls me up and lets go of my hand. I watch him, wondering if I should apologize or just pretend like maybe I didn't get his entire hand covered in wet dirt.

He looks over his hand, and I'm worried he might be irritated that I was so careless. But then he looks back up at me, and I can see the mischief in his bright eyes.

With one smooth movement he wipes the dirt onto the tip of my nose.

I find myself almost saying, *Why'd you do that?* But I stop.

It's all so achingly familiar, even though I'm sure he has no idea of the image he's just unearthed. He has no idea how often I've thought back to that single moment in my life, when I felt on fire and on top of the world all at once.

He's simply lightly teasing a colleague while I'm rooted to the ground, incapable of extricating a memory from the present day.

I have to snap out of this. I don't have the mental energy to embarrass myself even more in front of this man.

"Well," I squeak abruptly, "I should probably go get cleaned up. Thanks for helping me."

I turn around and bolt away without looking back.

When I get upstairs, I immediately wash my face.

CHAPTER ELEVEN

I pulled myself together for the rest of the day. I had to. Brigid invited a lot of the team from Galway for the afternoon, and it was one long series of meetings and PowerPoints that by the evening had started to make my eyes cross.

Everyone left by 11:00 p.m., after a dinner that was followed by more fluffy apple turnovers and whiskey than I could possibly track.

But now that I'm back upstairs, I'm restless. After calling Bash to say good night and getting ready for bed, I'm having a hard time making my body forget that it's still early evening back home, no matter how brightly the stars are shining against the midnight sky here.

Maybe I need a stray turnover to make myself feel a bit dreamier, the density of caramelized apples being dreamy enough on its own.

I tiptoe downstairs and turn into the living room in search of the kitchen. I see a small light glowing ahead, but I realize it hasn't been left on to help guide me toward middle-of-the-night snacks; it's lighting up a solitary board with only one player.

"What're you doing, Jack?"

He doesn't even look up. "I'm playing Scrabble."

"Against yourself?"

"Sure."

His hair is mussed up a bit, and I know to anyone else it would look like an intentional hairstyle, but it's definitely not. He has that kind of sandy swoopy hair that always manages to sit annoyingly perfect, unless he's been tossing and turning.

It's those little lost and retrieved intimacies with him that sometimes give me heartburn. Maybe I can blame that for why I sit next to him.

"Would you rather play an opponent whose mind you can't read?" I say.

He shifts his eyes upward without moving his head, and I'm suddenly not so sure my question is accurate.

"Of course. But maybe not an opponent who storms out when she loses."

"Okay, *one* time I did that," I say quickly, but he's already giving me one of those small smiles I crave, the ones that are so much bigger in spirit than they look.

"I'll redeal the tiles," he says, gathering up the game he's in the middle of—one that looks like both "sides" are incredibly organized, despite no one else watching—and puts the letters back in the bag before shaking it and handing out new ones.

We both set up and start playing in cozy silence, slipping back into a twenty-year-old Scrabble pattern. We go a few rounds before he finally breaks the stillness.

"You're really great with the sales team here. Having you in person has clearly been a huge boon to them."

It's a comment so offhand that he's still scanning the board, making plans for his next move. I'm glad he can't see that his words are making my cheeks blush.

"Oh, it's not me," I reply. "They were great even when we were only virtual."

I'm easily distracted by an open triple letter square right next to a spot I now can use. But apparently he's not even going to notice my little victory.

"Just take the compliment, Beatrice," he says, rolling his eyes. "It's not gonna kill you."

I tut, but he's not accepting my dismissal. I wish I'd become better in that department since we last knew each other. When people give me compliments, I'm like a vending machine trying to accept a wrinkly dollar. I've never managed to improve.

He puts down a long word on the board that gives him thirty points, and I have to hide the seething feeling it gives me. It takes me a minute before I can put down the only measly word I can manage after his slaughter.

"I'm kind of glad I started at the same time that Brigid stopped being in New York," he says finally. "It's good being able to put my head down and then have these check-ins every few weeks to make sure we're going in the right direction. But is it better or worse for you, having had it the other way for so long?"

I haven't really thought about it, but he's sort of right. The workflow is much easier when you're not constantly in meetings, and the meetings are more productive when you're not being interrupted every few minutes.

"No, I agree with you, actually," I say, putting down a middling set of tiles on the board. "Brigid is kooky, but she's kind of my icon, so this feels like a normal Brigid shake-up."

"Your 'icon,'" he replies, a little note of amusement in his voice. The roughness of the sound warms me from the inside, but I keep my eyes on the board.

"Yes," I reply, immaturely needing to double down whenever he teases me. "She doesn't care what anyone thinks and does what she wants, to the point where she insisted on leaving the country, and somehow that makes her employees work even better. *Iconic*." He doesn't respond, and I can't sit with the dangling silence. "Who's your icon?"

"No one—I hate everyone," he replies, seemingly distracted by the next word he's going to crush me with.

"You can't hate everyone," I say, letting out an exasperated sigh at this man who's allowed himself to go from aloof to practically quarantined over the past two decades.

"Sure I can."

"What about someone dead?"

"Should I find it *iconic* that they kicked the bucket?" he needles.

I don't reply, instead setting down a triple word score word and gleefully looking up at him, hoping he'll realize that I've finally tied it back up. "All that snark is distracting you into losing."

I can see him running the numbers in his head, and the scowl that follows is more satisfying than it should be.

We play a few more rounds, trading scores until we're both further along but still mostly even. I'm surprised when he speaks again, without even looking up.

"Is this situation bothering you?"

"What?" I ask, unsure where that came from.

"That I'm working with you now?"

Ah. "No," I dismiss automatically. He looks up and narrows his eyes at me, and I know I'm not going to get away with that. "I just . . . well, I was surprised."

"I could see that," he says with a small chuckle.

"Weren't *you*?" I ask.

"Yeah . . . ," he says, nodding and looking back at the board again, but maybe this time it's just so he doesn't have to look right at me anymore. "But it didn't bother me," he finishes pointedly.

"Well, I didn't rip your heart out at an impressionable age," I joke without thinking, and that makes him look up.

I can see he wants to say something else, and I instantly regret skating so close, so carelessly.

"I like seeing how little you've changed," he says, his voice quiet and impossible to read.

I huff, but I can't look away. "Please. I've changed."

"Still defensive," he says with a small smile. It makes my perfidious stomach flutter. Damn it.

"It's not 'defensive' to disagree with someone," I point out.

"You've smoothed yourself, but you're the same brash can-do kid underneath."

I'm not sure how to respond. I could say the same thing about him, I suppose, but it's clear he means it as a compliment, even though anyone else might misinterpret it as an insult. I don't want to open that can of worms, though, and my heart has already sped up too much for my liking.

It's only now, with his eyes back on me, that I realize we've been inching closer to each other as we play, gravitationally compelled toward the center of the game. We're so near now that our knees are touching. And that lightness, that pressure, zips all the way through me.

Should I move? Has he noticed? How long have we been sitting like this? If I move, would that draw even more attention?

More disturbingly, I realize I don't *want* to move. His proximity is making me feel flushed while somehow being so natural I haven't even noticed it.

He looks up, his irritation from the puzzle of the board distracting him until he catches my eye. And then I know he's seen it.

He always had this uncanny ability to tell when the moment had shifted, whenever my thoughts had relocated from school or mealtimes to crumpled sheets and bodies in line. He caught it every time, the open book of my dirty mind only visible to him. It thrilled me in public and infuriated me in an argument. As obvious to him as if I'd lit up the sky with neon lights.

I've always assumed that I was only such an open book because I was so young and inexperienced. But maybe no one else was ever able to clock me so effectively.

He's staring at me now, clearly wondering if what he thinks he sees is what he's actually seeing, and I can feel his eyes on my skin.

"You really don't know me anymore, Jack," I finally say, preemptively trying to ignore the way he's looking at me, trying to pretend like I don't know that he can see right into me.

"Don't I, though?"

"Well, look at *you*. Same sarcastic know-it-all."

"Deflecting again."

I sigh. "What do you want from me?"

"I don't . . ." He pauses. "I don't know really."

And there it is. We can familiarly poke and prod at each other all we want, yet neither of us quite knows what to make of the other in this current context, and that's making us both unmoored.

But it's clear neither of us can do this dance anymore, where we pretend like we don't know intimate secrets about the other, don't feel the current that hums between us. It's too fake for two people who've always needed to skip over pleasantries.

"I *have* changed," I admit quietly. "I think I was more optimistic and . . . unburdened maybe? When you knew me."

He nods, his eyes still not moving from mine, the air crackling with something I can't put my finger on.

"Time does that, I think."

"Yeah," I murmur, wondering if we're stumbling into a topic too heady for me to handle.

"That wasn't all me, though?" His voice is expectant, and I regret my earlier comment even more now; "rip your heart out" was probably a low blow. And from the confusion on his face, I wonder if our story wound a different path for him, if he truly wasn't invested enough at the time to realize how much he'd hurt me back then.

"No, Jack," I answer, suddenly aching to remove that doubt from his voice. "I've had many more relationships crash and burn since you, fear not."

I pat his hand, intending it as a friendly gesture, but instead the feel of it scorches through me. I rest my hand there, a ticking time bomb that I'm incapable of moving, no matter how much it'll burn.

"Me too, if I'm being honest," he says.

"Is that what we're being?"

He narrows his eyes at me, and I can see his mind whirring as he tries to parse my words. "But some things haven't changed."

"No," I say, unable to break this staring contest we've somehow entered into. I wonder if I even know how to blink anymore. "Some things definitely don't."

The air is heavy, and it's so silent I can hear my own slow intake of breath. The late-night light is shadowing his face in angles, and it softens him, making him look boyish again, as though all the years we've had in between have inverted, and we're back to square one.

I don't know what I'm doing here. I don't know how I've gotten sucked into this magnetic vortex again, but I'm not sure I can keep pretending like I haven't. This lure between us never went away; *we* just went away. And ever since we've been forced back into each other's proximity, it's been a taut string waiting to snap.

I can see the recognition register for him too. My hand hasn't moved, but his does, slowly, his thumb circling over mine, the slightest touch setting everything on fire and sending warmth pooling to my center.

Fuck it.

That's all I can think. Just, fuck it. It's late, I'm horny, I can't help myself. This itch is clearly in need of getting scratched, and the way he's looking at me is too transparent and tempting to ignore.

We're already so close that I only have to lean forward for it to be obvious now that I've given up every pretense. I'm close enough I can almost hear his heart pounding as quickly as mine is.

My gaze moves to his lips, and he reaches up and pushes a loose piece of hair behind my ears, the contact making me shiver all over, his fingers lingering.

I look back up at his eyes, and I can see that he's clocked my reaction to his movement, the lust in response written all over his face. It's so recognizable it makes me crack a small smile, but I don't even have a second to consider because in an instant his mouth is on mine. Burning-hot pressure on my lips, insistent tongue, his hands needy, skating down the line of my neck, every sensation delicious and lighting me on fire.

We're a powder keg exploding, unrelenting, and not holding back.

His kiss is a memory resurfacing after a long nap. Everything was a first for me twenty years ago—first kisses, first gropes, first wide-eyed realizations. Now it's all familiar sighs and searing awareness, a tactile recall.

He pulls me onto his lap, the movement insistent, and I let out a sound that is desperate, and *oh shit*. I arch into him as he grips me so tightly I wonder if it's going to leave a mark.

It's wild watching him unravel like this, after all this time. We're everywhere, all over each other, parched for touch, like downing water when you suddenly realize how thirsty you are. He may not have wanted me anymore *then*, but damn, it's pretty apparent he wants me *now*. That rush of being desired has every piece of me humming for *more, more, more*.

And I'm desperate to know more than just what it feels like to kiss him again.

"We can't . . . here . . . ," I breathe, unable to form a coherent sentence as his mouth moves to my neck, and my head falls back.

"We can't do this generally, or we can't do this *here*?" he hums against my collarbone, nibbling and causing every nerve ending in my body to react.

"No, we definitely can do this generally," I say in a rush, my hands tangling in that hair of his, mussing it up even more than when he couldn't sleep.

"Good," he says, a small smile forming on his perfect lips.

"I just—"

I let out a sharp gasp as his hands roam up my body and light me up from the inside.

"You were saying?"

He's enjoying teasing me, enjoying watching me be momentarily lost for words. I lightly swat him, wanting to be exasperated with his knowing smile and feverish looks across my whole body.

"Look," I say, pulling back and trying to regain some semblance of control over my brain. My want is crystalizing in front of me, so obvious down to the depths of my toes. I don't think I could resist this, even if some more responsible adult with better judgment tried to drag me away. But even if I'm not capable of stopping, I'm still me, and my unmovable underbelly of rationality is insisting that I justify any fears away. "This doesn't have to be anything," I point out. "We've already done this before, so it doesn't even count."

He leans into me and whispers, "Done what, exactly?" The pad of his thumb gently traces the curve of my neck, and it's a spike of pleasure direct to my core; even though it's the lightest of touches, it feels like an incinerating promise.

And any remaining logic jumps straight out the window.

"Do you want to go back to my room?" I ask. I'm surprised by my bluntness, but I guess he's always brought that out in me. I can't mentally hide from him right now, any more than I can physically stay away from him when he's nearby.

And the truth of the matter is: I need this right now. I need something with no consequences and someone as emotionally unavailable as he's always been. In a messed-up way, it actually feels like the healthiest gift I can give to myself at the moment.

"Whatever you want, Beatrice," he replies.

He lifts me off him and grabs my hand, and we quickly and silently make our way back upstairs.

CHAPTER TWELVE

"What do you like?" he asks, the words muffled from his mouth roaming in my cleavage, his hand gripping my waist.

We stumbled our way into my room, and within seconds we've pulled each other's tops off and tossed them away.

I'm so keyed up I barely hear him. It's sort of pathetic how turned on I am from simply kissing—my whole body is in hyperdrive from just the *suggestion* of sexual activity involving another person instead of a vibrator from a drawer.

"What do you like, Beatrice?" he asks again, crisply, pulling back to look at me, his tall frame looming over me. My face heats up immediately, like my skin has combusted and caught fire. I don't care what he thinks—I barely know him at this point—but for some reason I'm tongue tied.

"Everything you're doing," I quickly mumble, dragging his lips back to mine, letting my hands roam down his pants, nothing gentle or polite happening anymore. But even without looking at him, I can feel that I've lost him.

"What?" I spit out, a mild sheen of irritation undeniable at the slowdown.

"Why can't you just answer a simple question?"

"I did," I huff, still not looking at him, now focused very intently on unbuckling his pants and getting back to the scenario at hand.

His hand slides beneath the waistband of my skirt and heads south, gripping between my legs so suddenly that I jerk my head up to look at him. *That was hot.* He's always taken the lead. But it startles me enough to finally focus on what he's actually saying.

"You didn't," he says slyly. "Tell me what you want. I can take you right here up against the wall, or I can throw you on the bed and go down on you for as long as you want. What do you need to get off?"

If I was previously stunned by his actions, then his words are like a tranquilizer. *What the actual fuck?* Who talks to someone like this? And why is he asking instead of just . . . taking? The way all men seem to do.

"I like . . . all of that," I finally stammer, unsure of how to make this conversation end and get back to the part where I'm no longer a horny and alone almost-divorced and overworked mom instead of a woman who might actually get laid this evening.

"Okay, so," he says with a chuckle, one hand now slowly stroking and the other holding my back gently so I don't keel over from desire, "you're a grown woman, and you created a whole human from your body, and yet you're unable to articulate what turns you on."

It's hard to focus when his hand is clearly on a mission to melt my brain. But I'm still thinking clearly enough to understand the implications of what he's saying, and it's annoying me.

"I can articulate myself just fine. Maybe I'm just easy to please," I finally say, hoping that'll end the talking portion of the evening.

"No woman is easy to please," he says with a chuckle.

I roll my eyes. "Has anyone ever told you you're a jackass?"

"I think actually, in this particular instance, I was being *gentlemanly.*"

I snort out a laugh, although incredulity does not come easily when I'm also exceptionally aroused, and not fooling anyone.

"I don't think anyone would mistake whatever your hand is doing for being gentlemanly."

"Oh, okay, if it's bothering you, I'll stop."

He pulls his hand out of my skirt, so goddamn self-satisfied that I want to smack him. Or maybe I want to smack him because losing his touch only makes me crave it more. I'm both furious and desperate for him to keep going.

But his arched eyebrow and wicked smile tell me that he's really not going to let me off the hook.

"Call me selfish," he says, "but getting you off is going to get *me* off. And I'm impatient and don't feel like beating around the bush or trying to divine what you're thinking instead of saying. So just use your words, Beatrice. You don't give a shit what I think, so stop being embarrassed and help me help you to help me. Get my drift?"

He's so goddamn direct, like an arrow straight to the bull's-eye. I've never had a man speak to me like that. Yeah, sometimes women talk more in bed or check in more, but every man I've ever been with has charged forth like he knew the mission directive.

And weirdly . . . he's right? I'm not sure how I never really saw that before. It's always been a subtle move of a hand to shift gears or a groan of assent to indicate that something is working—but never outright openly saying that some moves might work better than others. And why the hell not? I think about all our fumbling, exciting, clueless high school sex and wonder what might have happened if we'd simply brazenly used each other as test subjects to learn our own bodies.

At least he's learned in the meantime. It makes me wonder how much *I* have. How much knowledge have I parceled out in twenty years of having sex that was more trial and error than deliberate honest conversation?

There's no reason to play coy. I mean, yes, I probably don't look as good naked as I did when I was a damn teenager, but on the other hand I'm definitely better at sex now than the last time we had sex. And clearly *he* also must be better if he has the audacity to cockily ask the questions he's asking.

And even just with his shirt off, he looks incredible. It's hard not to stare up at him, all hard planes and taut forearms taunting me with how much I want to take a bite out of all of him. *Damn.*

I take a deep breath and pull my skirt off. His eyes widen, and a thrill shoots through my body with the knowledge that I've clearly surprised him.

"Okay, fine. I usually need a fair amount of foreplay to be ready, so if the offer still stands, I'd say the 'throwing me onto the bed' option sounded great—"

Before the words are out of my mouth, he's already lifting me up and walking toward the bed. His mouth is on mine, and my hands roam across his body. I'm glad to have the conversation over so my mind can get back to dizzily ignoring reality.

He tosses me gently down onto my back and roughly pulls my panties off, slinging them out of sight. He smoothly drags me to the edge of the bed and kneels down.

"Don't think I didn't notice that you didn't *actually* ask me to go down on you, and for that I think I'm going to spend a long time torturing you from this vantage point until you've forgotten your own goddamn insecurities for long enough that maybe next time you'll actually just say what you want."

Next time.

But it doesn't matter because the words have all slipped away, and there's only sensation. There's his mouth on me, my fingers tangled into his hair, and an electrical pressure that coils around me so tightly I wonder if I might light up like a Christmas tree.

He's deliberate and he's thorough and he most certainly knows what he's doing. And when he shatters me the first time, he pulls himself up and moves onto me assuredly and slowly until we shatter together, and I'm seeing stars for the first time in a very long time.

I'm not sure I could move even if I wanted to. The postsex haze is heavy, and it's making every inch of my body feel gelatinous. I'm flan in human form. Maybe I'm too old to have that many orgasms in an evening. Although I shouldn't complain, since he's clearly not too old to have multiple rounds. If I wasn't so blurry and sex sedated, I'd be impressed.

I'm lying on his chest, absentmindedly stroking my hand across the divots in his collarbone, listening to his heart starting to come back down to normal speed.

But even though my body is calm, my mind is already whirring. I need to ask him to leave, right? He can't *sleep* in here when everyone I work with is down the various hallways of this house. Tomorrow, are we going to be able to pretend like this didn't happen?

I sort of hate my brain for needing to find answers right now, but there's no use fighting it because this is who I am. If anything could've knocked common sense out of me, it would've been the vigorous sex I've just spent the last few hours engaging in. Oh well, can't win 'em all.

All I do know in this moment is that as fun as this was, I need it to be a one-off.

I don't need anything complicating my life more than it already is, but hopefully Jack—who wasn't invested the last time we did this and now is a self-professed loner—is on the same page.

I turn over so my chin is on his chest and look up to see him watching me, unreadable. I let the comfortable silence envelop us for a moment, but I obviously can't let anything remain ambiguous.

"Well, thanks for the sex, or something," I say, and I love feeling his immediate laughter from the vantage point of being on top of him, like a kid lying down in a bouncy house.

It's sexy. *He's* unbelievably sexy, all sharp lines and toned skin, the blond scratch of late-night stubble making his face look like perfection.

"I don't really know what to say now," I admit, honestly.

"See, that's always your trouble. You don't have to say *anything*."

"Well, *I* have to."

"I know," he says, unable to keep whatever small reserves of affection he has for me out of his tone.

The intimacy makes me nervous, like I need a boundary, and stat. Like that *next time* is whispering in my ear again, and I need to make this situation crystal clear.

"I was trying to say . . . everything can be the same tomorrow. We're both stressed out, we're here anyway, it doesn't count—"

"You said that before—that it doesn't count—as though there's some mental tally of fuckable units we have to adhere to," he says with a small chuckle.

He slides one hand lower on my back, and it briefly short-circuits my brain again, but I'm determined to finish this conversation.

"I just mean, it doesn't change anything."

"Ah."

That small smile is back. This time he looks pleased with himself, and I need to poke at him again, now literally in his chest.

"Listen, let me justify my own shit in my own way. My life is messy, and if I want to believe that having a one-night stand with someone I've already slept with makes it less complicated, then please let me live in that world."

"Whatever you want, Beatrice," he repeats in a whisper, fixing me with a stare that's so heated I have to look away.

I'm glad that it seems like that settles things then.

"I'm going to hop in the shower, okay?" I say, with a yawn I've certainly earned from so much activity. "See you tomorrow for, ya know, normal work colleague things."

I give him a pat on the shoulder in the hopes that he'll interpret this as less kicking him out of my room and more *Thanks for the one-night stand, good night.*

I can feel his eyes follow me as I saunter naked into the bathroom, satiated by his scrutiny.

When I come back post-shower, the moonlight seems deeper, spilling onto the hunter green shades of the room and giving it an earthen glow. I feel cozy and relieved as I slip into my now empty bed.

I turn over to set my alarm and notice that a glass of water has been poured from the pitcher that normally sits on the desk, now gingerly sitting on a coaster on the bedside table. For all that bravado, I wouldn't have expected him to leave behind something so simplistically intimate.

But it's probably just a habit.

I turn out the light and immediately allow myself to drown in sleep.

Chapter Thirteen
Late March

This time, I wasn't able to sleep during the car ride.

It's been two weeks since the last trip, and my insides are doing a *delightful* mambo as my cab pulls up to the castle. The weather is being equally uncooperative, spitting light rain amid temperatures that say it *is* still March but somehow feel colder. The damp makes me pull the hood up on my windbreaker before bracing as I step out of the car.

I see Des approaching, wearing a windbreaker of his own (without my wimpy hood). He's holding an umbrella out for me, but I shake my head, determined to not be *that* pathetic.

It's striking how no matter the state of the rain, the castle always looks beautiful. Maybe it's beautiful *because* the rain allows things to be so lush. And now that spring is starting to peek its head out, we're getting the first inklings of a display. The grass is dotted with yellow wildflowers, encircling the property like a beacon pointing us all to the center.

"Beautiful dandelions," I say to Des.

"Coltsfoot, actually!" he replies cheerily, bending over to pick one up before handing it to me. "The stem is a bit scalier than a dandelion's, but they're similar in color. People mistake 'em for weeds, but we're not prissy enough here to get rid of a wee wildflower. And this one's roots can go three meters down, so it's hardy. Ye'd have to be, to bloom so early."

I roll the stem around in my hand, admiring this little weedy wild-flower making sunshine all on her own despite gloomy weather and low temperatures. Something to aspire to.

Des grabs my bag from the trunk. I try to stop him, but he won't hear of it. The cab pulls away, and I'm left outside with my wildflower and my windbreaker, willing myself to wake up enough to have the energy to get some work done.

I can feel eyes on me, like the shivering sensation I imagine you might have from inadvertently walking through a ghost; when I look up, I can see that Jack is watching me from the large wooden bay windows of the entry-way. That internal mambo is back, making all my insides twirl instantly.

How does he always get here before me? He must like a different airline with an earlier flight. Having him here all rested and showered isn't making me feel great about presenting myself as a rain-soaked, sleep-deprived thing the cat dragged in from the cold.

He definitely heard me loud and clear before he left my room a couple of weeks ago—the next morning and all the days after in the office, he acted excessively normal. Not avoidant, like I would have expected (and probably would have defaulted to if he hadn't been so deliberately unawkward). He was professional and amiable but dispassionate. It almost made me wonder if that whole night had been a fever dream. At least he'd made it clear that a one-night stand was really going to be one night.

But now, that look has me flustered. And I can't stop myself from staring back, his gaze making me shiver. He doesn't seem bothered, though. He's observing me, carefully, as if the glass isn't even there, and he might reach out and touch me. That awareness thrums through me, and it almost melts away the cold.

But I'm definitely not going to survive this day if I let my mind go in any direction other than work.

I break our eye contact, walk into the entryway, and deliberately make my way upstairs to my room before I can run into him on this side of the glass.

By the late evening, everyone has ended up at the pub down the road. We need the break after a long day of collaboration.

This pub is the perfect antidote to Brigid's meticulous house: rough-hewn wood paneling and tables lit by a roaring fire in the corner; peeling currant-colored cushioning over flimsy chairs and dark banquettes; sports memorabilia and old Irish spirits posters lining the walls. It's comforting in a lived-in way.

We've coupled whiskey with strong Irish tea, and Des brought along a boatload of fresh currant scones that are as fluffy as the clotted cream we've been encouraged to lather onto them. Pillows of carbs washed down with a bristle. The pub owners seemed delighted at the delivery, which makes me wonder if Des himself makes the scones and doles them out whenever he needs some goodwill.

And I'm grateful I have food and drinks to keep me busy because Paul, one of the sales guys from Galway, has been rambling on for at least twenty minutes about various national parks I *have* to visit for a hike. There's no world where I would possibly be interested in a conversation about hikes, let alone when I'm jet-lagged. I'm worried I might face-plant asleep into my whiskey.

"So that one's a slightly shorter drive from here, but you could manage it in a day," he says about the tenth (probably?) place he's mentioned enthusiastically. *How do I make this stop?*

"Oh," I finally say, realizing my best out as a New Yorker. "I let my license expire a while ago, so I can't rent a car."

"You don't drive?" he sputters, as though I've just told him I murder puppies in my spare time.

"Well," I begin, realizing too late that this revelation was not as innocuous and conversation-ending as I might have hoped, "I had a license when I was younger, but I just let it lapse, I guess."

"But surely you need to get out of the city sometimes?"

"Trains?"

"But what about the countryside?" I don't have the heart to tell him that I don't exactly need the countryside to survive. "How'd you get here tonight?"

"I walked over from the castle," I explain. "It stopped raining, and us New Yorkers love a long walk."

At least at that he looked impressed. Good, apparently my urban trot can translate into scenic strolls when needed.

He turns to Jack, who's been avoiding everyone and typing on his laptop the entire time we've all otherwise been taking a break. (*Who brings their laptop to a pub?*) "Jack, you live in New York. Do you drive?"

"Of course," he says, not looking up. But from the slight twitch of his lips, I can tell he's enjoying making my conversation worse.

"Are most New Yorkers able to drive?" Paul continues.

"Yes," he replies dryly.

I narrow my eyes at him.

"Well, I *can* drive," I counter. "But I just don't like it. I didn't have a car in college, and then I lived in New York. So I never really needed to get very good." I say this all to Paul, deliberately not looking at Jack while sharing this fact that he's keenly aware of. "So I didn't."

"What a coincidence, so did I. And I did," Jack says, finally looking up, a light grin lurking below his professional veneer.

"Well, you don't count," I finally say in a huff, unsure of why I'm letting him goad me.

But I do enjoy the little laugh that escapes from him at this small bout of petulance.

"Sorry, I didn't mean to interrupt your conversation," Jack says, refocusing away from us and back on his laptop. "Maybe Paul can explain to you the different national parks you could get to by taking the train?"

"That's so true, Jack!" Paul says, turning back to me, invigorated to begin his unknowing torture again.

And even though he's now appearing to no longer be listening, Jack's slight smirk is a secret indication to me of his enjoyment of my being cornered.

He knows I'm never going to escape either. I've always been totally unable to extricate myself from small talk because I'm wired to avoid any trace of rudeness; it makes me so uncomfortable to feel like I'm leaving someone in the lurch. It's always been that way for me, and I keep expecting to get better at caring less as I get older, but I'm yet to see the fruits of that theory bear out.

Whereas unlike me, Jack is comfortable being completely antisocial and sitting in a pub doing work, a solitary beer his only companion. I'd respect him if I wasn't annoyed that he's squandering my only hope for escape. I'm otherwise trapped because Lane, Brigid, and Greg are deep in conversation next to the fireplace across the room, and the rest of the Galway contingent is off to the side, playing pool.

But maybe Jack's solitude is intentional and not oblivious, because after another ten minutes, I can see from the corner of my eye that he's starting to sneak looks at me.

He's watching me again in that way only he seems to know how to do—that way he's always been able to make every inch of my skin feel aware, just from looking at me. The dull topic Paul is droning on about isn't helping my mind to not wander back to that night two weeks ago.

"Hey, Beatrice," Jack finally says to me after another few minutes.

I instantly swivel toward him, a student enthusiastically being saved from unending detention. He purses his lips together, presumably to stop himself from laughing at my desperation.

"I know it's late, and I'm so sorry to interrupt your conversation to talk about work, but do you mind going over some of this copy with me?"

He raises one eyebrow, and I can't decide if he's just that sexy or if he appears sexier because he's granted me an ironclad excuse.

"Sorry, Paul," I say, making a *What are ya gonna do?* face at him before standing up and sitting next to Jack.

In hindsight, maybe I didn't need to sit *so* close to Jack, but since he made it seem like his fictitious question was on his laptop, and I wanted to decisively end my previous conversation, there was sort of no way out of it. The old booth dips, and our involuntary curve we have to make toward each other causes that magnetic current to zap me instantly to attention. His eyes dip to my collarbone, and that one look makes it so I can practically feel his teeth on my skin.

But just as quickly he looks back at his laptop.

"Right," he says, coming back into the moment, like a swimmer shaking his head to get water out of his ears. "Uh, can you look this over and let me know if it seems right to you?"

His laptop has one of those privacy screen protectors where you can't see anything until you're close enough to view it straight on. I tentatively lean toward him, skin humming the closer I get, and I have to stop myself from laughing when I see the document on his screen.

I was tinkering with a presentation and didn't have time to make up an entire document. So pretend this is interesting.

"Very important work stuff," I say under my breath, although by now Paul has wandered over to the rest of his crew at the pool table, so we're out of earshot of anyone else on the team anyway.

"Let the record show I eventually saved you," he murmurs.

"'Eventually' is doing a lot of work in that sentence," I reply, parroting back his own barb.

He laughs, but we're interrupted by "Just the Two of Us" blaring from the phone in my purse. I immediately grab it.

"Hey, Bash!" I say as I stand up and move toward the edge of the pub to find a quieter spot.

"Mommy! I—"

His voice is crackling so much I can barely hear what he's saying. And it's not from the noise of the pub. I look down at my phone and realize I'm barely getting any signal.

"Hold on a sec, Bash, I can't hear you. Let me try . . ." I swipe across my phone, looking for Wi-Fi, but nothing is coming up.

I walk back to Jack. "Hey, were you getting Wi-Fi on your laptop?" I ask, since he's been doing work ever since we arrived.

"Oh," he says, looking up. "No, there's nothing here. I was just working on stuff I already had saved."

I nod, frustrated, and look back at my phone.

"Bash?" I ask hopefully. But his answer is garbled.

I walk to the other side of the pub, in hopes that maybe I'll get another bar of service, but nothing changes. I open the door to walk outside but am confronted with a new torrential downpour. Well, *that* wasn't in the forecast. Shit.

I step inside to escape from the rain and stand on my tiptoes, as though somehow that's going to make my service better. "I'm out, but I'm going to get back to Brigid's and call you back, okay, Bash? Bash? Can you hear what I'm saying?"

"Okay, Mommy!" I hear come through, still garbled. I hang up and look out the window, as though the rain might've been a figment of my imagination. But nope, it looks like I'm about to get completely soaked on a cold, dark evening. Great.

"I'll drive you back."

I whip around at Jack's voice.

"Oh," I say, surprised that he's still paying attention. "You don't have to do that."

"You'd rather get drenched than sit in a car with me for five minutes?"

I can't tell if he's joking or not, and I feel a twinge of guilt, wondering for the first time if *I've* been standoffish the last few weeks.

"No, of course not," I rush out. "I just didn't want to ruin your evening."

He scoffs. "I'm sitting in a pub doing work. You're giving me an excuse to call it an early night. I should be thanking you."

"Okay then. Thank you," I say quietly.

He nods and packs up his laptop.

I down the rest of my whiskey and follow him outside. We run to the car to try to avoid getting soaked, but by the time we shut the doors, it's clear that was a futile effort.

"Well, you're still as wet as you would have been, but at least you don't have to walk the whole way in it," he says with a laugh.

"Or swim, more likely."

"Exactly," he replies, turning on the car before starting the drive back to the castle. It would normally be only a couple of minutes, but he's going slowly because the darkness and heavy rains are making it almost impossible to see anything.

When we pull up to the house, we both stare at the distance between the car and the doorway. It seems so much farther in a downpour.

"At least a little more rain isn't going to change anything at this point," I joke, waving my hands over my drenched hair and clothes. "I'm already a wreck."

"You always look beautiful," he murmurs offhandedly, and my eyes widen. I can see he immediately realizes what he's said, and his cheeks flush. "I just mean . . . sorry. That wasn't a . . . I'm not trying to . . ."

"I know," I say quickly, trying to wave the sentiment away like it's no big deal. Although, frankly, the stumbling is adorable, and it's doing something to me. My pulse is suddenly racing faster than if I'd run a marathon, and it's taking a *lot* of self-control to resist smoothing my hand across the light-golden stubble that's dotted across his face.

"Okay," he says, as though he's trying to gain back whatever composure two people who've slept together recently and are soaking wet in a car could have. "We should get inside, right? You need to call your son back."

"Right," I reply, and we both open our doors and make a run for it. When we get in, I'm about to say something else when "Just the Two of Us" starts blaring again from my phone. I look over at Jack, and he nods, silently letting me know it's okay to answer.

And even though I'm happy to have Bash's voice coming through crystal clear now, I can't help but feel sorry to watch Jack walk away.

CHAPTER FOURTEEN

I'm always smiling when I get off the phone with Bash. He cycled through stories from his school day of recess zombie games, math worksheets, and facts about the exoskeletons of ants.

But now that I'm alone, all my nervous energy from earlier creeps back in. I don't like that I didn't get a chance to thank Jack.

I should thank him for driving me back.

But what am I going to do, knock on his door late in the evening? As though that wouldn't send the wrong kind of message?

Do I *want* to send that message?

Anything with Jack is playing with fire. Even though time has made it hazy, it's impossible to forget that he hurt me so many years ago. I can't stop myself from drawing a straight line from accepting someone who kept me at arm's length to letting myself marry someone who also wanted me conditionally. It's dangerous to let my relationship with Jack be anything but professional.

But I don't know how to fully relegate him to that side of my mind. *You always look beautiful.*

Crap.

I do need to say thank you, right? I kind of ruined his evening?

Oh, who am I kidding.

Before I can stop myself, I'm walking down the hall and knocking lightly on his door. Maybe he's asleep, and that'll be the answer for me.

But instead the door opens, and Jack is in front of me, freshly showered, standing in shorts and no shirt. It momentarily short-circuits my brain.

"Oh. Hi, Beatrice," he says, the confusion crinkling his nose and making me even more distracted. "What's up?"

"Um . . ." How does he *look like this*. I've forgotten what I'm doing here. Oh, right. A thank-you. "I just wanted to say thank you for driving me. My phone rang, and I didn't get to say it, and I wanted to tell you. And . . . yeah. Thank you."

He's watching my little meltdown with one of his small secret smiles, and I can't tell if he thinks I'm completely pathetic.

"You're welcome," he finally says.

There's finality to the conversation, but neither of us moves. And I'm also realizing this was probably a bad idea. I haven't showered after getting caught in the rain, so I'm far from looking my best.

But also . . . he's looking at me like none of that matters. He's looking at me like a one-night stand maybe was too good to be one night after all. He's looking at me like he thinks I'm always beautiful.

And I know I've already cracked. Just like Rika laughingly said I would.

"Can I um . . . can I come in?" I hear myself ask.

He nods and takes my hand, guiding me inside before shutting the door.

He walks into the room, but I lean against the door, as though I haven't quite decided what I want to happen. We're sizing each other up, waiting for someone to take the lead, even though we've run well through the wall of plausible deniability. Just having him standing here is making my entire body pump with awareness. I don't know how he has such an intrinsic physical effect on me.

"So," he says, still not coming toward me. "You don't drive, huh?"

I smile at the absurdity of *that* being the most pressing question between us.

"Is that a major aversion for you?" I tease. "Women who can't handle major machinery?"

"I'm wondering if I graduated from high school twenty years ago, and you stayed there locked in a time loop of Peter Pan–like lost children who never grow up."

"That's me, still underage, while you get unfortunately old," I needle.

"Cute. Like all the cute people who can't drive."

"I *can* drive. I just let my license lapse. Plenty of people don't drive."

"You've lived in New York too long if you think that," he says, finally moving toward me. My breath catches. I'm trapped against the door, but I like being bracketed in by him.

He softly grazes my hip with a single finger, and even with all my clothes on, it makes my stomach tighten and my insides scorch like they've been prodded with a hot poker.

But he's waiting for me to decide what I want.

There's moonlight drifting in and shadowing his face, making his profile golden. I don't have to stop myself now from lifting my hand up and caressing his jawline, the stubble that distracted me earlier rough across my hands.

I pull him to me. I have to.

The last time we were alone was fire and speed, rasping and feral. Now it's lingering touch and torturous glides; it's recalibrating a lost map of another body and studying it.

He wordlessly removes my clothes, one item at a time, and gently leads me to the bed, slowly pushing me onto my back. I watch as he undresses and gets down on his knees again, studying me, taking small bites out of soft patches of my upper thigh. Until just as slowly, he's unraveling me, and I allow myself to get taken away on this second trip down memory lane.

My fingers are tingling, the way they do when you sit on your hands the wrong way and they fall asleep, except this time I think it's from having what might be the most intense orgasm of my life. Is that possible? Or is this what a minor heart attack feels like?

I'm flat on Jack's chest, and we're both attempting to bring our breathing back to normal. He's tracing little circles on the curve of my lower back, and I'm not sure if it's helping to bring me back to reality or sinking me deeper into a sex fog.

"I think you broke my brain," I say finally.

"What defines 'broken'?"

"Describe something to me. Imagine I'm a person whose mind has been melted and now won't be able to sleep, and you need to help me get my brain back on something mundane."

"Hmm," he says, taking this thought experiment seriously. With my ear to his chest, his voice sounds like a purr. He's quiet for a minute, and I wonder if he's fallen asleep, but then he starts talking. "There's this dessert I absolutely love. It's a lemon torta at that restaurant Ci Siamo. I don't know how they get it to be so intensely lemony, but it's like they took the flavor of lemon and condensed it until it was the perfect balance of a little sweet but mostly tart. And the crust is simple, maybe a graham cracker crust? The whole thing is sort of like a lemon version of a key lime pie, but I think the base has more meringue or something that just makes it exceptionally fluffy. I'm not sure there's a more perfect bite anywhere."

The description is so good I can practically taste it. I can't believe the man can barely get two sentences out when I need him to in a meeting, but lying here naked in the middle of the night in Ireland, he can wax poetic about a lemon torta that exists across the sea in New York.

"Definitely not what I would have expected you to say," I finally reply.

"And that would be . . . what?" he asks, maybe a little curious.

"It's funny thinking of you in New York. In my mind you still live in suburban Boston with all your brothers."

"I'm not the person stuck in an ageless time loop who never learned how to drive."

He's teasing, but it feels emptier. I pause, not sure if I've tapped too hard on the glass of this Irish experiment by mentioning his family.

We lived in that weird high school bubble where we never really did know each other outside our school lives. I knew his mom stayed at home; I knew his dad was a hard-ass; I knew he was the youngest of four boys. But I never knew *them*. I always got the sense that even thinking about his family made him want to burrow away, a skittish crab looking for cool refuge in a cave of his own making. That was all I ever got about his outside life when we were younger.

And now we're in a bubble of a different kind, caught between professional lines and an opened can of worms. Maybe I wanted to know more when we were younger and I had the mental space to inquire, but I really don't need to get that kind of insight now. This bubble is a freedom and a cautionary tale, a champagne tower that hinges on no single piece being removed. Neither of us needs to have anything fall down right now.

So I happily give him the out.

"At the very least, one of us needs to be using their brain and point out that I can't sleep here," I reply, shifting the narrative.

"Jeez, let a man regain some strength before he walks a girl out."

"That's not what I'm—"

"Relax." His eyes are on me again, reading me. "I know you want to go back to your room."

"I really wasn't running away," I explain, grimacing internally at potentially having broken the bubble. "I just think it's good to draw some boundaries."

At that his wry smile is back, and he sits up and shifts me off him, and I want to pout a bit because he'd made a comfy body pillow.

"Okay, tell me your *boundaries*, Beatrice."

"Don't mock me."

"You made a mockery of yourself; I'm merely pointing it out."

This is good, this light teasing. I didn't want to offend him, but I also don't have space in my brain for him to misinterpret where I stand.

"Okay, well, I just need to be clear that this"—I point between him and me—"cannot be a *thing*."

"I didn't realize I'd proposed to you and tried to whisk you off to the castle next door."

I roll my eyes. He really doesn't make things easy.

"Shut up, Jack. Seriously, I don't know what your life is like, but I definitely don't have space for anything taking up any mental energy right now. I have work, I have my kid—that's plenty."

His gaze turns thoughtful, and I wonder what part of that soliloquy has him churning. He's silent again for long enough where I wonder if I've exasperated him.

"I'm the same way," he finally says. "Well, opposite from the kid situation, obviously, but same in that I don't really do relationships. So I get that completely." He pauses. "But maybe what happens in Ireland stays in Ireland."

"Yeah?"

Can it actually be this easy? The other shoe isn't going to drop directly on me at some inopportune moment?

"You said it yourself the last time—it doesn't count. Sex together is old news, just with a new round. But obviously trying to keep it to one time . . . didn't work." I snicker. Yeah, that was probably never realistic. But he continues. "So we can simply . . . keep it here."

There's a niggling feeling in my chest, like a postsex sting of hearing him throw my own words back in my face. Yes, I said it doesn't count, I know I did . . . but why don't I like hearing it said back to me?

It's probably not that.

It's just the lack of clarity, and I can solve that.

"Keep it here, meaning what?"

"You tell me."

The ball is in my court, and I think that's on purpose. I want to crack him open like a walnut and root around to get the meat inside. I want to know what he's thinking, even though I'm the one who pulled out the nutcracker first. But there's power in getting to set the boundary, so I need to take it.

"I think in New York, anything personal outside of work is off the table. But if we're here and we need some stress relief, then this is fine."

"Wow, *fine*, what a searing compliment." I groan and roll away from him, but he instantly grabs me and pulls me back. "But yes," he whispers, "I think that's a good idea."

His fingers on my back are a balm, soothing me from the inside out. There's something glorious about already having spent so much time with someone else's body; there's a comfort here with him that I haven't ever felt before. Clearly the physical muscle memory of being together never went away, even if—thank goodness—all the emotions have.

"So this is normal for you?" I ask, unable to not pick a little bit more.

"Bedding women in my boss's house?"

"Noooo," I reply, lightly hitting him with a pillow. "Sex with no strings, I mean."

"At this point in my life I wouldn't know how to have strings," he says honestly.

"I think I'm the opposite," I say, turning the idea around in my mind. "I'm tangled up in so many strings the thought of adding any more makes me feel panicky."

"That makes sense," he says, nodding.

"Does it?"

"It does," he replies succinctly, letting the sentiment sink in. He's once again employing his most incisive skill: knowing when understanding is as simple as listening and saying little. And for once I know I don't need to ask anything else.

This could be good. I don't actually like him, and I need release. There's no way for this to get messy or complicated, and it saves me from having to try to get laid using whatever dating app Rika eventually shoves down my throat when she decides I need it. Home can be home, and then I can combine my biweekly work trip with a side of sex with a person I have no interest in outside of the physical.

And okay, he damaged me before. But that actually makes keeping it casual so much easier—yes, it was literal *decades* ago, but the man fully ghosted me. I don't need to get emotionally involved in the same mistake twice. I've had too many larger disasters since Jack, and those battle scars make whatever Jack did to me feel like a paper cut. I'm smart enough to know this backward glance is only ever going to be physical, and I'm too exhausted to even contemplate sharing any piece of my emotional state with another person. I don't need to worry about investment in a person whose emotional capacity rivals a turnip's.

Yup, this is a solid plan. I just have to find a polite way to kick myself out of his room now.

CHAPTER FIFTEEN
APRIL

"And then the fluid kind of like, *eats* the caterpillar's body and makes it also turn liquid, and *then* they turn into these things called 'imaginal cells.'"

"That has to be made up." Clem's eyes are wide as Bash hooks her in with his gross caterpillar stories.

"No, it's really not! But I haven't even gotten to the best part. So the imaginal cells can basically decide what they want to be. They can transform into *anything*! And so they decide to become butterflies."

"So inside of a cocoon is just a gross dead caterpillar liquefying and then turning into a butterfly?"

"Basically," Bash says, taking another huge bite out of a cookie Clem brought over tonight.

I'm a pretty average cook, but I can get away with throwing a dinner party at my apartment. I justify that I'm providing the space and Clem loves to bake, and I can sweet-talk Rika into cooking for all of us and letting me clean up.

I'm relieved she agreed to come over because, beyond my own selfish desire to enjoy Rika's cooking, it means she really is turning the corner on sleepless baby nights and is finally becoming herself again. Getting the three of us together with my constant travel, the five kids between us, and life in New York sometimes feels like trying to balance alligators on a seesaw. I've been to Ireland three times since I last saw Clem, and she's usually the easiest to wrangle.

So it's not really my fault if maybe I haven't shared my casual colleague-with-benefits situation with my friends. Not that it's anything even worth sharing; biweekly sex is hardly a major announcement. Even if it's been exponentially excellent sex, and even though it's now happened more than a handful of times.

But after all, it doesn't exist here in New York.

"Bash, time to go to bed," I say, scooping up my pajama-clad boy and getting a giggle out of him.

"But Moooommy, I want to tell Clem more about the butterflies."

"I think she's gotten the gist of it—come on. Brush that sugar off your teeth and hop into bed. You've got school tomorrow."

He sullenly accepts his fate and marches off into the bathroom. Clem immediately fills my free hands back up with a glass of wine and one of Rika's signature appetizers, a cheesy puff that she insists on calling a *gougères* that she popped out of the oven moments ago.

"I made these with Irish cheddar in honor of your new favorite place," Rika calls out with a grin from behind the counter.

"Hardly my *favorite* place," I say.

I don't know why I have the jittery need to play it cool on Ireland. I can't quite gauge why admitting I'm actually happy to have the breaks feels traitorous.

I pop one of Rika's fluffy cheese creations into my mouth and let the comfort of carbs lull me.

"I feel like I've missed everything you've been up to, Bea," Clem says. She's sitting at the kitchen island so she can be closer to everything Rika is making. "Whatever happened with working with Jack?"

It's an innocent enough question, but immediately my face starts burning, and I can tell both of my too-observant friends have clocked the rising flush.

Rika puts the tray down and narrows her eyes at me. "Yes, Bea, whatever *happened* that Clem has clearly missed?"

Her words are clipped, and she is not playing. I could feign ignorance. I could tell a half truth where I claim I haven't told her yet because it only just started happening. I could make a run for it, although that seems like the least appealing option, since everyone is currently congregating in my house.

What am I so afraid of, anyway? I'm allowed to have sex with whomever I want. These are my friends.

My very honest friends.

I take a deep breath. "So, okay, I think you should both remember that I'm in sort of a . . . well, I'm in this in-between stage in my life where I need familiarity . . . and, uh, I also am finding a balance between healing and putting myself out there . . . also, you know how you're always saying you have to find—"

"So how long have you been banging Jack?" Rika says, cutting off my rambling like I'm a flailing wounded animal being put out of its misery.

"Let's not say 'banging' with a child in the next room," Clem whispers.

"'Fucking'?" Rika asks, her wide-eyed simper directed toward a visibly cringing Clem. "'Lovemaking'?"

"Okay, no, please, dear god, no," I finally cut in.

"Oh, so the f-word is fine, but we draw the line at 'love'?" Clem says, downing her wine and looking deeply disappointed in me for desecrating the linguistic overlords.

"Well, yeah, because one is a better descriptor," I say matter-of-factly.

"Glad we're not obfuscating here," Rika says, chopping up some vegetables with a force I'm not sure I want directed toward me. "So you've been 'hooking up'"—("Thank you," Clem says under her breath)—"with Jack for what, six weeks? Eight weeks? And you just weren't going to mention anything because what? We're all so notoriously out of each other's business?"

I purse my lips and fidget, pulling apart the cocktail napkin that's resting in my hand. I'm not totally sure why I haven't wanted to tell my friends about Jack. Yes, I knew how they'd all react because, *yes*, they watched everything go south the first time. But it was easy enough to explain, and definitely after all these years, there was a simple way to spin it as not being a big deal. It *isn't* a big deal.

But maybe there's also something about keeping things ensconced in Ireland that maintains the protective sheen.

"Are you afraid something will change if you say it out loud?" Clem articulates for me, her voice soft, her fingers gently smoothing across the rim of her wineglass.

I watch her movement and consider the simplicity of her question. "I guess so, yeah," I say finally.

"If you're afraid of it, that's not a great sign," Rika says, throwing the rest of her vegetables into the sauté pan with barely a glance. "He always had that ability to make you question yourself."

"I'm not sixteen anymore, Rika, for god's sake," I snap at her.

She stills, and I immediately deflate, wanting to dislodge my own discomfort enough to not wreck our dinner.

"I just mean it's not like that now." I can see the skeptical glances from everyone and resign myself to the inevitability of explaining. "It's not becoming something. I'm not in a place for dating, obviously, and he clearly isn't either. It's just . . . easy. And fun. Sex hasn't been easy and fun for me for so long, you guys." I can feel myself heating up. "Can't you lay off this one particular thing? Can't I let sex be fun again and not some soul-crushing, heart-wrenching, baby-expectation, pressure-filled cannonball?"

There's a static silence, and all eyes are on me while the verbal confetti I spewed on everyone slowly drizzles down. I sit down next to Clem at the counter and defiantly stuff another gougères in my mouth, tantrum completed.

Rika wordlessly pushes the plate toward me, a peace offering in my favorite form of baked goods.

"Fair enough," she says. "So tell us about the sex."

I'm so grateful I could kiss her. I love that my friends can change course at a moment's notice when needed, like a scene from an old movie where everyone's running to catch the train as it leaves the station, and they get pulled up by the skin of their teeth.

"I guess . . . ," I start, trying to put this thing between Jack and me into words. "It's like I've found the cheat code to combining chemistry with expertise and a willingness to listen."

"Listening sort of implies more than just sex," Clem says.

I shake my head.

"I don't mean like listening in a conversation." Although, to be fair to Jack, in a work context at least, he's pretty good at that too. But I'm definitely not explaining that to two women who are already skeptical of my ability to keep things with this particular man casual, and who saw firsthand how much he hurt me so many years ago. "I mean, he listens in bed. He asks what I want. He asks if what he's doing is working. I . . . I've never had anybody who's actually prioritized that."

Although with the looks I'm getting, I might as well have three heads. I'm surrounded and suddenly a little nervous that I'm about to be part of an intervention. Rika is probably going to let the food burn, she's staring at me so intensely.

"But why haven't *you* been saying what you want in bed? Like, who gives a damn if they're asking you?" Rika asks.

I see Clem nodding along, and I know whatever answer I give, it's definitely going to be the wrong one.

"I mean, you know, I make . . . noises and move a hand or whatever needs to be to sort of . . . get it where it needs to go."

"And so the person is just supposed to intuit what you need?" Clem asks.

Okay, damn, if I've lost Clem, I've really lost the plot.

"Well, obviously with women it's easier, since they know more on a personal level," I reply huffily, as though my queerness can be used as a trump card of some kind.

"Okay, but still—well done to Jack for being a talker and good in bed and everything . . . but you've never actually dated anyone else who gave a shit about getting you off?" Rika presses.

"I wouldn't go that far—"

"But how far? Like, what percentage of the time would Lucas finish you if he finished first?"

"Oh, never, obviously," I say automatically, before realizing this is not the answer everyone was looking for. "But we got married for the wrong reasons. I mean, Bash is not a *wrong* reason. But you know what I mean."

They do, of course. They helped me breathe when I found out I was unexpectedly pregnant; we all swooned collectively when Lucas got down on one knee. They brought food and soothing whispers when I was in the trenches of newborn Bash. They held my head in their laps through every miscarriage; they took cotton balls to my thigh to stop the bleeding after another round of estrogen shots during IVF as Lucas pulled further and further away.

"So now you're having fun," Clem says, all that history sitting in front of us so clearly I could practically reach out and pick each memory up as swiftly as I can one of Rika's appetizers. The mention of fun pierces through the cloud.

"Yeah," I reply quietly. "For so long it felt like my body was a battlefield, you know? Like it was representing everything disappointing about my life—unable to *sustain* life. Sex couldn't be extricated from all of that baggage. Now, though, I don't know, with Jack—almost because he's so detached from anything beyond the physical, but I know he's trustworthy—it's like I'm free again. I can just fuck a guy and not have it be about a family or babies or womanhood or whatever. I really am sorry I didn't mention it before, but I needed to keep this uncomplicated thing uncomplicated." I see a small tear roll down Rika's cheek, and I immediately hop up to wipe it off. "Oh, honey, I didn't mean to make you cry."

"No, I know," Rika says, grabbing my hand. "I'm so sorry you were still feeling like that after so much time. I had no idea."

"Grief can take a long time to process," Clem concurs. "You cycled through miscarriages and IVF so fast and then a separation. Of course you're still coming to terms with it."

Even hearing Clem verbalize the sentiment makes my heart lift. I'm getting some advantage of hindsight, and that in itself feels like a step forward.

But Rika breaks the stillness Clem has evoked. "Okay, can I just say that, like, I would not have put *Jack Sander* on the bingo card for the person who fucks you back to life?"

"Come on, *Rika*," Clem hisses. "Can we please stop with the language. You know I hate it."

"Bea said the same thing literally only a minute ago!"

"Yeah, but she's processing some stuff."

"So?"

"So, she can say whatever she needs to," Clem responds.

I smirk at Rika, silliness rising back to the forefront. She rolls her eyes, then turns swiftly back to her pan before everything burns.

"So I guess it's good I made extra cookies tonight?" Clem says, chuckling.

"*Definitely*," we both say in unison.

CHAPTER SIXTEEN

So while I do not regret spilling my guts to my friends yesterday and all the banter and conversation that followed late into the night, I *do* regret the copious amounts of alcohol the evening involved.

By the time Bash and I leave for the bus, even the refreshingly brisk late-April weather and the lingering cherry blossoms on the trees can't stop the morning from feeling bleak.

When Bash sees his friend Ella running across the street and breaks out into a run, I'm too tired to even pretend to try to catch up.

"I win!" she shouts gleefully when she beats him to the corner.

He smiles and shakes his head. I can never get over how easily Bash lets things roll off his back. It took me years to develop a cool exterior when I needed to focus. He simply has it naturally. And thank goodness, because Ella is always somehow getting into detention for whatever bus shenanigans she has going on.

I wave silently to Ella's dad and lean up against a wall, counting down the minutes until the bus arrives and I can go slink away. Thankfully, Bash and Ella are in their own little six-year-old self-involved cerebral worlds enough to not really care that my only responses to their stories are grunts and mmhhmmms.

But apparently that streak is ending. He and Ella are directing a question at me now, and the bus has unmercifully not shown up yet.

"Sorry, what?" I ask.

"Ella says 'zax' is the best short word for Scrabble because it has nineteen points, but I'm not sure if that's actually a word. Is it a word, Mommy? Is it? Is it?"

Is "zax" a word? How the hell would I know. But I can't say that.

"I'm not the best Scrabble player. I really don't know."

"Well, ask the best player you *do* know."

"Okay," I say, pulling out my phone and blithely following instructions. I shoot off a text to Jack—Is zax a word?—since he for sure fits that description.

It takes me a minute to realize that my autopilot has committed a crime against myself. *Shit.*

I've never texted Jack for anything outside work. We text and email all the time now that he's up to speed on everything in the office and a lot of our job stuff overlaps. But this is not that kind of text. I set those boundaries the second time we slept together, and ever since, our unspoken understanding has stood. Work is work. Except the one night every two weeks when we're already sleeping in the same house on another continent, and then that particular evening involves one of us pulling the other into their room for a few hours before never acknowledging it again in the light of day.

Shit, shit, shit. I do not need to complicate my one uncomplicated thing. I spent practically a whole evening convincing my friends how uncomplicated it was. I don't need Jack to now get the wrong idea because I'm one step from unconscious this morning.

But before I can whirl out into a panic spiral, he's already texted me back.

Is this a Scrabble-related question?

His immediate answer makes me smirk. Of course he would know useless Scrabble words. Yes, I type back. Keeping it simple. I'm allowed to ask him a friendly question, right? It's not an invitation to something or an attempt to get into his deepest, darkest desires. It's a Scrabble question.

> Technically, yes, a zax is a small axe for cutting roofing materials. But mostly it's just a bullshit Scrabble word for getting points on useless letters.

I quickly shoot off thanks to Jack and show the text to Bash. "My work colleague Jack concurs with Ella," I say, and she starts hopping up and down in delight.

Thankfully, I'm saved by the bus pulling up. Ella's dad gives her a hug and lowers his voice. "Make good choices today, sweetheart. We all have to play by the rules, even if we don't always agree with them."

Truer words could not be spoken, especially on a day that involves a pounding headache.

I give Bash a kiss on the head before he and Ella bound up the stairs onto the bus. And with that, my little morning home bubble has broken, and I have to face the day. Or at least, look at my phone and finally respond to some texts. *We all have to play by the rules, even if we don't always agree with them.*

And when the bus pulls away, it's time for that instant changeover from parent mode to work mode.

Or at least, normally it would be. Today I'm more in hungover mode. And even my regular walk to work can't shake it.

At least the sandpaper mouth and the pressure emanating into my eyeballs are making it impossible to dwell too deeply on my text to Jack. And at least he wasn't weird about it.

Besides, maybe calling him my "work colleague" to Bash was a little cringe, but that *was* the kind of thing I could text to a work colleague. No innuendo in Scrabble questions. We're friends, sort of?

I get to the office and immediately pour myself the largest cup of coffee I can find before my daily morning catch-up with Brigid. I join the Zoom call and try to sit up straighter, as though that'll make me look more ordered.

"I don't need to hear about why you look like a bedraggled raccoon today, Bea," Brigid says the minute I show up on the screen. *Excellent.*

Of course, she looks amazing, in a silk orange shirt and an even darker lipstick than usual. I automatically minimize my own face on the screen because I don't need the comparison.

But she just barrels along. "And I only have two minutes, but I wanted to mention that you should notice I put the board meetings in June and September on your calendar."

I *did* notice that and was surprised. I'm not normally invited to the quarterly board meetings. Maybe Brigid really is taking this potential actual promotion and raise seriously, even though it still doesn't feel like she's changed anything in my day-to-day job other than overseeing the office stuff.

"We just had the end-of-first-quarter meeting and were discussing the three-year plan and your role. I know I promised you a raise and a real promotion beyond just a title change when we talked in Ireland in January. So I now have a plan in place, and this is how we'll do it. I want you to give a presentation to the board about growth strategy at the next meeting. I wanted to give you the heads-up now so you'll have a few months to prepare."

"Well, thanks for that, Brigid, I appreciate—"

"It's not for your appreciation; it's because I need you to nail this so the board can see how valuable you are to their bottom line. You can give the presentation in June, and then the board is going to do the September meeting in Ireland, where we'll have a lot longer to talk through their impressions and really delve into it. So start thinking about it now, okay? Okay. Talk soon."

She's already hung up before I can get another word in. Without her in the office, with its typical New York glass walls separating our spaces, it's much easier for her to vanish. Lately it's felt distinctly emptier when I look out from my office and onto the expanse of cubicles beyond.

Typical of Brigid to give me marching orders and then disappear; she knows that we approach everything the same, anyway, so—to be fair—there's no point discussing it further.

I'll need to take time in the next month or so to interview various team members and come up with a longer-term and more detailed plan than what we've been operating on. It's a lot of extra prep on top of what I'm already doing, but on the other hand she's given me two months to get everything in order. Plenty of time. This is just another step-up moment. I can handle it. I *need* to handle it, now that Lucas has his hackles up. The stakes for me are too high to have anything go wrong with my job.

As I'm staring out of my glass cage, I see Jack saunter in and wander to his. He's typing away on his phone, probably already knee deep in emails from Ireland, a hank of hair curling a bit too far down as he walks while gazing at his device, and he has to bat it away from his eye. He doesn't look up for even a second, though, before pulling on his headphones and opening his laptop.

But I notice that my phone buzzed while I was talking to Brigid, and I see that maybe he wasn't working on emails after all.

Jack Sander has invited you to play Scrabble Go! Click here to join the invited game "Zax"

I look up, but he's still staring at his computer, seemingly oblivious to the message I'm only just now seeing but that he sent before walking in the door.

He's chewing on his lower lip, lost in thought, and it's immensely distracting. He has one of those mouths that's all lower lip. Sharp curves on top and full lip on the bottom. How does he just wander around *looking like that?*

I dart my eyes back to my phone to get the image out of my mind, since I feel a little guilty for objectifying him at work, even if it's from behind the safety of glass walls. Not to mention that it's a week until we're back in Ireland, so I don't need to make my week feel longer than it already is. I click to download the app and log in to pull up the game he's already started.

"Lame." That's his first word. Twelve points. He's usually better than that, so I'm guessing the desire to start with a funny word was probably too tempting to pass up. The corner of my mouth arches up slightly.

I look at my letters, thrilled to see that I can keep the antics going *and* take the lead instantly.

"Joke." I push *submit* and see twenty-eight points float to my score-board. I watch as his phone buzzes next to him. He clocks it, pulls it up, and grimaces. I quietly chuckle, knowing exactly what he's thinking. He's regretting his initial word, and now he'll take his next answer more seriously.

But he looks up and catches my glee, raising a sardonic eyebrow at me. *Competitive Beatrice,* I can practically hear him thinking. I really cannot give him the satisfaction. I need to not get sucked into a vortex of playing Scrabble all day with Jack instead of focusing on the extra pile of career-defining work my boss just gave to me.

I point to my computer and shake my head dramatically at him, continuing our wordless conversation and indicating that I have *very* important things to do. I turn my phone over and go back to staring at my computer before he can have the last "word."

CHAPTER SEVENTEEN
EARLY MAY

"Why are you awake?" I ask Mona without even saying hello when my phone rings. I was already staring at it while responding to a new Scrabble notification.

"I'm walking home from a date."

I hear horns in the background. Only Mona could manage to stay out so late on a Monday and feel so casual. I, on the other hand, feel like a truck has run into the side of my body from sleeping face down on a plane and dealing with an earlier flight than normal. "Besides," she says, "six a.m. for you is only one a.m. for me, so you're really the one with a shitty schedule today."

Isn't that the truth.

I'm sitting on the tarmac, having just landed in Ireland. I certainly have time to kill. "Well, what's up?"

"I had a *lovely* run-in with Lucas earlier."

Oh, dear god.

"And he told you how nicely he accepted me bringing by Bash a little earlier when my flight got changed?" I ask.

She snorts and I smile, knowing that at least Lucas can't escape from his sister's rational opinions instead of only stewing in his unreasonable ones.

"Let's just say I wanted to check in on you when you landed."

"Thank you," I say quietly.

I really don't know what I would do without Mona in my corner. She's the only person who can talk smack about Lucas while also reminding me he isn't a piranha when I'm out on a ledge.

"Next time, call me first. I can always come home and watch Bash until it's the exact time my anal-retentive brother has indicated in his calendar. You could do without these little things setting him off."

"You didn't sign up for my problems to be your problems." I sigh as I pop a headphone into my ear so I can grab my bag seamlessly once the line of people starts moving off the plane.

"Don't call my nephew a problem, Beezus. So rude of you."

I smile. I love how easy she sometimes makes things for me, even as she taunts me. Is it possible to divorce the man but keep the sister-in-law?

To be fair, I guess I've effectively done that.

"Okay, Ramona. I'll let you joke your way into this one. Next time I'll call you." I take a deep breath. "I appreciate it, really I do. When he gets angry, I can't help but let it get *me* angry because the only other option is to cry, and that seems worse. I hate leaving Bash and getting in the work zone when I'm all riled up."

"I hear ya. Hence the suggestion."

"Thank you."

"Speaking of things you should've told me first"—I groan; Mona always has some extra agenda—"Randall says you're getting Irish booty calls on these trips, so I would've thought that *that* could help when you're riled up."

I can sense her glee to be springing this on me, even though I can't see her face.

"Rika really doesn't need to share *every* detail of my sex life with her husband, you know."

"Hey, that's between the two of you. I'm just the interested extra party who would like to get the same level of detail as the women you aren't related to."

"Okay, being related should theoretically make me *less* likely to share my sex details with you. And besides, Rika guessed it, so it wasn't like I *told* her."

I hear her open the door, and I'm happy picturing her back in our apartment, holding down the fort, swaddled by our nook of a home even when I'm not there. "Well, whatever excuse you want to make for being cagey, I'm just happy to know you're getting some action. Is he hot?"

I pause. "Yes."

"Is he good in bed?"

"Yes."

"Then thank the fucking lord, because I can't feel sad every time I see you charging your vibrator again."

"Gee, thanks."

"Anytime, my dear. Always here to champion your vagina."

"Please never say that to me again."

"Can't make any promises," she says, laughing. "All right, I'm jumping into bed. Love you, miss you, enjoy getting laid."

She hangs up before I can even respond, and a smile emerges, the fog of my sleepless night made a little bit lighter by Mona's sheer charisma.

But I get another jolt to the system as I look up at the baggage claim and realize Jack is standing in front of me, eyes looking down on me from his taller vantage point. Did he hear . . . any of that? Were we on the same plane the whole time? I guess we're both so used to arriving at different times that it didn't occur to me to look for him.

"Hey," I say tentatively, fidgeting from the light of day.

"Were you on my flight?" he asks, obviously thinking the same thing as me.

"I guess so. My normal flight was oversold, so they switched me to the one two hours earlier."

"Well, now you know the secrets to my schedule." He says it innocuously, but it does feel a little weird to be here this early in the morning, alone together.

I'm trying to think of how I can feign an excuse to take a cab by myself when he cuts in with "Do you want to drive with me? I know you usually take a cab, but I'm driving anyway."

I stare at him, unsure of how to politely decline. There *is* no way to politely decline, so I guess there goes my extra hour of snoring in the back seat of a stranger's cab.

But before I can muster up the enthusiasm to be polite, he flummoxes me by coming closer, like he's going to whisper something in my ear. I'm not sure my brain is in a state to register his scent of simple soap mixed with overnight sleepiness without short-circuiting.

"You can sleep, Beatrice," he says in my ear, the extra syllables of my name coming across like strands of silk. "I won't tell."

He pulls back and gives me a small lopsided smile. It makes my insides fizz. I hate that he's able to read me like a book with no nuance or plot secrets.

But I'm sure it must be the same with my older friends too—it's easier to see under the hood of someone you watched being made.

A little voice is tapping at the windows of my jet-lagged brain, though. I'm surprised at how easily I always accept his little gestures of help, even when no one else would even know I needed it. It's surprisingly easy for me to picture falling asleep next to him while he drives, disheveled and exhausted and without a care about what he sees of me.

I shake off the image of that little intimacy.

"Okay," I say. "Thank you."

"Thank goodness I have my license," he says as he walks away toward the car rental counter, and I find myself muttering after him, cursing myself that I walked right into that one.

I wake up to the car door opening. Des is looking down on me, amusement etched on his face.

"Y'all right there, Bea?" he says.

"Yeah," I mutter. "Just was on the earlier flight, so think I slept longer than I normally do."

"Well, it's nice you and Jack were able to come together this time."

"Not together. Just a coincidence," I say as I sit up. Thank goodness I'm wearing an olive green canvas jumpsuit that's impervious to wrinkles or disheveling of any kind. "Nice of him to drive, though," I add when I realize he's still within earshot.

"She's much less chatty when she's conked out, so it was a blessedly peaceful journey," he cracks. He ambles into the house with his bag and leaves me to catch up, even though Des has already got my bag.

"You should come see the lambs later. May is really peak cute time. Either of you can drive the car just down the private road and park in front o' the barn house if you want to see 'em."

I see the glint in Jack's eye, and I'm about to cut him off before he can make the obvious joke, but then he surprises me by saying, sincerely, "If it's a private road, maybe it's a good opportunity for Beatrice to practice driving so she can get her license back."

"What a wonderful idea," Des says with his patented enthusiasm, ruining my opportunity to explain that I'm actually being mocked. "I know there's a lot of work here in the mornin', but maybe before dinner around five, take a break and come see 'em gettin' fed. Ya need to go outside to mix up the day when you're here."

I trudge upstairs. I can't think about the evening when it's this early in the morning outside but still the middle of the night in my brain. Nap time comes first.

CHAPTER EIGHTEEN

The day rolls along, and it's actually been good to have everyone in a room so I can go over questions that will help me with my presentation to the board in a month.

The minute Brigid mentioned it to me, I started outlining. I want to *kill* this presentation. I want to ooze competence. I want to show the entire board that I'm worth promoting. I want to show *myself* that all my hours secretly enjoying being a workaholic are because I'm genuinely meant to be doing this. And, okay, maybe I also want Brigid to smile (even though perhaps that one is a little far-fetched).

But today is the first time I've gotten to run ideas by the team and escape my own self-imposed mental isolation. The feedback is super helpful, and I feel satisfied from a day well spent without any distractions.

Well, except one.

As we're all packing up our laptops after a long brainstorming session, I see Jack standing above me, waiting, still as a totem and somehow always able to strike that perfect balance between annoying and distractingly good looking. He's giving off those Harrison Ford vibes I've always attributed to him, but now he's approaching the gruff middle-aged version instead of the fresh-faced earlier iteration.

"Can I help you?" I finally say.

"Uh, yeah, it's driving time, and apparently also baby sheep time."

He's so blasé that it's hard to reconcile that grumpy face with any conversation about baby animals.

"Lamb time," I reply, unable to stop myself from correcting him.

"'Lamb time' makes me think it's dinner," he counters, gently grabbing my arm and steering me toward the door.

"Fair enough," I breathe as he pulls me out to his car and throws me the keys.

"Not driving at your age is absurd; how do you go on a vacation or do anything outside of a major city?" he mutters, almost to himself, and I try to tuck away the smile that's emerging from how irked he seems by the thought of anyone flouting conventions in such a dramatic way.

"I don't know—I got married right around when my license lapsed, and Lucas always drove, and I hated it, so I just let it go," I reply truthfully.

There go those eyebrows again, shooting up.

"That doesn't sound like you," he says, and I'm surprised.

"You don't know me," I retort defensively, although immediately I cringe at the immaturity.

"You're a single mom," he continues, ignoring my rejoinder. "What if you want to take your kid to Disney or something?"

"Cab from the airport, then stay in a hotel that's on the wonder of technology that is the monorail."

"Okay." He pauses. "Summer weekend to somewhere upstate too far from the train?"

"You literally just pointed out I'm a single mom. When would I have time to do that? It's not like I *deliberately* let it lapse. I just didn't need it, so it lapsed," I respond, hoping that's enough. Although I need to mutter the other basic truth: "And the DMV is such a pain in the ass."

"Oh my *god*, Beatrice, that's the laziest thing I've ever heard."

I sort of hate that every time he verbalizes my name, it gives me a little shiver. He gets into the passenger seat of the car, all his long limbs crammed adorably into the small European vehicle, and he waits for me to take over the driver's side. I huff, but I get in.

I put my hands on the steering wheel and realize I'm nervous to start the car. The reality is it really *wasn't* intentional to stop driving. It's true that I didn't drive very often anyway, so it wasn't like I was missing something essential in my life.

But I think about a road trip that Clem, Rika, and I took up to Maine before any of us had kids, our neon-blue rented convertible's top down, even though it was probably slightly too early in the summer. We belted out eighties pop songs while dense trees and flowers zoomed past outside. I've let that freedom go somehow.

I wish I could blame Lucas for it (it's always so much easier when I can blame Lucas), but the truth is I've let that side take a back seat all on my own. You have to give up some independence when you have a kid, sure, but maybe I've allowed too much to be shed away.

I can see Jack considering me out of the corner of my eye, some comment on the tip of his tongue, holding himself back from over-stepping. But I can hear it anyway. I know it's encouragement and not mockery that he's unable to articulate. I know he's rooting for me to start the car.

I turn the key in the ignition. The car thrums to life, and I roll down the windows and put my foot on the gas.

It's a quick five-minute drive down to the barn, but just the knowl-edge that I'm taking back some small piece of my former self is exhila-rating. The dirt path is well worn as we drive past hand-cobbled stone fences, with metal gates hastily added in. It seems like miles and miles of excessively green grass stretch in front of us, with freshly shorn sheep trotting along every corner. The wind is blowing in the vegetal scent of all the shrubbery, and it's hard to pay attention to the road when all this vivid, windswept landscape is yawning out in front of me.

But it's like riding a bike. There's nothing to driving, especially since Jack has rented practically the only automatic car in Ireland, a fact I'm exceedingly grateful for at this moment, even if it is weird to be driving on the opposite side of the road.

I park the car and can't stop the grin that breaks out across my face.

"You can thank me later," Jack says, a small smile of his own unable to be contained. I roll my eyes to stop my heart from squeezing unnecessarily.

"You're just trying to get into my pants later," I retort, handing him back the keys and getting out of the car.

He moves faster and is already walking toward the barn when he turns around and whispers, "You're wearing a jumpsuit. There are no pants."

"Oh, you think you're *so clever*," I say to his back, but he fully ignores me as he gets roped in by Des instantly.

I try to ignore the way his whisper has made every hair on my arms prickle with anticipation.

Des wasn't lying when he said it would be fun to feed the lambs. They're at that perfect age where they aren't newborns but still bounce around like toddlers. They're partially drinking milk, but Des is weaning them onto solids—hay and grains mostly.

So he's showing us how to put the hay out for them and how to clean out, then fill the troughs with water so they can start getting used to drinking that. It's a delicate dance Des is managing, and it's fascinating to watch. Not to mention impossible not to pet every lamb in sight. Their woolly coats are rougher than I would've expected, but their little faces are just too damn cute. I'm having actual, honest-to-goodness fun, smiling like a goof at every lamb that looks my way.

I get a little pang thinking about having fun in a place Bash would love without him. But I will myself to shake off the guilt. He's perfectly fine, probably running around the schoolyard at recess right now. There's a relief that washes over me at even the thought of accepting that it's okay for me to keep some things for myself.

We finish up with many thanks to Des, and I drive us back, a slight chill more noticeable in the air as the sun starts to set and turn the sky a dramatic orange that tinges the fields with a golden hue. I've got mud splattered all over the canvas of my jumpsuit, and my hands are caked in dirt, but I feel so awake and in my skin now. The work high from earlier in the day has seeped into the rush of driving and the unusual manual labor. It's impossible not to breathe it all in.

After I park the car, I sit still for a moment in the quiet, breathing in the cool air and all the sweet earthiness contained in the countryside breeze.

But instead of getting out of the car, Jack turns toward me, and our eyes catch, piercing and unable to break away.

Suddenly everything feels like the slow motion of trying to walk surrounded by water in a pool. Whenever he looks at me like that, it's as though a thread is unspooling in my center, a flush rising rapidly. I don't know how I ever described those eyes as "icy," because, while it always seemed to fit his detached demeanor, the descriptor also let him off the hook of everything that's whirring beneath. Solid like a robin's egg, deep like the ocean, ephemeral like a blue gas flame. And my insides are caramelizing underneath them.

He reaches his hand into my hair, and I can't breathe for a moment. He lingers, slowly wrapping the strands between his fingers. My dirty palms still grip the steering wheel as though I might implode otherwise, set on fire by a single touch.

What are you doing? I think as we keep staring at each other. The sun is setting, but it's still light enough to see, and if anyone walked by us right now, I'm not sure we'd look like anything but two teenagers on the brink of shoving their tongues down each other's throats and getting caught on a gearshift. This is *not* supposed to happen at this time of day.

But he breaks the spell as quickly as he started it, pulling a bit of hay out of my hair and gingerly handing it over to me.

He gives me a last unreadable look and gets out of the car.

I look down at the stray piece of hay he retrieved. It's rough and weedy, and holding it in my hand tamps down everything that'd been building inside me. Except for confusion over what the hell just happened.

My phone beeps, and I look down. I see two little emojis—a small car and a sheep—and the words You did good today.

What. Was. That.

Sometimes when I'm in Ireland, I feel impressed by my sixteen-year-old self, and simultaneously deeply grateful to not be sixteen anymore. In this particular moment, I'm glad we didn't have texting then. The levels to which I analyzed his Away Messages—*Jeez, that thought dates me*—are not something I want to aspire to today. It's hard not to feel sympathy for my former self, pining in my teenage room at my shoddily cobbled-together desk holding an ancient iMac, surrounded by tapestries pinned up to the wall.

Jack and I were that polar-opposite high school cliché, the athlete and the debate team nerd who bonded in private but could never quite make it work as an actual couple. All the unexpressed angst and attempted unbothered cool girl vibes brimmed off me, as I convinced myself that having lost my virginity made me an adult of some kind. I wish I could go back in time and tell that girl it's okay to wait for life to happen.

But on the other hand, that comfort I always had with him in private—away from jockeying over which tables to sit at during lunch and our diverging group of friends—I can no longer pretend that that wasn't real. It was as real earlier today—eyes locked, senses churning, understanding unspoken—as it was then.

After he graduated and we lost touch, I convinced myself it was all just an infatuation—all those easy silences weren't understanding; they were two people sated on the drug of sexual exploration without any sense of where their futures would go. Time didn't stretch out yet, no context to the horizon.

I'd bloomed with expectation, only to be shaded into self-doubt.

Maybe I'd sold my younger self short, and she'd been onto something with that first infatuation. After Jack, I always assumed that that comfort, that desire, that unspoken trust would exist with anyone I was sleeping with. I forgot what that ease felt like, or figured it was youthful inexperience and not specific to Jack.

But that was selling *him* short. Maybe we've needed each other at these inflection points in our lives, two unromantics who really look at the parts no one else wants to see and keep ourselves honest.

Thanks for getting me back on the horse, I reply to his text, not wanting to let whatever combustion has just been averted between us take hold and change our status quo.

It was baby sheep, he responds.

I roll my eyes, even as a quirk of a smile tugs at the edges of my lips. I meant the car dingdong.

And then I put my phone away. I have a shower to take, a dinner to get to, and a presentation to work on. There will be no pining in this iteration of friends with benefits. We may have the same chemistry, but I'm not sixteen anymore.

Chapter Nineteen

Late May

I only have a few weeks until my board presentation, but I know I'm prepared. I'm not a person who leaves things to the last minute—I was the kid who always turned in reports early at school, much to the chagrin of everyone else around me. I know this presentation is a big moment for me, but I also know our business from the inside out. I know our data; I know our customers; I know our partners. Nothing can trip me up.

So I'm a little surprised that Brigid wants to have a meeting after our dinner to go over everything. She's never looked over my work before.

But then again, I've never presented to the board before.

"Knock, knock," I say as I push the door open to the library.

Brigid is already seated in one of the midnight blue velvet wingback chairs, engrossed in her laptop, so I sit next to her and wait. She takes her time. The meticulous way Brigid always presents herself—today's look is typical maroon lipstick, a silk navy button-down, and chocolate-brown tapered jeans—is the same way she approaches completing any task. I'm not going to get her attention until she's done and ready to give it.

"Okay." She finally looks up, closing her laptop and immediately giving me her undivided attention. "Give me what you've got."

I hand her a hard copy of some of the projections, but I don't even need to reference it. I share what I've compiled from our US and European sales teams, the market research studies I'd commissioned and their results, as well as the client feedback I've organized over the last few weeks. There are actually a *lot* of potential areas for growth for Breck, but I've narrowed things down based on all the new materials and some helpful advice from Jack on what's feasible, tech-wise. I already know Brigid is going to love how much data I've proactively sought out to back my recommendations.

When I finish, I look at her expectantly, a teacher's pet hoping for praise after her book report.

"I would claim to be impressed, but I expected to be impressed," she finally says. "I am glad you've nailed it, though."

I beam. For Brigid, that's about as high a compliment as she can muster.

I still want to make sure it's completely ready. "Do you think the handouts are the right level of detail? I know it gets a bit in the weeds there when I'm talking about the Midwest gains, but I think it's a really key portion of—"

"I have no doubts about you carrying this off seamlessly, if that's what you're worried about. I think you know me well enough by now to know that I have no patience for hand-holding."

"I do know that, yes," I reply softly.

"Good. Because *when* you nail this, your role is going to grow substantially."

I'm not quite sure what she means about my role, but it's hard to focus on anything but the positives. This kind of feedback from Brigid is about as effusive as she gets.

I figure I should stop pressing her, accept the win, and change the subject already. Maybe it's the confidence boost or the cozy library setting, but somehow I find myself asking, "Are you happy with the move to Ireland?"

She looks surprised that I'm bringing up something so personal. "I think the team is actually working really well with these condensed spurts coming here."

She knows that's not what I meant, though—of course her response is deliberately about the company. She's always such a pillar, with ironed shirts and ramrod posture. She doesn't give anything but strength. But as she cocks her head to the side a bit, I can tell that *maybe* she's considering giving me an inch of the interior.

"And yes," she finally says. "I am happy here. I know you know that divorce is never easy"—I have to admit I'm surprised she even *knows* to say that—"but this was the right choice for me."

"I'm really glad to hear that," I respond sincerely.

She nods and sits back, such a different reaction from her usual curt dismissal when she's done with a conversation. I hold my breath, wondering if maybe for once I'm going to get just a touch more of Brigid's particular perspective.

"You're strong, Bea," she says with her distinct succinctness. "Sometimes being strong means making the harder choice. My husband thought he was strong enough to marry an ambitious woman, but he wasn't. And so I had to choose myself."

The sentiment sinks slowly into my chest, a rock thrown in water winding its way down to rest.

"And the castle?" I ask, wondering if I'm pushing my luck.

I almost get the beginnings of a small smile. "Oh, the castle was just because I'm successful and I wanted to live in a castle. Without a husband's opinion on my life, I could do that."

She reopens her laptop and goes back to her emails without another word. I'm dismissed, per usual, now that she's done with the conversation.

As I leave the room and make my way upstairs, I wonder if there's a world where I could get more of that story. Maybe our no-bullshit work symbiosis could be a balm in a personal context too.

Or maybe I love Brigid precisely *because* she doesn't let work bleed into her personal life, and vice versa.

Although since I'm standing in front of Jack's door, debating whether to knock this late, the irony is not lost on me.

I hear a muffled voice sigh from inside the room: "Stop lurking and just come in." *Oops.*

"Sorry," I say, coming inside and then quietly closing the door behind me.

Jack is sitting on his bed in his boxers, also typing away at his laptop, but he motions for me to sit down as though he only needs to finish his thought before engaging. I'm beginning to wonder if Brigid's grand scheme is to trap a bunch of workaholics in a single place so they can get even *more* work done.

At least it gives me a chance to look around. I haven't been in his room much, and I'm struck by how orderly everything is. Clothes hung neatly, pens and pads lined up, shoes perfectly aligned in the corner. He's such a deliberate person. I have a strange urge to imagine what he looks like in a more casual context—if he even *has* a more casual context. But I push the thought out of my head.

"My meeting with Brigid went well. I think the presentation is in good shape," I say. I walk over and sit in the chair at the desk, since he's still not quite finished. "Although maybe I'm overestimating my adroitness."

He looks up.

Can you be attracted to the line of someone's neck? Because I very much am. Or maybe it's the way the line smooths and curves into his shoulder. Whatever piece of him is attractive, it's working. It's all working. But he obviously can't tell that I'm objectifying him now instead of talking about a meeting.

"Your adroitness?"

"I mean, my ingenuity on this topic."

"I know what 'adroitness' means," he needles.

"Are you sure?" I tease, desperate now to get an elusive smile out of him, since he's at least more reliable on that front than Brigid, even if they are both killjoys of the first order.

"*Yes*," he says, deliberately denying me the smile I know he knows I want. "That just wouldn't be the word I'd use."

"Oh, so like, you'd probably say I'm a genius."

"Not what I was going for," he huffs.

"'Irreplaceable'?"

"Eh."

"'Masterful'?"

"Not really, no."

I scan my mental word bank for another synonym. "'Dexterous'?"

"Are we talking about work or sex now?"

I bark out a laugh but then quickly purse my lips, trying to rewind the part where he clearly won this particular verbal volley.

"We can't all be Scrabble word masters," I say, with as much nonchalance as I can muster.

"I only meant that I can't imagine you of all people overestimating anything about yourself."

Oh.

"Because I'm already too full of myself?"

I always have to do this. I have to joke my way out of a compliment or assume it *wasn't* a compliment.

"No, because you're exceptionally effectual at your job, and anyone who makes you think otherwise—I'm guessing yourself included—is a total fool."

Oh. Oh. Ohhhh.

I'm sizzling. This is like my very own competence porn. He's standing up for the honor of my brain and abilities, and it is *doing* something for me. Although . . .

"So that's a compliment and an insult all rolled into one?" I finally say, latching onto the *I'm guessing yourself included* part.

"Take whatever you need from it," he says, moving his laptop onto his side table and then standing up.

He comes over to where I'm sitting and hovers over me. I have to crane my neck to look up at him, like a tree suddenly casting a shadow. I'm unable to decide if I'm more turned on by his particular zinger of a compliment or the proximity of his bare chest, but awareness is zipping through me, and I stand to get nearer to him. He moves the chair out of the way, and in one fluid movement I'm up on the desk and his hands are in my hair, reverent, like he can't wait to touch me. It's as though we're back in the car, strands making their way around his fingertips, but this time he doesn't let the moment go.

In an instant, his mouth is on me, needy and urgent. I love the lingering taste of whiskey on his breath. It's raw and spicy and somehow makes him taste even more like himself. I can't stop from tracing the line of his neck down to his shoulders, the perfect curve of cursive, responsive to my touch.

"The difference in our states of dress needs to be remedied," he rumbles after a while, pawing at the little straps on my shirt, and I love that he's somehow able to say such an unnecessarily flowery sentence while also being mentally incapable of removing my top.

I help him out and pull it over my head, and he groans at the sight of the black lacy bra underneath. His hands skim across it, the pads of his fingers lighting me up like a pathway in darkness as he moves from my shoulder to the side of my breast and onto my nipple. I suck in a breath, and the sound makes him react, like a Pavlovian indication to move faster. His hands are on my pants, unbuttoning, and I'm leaning back, my arms holding me up on top of the desk as he tugs at the fabric.

"Can I have you here?" he whispers in my ear, always asking, always somehow finding the capacity to give me agency, even when he's so in control over every part of my body.

I nod, and he lowers his mouth and nibbles my shoulder; it makes me arch into him. *That* gets me the glimmer of a smile I was hoping for before. Or maybe an even better one, because it's drunken and soft and admiring. It's magnetic between us, again and again, but every time still feels like a lightning bolt against a starry sky, unique and perfect in its particular moment.

I pull down my underwear, and he follows suit. His hand skates up my thigh, and I shiver, pulling him toward me just to feel his heat against me. He pulls open a drawer for a condom (*jeez, the man is so organized he even has a particular place for his condoms*), tears at the packaging, and rolls the condom on. I wrap my legs around him and skim my lips across his forearms, lusty and wanting and wishing his hands would come back onto me. But I get my wish soon enough—his hands are under me, angling me, and I move with him until we're so close that I'm aching for pressure.

"Is this okay?" he asks, and I can't even form a coherent sentence; I just pull him toward me, bringing us together slowly, but the relief I feel is palpable. "Beatrice? Use your words."

"More than okay, Jack," I mumble into his shoulder as he exhales into me.

We're moving together, gaining speed and both a bit crazed, each other's names escaping from our lips, tongues scraping across each other, fingernails pressing into flesh. Every time we come together, I feel more urgent, more manic, pressure building and not yet satiated.

But it's like he can read my mind because he lifts me off the desk, and I wrap my arms tightly around him, and it's just the sensation I need to let go, to feel the pleasure rip through every inch of my body, to ricochet from my toes to my ears and leave me breathless. There's a beautiful blankness to these moments, all sweaty skin and hot breath and nothing else in the way. It's the moment and nothing else, sensation overtaking logic, the one person I can let go completely with.

And boy, do I let go.

When he can tell I'm done, he moves us onto the bed, and he's on top of me, groaning and moving in and out until he reaches his apex. As buzzed as I am from my own orgasm, there's something thrilling about watching the way he loses control at the end, as though once he's gotten me where I need to go, he can abandon all restraint and just let his own pleasure overtake him. It would turn me on more if I wasn't physically incapable of moving again.

And then as suddenly as it began, we're both slack, letting our breathing slow and bring us back to earth.

Chapter Twenty

It takes me a moment to become aware of my body again, as though I've traveled outside of it and have to readjust to fit my skin back on. I'm sated and comfortable, the pressure of him lying on top of me like a weighted blanket that also happens to smell really good.

It's sort of perfect except for one thing—I unfortunately am coherent enough now to notice that I have one of those impossible itches, right behind my shoulder blade. I attempt to get my arm to it, and the contortion I'm trying to do to reach it is probably going to hurt in the morning.

"What the hell are you doing?" Jack says, his voice gravel from still being a bit winded.

"Trying to scratch this itch."

"Jesus, Beatrice," he says, moving my hand away, then moving his toward the spot. "The universe isn't going to implode if you ask for help."

I want to say thank you, but the sensation is instantly ruined by whatever he's doing that he considers to be back-scratching.

"Jack," I say, almost laughing at how hard he's digging into me. "Who told you this was something anyone would think is nice? This *hurts*."

"This coming from the woman who bites my shoulder so hard I'm surprised it hasn't turned black and blue," he says, and I roll my eyes.

"That's sexy," I reply, and he practically snorts. I ignore him. "Who taught you this violence?"

"Please, I have three brothers. This doesn't come close to violence."

He kisses my neck and stands up. He says it so matter-of-factly that I'm not sure he realizes that any of these little insights into his personal life seem larger when he shares them. He goes to clean himself up in the bathroom, and I wonder if merely the mention of his brothers has made him antsy. It's like he lives in the glass box of our office, and anything outside of that would break the walls.

Note to self not to breach those barriers.

I sit up and still feel a little dizzy. A goofy hypothetical comes into my mind, and I shout out toward the bathroom, "Okay, would you rather never have an orgasm again but also never have a bug bite, *or* would you rather keep your orgasms but also never be able to scratch another bug bite as long as you live?"

"Has anyone ever told you you're nuts?"

He walks out of the bathroom shaking his head and lies back down on the bed.

"Yes, you, plenty of times."

"That's just about the worst hypothetical I can possibly imagine, and I refuse to choose."

I lie on my back and stare at the ceiling. "Well, you're lucky you're a man, and endless orgasms are always on the menu," I blurt out honestly.

He shifts next to me, and when I turn my head to him, he's moved closer.

"It's not hard to get you off. You acted like it was going to be some big effort that first night, but I'm not sure what the big deal is."

My face heats up. This wasn't the direction I intended that comment to go—I *hate* talking about this kind of stuff.

Maybe flattery can get me straight out of this line of discourse. "Well, maybe you're just good in bed—have you ever considered that?"

I can see straightaway that he isn't going to let me off the hook with that. He furrows his brow, and it's so cute I want to kiss it right in the spot where it wrinkles.

"What the fuck was wrong with your ex-husband?"

Okay, *that* was not what I expected. I know he's direct. I know he only speaks when he actually wants to. But for a man who hates extra chatter of any kind, that's certainly quite the question.

"In which of the many ways?" I ask with a chuckle, more comfortable with laughing it off than scratching the underbelly of wherever he's trying to take this suddenly personal conversation.

"I mean, you're not prudish in *action*. Obviously," he says, his eyes skating across my whole body·and making me shiver. "But you get skittish talking about sex. I know I have no experience in marriage, but come on—you were married to someone and had a kid. What's up with that?"

The question is startling in its candor and lack of judgment—only the curiosity to understand.

I turn onto my side and stare at him. I'm sort of wild for seeing him this close because it's the only opportunity to take a real assessment of his face, like a map showing a few new roads built in the intervening years since I last visited. And it's soothing to stare rather than actually think about his question. But I know he's waiting.

"You're the only person who's ever asked."

"Why you get skittish?"

"No . . . what I like, or what feels good."

This close, it's easy to see him regulate his face. His eyes *want* to go wide. But he doesn't want me to feel embarrassed. It's such a little movement, but it's endearing.

"My marriage was . . . not good." I finally say.

He stays silent. Damn it, why does he have to be the only man in the history of the universe to hate talking over women? He isn't effusive, and I wouldn't say he's quiet exactly, but he'd never use ten words when five would suffice. He's exacting. And he's not going to talk until I answer his question.

I don't owe him an explanation. But somehow in this moment it feels okay to be honest about this kind of stuff with him. It's like the distance and the darkness can hold these kinds of intimacies, and they don't have to ever leave this room or mean anything outside of it.

But I turn onto my back again so I don't have to see him while I explain. "Lucas and I only dated for a couple of months before I got pregnant. When I found out, I was scared, frankly. And when he asked me to marry him, I said yes because it felt like the right thing to do. The sex was always fine, but it wasn't a priority. And it never really reached a level of that kind of intimacy because . . . well . . . it was always sort of tainted, you know? I was pregnant and hormonal, and then I'd just had a baby and then I was breastfeeding. My body wasn't exactly in the most beautiful state for the majority of our relationship." I hear him scoff next to me, and I don't want to ask why. But knowing he's listening fuels me to lay it all out there. "Then he really wanted another kid. So we kept trying, but I just . . . my body couldn't do it. I had a lot of miscarriages, and then we did IVF, and that didn't work so . . . yeah."

He's silent, and I don't know whether he knows I'm finished. There's of course so much more to say, but it hurts to say any of this out loud.

I'm about to get up and make some excuse about an early morning when I feel his hand on my shoulder, stopping me from the quick exit he clearly understands I'm about to make.

"I'm sorry you went through that," he finally says quietly.

Neither of us moves; I'm still on my back, and his hand is still on my shoulder, and I listen to both of us breathing, a soothing metronome. I like that we can sit quietly like this.

Sometimes, when I was deep in the infertility years, I felt like everyone else was standing in the sunshine, and I was hidden in a shadow. All I ever wanted was for someone to stand *with* me in that darkness. Everyone was always trying to pull me out, giving advice or attempting to buck me up. But this is the only thing I actually needed—friends to stand with me and help me exist outside of the light. And say, *Sorry you're going through this.*

"When you say 'he' wanted another kid . . ." He trails off.

I know what he's getting at.

"I'm an only child, and I liked it, so I was perfectly fine with just Bash."

"So it ended because you didn't want to keep living as a human hormonal roller coaster for his sake." Nail, see head.

"I shouldn't have accepted his proposal in the first place."

He scoffs again, and on that I finally turn back onto my side and look at him. "What?"

"*You* weren't sexy enough; *your* body couldn't have more kids; *you* shouldn't have accepted his proposal. Give me a break."

I sit up. "So what?"

"You didn't do anything wrong. Sometimes shit just happens. Him pressuring you is not your fault."

His eyes are on me, challenging me. I don't know whether to be offended or relieved. But mostly I'm speechless at how simple his solution is. I *wish* I could believe that. I wish I could dismantle the entire bridge I've been sold as a woman my whole life and believe that women's bodies and minds aren't expected to live up to unrealistic standards. What would it even look like to give myself some grace? To believe that my failure of a marriage was no one's fault?

"Besides," he continues, "I bet your kid is thrilled to have all your attention instead of duking it out with a bunch of siblings."

I appreciate the admission; the vote of confidence in my parenting; the vulnerability of lightly admitting his childhood was hard for him, even if he's never let me shade in the specifics. We're both complicated little onions, layers and layers hiding the astringency underneath. Maybe tonight I'll get an extra little layer of his, since he's shed even more of mine.

"Do you spend a lot of time with your brothers now?"

"No, they're all still around Boston," he says, and I can tell this is a bruise that twinges even with the slightest of prods. Boston and New York aren't far away at all—I see my parents plenty—but from his tone, it's clear it might as well be the moon.

And since he was willing to stand in the dark with me without much explanation, I'm not going to berate him about pulling anything into the light either. I quickly drop it. "So that's why we're both in the office so much on weekends. Doomed workaholics with families out of state," I quip, trying to alleviate the mood.

"Oh, I thought we pretended we didn't notice each other in New York?" he lobs back, jokingly calling me out on my staunch adherence to our rules at home.

"Like I have enough time to notice *anything* with my schedule." I give him a lighthearted nudge, stand up, and begin putting my clothes back on. "You're just mad I don't have enough time to respond to your Scrabble games as quickly as you do."

I love that after all that, *this* is what gets a smile out of him.

"Guilty as charged," he says, eyes scanning every movement of my hands, appreciative, like I'm doing a reverse striptease as I button up my pants and hook my bra back on.

Once I'm dressed, I walk over to the bed and give him a kiss on the forehead. "Good night, Jack. Hope I've sufficiently tired you out," I vamp, trying to keep things light as I leave, even though there's a nagging flare going off in the back of my mind.

"Night, Beatrice."

Those extra syllables again, always somehow luring me in. I walk toward the door, but before I open it, the nag gets the better of me.

"Thanks for listening earlier," I find myself saying softly.

And because he understands that exposing that squishiness is hard, instead of making a big deal of it, he simply nods. And it's enough.

CHAPTER TWENTY-ONE

JUNE

I hate being late even on a normal day. But on the day of the board meeting, it's *really* throwing me off.

Even though I'm not going to Ireland this week like normal—because Brigid's in town for the meeting—I still let Lucas keep his extra day with Bash. I don't want to upend either of them (or, frankly, poke a sleeping, semi-friendly-for-now bear).

But Mona slept over at some date's house last night, and the double whammy of both her and Bash being gone means I've been behind the eight ball all morning. I haven't had my obnoxious multiage twins to keep me in line.

And since I changed my outfit about seventeen times, I'm late even without having made breakfast.

I throw my stuff down in my office and sit, forcing myself to close my eyes and breathe. I keep hearing Brigid in my head saying, *When you nail this.* It makes me gulp from the expectation, edginess quietly tapping away at me.

But I have to remember: everything is all set; I could give this presentation in my sleep; I've read and reread my slides a thousand times. I've got this.

When I look up, I notice a neat little army of fortitude staring back at me on my desk. A steaming to-go cup has been placed precisely in the center of a napkin; there's a fluffy scone like the ones Des makes in Ireland; a good pen sits straight on top of a notepad.

There's only one person who could have set this up on my desk. This level of anal retentiveness has Jack written all over it.

But why?

Yeah, he's gone over my presentation with me a few times and helped to ensure we're aligned on what technological changes would be realistic for his team to accomplish. But everyone's done the same within their roles. I *have* been nervous, even though I don't have a real reason to be. But I haven't said that to him.

Maybe it's been obvious to anyone who works with me. Perhaps I've been a little too obsessed with this presentation. It clearly hasn't gone unnoticed by all my colleagues that I've asked them questions from every direction and angle over the last few weeks.

But not everyone got you your morning sustenance, says a little voice in my head that I swiftly bat away.

He's being a friend. We're friends. I haven't given a board presentation before. That's a big career day for anyone. He's being nice.

I pick up the cup and instantly smell the Irish breakfast tea wafting up. I open the top and let the now familiar beverage warm my insides.

I shoot Jack a quick text. Thanks for the breakfast, you saved me from my harried self this morning.

I look across at his office and see him already at work on his laptop, his phone abandoned on the corner of his desk. I guess he'll see my text later. And I'm too late anyway to focus on this.

I scarf down the scone and take the rest of my items with me to the conference room. An assistant is finishing laying out hard copies of the presentation, and she's already got a laptop queued up.

I flip through the presentation one last time as everyone starts filing in. Brigid's board is, naturally, an all-woman powerhouse: seven professionals—some investors, some data experts—who've helped her steer the ship this far. I've only met a couple of them before, so I try to project confidence as I shake hands and make small talk.

Brigid comes in with Jack and Lane and says hello before indicating that everyone should sit down.

It's funny seeing her back in New York mode—I've gotten so used to her Ireland look. I've never thought of her sharp outfits as armor, but that's how it appears here. She always looks sleek in Ireland, but it's not like this. Today she's in a fitted asymmetrical marigold pantsuit with a chunky bronze necklace, perfectly complementing her New York–preferred shade of maroon lipstick.

It makes my all-navy ensemble feel exceptionally muted. But then again, I'm not meant to pull the focus from Brigid, so hopefully my simple professionalism is the right note to strike. Although I probably shouldn't be letting my mind wander about clothes so much when I need to get my mind on the presentation.

The board stays mostly together on the far side of the conference table, so that leaves me with Lane and Jack, who sit on either side of me. I don't look over at Jack because I'm still a bit restive over the tea and scone; I turn to Lane to say good morning. But I shouldn't have even bothered, because of course Brigid doesn't waste a second anyway.

"I know everyone's busy, so let's get started," she says. "We'll have Lane go over the quarterly earnings first, and then, as I mentioned at our last meeting, Bea will give us her presentation on where she sees Breck's potential areas for growth in the coming years. I think you're all going to be really impressed with what our newly designated chief revenue officer has come up with."

She sits down and nods to Lane, who gets up and starts talking.

I tune Lane out and try to mentally prep for my presentation. But now that I'm on deck, I'm a fidgety ball of energy. I can't stop my leg from bouncing under the table, and I'm trying to make myself breathe slowly so that my heart rate will stop accelerating.

This group is so impressive, and that small introduction Brigid gave oozed confidence in me. What if I can't live up to it? What if they ask me questions I'm not ready for? What if I choke—metaphorically or maybe even literally?

I see Jack shift next to me out of the corner of my eye. I want so badly to ignore him because I don't need something else making me feel out of sorts today. But he's pushing something toward me on the table. I can't look at him, but I do glance down at what he's moved in my direction. It's a little notebook—same as the one he left in my office this morning—open to a mostly blank page. At the top, in his distinctive orderly handwriting, is a single sentence: *You've got this.*

I look up, but he's still watching Lane, no indication that he's simultaneously giving me a wordless pep talk on the side. It distracts me enough to slow my breathing.

And it's at just that moment that Lane sits down and gestures to me. I stand up and smooth out my skirt. I smile.

It's true. I *do* have this. I know I have this. I get started.

CHAPTER TWENTY-TWO

"So what you're saying is . . . you crushed it?" Mona grins as she hands me one of her perfect gin and tonics, and I could not feel more relieved to be sitting down at my own table right now.

"You're saying that," I reply, taking a long sip. "I'm simply saying that I got all my points across and they asked good questions, and I think I answered everything without ruining it. That's about as good as it gets, from my perspective."

"You don't have to be modest in front of us," Rika says.

She's at the counter, mixing up something that already smells delicious. Her husband, Randall, is seated next to me and raises his glass at the sentiment. He's barely touched his drink anyway because he's mostly just staring at Rika—even after they've spent a decade together, it's amazing to watch how much he adores her. I've obviously adored her forever, but you never assume that your favorite women are going to find partners who actually realize how incredible they are.

I get to see Randall on his own more than the average spouse because he and Mona have been best friends since business school (and he's the reason I actually met Lucas . . . but let's not dwell on that one). So I get him as a bonus family member across multiple angles. I clink our glasses together and silently whisper *Thank you* to him.

I'm grateful Rika volun-told me she was cooking dinner for us all tonight. Either way, I would've wanted them here—if I'd bombed the presentation, I would've needed support, but now I just get to feel proud because my friends insist on celebrating and won't allow me to downplay how it went. And I always hate it a little when Bash isn't here, so the company is especially welcome.

My phone chirps next to me, and I see a Scrabble notification.

"Uh, what's happening to your face?" Mona says to me, and I look up sharply.

"What?"

"Who texted you?" she asks suspiciously.

"Actually, no one." I'm very pleased with myself for being able to truthfully evade, but Mona is having none of it.

"It's your sex friend."

"I don't have a 'sex friend.'" I whisper the last two words, embarrassed.

"Oh, are you actually dating that Irish guy now?" Randall asks, so sweet and yet *so* unhelpful to this particular line of questioning.

"He's not Irish. And we're not dating. And he's not a 'sex friend.' He's just a colleague and friend—"

"—who you consistently have sex with," Mona cuts in.

"Who you literally lost your virginity to," Rika adds.

"Okay, but please, Rika, can you add in that that was *twenty years ago*. I'm too old to make this sound that tragic."

Randall is chuckling, but I'm not amused. Rika shoves one of her delightful gougères into my mouth, presumably to shut me up and/or make me happier with carbs. Randall takes two and then tries to grab a few more, but Rika bats his hand away.

"Okay," Mona continues. "So your friend, who you have sex with on a scheduled basis in another country, who you also used to have sex with twenty years ago, but who is definitely not someone you are dating, is texting you." She's not letting it go.

I hold up my phone to show her the screen. "He's not *texting* me; it's a Scrabble notification. We play online Scrabble. It's nothing. And that's about the least sexy thing imaginable, so you can take that self-satisfied look off your face as though you've discovered something."

She snorts. "Okay, well, the goofy look that took over *your* face when your *Scrabble notification* showed up was like a biological response to nerd flirtation, and it was clear as day to me who it was."

I don't even know what she's talking about. I like Scrabble. And yeah, Jack really was nice to me today, okay. But I don't make faces for him.

"So you're dating him?" Randall asks, clearly trying to stay on topic.

"When would I have time to date someone?" I respond, standing up to help Rika bring everything over to the table.

We sit down and dig in; for a moment we're all consumed with Rika's creations.

But now Randall is the one who won't let it go. Why do I have so many stupid inquisitive friends hell bent on extracting every last detail in my life?

"You don't like him?"

"It's not that I don't like him," I say, churning internally at the thought of still pretending to remotely dislike Jack at this point. It doesn't feel right. We've turned a corner from that, even if it's still a small corner. "I'm just . . . not in a place to date anyone. And even if I was"—I can already see Mona lifting her hand to reject that premise—"he's not someone I *would* date. First of all, he completely ghosted me twenty years ago, so, ya know . . . once a ghoster, always a ghoster. No thank you. But aside from that, we're super different, other than both being workaholics. And he's not a sharer, so I barely even know anything about him personally, really. But that's kind of why it's good, actually. Two emotionally stunted and unready people blowing off steam every couple of weeks. Neither of us wants a relationship, so this is easy. It's not a thing."

"So like . . ." Randall is still trying to wrap his mind around this particular arrangement. "You don't talk to each other? You work together all day, and then silently go have sex and then walk away?"

"Well, no, obviously not," I say quickly. I feel weird at the idea of selling Jack short in that way. "I like talking to Jack. But that doesn't mean we talk about anything substantive the way I would if I was actually trying to get to know someone. But it's not like . . . wham bam, thank you, ma'am. We talk to each other. And we help each other out at work."

"How does he help you at work?" Mona chimes in again.

Lord, these nosy, nosy people. I don't grill Mona on every person she goes to bed with. Hell, I haven't even heard a single thing about whoever she was out with last night. It's like my friends are so desperate to get me to date again and be "over" what happened with Lucas that they're grasping at straws.

"He helped me narrow down what was technologically feasible for what I wanted to suggest in my presentation. But he's the CTO—he would need to sign off on anything eventually anyway, so that's just a positive coworker situation. Or like, this morning he left me some breakfast in my office before the presentation. And he wrote down some encouraging things when I was nervous to get started." Mona and Rika give each other a look, and I roll my eyes. "Please stop reading into things that do not exist."

"Oh, honey, I'm *all* for you having a sex friend," Mona says with a laugh, even though I'm distinctly not going to laugh at her continued characterization. "And a sex friend who brings you food? You must be horny without Ireland this week! Screw the Scrabble and make him send you a dick pic instead."

I'm about to interject, but Rika beats me to it. "Oooh, yeah, has he sent you any good dick pics?"

"I don't do that," I say, feeling a flush rising on my cheeks.

"Of course you don't," Mona says, standing up to get another drink. "You don't have a dick."

Can you hurt yourself from rolling your eyes too much? Because if you can, my eyes are in danger of falling out of my head. "Cute, Mon. Seriously, this is not a *thing*. When we're trapped in the same place, we have sex. The end."

But it's clear I've already lost the plot, and my friends are now fully ignoring me while also talking *about* me.

"Do you think that means she's never sent him a nude?" Rika asks Mona.

"I don't know, sex once every two weeks but ignoring each other at work feels like some extra-kinky shit, so maybe that's enough."

"Ah, so the ignoring each other is kind of the foreplay?"

"Okay," I interrupt, not sure if I'm about to burst out laughing with them or kick them all out of my home. "You're all very funny and nosy, and I would like to know what it will take to make this conversation end."

"Ooooh," Mona says, as though I've offered something, and I already know I'm going to regret whatever she's thinking of. "Okay, I will let it go and believe you that you actually don't care if you send him a naked picture."

"What?" I say, fork midair, food abandoned. "No. Mona, no. He doesn't want that." I hear Randall snort, and I turn toward him, glowering. "Oh, now you have thoughts on me taking nudes?"

"Okay, absolutely not," he says sincerely. "Just that, all men want naked photos. I mean, you can say you don't want to and that's not your thing, but you can't say he wouldn't *like* it."

"No, okay," I say, feeling a bit cornered. "Yes, men like naked photos. But that's . . . intimate."

Rika and Mona are full on howling now, and I cross my arms, pouty and definitely not enjoying being mocked.

"You literally allow this man's penis into your body—"

"*Mona!*"

"—and you're worried naked photos are *intimate*? What is wrong with you?"

"Just for the record," Randall says, butting in, "I think you can do whatever sexual things you want in private and also not want to send someone digital evidence of it." He's *such* a buttoned-up banker to his core. I pat his arm in thanks for his very particular Randall brand of defense.

But Rika isn't even listening to him. "Nonsense. The man brought you breakfast. He saved you. He deserves a reward."

"My *colleague* brought his *colleague* some sustenance before a presentation," I counter. "Stop trying to make this a thing! I'm tired, and I *like* having sex with someone who has no emotional bandwidth to harass me, since you guys clearly are taking up all of that energy. I have Bash, I have you clowns, I have work, I still have to deal with Lucas. Let my sex friend just be a sex friend."

Mona is practically levitating with happiness that she's clearly won by getting me to call him my "sex friend." But I can see that Rika has clocked that I've had enough of the ribbing.

"How did Brigid react to your presentation today?" she asks, deftly changing the subject.

"Good, I think," I say truthfully, grateful to be talking about anything else. "I feel like Brigid has some agenda, but she tells me nothing. Whatever she's plotting for me, though, it can only be good things, since she brought me into this meeting today."

"Will they implement your ideas?" Randall asks.

"I gave them a lot of supplemental materials, so they're going to take everything home and review, and we'll discuss their thoughts at the next meeting in September."

"Ah, because you love waiting so much," Mona says, smiling.

I wrinkle my nose at that sentiment being caught. But I'm glad my friends can see both my giddiness and my impatience, the swirling balance of being me.

The conversation swims along like this for the rest of the night on a sea of laughter and gin. I share details about some of the board members I talked to; Randall whips out photos of the kids and finally has to be nudged to stop by Rika; Mona finally regales us with tales of her sleepover last night and complains about having to battle Brooklyn traffic back into Manhattan this morning.

When we've dragged the evening as far as it will go, Rika and Randall head back home. Mona and I finish washing up, and then I finally say good night and collapse into bed. The day's frantic start and the rush of adrenaline is all catching up with me now, and I'm exhausted.

The conversation from earlier is still buzzing in my ears. I spent so much of the night fighting off my friends' playful jokes, but I can't help but hear Jack's voice from a few weeks ago ringing in my ears. *You get skittish talking about sex.* When did I get like this? Have I always been? Or have the last few years taken something away from me—something free and open, some piece of spontaneity, some sexual well that emptied when fertility entered the equation? I *am* loosening up, though, right? I'm having casual sex! Surely that counts for something?

But I'm too tired to go in those mental circles.

I pick up my phone to start my definitely-good-for-me evening doomscrolling and see the Scrabble notification again. I open the app and look at my letters—*NRESDLU*. It's impossible to stop myself from laughing.

I add NUDES into the board and don't even care that I've punted on getting more points in order to make an inside joke to myself.

CHAPTER
TWENTY-THREE
JULY

I'm standing in Bash's doorway, wondering when he's even going to notice that I'm there. He shooed me away twenty minutes ago, irritated that I didn't think he could get ready alone. (*Moooom, why don't you trust me?*) I didn't want to point out that he always inevitably gets sucked into some book, but since he used a trust bomb on me, I had to suck it up and pretend like I totally believed he could get dressed without getting distracted.

But now he's sitting on the floor, shirt on with no underwear or pants, reading a science book about extreme weather. *Fun.*

I clear my throat, and he still doesn't look up. Finally I can't wait any longer. "Earth to Bash; you've got to get ready."

He looks at me, a big *oops* written all over his face, and he springs up to pull his pants on. I hand him a pair of underwear, and he quickly rips off the pants and puts on his clothes in the proper order.

"If you want to make Open Studio, we've really got to go," I reiterate to him, and he follows me out of the room.

I love this little tradition we have on Saturday mornings when Bash is with me; we go to the Whitney Museum together. They have this program where they pick a piece for kids to draw inspiration from and then the kids make their own artwork. This week they have an artist from the Biennial coming in to talk to the children, so I don't want to be late.

We hotfoot it across town, stretching the definition of "walking" to get there as fast as we can without looking like fools. The muggy July heat is seeping in fast, even though it's still pretty early in the morning, but thankfully we get to the museum quickly. I'm in the front, digging through my purse looking for my membership card, when I hear a familiar voice behind me.

"Did you win the speed-walking competition?"

I look up and am momentarily jolted. I'm having an out-of-context moment with Jack again, although now it's happening blocks from my apartment, at the Whitney. The sandy hair, the plump lower lip, the perfect shoulders are all as familiar to me as entering my front door at this point, but it's all in the wrong place. He's wearing a T-shirt and shorts (both of which are truly, truly working for him) instead of his typical work shirt at the office, or corded sweater in the cooler Irish temperatures.

"What're you doing here?" I finally say, not loving that I'm suddenly a little out of breath with him towering over me.

He looks around the museum, as though it should be obvious what he's doing here. Duh. It's a Saturday at an art museum.

I change tactics. "Well, that's . . . that's just how I walk."

"Yup. Could spot you three blocks away."

"Maybe walking is my exercise."

"Walking from your apartment to museums doesn't count."

I want to retort, but my mind is too blank from the surprise of seeing him here. I'm fidgeting; I try to grip my hands together to stop them from nervously moving. It's so damn bright in the entryway, surrounded by glass on every side, and his eyes are lighter than usual because of it.

The room is cavernous, but I feel trapped nonetheless, unable to move in my total awkwardness.

"Hi, I'm Bash."

I hear a little voice beside me and jerk toward my son. He's looking up at Jack, holding out an outstretched hand. Ugh, I really am regretting teaching my kid to be polite.

"Nice to meet you. I'm Jack. I work with your mom," he responds, gripping Bash's hand and looking way less uncomfortable than I would've guessed he'd be around a child.

He has that vibe that some adults have where he almost ignores that Bash is a kid, as though every person is a person and this one's no different from anyone else. I *do* dislike it when adults try to get all kid-like when they're around Bash, since he usually hates it. But the whole situation is still throwing me off.

"Oh," Bash says, eyes widening, "is this Jack your work colleague who's the best Scrabble player you know?"

Damn children and their spongy elephant memories.

"The 'best Scrabble player you know,'" Jack says slowly, turning his gaze back up to me, mischievous delight written all over his face. "Better than yourself?" he asks.

It would come across to anyone else as an innocent query, but I know underneath that is a gloating, competitive degenerate.

"Yes!" says Bash, unaware of the silent conversation happening over his head in narrowed scowls and wicked grins. "I asked her a word question, and she said she's not the best Scrabble player, so I asked her to ask the best one she knows. I think that was you, right?"

"Indeed it was. That is I. I am Jack, the *best* Scrabble player Beatrice Leal knows." I glower at him. "What are you planning to see at the Whitney this morning?" he asks Bash, ignoring me now.

"We come here for Open Studio. They let the kids make art inspired by a piece in the latest exhibit. You should come—it's really fun."

"Oh."

I enjoy watching the bravado slip off him a bit. I know when he initially saw me, he couldn't give up an opportunity to rib me, but I think the reality of the situation is now hitting him. He's just inadvertently introduced himself to the kid of the woman he's casually sleeping with, and now he has to find some way to wriggle out of being saddled with her baggage.

But I don't want this to get uncomfortable. "Jack isn't here for Open Studio, Bash," I interject, trying to save him from having to say no to Bash's eager face. "He's . . ." *Ugh, what do I even say here? "He's a dude who clearly likes going to art museums on a Saturday morning? Alone? He clearly relishes his peace and quiet and does not want to partake in an activity with a bunch of wiggly kids?"*

"*Mom*, adults like Open Studio too," he says back at me, obviously exasperated by my closed mindedness. "It's painting today. Do you like painting, Jack?"

I can feel my face start to go red because I know the answer to this one. Or at least, I did. Jack could sit and paint for hours. He could focus no matter the noise around him. I can picture him, one hand on a hip and the other with a brush in the air, staring at a canvas, just thinking. So much of our past time together is blurry, but that's an image I can't forget.

"Well . . . yeah," he finally says.

"Then you have to do it. It's so fun, come on."

He grabs Jack's hand and is already pulling him forward, his tiny body taking control of a much, much larger one. Jack swivels his head and gives me a questioning look. I can't tell if he wants to apologize or have me get him out of this scenario, but either way, there's no extricating yourself from Bash once he's made up his mind.

I figure the best bet is to let him get started, and then Jack can slip away once Bash's kid-size attention span grabs hold of something else.

But that opportunity doesn't quite materialize. Bash pulls Jack over to a square table, and I watch as the two of them organize and discuss the art supplies that have been placed there. I sit dumbfounded at the table while they go to collect more items—different brushes, a few colors our table doesn't have, four Dixie cups with water.

There's an uncanny familiarity at seeing Jack in this mode, organizing paints, distributing palettes, and lining up brushes, a little ritual unchanged. Before the talk has even started, we're like chefs with our mise en place laid out perfectly, no recipe shared yet but at the ready to begin whenever we receive our assignment.

I do a double take when I notice that two of the cups of water have been placed in front of me. I peer over at Jack, but he's looking forward, listening to the artist, who's started giving her short talk without me noticing. I try to snap into it; she's a willowy gray-haired elderly woman whose abstract paintings are a key part of the Biennial exhibition this year. She talks about children and parents as her inspiration, which is why she was so keen to join in with this concept and speak to (as she says) "budding artists while they're still young and interesting."

Bash is nodding along, but I'm distracted, unable to stop looking at those two little cups. This day has taken a weird turn.

And then just as suddenly, everyone is silent, painting commenced, abstract masterpieces apparently ahead of us, and I'm the only moron still staring off into the distance.

"What did she say to do?" I whisper to Bash, who looks over at me and rolls his eyes. *Hey, that's my move.*

I notice Jack wearing one of his small smiles, even though he's also looking down at his paper as he strokes his brush across the page.

"Come on," I say quietly, turning my attention toward him. "I wasn't listening to what she said."

"Clearly," he whispers back. "I'm surprised you're admitting it so openly."

I want to roll my eyes at him, but since the six-year-old in our midst has just used that particularly mature reaction moments ago, I hold it back.

Jack sighs, seemingly not totally impervious to my silent pleading. "She said to paint yourself in your family unit, as abstractly as you can."

He glances over at my blank paper. I nod and mouth *thank you*. And I get to work.

A little while later, our "paintings" are hanging up, and we've been given instructions to wander the museum for at least half an hour until they dry. In the meantime, the artist is letting some of the kids talk to her about her paintings in the exhibit. I watch Bash as he excitedly peppers her with questions. It's moments like these that I'm grateful to be raising him in the city, even if that sometimes comes with its own baggage.

I peer at all three of our little paintings. Bash—who, for all his mental acuity, isn't exactly the most dexterous with his hands—has painted abstract versions of what seems to be himself in the center, me on one far side, and his dad on the other, although I'm not sure I love the clear division, even in the abstract.

I look over at what Jack's painted, more precise than anything the kids have made: sharp triangles locked together in the center of an otherwise blank page. It's a tumble of a memory seeing a painting of his again. The sensation is familiar both visually and in my own internal intrinsic desire to want to dissect every brushstroke and understand its meaning.

Even without seeing him, I can feel him hovering behind me, his tall frame lurking just out of reach.

"What's yours supposed to be?" I ask.

"Didn't anyone tell you art is subjective?" he says, his voice low and far too sexy for this early in the morning.

I spin around to look at him. His hair is a little scruffier than he keeps it in the office; this weekend look is more like a late night in Ireland. I want so badly to run my hands through it. We're in New York, but in this more casual setting, I'm disoriented by how much that's somehow blurring the line for my insides.

I need to stop *noticing* him so much. Or at the very least thank him for being nice to my kid and somehow get him to scuttle off.

I ignore his previous comment. "Well, it was nice of you to humor Bash." He shrugs with a nonchalance that belies no rush to escape. "He's chronically incapable of recognizing that other humans might not share every single one of his interests," I continue.

"Yeah, there was twenty minutes or so of straight monologue about the patterns of monsoons. It's no wonder his painting didn't get the attention it deserved."

I snort out a laugh. "Yeah, sorry."

"No, no, it was interesting."

"The monsoons?"

"Sure."

He's quiet, and while that's not unusual for him, I'm not used to being in this strange sort of social weekend setting with him, so the quiet makes me feel awkward.

I know we should be able to stand here and look at these atrocious paintings without talking, but I can't. I wish I had that ability with anyone, but I don't, and especially—*especially*—not when my insides are taking me for a ride down the roller coaster of embarrassment to attraction, up toward discomfort, whiplashing near contentment, and then taking a deep dive into confusion, all in the span of five seconds.

"Why is yours so tiny?" I hear myself asking, still focused on the varied deliberate shades of blue within the small central spiky figure in his rough painting.

"Our paper is the same size, Beatrice."

"*Jack.*"

I get that small, barely perceptible upturned corner of his mouth that I feel so triumphant over.

"It's me, I guess. I'm my own unit. My own contrarian little island."

"Blue because of your eyes?" I ask, unable to stop myself.

He sighs a little bit and looks back toward the paintings, pinned haphazardly on a clothing line.

"I don't know; it felt sort of calm and neutral."

"I'm not sure I'd describe you as 'calm and neutral,'" I say, letting the words roll around my mouth to see if they sound any better. It seems too boring for Jack. Too surface. Too much like his externally facing persona but not who he actually is.

I feel an urge to tell him that; I want to reach out and grab his shoulders and shake him, and tell him he is funny and warm and that this quiet fortitude he projects isn't fooling me.

But I immediately shake off the thought—here I am, once again, still that teenage girl in the art studio, wanting to believe he's so much bigger than what he lets me see. I want to believe in that gut feeling and in those quiet moments we have in the dark. But he is who he says he is, and I'm too old to keep wanting him to be someone he's not.

Jack's voice again breaks me from that particular mental spiral. "Bash's painting certainly keeps a lot of space between his *units*."

"Yes, even in the abstract, Lucas and I have to be as far apart as humanly possible."

"Do you think it bothers him?" He turns to look back at me.

"That his dad and I don't really get along?" He nods. I breathe in deeply, hating the thought. "Yeah, I'm sure it does. He's a perceptive kid, even if we try to keep it away from him. But Lucas is a really good dad. He's attentive and loving to Bash, so that's what's important."

"Definitely," he says with more force than I would have expected. "Parents who are separated but make an effort is way better than parents who are together but don't."

I can see the truth of it storming in those blistering blue eyes. I put a hand on his shoulder, and he leans into it ever so slightly.

"Better to be a contrarian little island than have to be around some parents?" I ask.

"Yeah," he says, nodding. He's biting his lower lip while he looks at all three of our paintings, and it's distracting as hell. Maybe it's why I'm so surprised when he keeps talking. "My dad wanted everyone to do things his way, and my brothers always bought into it. My mom didn't, and neither did I. But I guess the difference is she just stayed and put up with it, and I . . . didn't." I nod, forcing myself to say nothing since I know this admission needs quiet. "Anyway," he continues, shaking the thought off, "it just made me think Bash is lucky to have two parents putting him first, even if it's hard."

"Thanks," I mumble, and he shrugs, like once again it's no big deal. My hand is still on his shoulder, and I can feel his whole body ripple through that shrug. It's too intimate. I have to move it away.

"Just because your dad sucks doesn't mean you have to be an island, though," I say, and he closes his eyes at my bluntness. Sometimes I really just can't stop myself.

"It's easier," he says.

"Is it, though?" I'm teetering too close to being that poking teenage girl, but I can't stop it.

"Being financially independent and not needing to rely on my dad or take his opinions seriously has made adulthood infinitely more tolerable."

"Jack, don't threaten me with 'tolerable'; I can't take the excitement."

He snickers, and my insides bloom at the almost-smile. *Get out of here, giddy teenager.*

Thankfully, Bash runs back up. "Did you know she's been painting professionally since the sixties? Did you know she worked with Picasso? *And* did you know that she has—"

"Bash, you gotta slow down," I say. "Why don't we go walk through the rest of the exhibit, and you can tell me all about it."

"What about Jack? Can he come too?"

I look over at Jack, his expression unreadable once again.

"No, I've already taken over too much of your time with your mom," he says, ruffling Bash's hair, to his delight. "Thanks for letting me crash your class, though. I never knew I could learn so much about art and monsoons in one trip."

"But what are you going to do, Jack? Just wander around the museum *alone*?"

Ugh, I know kids have no filter, but after the conversation we've just had, it's like he's continuing to chip away where I've already started picking.

"Yeah, actually," he says, seemingly not offended in the slightest, and suddenly Bash now looks intrigued. "I go to a museum alone every Saturday morning. It's more peaceful."

"Okay," Bash responds, evidently mollified. I wish I could accept things as simply as this kid. "Thanks for painting with me."

"Anytime."

"And, I bet you didn't even realize it, but you even gave my mom two cups for her water, which she always does too! She has this weird thing about light and dark paints mixing, and I think it's cuckoo."

I can feel flames burning across my face, although Jack doesn't seem to have noticed because he's still zoned in on Bash.

"Every artist has their preferences, Bash," he says, still not looking at me. "Your mom gets to do things her own way. We all do."

And with that, he gives Bash a last high five and walks out, back to his solitary Saturday communing with the arts.

CHAPTER TWENTY-FOUR
AUGUST

In the two months since the board meeting, Brigid's vagueness has only proliferated. She's always been sort of a weird boss, obviously, but at least she's been direct and predictable. Now she's like a slippery eel whose trajectory is harder to pin down.

It's not that her behavior would strike anyone who doesn't know her as abnormal, per se. But it's abnormal for *her*.

When I arrived at the castle this morning, she was . . . chatty. Instead of heading upstairs for my usual shower, I got harangued into breakfast and tea while Brigid asked me about my life.

But, of course, since Brigid never asks me about my life, she didn't really have the context to ask normal questions, so it was all sort of clumsy. *How's school for your kid?* (Don't mention it's only August, so it hasn't started. Don't mention that she clearly doesn't know his name.) *Are you taking any vacations this summer?* (Don't mention that it's nearing the end of the summer, and she should have already known I'm not.) *How's your charming roommate doing?* (Don't mention that Mona is the only friend Brigid ever remembers, since she's the loudest and least appropriate, and that this is the first time she's said "charming" instead of "egregious.")

When I try to take her lead and ask her something personal and friendly in return, she ignores me, her typical demeanor returning to make clear she isn't going to play at her own new game.

But the weirdest thing is when she insists on spending the afternoon taking us all on a fishing expedition (and by "taking us all," I mean Des is planning and executing everything on Brigid's behalf, but Brigid will be there).

After those first few trips to Ireland, where she organized (Des organized) activities like the clay pigeon shooting, Brigid has mostly left us all to our own devices during breaks in work. Since it's summer, the warmer weather has meant we can take long walks around the property or bike rides into the town, which has been truly lovely.

But even early on, when she *did* insist on activities, it wasn't like she was actually joining in.

This afternoon, she's joining in.

She's standing at the edge of the lake, wearing an outfit that makes her look like the photoshoot version of a model who's pretending to be going fishing but really is trying to sell you a casual but very expensive watch. From the olive vest covering a crisp cream sweater to the heeled Wellies (and, yes, expensive-looking watch), Brigid is cosplaying enthusiasm for fishing.

I'm trying to stand as far back as possible, in case maybe there's a world where I can escape this activity and instead go catch up on all the work emails I've missed in our morning meetings. Des is giving the group instructions and demonstrations for how to use a fishing rod, and I'm trying to feign interest.

But then I see Jack lope up to the group, late but unhurried, and he is, as always, distractingly sexy. I'm not sure how he so effectively pulls off office wear when we're in New York but then also casual outdoorsman attire when we're here. Maybe it's something to do with being tall.

Tall men always seem to wear clothes properly. *He* always seems to wear clothes properly.

He sidles next to me, and we stand, inches apart, both probably pretending to listen to Des as he yammers on. After a minute, he turns his head, and out of the corner of my eye, I can see he's giving me a look that's so latently heated that every thought I've been having about the woes of fishing swirls down the drain instantly, and my skin starts pulsing. *How does he do that?*

I swallow thickly, unable to contain my curiosity. "What are you thinking about?" I whisper, unsure of whether I'm inventing things in my head because the boredom of fishing has probably caused me to create sexual innuendo where none exists.

"You on top of me."

My head swivels up to him as heat shoots through me. "Right now?" I whisper more feverishly. "You're thinking about that while we *stand here listening to Des talking about fishing?*"

"Well, I know how to fish. So my mind . . . wandered."

"Wandered," I say, irritated with how much my whole body is now thrumming to touch him, even though we're standing idly with all our coworkers, none of whom (thankfully) are close enough to hear this conversation.

"Yup," he says, popping the *p* with a touch of frustration, clearly also realizing the total impracticality of voicing this topic in this setting.

He's no longer looking at me, but I gape at him.

Ever since the other weekend's museum coincidence, I've been wondering if he would act weird. I've successfully batted away the feeling that it was a strangely nice Saturday because, once again, after we were back in the office, he took the lead by being exceedingly normal. But as I arrived in Ireland this morning, I felt more anticipation creeping in than I normally would.

It's probably just the sex. I'm anticipating sex. Anyone would anticipate sex. I mean, come on, look at him. He looks like a tailor-made Irish fantasy, standing here in his oversize boots and windswept hair with the crystal-calm lake as a picture-perfect backdrop. Who wouldn't make these trips totally and completely about work with a side of sex? It's very understandable that I look forward to that.

All the sex pondering makes something from earlier pop into my mind, and I, unfortunately, have no filter to stop the inevitable question. "Do you have expectations of naked photos?" I ask under my breath, suddenly remembering my friends' advice and thinking that might be a definitely positive way to keep my sex-addled brain *anticipating*.

"Excuse me?"

"Oh, okay, you can say you're picturing fornication, but I can't ask about nudes?"

"'Picturing fornication'?" His voice is even lower than a whisper, but I can still hear all the shades of disbelief and mockery underpinning it.

"Yeah."

"I'm trying to suss out how your mind works," he replies.

"As dirtily as yours, apparently."

"Touché."

"Never mind," I finally mumble, realizing that any man who isn't jumping at the chance for what would clearly be my superior naked photos probably isn't as interested as Randall *insisted* he would be.

We aren't looking at each other, and I can feel his hand softly grab my wrist.

"Obviously any person would be *thrilled* by . . . that," he says. *Okay, so one point back to Randall, I suppose.* "It's just not what I was expecting you to say."

"Well, I wasn't expecting you to say you were thinking . . . you know," I mumble, still unable to articulate myself, as usual.

"Oh, so tit for shocking tat?"

"I'm not sure talking about tits is going to get us anywhere." I hear him snort next to me, and I get a zing of pleasure. "And no . . . my mind sometimes wanders too," I say with a shrug.

His thumb grazes slowly over the inside of my wrist, his light touch probably picking up the sharp uptick in the speed of my pulse, before letting go completely. It feels like I've been singed.

"Good," he finally rumbles softly. And now I'm the one picturing fornication.

"Can we blame our trains of thought on Des for being boring?"

"Definitely."

"All right," I say, mollified.

"Have you ever been fishing?" he asks, changing the subject.

"Uh yeah, of course," I say, watching him hold back the expression of skepticism I know he wants to let take over. "Well, my friend Rika taught me how once on a trip to her grandmother's house in Maine, so that counts for something?"

He's mentally searching, but I doubt it's for whether my fishing experience is adequate. "Rika from school?" he asks. I'm surprised.

"Yeah," I respond, not knowing what else to say.

"Huh," he says, as though he's not surprised. "She was originally from there? Or her dad was or something?" Surprised again.

"Yeah," I answer. "Good memory."

He gives one of his reluctant half smiles, like he's unable to ignore the compliment as much as he wants to. It's adorable. And still totally distracting.

Thankfully, though, I'm saved from that particular torture when Des divides us into two boats. I'm with Des, Brigid, Greg, and Samson, one of the VPs from Ireland who always drives up whenever we're in town. Lane, Jack, and a few of the other members of Jack's technical team are pointed toward the other one.

"Boat" is probably a strong word for what we're going out in. It's like one step up from a large canoe but with a much more beautiful design. It's all polished wood and hand-joined craftsmanship, with little flourishes of filigree on the front and back. A small motor hums at the rear, and I hope that means the oars on the sides are more prominently used as decoration.

I settle myself on one of the wooden slab benches and gratefully take one of the life jackets Des is insisting we all wear. He's already arranged the fishing rods in their holders, and the center of the boat has all the nets, tackle kits, and bait at the ready. I guess we're really doing this.

After everyone has wobbled their way aboard the boats, we motor out slowly to the center of the lake. I let myself relax—it's an incredibly peaceful setting. The lake is large enough where I can't fully see the other side, and the glassy surface reflects the billowing clouds off the blue sky like an impressionist painting.

"It's mostly trout in here," I hear Des explaining as we putter along, Brigid no longer listening and Greg looking a bit seasick. "We like ta use *Dendrobaena* worms because they're a good size, and since we're not in salt water, they'll wriggle for a wee bit longer." *That's not going to help Greg's seasickness.* "We're going ta turn the motor off here and get set up."

He signals to the other boat to cut their motor, too, and soon we're bobbing along, within sight of each other but far enough away where, thankfully, certain people are no longer distracting me.

Des encourages us to hook some worms, and I try to stop the wriggling creatures from continually squiggling their way out of my hands. Brigid refuses on principle—*I should really let you all have the pleasure of this experience; I could do it anytime*—and soon we're simply floating along, rods in the water, waiting for something to bite.

It's a tranquil way to enjoy the late afternoon, if you can ignore that everyone is still completely unable to talk about anything other than work. Greg and Samson are chatting about operational deliverables, which seems to be enough to keep Brigid listening with one ear while furtively glancing over at me every so often. Des distracts her a bit with some updates on tree plantings around the grounds.

I take the opportunity to watch her. It would be impossible to explain to anyone else that a person being *more* interested feels colder, but that's the biggest takeaway I'm getting from Brigid's change in behavior. When she was direct, pushy, and to the point, it was like I was getting the real her. This papered-over polite version is guarding something.

Maybe I've done poorly? Maybe the presentation was a big red flag wake-up call, and I'm going to be demoted or layered? I know logically that we aren't going to implement anything until the board has had time to consider all my proposals, but it *is* a little curious that we haven't discussed any of it since the meeting. Surely if they're going to be moving forward on some of the long-term planning I suggested, we'd be setting things up more effectively to get started?

I shouldn't be spiraling as I sit here on a rickety boat in the middle of a lake *with my actual boss*, but that's what it's come to. I'm on edge now, and I can't quite make myself stop.

Which I *think* is why I startle so forcefully when I hear a shout from the other boat. Specifically, Jack's voice saying *Oh shit*, which I guess, unfortunately, triggers something in me to whip myself around to make sure he's okay. Which has the unintended effect of making *myself* not okay. I lose my balance and—in that sick, sad, horrible slow-motion kind of extra-schadenfreude way—find myself tipping completely out of the boat.

"Bea, what are you—grab my hand!" I hear Brigid shouting, and before I can go crashing into the water, I feel a hand come around my wrist to try to steady me. But the effect it has is just to pull Brigid into my unstable vortex, because the boat has tipped enough where she's following after me.

I'm suddenly engulfed in icy brackish water, and I'm sincerely regretting the heavy boots weighing my feet down. My head is bobbing inelegantly from within the neon blue of my life jacket, which, I'm realizing belatedly, is too large in practice, so I probably resemble a drowned cat being held aloft by a teetering preserver.

I hear a splash behind me and turn around to see that Jack has jumped into the water and is swimming toward Brigid and me. *Great.*

Is it inappropriate in this moment to enjoy how speedily he still moves in the water? To be honest, I never saw him in a swim meet when we were in high school because I was too embarrassed to even hint that I liked him that much. My blasé too-cool-for-school self would not have been caught dead cheering at a sporting event.

But maybe I made a gargantuan mistake on that front, because the way his arms are moving is pretty enticing, and that's *with* his clothes still on.

"Jack, what are you doing?" I shout as he closes in on us.

"You fell," he says, looking at me like I'm a desk with too many papers out of place, messy, and in need of serious help. "And . . . Brigid fell. Or you pulled her?"

"I didn't pull her! She was trying to help me."

"How'd that go for you two?"

"I've never regretted having employees that I gave two shits about until this moment," Brigid shouts at him from behind me.

I know I should be focused on being freezing or how I'm going to get back into a small boat while weighed down by heavy clothes, but all I can think is *Aww, Brigid is admitting she gives two shits about me. Maybe I'm not being demoted.*

"Well, let's get you both back into the boat to start?" Jack says.

Des has stood up to get a better look at us, concern etched into his face, but he's watching Jack and seems to be awaiting instruction.

"Des, sit down, okay?" Jack says. "I'm going to need you to be a counterweight while Samson and Greg pull each of them in. You sit on the far side, and then they'll sit in middle so they don't pull themselves in along with Brigid and Bea. They can use me as leverage to get far enough up, and then you can grab them and pull them back."

All three men nod and move accordingly.

"Okay, Brigid," he says, turning to her. "Use my shoulders as balance and pull yourself up as far as you can go, okay? And then they'll pull you in. When you get in, go sit next to Des so Bea doesn't tip everyone over when she gets in."

"I'd say no one likes a hero, Jack, but I'm preposterously cold, so let's get a move on," she replies, and I chuckle at her ability to still pull off haughty even when soaked to the bone.

She wriggles her way onto Jack's shoulders, and I'm not *not* impressed by his ability to tread water and somehow lift an entire person and help her back into a boat.

After she's safely in and everyone is fussing over her, Jack finally turns to me. "What the hell happened to you?" he asks with an impish glint in his eye.

"I . . ." I suddenly realize why I fell out of the boat in the first place. "I thought something happened to you. You said, 'Oh shit,' and I think I turned around too quickly to see what was wrong."

"Ah."

"What *did* happen?"

"Oh, Lane dropped some of those bait worms, and they were wriggling everywhere."

"Oh," I say, feeling even more foolish, which I hadn't thought was possible, considering I'm currently a soaking-wet klutz in front of my entire team.

"Well, let's get you out of here, okay? On the count of three, try to launch yourself off of me and back into the boat, all right?"

I follow his lead and scramble my way back into the boat without managing to tip us all over again. Des rightfully decides that this is the end to our short excursion, so after Jack has managed to hoist himself back into his own boat (with no trouble on his own, naturally), we all silently make our way back to the dock. The combination of wind and sopping clothing is, understandably, not super pleasant.

The instant we're tied up, Brigid launches herself out of our boat, clearly ready to make a quick escape.

"I'm really not cut out for this togetherness," she mumbles to herself before swiftly turning to face all of us. "Let's agree that everyone can watch a movie or whatever and have dinner in their rooms tonight. I'll have everything sent up." We all nod, probably relieved to not have to feign excitement for any more group bonding. "Bea?"

"Yes?" I say expectantly, hoping this is either the part where she tells me she hopes I'll be okay or where she says she totally doesn't blame me for her own adventures in the water.

"You really need a much more proficient waterproof mascara. You look dilapidated."

And with that, she turns and walks back toward the house, still somehow maintaining an air of dignity even when wet from head to toe.

Well, at least we know Brigid is still herself underneath her weirdness.

I turn to look at Jack, but he's already wandering back toward the house with everyone else. I wonder if he's annoyed that I ruined the afternoon.

But before I can dwell on it, Des pulls me aside. He wraps me in a large woolen blanket.

"I'sa little chilly out here, Bea. Ya don't want ta leave it too long," he chides.

"Oh yeah, because I was planning on moseying around the grounds rather than showering off all the kelp and fish guts I've got covering me."

He smiles. "Eh, I just meant don't go wanderin' off with yer man instead of getting yerself settled."

"My—" I look over at him, horrified. Was I really that obvious looking at Jack while he walked away? What . . . what does Des know exactly? Well, first rule of thumb is always deny, deny, deny. "I'm not sure—"

But Des waves me off. "I'm not sayin' nothing. I just notice tings."

"Hardly anything to notice, Des," I say, attempting to minimize.

But he chuckles.

"Men usually jump in a totally calm lake on a clear day ta rescue a woman wearing a life jacket, do they?"

Soaking through my new blanket, I'm left without a retort as Des chuckles and walks back up, following the rest of the group.

Chapter Twenty-Five

I *want* to prove Des wrong and not care what Jack is doing.

But I should say thank you.

And see if he's okay.

He jumped into a freezing lake to make sure I was okay. And Brigid, obviously. He jumped into a freezing lake to look after his colleagues. And that's a nice thing to do. Someone should look out for him too.

Ugh, what is wrong with me.

I thought things weren't weird after the museum, but maybe *I'm* the one who's weird. I'm already always too in my head, and now Des is poking around in there too.

But thankfully I don't have a lot of time to dwell on it because as I'm standing outside his door, I hear a voice from the other side.

"You're lurking again."

Damn it.

I open the door and step in, ready to apologize for the now-consistent lurking, but I'm instantly distracted by the fact that he's wet and has only a small towel wrapped around his waist. *We've got to stop meeting like this.*

Who am I kidding.

He's oblivious, though, since my outfit is apparently the more surprising one here.

"You haven't taken a shower yet?" he asks.

I look down and realize that wandering around in my wet clothes, even covered in Des's blanket, is probably not the most thought-out decision.

"Sorry," I say, realizing I must look deranged for coming here before changing. "I just . . . you left, and I didn't have a chance to say thank you. And I'm now realizing I probably look ridiculous."

He walks over and puts a hand on my arm. "You're freezing—you need to get in the shower."

"Oh," I reply, looking down again and now feeling even more ludicrous for coming straight here. "Sorry, I'll go—"

"Just take it here," he says, interrupting me, but not unkindly. "I mean, since Brigid mercifully gave us the night off, there's no rush to go anywhere."

I'm staring at him now, partly because, well, yeah, he's half-naked in a towel, and I'm a little envious of the water droplets that get to cling unabashedly to his undeniably perfect chest. But also because I don't know why my stomach is reacting like this to him right now. It's not the set-on-fire feeling that I normally get around him, but more swoopy and disoriented.

Maybe the cold lake really has knocked some water in my ears.

"Okay," I say, ignoring the fact that I could easily walk down a long corridor, take a right, and be back in my room within three minutes. And ignoring that this strangely feels like I'm being looked after rather than . . . well, just being sex friends (which, annoyingly, now that Mona has said it, is the only way I can think to classify this thing, and I really, really blame her for getting it stuck in my head like an earworm on repeat).

I walk into the bathroom, still thick and warm with the steam from his shower, and turn the water back on. I peel off my wet, dirty clothes and stand in the bliss of being drenched with heat. I hadn't quite noticed how numb the cold was making me until suddenly it's being thawed away.

After what's probably an excessively long time, I step out of the shower and realize, belatedly, that I have no clothes to put back on. And while I'm certainly not above walking out naked and turning this evening distinctly back toward sex-friends territory (*come on, there has to be another phrase*), for some reason it doesn't quite feel like the right way to handle this particular moment.

I grab a robe from the hook and luxuriate in the squishy softness of it.

"Thank you, again," I say, walking out. "That definitely was a much better plan for a post-falling-in-a-lake first priority."

He nods at me, waving away the compliment like it's all no big deal. He's sitting on the bed in his boxers, reading a book, legs stretched out in front of him. He's so composed; a serene image. I can't stop myself from joining in and relishing in the laissez-faire scene. I lie down on my stomach and prop myself up on my elbows. "Whatcha reading?"

"Oxford History of Art's *Portraiture*," he says, setting the book down.

"Oh, so some really light evening reading then?" I tilt my head and grin. I can see him softening.

"I saw it in Brigid's library here. I got sucked in. It's all about, you know, how the visual of a person has changed over time. How we represent ourselves."

His words feel like such déjà vu. It could be twenty years ago, this conversation. Except it would have been us side by side at easels after not talking for an hour while we initially worked. Maybe this is the adult version of that, lying on a bed, having gone through the motions of a seemingly unusual but now almost routine workday.

"I always liked the portraits you made," I say, unable to get the past off the forefront of my mind.

"In high school?" He's clearly not convinced.

"Yeah," I say sincerely, sitting up a bit.

That constant energy thrumming between us feels today more like a heartbeat—slow and steady and reassuring—rather than the usual pulse-racing craving that travels up my spine whenever I'm close to him. Maybe I just needed to be dumped in cold water and wrapped in excessively soft terry cloth to feel more serene. Maybe that's why my mind has circled back to our past. It reminds me of those quiet evenings together years ago, placid as today's lake.

"Do you still paint?" I ask. "You know, other than when a kid unwittingly browbeats you into it?"

He gives me a small smile, and I secretly adore that the mental image of Bash brings that out so easily in him.

"Not really, no," he says, sounding a bit wistful. "It was just a hobby."

"You say that, but I remember being so impressed by that final self-portrait you made. It was *brave*."

The final project for our art class was to make a self-portrait in any medium; his was a painting of just his face, features daring you to watch them, like you'd stumbled on a truthful scowl. At the time I was so keenly aware of not letting him *know* I loved it. But maybe today I don't care about showing my hand as much as I did then.

"This is what old age is doing to your memory," he says dismissively.

"No, seriously! It was visceral. I wanted to make something cute and flattering, and yours was so close up and . . ."

"Unflattering?"

"Noooo." I swat at him. "I remember the feeling it gave me, like you were letting everyone see right into you. That's heavy shit for a teenager."

"You don't remember that," he replies softly.

"I do," I press. "I really do. Your ego just didn't need the fawning at the time."

I always do this with him; I always downplay, always obfuscate so the pit in my stomach doesn't grow. And saying I remembered a painting he made from twenty years ago already feels like a confession that I'm only mildly comfortable admitting. It makes me feel like I'm on a ledge.

"That's really . . . funny." He's contemplative.

"Why?"

"Oh man, the feeling *I* remember was sheer nerves to show it to anyone. Especially to you. I wanted to do the opposite of what people do in self-portraits, you know? I wanted it to be all the flaws up close. And that was . . . scary."

"You were never scared," I say with a featherweight dismissiveness of what feels to me like hyperbole.

"I damn well was." He's serious, with a shade of self-consciousness that makes me wonder if maybe he's out on a ledge too. "All the time."

That makes me sit up. "Could've fooled me," I say, wanting suddenly so badly to touch him, anywhere, a hand on a hand or a shoulder brushing conspiratorially. Comforting. But I can't bring myself to.

"Well then, my plans to be a really cool and aloof man about to graduate high school really won over all the ladies." He halfheartedly chuckles.

His eyes look grayer in this warm light, soft and reflective. His words are teetering on bowling me over, and it doesn't help that he's projecting a palpability I'm not used to seeing on him, as bare as most of his body. Part of me wants to break the moment and straddle him, kissing him senseless so I can put away that exposed sentiment he's shared and swerve our conversation back to the nonconversation of sex. But another, more tender part can't stop from lightly picking at it.

"Why were you scared?" I finally ask.

He's quiet for a minute, like he's deciding whether to answer. "I hated that feeling of being so exposed. I don't really know why I did it."

"Did what?"

"Painted like that."

"Why do you think you did?" I shift closer.

"I wanted to be like you."

He's twined his hands together, fidgeting, and he's not looking at me anymore.

"Like me?" I'm confused.

"Sitting with you and painting felt so much more honest than the rest of my life at that point." He sighs and still isn't looking my way. "I mean, I know that sounds like such a dramatic teenager thing to even remember, and it probably was"—I bristle a little bit at his own minimization of himself, but I stay silent, aware that this kind of confession doesn't come easily to Jack—"but you always seemed to be able to sit down and start and go. I wanted to be like that too. I wanted to simply let out whatever I was thinking. So that last assignment, the self-portrait one, I just did it. I wanted to put onto paper everything that was confusing and dysfunctional and crooked. I was surprised, honestly, that it came out the way it did. I never really thought you liked it."

"I did," I confide.

"Well, I guess that's good to know," he says, unfolding his hands and dispassionately patting me, like a buddy. I'm not sure I like this: like we've opened a delicate box, and then he's suddenly rushed it closed.

"Was it your family?" I say, and his eyes swerve toward me, looking surprised. "I mean, then . . . was your family what made things complicated for you? It always seemed like . . . then, you know . . . that you were . . . burdened?"

Well, that was as inelegantly as I could possibly have asked a question I've thought about for the better part of two decades. But he doesn't seem offended. More curious than anything. He shifts his whole body toward me, and, like the magnet I inevitably am, I turn on my side, too, facing him for whatever this answer seems to take from him.

"My family is fine," he says, not looking at me again, which makes me know that this is the lie he tells himself. This is the lie he's probably always told himself. "My brothers and my dad are all really similar. I told you the other day that he was sort of 'my way or the highway,' but it wasn't just him. They fed into it. They've always wanted what he wanted. Go to the same college he went to, play sports, get a job in sales or something utilizing their shining personalities."

I scoff at this, which wins me the tiniest of buried grins. A moment passes, and apparently my scoff has also won me a single pinkie against mine, a little tether to be able to hold on to as he shares. I thought I was warm after my shower, but now my body's blooming from the inside.

"At that time, my dad kind of expected me to do the same thing. I was getting recruited for soccer as well as for swimming, so I was in his good graces. But I was really sick of the way he pushed everyone around. I wanted to go to college where I wanted; I wanted to study math and programming. I didn't want to have to focus on a sport. So taking an art class and putting more effort into it felt like my own little rebellion."

I can almost hear the echo of his words to me from twenty years ago. *Just for once I wanted to do what I wanted.* I never really knew how much he was shouldering. A swirled-up, confused, undecided boy just trying to carve out the space to find himself. The realization makes my heart feel achy.

I put my hand softly in his hair and brush small strands behind his ear. I'm considering that feeling I had earlier—the sense that he was taking care of me—and wonder if that's what I want for him in this moment. Maybe this means the "friends" part of "sex friends" is just as important right now as the actual sex. The thought simultaneously makes me feel panicky and mollified. I try to breathe past it. Maybe this is something we both need in this particular moment.

"And what about now?" I ask, fingers now gently trailing behind his ear as I give in to trying to soothe whatever it is inside him that usually keeps all these things under such decisive lock and key.

He reaches out to brush his thumb along my hip bone, like we're in tactile communication. Like these little grazes can help connect this conversation back to what our bodies are now used to doing together.

"Well, I did what I wanted. I went to my own college, I got my own job, I moved away from Boston, and I get to blissfully be—what did you call me the other day?—my own island."

It sounds nice, to be honest. The thought of being free of obligation, free of other people's expectations. And I don't mean Bash, because his expectations don't weigh on me the same way. But everyone else— what I *should* be doing; what I *should* be accomplishing; what I *should* have done to have a family and keep my marriage instead of falling apart. What would that feel like, to wake up every day and just not give a damn?

"Do you miss having them around as much? I mean, if you grew up with a big family . . . ?"

"No," he says, once again his gaze darting away whenever he doesn't quite want to let me see the answer on his face. "I spent so much of my life walking with guardrails directing me. And going home for Christmas or family obligations is like stepping into the alternate universe where I watch my mom resentfully compromising, and that just makes me glad to leave."

I nod. "I certainly understand that. I was like the literal embodiment of that metaphor after years of jamming myself with needles to give my husband the thing that would make *him* happy, even if it was making me miserable."

His hand moves swiftly from my hip onto my wrist, once again thumbing the soft spot where he can feel what he does to my pulse. He's looking at me now, the melancholy of the color blue seeping through even with the warmth of the evening light on him. He's close enough for me to detect the soap I now know (after getting a look in his bathroom) that he clearly brings all the way here every time, and it's comforting.

"Right, yeah." He sighs. "I hadn't really considered how much that would make sense to you."

"The most unwanted earned insight." I lightly laugh, trying once again to steer toward more frothy pastures.

"But you got Bash out of it," he adds gently. "So now you get to direct your own path but with an entertaining little person by your side who you can tell what to do." That gets a genuine smile out of me, maybe if only for the amusement of thinking I can ever tell Bash what to do. "And that's never lonely."

"Ideal, really," I say. "Determinedly independent but with a mouthy sidekick."

"Exactly."

His hand on my wrist is having an effect on me. It's like the consistent contact is speeding up my bloodstream, and I can't stop myself from reaching out to him, just so I can put my other hand flat on his chest, tangible and solid in front of me.

"I was before, when I was married," I confess quietly. "Lonely."

That singular word reverberates in the air for me. I turn it around on myself, because the word feels so foreign now, with the freedom that deciding to get divorced has given me. I was shut in and small when I was in a relationship, but now this freedom feels expansive.

"Is that . . . is that how you feel now?" I ask, without judgment.

"Maybe," he says, genuinely considering. "But I'd take the trade-off over the example I saw." I certainly agree with that. "I mean, the only flaw is the dying alone part."

"The 'dying alone part,' huh? Dark." I can't help but smile.

"But I can probably solve that with a retirement home in Boca, playing mah-jongg."

Okay, now I'm laughing.

"First of all," I say once I catch my breath again, "you could not handle the abrasive loudness of Florida." *Yessss, a real smile.* "Second of all, you're too young to be dreaming about sitting around with old ladies playing a game requiring knowledge of mathematical odds."

"Don't thwart my foolproof plan," he says with mock seriousness.

"Okay," I say, affection coloring any ability to question him. "I'll let you go through life believing that the answer is in a mah-jongg board for you."

He gives me a quick kiss on the lips. "Thank you for preserving that truly sexy old-age fantasy for me."

I know his smiles now; I collect them; I file them away. And so, even though he's giving me a larger smile than usual, I can tell that underneath it is a twinge of sadness.

And I hate that. I want to shake the sadness out of him, like apples from a tree. But this conversation has already been skating a little too close to the edge, and I'm not sure I'm brave enough to mention it. So I do the one thing I really *do* know I want to do.

I untie my robe and kiss him for real this time. I press myself into him in the hopes that we can make each other feel better, in this one way I know we both know how to do. Two lightly lonely people who've learned how to make their lives make sense in an imperfect world. And sometimes, that requires having friends—of all kinds.

Like a moth to a flame, his hand is under my robe in an instant, pulling me closer into him and letting us both slide away on a sea of comfort and satisfaction.

CHAPTER TWENTY-SIX
SEPTEMBER

It's weird having so many people at the castle this morning (*a sentence about castles I could not have conceived thinking last year*).

But I can see why Brigid wanted her board to come out this time of year—every inch of ground is still earnestly, vibrantly green, as though the grass is yearning to prove the point that we live in a Technicolor world. The days are defiant in their length, reminding us that it's still officially summer for a few more days.

But there's a quieter tone to everything; school is back in session, and the tourists have dissipated. I took a walk this morning after my shower, and there was something comforting about having the sun on my face but a streak of cold already winding its way in the breeze.

I waved at all the board members while they spent the early morning sitting on the outdoor deck, taking in the view for the first time with teacups held fast to warm their hands. Blankets were perched on each side of the wicker couches, ready to swaddle anyone who needed them. (Des really is always ten steps ahead.)

This meeting is a world away from the one we had in a sterile conference room just three months ago, when every woman exuded sharp competence. Stripped down to the casual elegance of Brigid's home, the air now feels more like peace and purpose. I'm hopeful that we can actually dig into the plans I presented and have real time to get some productive feedback in a setting where these women aren't rushing to the next item on their calendar.

Although now that we're all gathered in the drawing room, some of that optimism has curdled, like milk sitting out too long. The chandelier and the butter yellow curtains are painting everyone in a warm light, which makes the room seem a little too cozy. Is this where everyone kindly tells me my ideas are terrible, and I get a scone as my parting gift? Is this why Brigid has been so uncharacteristically supportive and, frankly, weird in the last couple of months? Because she's actually going to feel bad when she has to admit that the board hated all my suggestions?

Before I can spiral, Brigid stands up sharply and claps her hands together, immediately bringing silence to the room. She really does have an uncanny ability to project a commanding presence, whether we're in a boardroom or a tearoom.

"This year has felt incredibly productive with these bimonthly retreats, and I thought it was important for the board to get to see everyone in action. So I'm very glad you're all here. After our last meeting in New York, we had quite a bit to discuss, and I'm excited to share that a few things are going to change moving forward. Both myself and the board feel confident that after this year of transition, we'll be even better situated to expand going forward."

I hate that Brigid's words are making my palms clammy. No one else can see it, but I don't even want the hint of nervousness in front of this group.

I try to keep my head still while moving my eyes enough to glance over at Jack as subtly as I can. But he's focused on what Brigid is saying, clearly unaware of my internal state of haywire. Not that there would be anything he could do about it even if he *was*. Brigid is barreling on, and I need to focus.

"I'm proud for having steered this ship to build what we have here. Breck Data is more profitable than ever, and our client satisfaction is exceeding all projections. Which is why I believe this is actually the perfect time for me to step back as CEO and instead become chairwoman of the board. I'll still be heavily involved, but I can pass off most of the day-to-day to someone who's more equipped to be on the ground."

The surprise in the room is palpable on everyone other than the board members. I'm a little embarrassed by how far my jaw is hanging open. Lane has a scone halfway up to her mouth and is completely frozen in place. Jack is the only one of us who isn't openly gawking, but I can tell he's surprised by the single eyebrow he's raised.

Brigid is stepping away? To do *what*? Flounce around on her countryside estate and *not work*? How is that even possible? Who is this woman, and what cave has she buried my boss in—my workaholic, pristine, blunt, and frankly indispensable boss whom I rely on to keep me feeling ordered?

"What . . . what?" I finally say, piercing the silence with the most inarticulate response I can come up with.

And suddenly I'm keenly aware that now I've got every eye on me. Great. I guess now the whole board is anticipating the awkward part where Brigid announces her new CEO, who's going to want to go in a completely different direction from what I proposed. I shouldn't have gotten my hopes up from all the months of planning.

"Bea, I think this might have been a better moment for you to listen instead of squawking, but at any rate I'm glad that you've so eloquently raised the question of what happens now." *Ugh*. Brigid really knows how to kick you when you're down. "And I would hope that the obvious answer is that the board loved your plan for moving forward, and they've agreed with my suggestion that you should take over for me as CEO."

"What . . . what?" I say, again, like a moron, because now I really am flustered.

Am I being punked? First Brigid shares the completely ludicrous concept of her stepping down, and now she thinks it's funny to pretend like I could be in charge?

"Did you fall in the lake again?" Brigid asks, maybe not entirely joking.

"No, I'm just . . ." I look around, internally flailing, wanting someone else to step in and save me from this. My eye catches Jack's, finally, and for some reason the lack of surprise on *his* face bolsters me enough to pull myself together. "I'm just a little taken aback, is all. I didn't have any inkling that you were thinking of stepping down."

"Well, much as I love sharing all the inner workings of my life with my employees, you might be shocked to know that that was a decision I made privately without input from anyone who works for me."

"Of course," I reply, knowing I'm not getting anywhere. "I meant more . . . I'm a little stunned, is all."

"Oh, come on, Bea, I didn't realize I couldn't surprise you with positive career news." I don't think I've ever seen her look so exasperated with me. "Thank goodness you were brimming with ideas for the board at the last meeting, because otherwise *this* display wouldn't instill confidence."

It's taking a minute for my brain to catch up with the words she's saying. I've always assumed Brigid would work until she was dead—or at least until the rest of us were.

Thankfully Susan, the current chairwoman of the board, clears her throat. "I mentioned to Brigid this was probably something you'd need a bit of time to consider and take in. We'll go over the package that the board has approved, but you can have your lawyer look it over and take whatever time you need to decide if you want the role—"

"Of course she wants the role," Brigid interjects.

"As I'm sure you've surmised," Susan continues, although now with a hint of a smile toward me, as though we're two parents commiserating over a precocious toddler, "Brigid wanted to do it her way, and her way was to wrap her own mind around all the logistics and have them sorted out before even mentioning this to anyone. But that being said, we do agree with her. You've done an amazing job growing the company, Bea. Your plans to continue in that vein were very impressive and thorough. We feel confident in Brigid's instincts, and her instincts are that you have the deepest well of knowledge about Breck Data and the most clear-cut plans to keep it on the right trajectory."

"Thank you," I say quietly.

Having so many eyes on me is disorienting, as though each one is unintentionally a tiny flick of impatience to see what I say next. I feel so utterly unequipped for this. I'm the person who executes, sure, but it's always behind the scenes. I'm the woman behind the curtain, not the one people come to see. But I know I don't want to let Brigid down, even with this inane proclamation.

"I appreciate your faith in me," I continue. "And I'll definitely think about it, of course. Thank you."

Brigid looks as though I've already said yes, based on her self-satisfied expression. Lane and Greg are both beaming at me and giving encouraging thumbs-ups—that in particular helps shove aside a bit of the imposter syndrome, and it starts to infiltrate my center with something a little gooier. Jack is still looking at Brigid, and I wish it didn't sting so much that I have no idea what his reaction to all of this is.

But as quickly as this strange fever dream started, Brigid just gives me a nod and continues with the rest of the day's business. You wouldn't think this woman was on the brink of slowing down based on her laser-sharp focus today. She cedes the floor to Lane, who details the quarterly earnings, while I zone out.

My mind is whirring. Is this really something I could take on? Sure, at this point I could do my job in my sleep, and I know the company like the back of my hand. I've exceeded projections every year, to the point that it's almost now expected.

But being proficient at my particular job does not mean I'd be an effective CEO. It's not my company. Brigid is the engine that keeps us all going. I'm tactical, but she's the leader. I organize the nitty-gritty details, but she's the big-picture executor. I'm the meticulous planner, and she's the charge ahead. That's always worked for us. I've loved it for a decade. Where would she get the idea that I could do this on my own?

Maybe keeping my personal crap from her has had the unintended consequence of giving her the impression that I have things a bit more together than I actually do. If I'm already floundering to simultaneously do a good job as a mother and a professional, imagine how much worse I'll be when I have even more responsibility? I want to keep my head above the water in this sea of insecurity, but the riptide of questions is pulling me under.

After another half hour of back-and-forth that I'm barely listening to, Brigid insists on a break. As everyone files out of the room, she pulls me to the side.

"Obviously there's nothing to think about—you know you're the right person for this role."

"I hadn't ever really considered you leaving, Brigid," I deflect honestly.

"Well, I'm not *leaving*; I'm just taking on a different role. It's time for some new blood."

"Why, though?" I hate how whiny my voice sounds.

"Oh, honestly, Bea, take the win. I need to mix it up, and you can make that transition seamless for me."

Well, at least now I feel like the world is a little more ordered. If there's a self-interested motivation, at least the choice of me as her path of least resistance makes for a much easier narrative.

"I need to give it some thought," I reply, "but I *am* very flattered. And grateful. And just, surprised generally—"

"It's not an Oscars speech. Go over the package with Susan and the rest of the board. Let's have a meeting in a few weeks to answer any questions you might have once you've wiped that look of shock off your face that, frankly, is unbecoming for someone as talented as you are."

"Okay," I mumble, even though I still feel definitively untalented in this moment.

"And then think about timing, because you'll have to move here for six months or so to shadow me for the transition."

"I'm sorry?"

"Don't be sorry. Well, you can be a little sorry for how slow you're being on the uptake. But we'll get over it."

And with that, Brigid's left me gaping at her for the second time today.

CHAPTER
TWENTY-SEVEN

I can hear the door open and shut softly behind me, but I'm too engrossed in the spreadsheet on my computer to turn around.

There's really only one person it could be anyway.

Out of the corner of my eye, I see him sit down on the edge of my bed, patient, not interrupting me, even though I'm probably being a little rude by not saying hello. Although, based on the way the sun is still creeping over the horizon, it's not nearly late enough for this particular visitor.

"You can't just wander in here while I'm working when you don't have a reason," I say, still facing my computer but trying to modulate the huffiness out of my tone that I know is waiting to erupt after the day I've had.

"I did have a reason. I wanted to grope you a little bit," Jack says, and *that* gets me to turn around. The cheeky look on his face softens me.

"Very cute," I say, rolling my eyes.

"Well, it's not *totally* untrue, to be honest," he replies with a smirk. "But no, actually, I hadn't seen you since Brigid's bombshell and wanted to see how you were doing before everyone is crowded around for dinner."

I breathe out a heavy sigh, appreciative of the question but unsure quite how to answer it.

I should be feeling a lot of things, but for some reason the main emotion coursing through me is that I'm just sort of mad. Susan and a few other members of the board sat down with me earlier this afternoon to go through the overarching details of the offer. It looked generous and well thought out on paper—more equity and a salary bump would come in phases, first for a six-month overlap with Brigid and then for me taking over after that. They said it would take a few weeks to get a contract written up, which will give me some time to think about it. It was all more than fair.

But for some reason the only thing I can focus on is how annoyed I am at Brigid, even if I can't quite articulate why. I don't want to say that out loud, though.

"I'm good. I'm flattered. I need to think about it."

He raises his eyebrows. "You're really selling it there."

"Well, what do you want me to say?"

He gets up and walks over to the desk, then sits on it, blocking me in from my obfuscations. "Whatever the truth is. Just use your words."

"Oh, is it time for a pep talk?" I say sarcastically, leaning back in my chair like a defiant teenager.

I don't have the energy to let every emotion about this day tangle into an even larger mess.

"If that's what you want."

He's smoking me out with quietude. He's waiting. I know deep down that he's trying to do the right thing, but for some reason today it's irking me. And, irrationally, I know he's the only person safe enough to actually blow up to the way I sometimes want to but never let myself in front of other people.

"It's a ridiculous idea, and I'm sure you and everyone else knows that," I finally say, snapping out of my silence and letting the words tumble out. "Waving a magic wand doesn't make someone into a CEO. She can't throw out unearned promotions like she's Oprah handing out cars." He snorts a laugh but doesn't otherwise say anything, which fuels me further. "She's selfish. I'm usually happy with her shtick—it's uncomplicated, and I always know what I'm getting, even if she's a constant pain in the ass. But at least it's a known quantity of pain in the ass. Now she thinks she can spend months making a decision about my life without running it by me first? Did you know she wants me to move to Ireland for six months to follow her around? Like I can uproot my life for her in an instant. Like Lucas wouldn't blow a gasket and try to permanently take custody. Like I don't have a kid who goes to school and can't leave. Maybe she should have *asked* if I wanted the job before telling the entire board. Like maybe I'm actually not equipped for this, and she didn't even fucking ask me—"

"Okay, let's back up a second," Jack says, brow furrowed.

"What?" I snap.

"Why are you so . . . angry?"

His eyes are searching mine, and I'm surprised by the puzzlement in them.

"I'm not angry," I counter.

"You are, though."

"I'm *not*!" I say in a way that is completely negating the point I'm trying to make.

I stand up and start pacing because I can't look at him anymore.

A full minute goes by before he speaks again. "Sometimes it's easier to be angry than scared." He shrugs, a gentle timbre etching into the softness of his words.

It flashes me back to something Lucas said a few months ago, in a markedly different tone. *You decide you're angry so you won't have to actually feel bad.*

"That's not what's happening," I retort, although I'm not sure I'm even convincing myself with that answer. Mostly I'm bristling at the thought of Lucas and Jack agreeing on something together in absentia.

"You *can* do it, you know. You'd be great."

I turn around and look at him.

"That's your takeaway? Not that she ambushed me, not that I clearly can't live here for six months—"

"Yeah, but that's all solvable. I mean, Brigid having no boundaries and trying to decide things for other people isn't going to change, but you can obviously push back on the parts you don't like."

"No, I can't?"

"Of course you can. It's a job offer. It's a negotiation. And she played her hand poorly, by the way, because instead of you having to apply for the job and concede anything, she's actually already told you she has no other candidates, her board has already approved you, and she's counting on you doing it." I hadn't really thought of it that way. "But none of that's important if you don't start with realizing you can do it."

I shake my head, the idea still seeming so unreasonable to me. "I'm not a CEO."

"Neither was Brigid."

"Yeah, but now this is a huge company."

"That you know every inch of."

He's earnest, and I want to believe him, but it seems so ridiculous that I want to swat the whole thing away. I sit down again, drawn back to him sitting there, like I always am when he's in my orbit. I put my head down on my desk to try to think. He coils a finger through my hair, and all I can hear is my own breathing.

"Look, I get how it's easier to be mad than it is to actually look this thing head on," he finally says. "But don't avoid it, okay?"

"I'm not avoiding," I mumble into the desk, clearly avoiding even so much as looking at him.

I wait for him to say something else, but once again he's letting silence worm its way in until I can't stand it anymore. "Okay, fine, I'm avoiding, but not without reason."

"This isn't a zero-sum game. Yeah, you've had a lot of shit go down in the last few years. Your ex took some of your confidence and energy, and by the way, you allowed him to for a long time. Hell, you've literally allowed for your ability to drive away to expire—"

"Horrible pep talk, Sander."

"I'm not finished," he says, pulling me to sit up and get my head off the damn desk. "*But*—I was going to say before I was rudely interrupted—you pushed ahead. You had a kid, then got out of a bad situation, even though it might've been easier to take the path of least resistance and stay in it. We all go through periods of stagnation in some parts of our lives. But it's time to move forward. You can move forward."

I'm always a little caught off guard when Jack talks for any prolonged length of time. He's not a man of excessive words and certainly not about the personal stuff. I *want* to believe him because he's not the kind of person who ever bullshits me. He's been a startlingly incisive friend since he's come back into my life. But even if he somehow has become the only person I probably *could* have this conversation with, I still want to wriggle out of it.

"That's a lovely speech, but if you haven't noticed, I'm a mess. I can barely make this two-days-twice-a-month work."

"You know you can do it."

"I don't know that."

"You can ask for what you want. Give them your terms. The company's always been in New York; it should stay in New York. You can say that."

It's tempting to listen to him. But it's so much easier to stay annoyed. "What do you possibly know about how I can manage my life, huh?"

"I know you, Beatrice."

"Why? Because you're fucking me every other week? That's some great insight?"

I regret it the minute I say it.

An instant frisson of tension is erected between us. His lips press into that smooth line he makes when he's holding something in, and he takes a deep breath, as if willing himself not to snap back at me.

"I'm sorry, that was rude," I finally say quietly, ashamed at my outburst but unable to bring myself to say anything else.

"It was."

He's giving me a look that gives away nothing. And his retreat back into silence—his normal state with everyone else; the opposite of how he's been in this entire conversation—feels like a stinging rebuke.

"I'm just . . ." Everything I want to say is muddled. Sometimes our differences feel like a chasm. I talk things out; I throw ideas up against the wall; I charge ahead. He's all listening and waiting, thinking things through and holding back. "I appreciate you checking on me," I finally say, settling on some version of the truth without having to actually delve deeper into this. "I'm just a little overwhelmed from thinking about it. I didn't mean to lash out at you."

He's silent for a minute, his expression looking as though he wants to say something else, but he's decided against it. "Apology accepted," he says quietly.

He puts a hand on my shoulder and squeezes. And then he walks out.

I put my head back on the desk. *Damn it.* The one person I actually *should* be able to talk to about this, and I'm pushing him straight out the door.

He was trying to be a friend. He came here in his free time to talk things out and make me feel better, and I lashed out at him. I've taken the first person who could ever slide past my angry defensive bullshit and made him regret it. *Oh, you want to kindly wait and listen and challenge her to see her own value? Well, too bad, she's going to come back at you even meaner than before!*

I spend at least twenty minutes like that, head on the desk, feeling even more pathetic than I did this morning.

But to my surprise, when I come downstairs, it seems like nothing's happened. Maybe I've miscalculated how badly I've screwed up, because throughout dinner, he acts totally normal. If he was the one who lashed out at me, I would've sulked in the corner all evening, avoiding him. But he's engaged with everyone and doesn't seem the slightest bit bothered. Maybe I've let myself get more worked up about this than I need to.

See, *this* is exactly why this friends-with-benefits thing is such a good idea. He doesn't care enough to actually get hurt by my whirlwind.

You can't cut someone who doesn't actually have skin in the game.

When he slips into my room after everyone else has gone to bed, though, that last little piece of me that was secretly worried I'd ruined . . . whatever this is . . . lets out a sigh of relief.

I'm too cowardly to apologize to him again, even if I want to. I know he said he'd accepted my apology, but an unfamiliar unease of regret is snaking through me. I don't want to examine why I can't shake it, why it matters to me so much to know I haven't actually hurt his feelings.

But we don't say anything. He comes to me in bed and undresses quickly, our eyes locking. I don't say anything when he moves slowly on top of me. I try not to read anything into the way he watches me, never taking his eyes off me as I come undone; the way he kisses me so deeply, even after we've finished; the lightness of his touch on my hands as he pulls me in closer. I fall asleep in his arms and don't let my mind go down any paths that I'm not capable of imagining.

CHAPTER

TWENTY-EIGHT

EARLY OCTOBER

I'm antsy. This would normally be an Ireland day, but Brigid had some prescheduled something that she didn't care to explain, so we're taking a rain check on this particular trip.

I'm happy to avoid the travel, especially because New York in October is like a fall postcard come to life—all the crisp air and crinkled, brightly colored leaves you can imagine. But I can't brush off the feeling that by not going to Ireland this week, I'm kicking the can down the road instead of talking to Jack.

My incivility, or our disagreement or whatever you want to call it (*or, let's be real: the "Bea being extremely rude" incident*), is like a fish. The longer it sits, the more it smells. It *seems* like everything is basically normal. But . . . *yeah*.

The more time goes by, the more I get the sense that he's just ever so much at arm's length. And that undertone grows. We had another Ireland trip after *the conversation* (or, more accurately, my temper tantrum), and we spent the night together, but the late-night chats and the small daytime jokes were missing.

Whatever little pieces of the normally quiet and reserved Jack Sander I was able to slowly pull out of his box feel like they've started retreating back inside.

And I don't know why that bothers me so much.

I think it's because I hate being rude. He was trying to give me advice and be a good friend, and I bristled. It was too personal. And it's normal to not want to hurt the feelings of someone who's trying to be nice to you.

But it bothers me. An inexplicably inordinate amount.

At least not going to Ireland this week means I don't have to get ambushed by Brigid again. Last time it felt like she was lurking around every corner, a perkier and attempting-to-be-genial version of my boss, for whom "perkiness and geniality" is not a natural state. I told her I needed a few weeks to think about her offer—and needed to get more actual paperwork detailing what the full offer would be—but that didn't stop Brigid from her unsubtle nudging.

So now it's all sitting on top of me. My friends are bustling around my apartment making dinner, but all my internal messes are distracting me—Jack. Brigid. The job. How Lucas is going to react to even the *idea* of the job.

I'm a smidge off balance from all the wonkiness in my normally even work-life, as though I accidentally put on two different shoes, and one has a slightly higher heel. In my personal life, sure, I'm inured to this kind of friction. I could practically heat my house with the friction Lucas and I generate. But the counterweight has always been work, and it feels weird to have that part of my life swirling.

The smell of whatever Rika is making is almost enough to make me forget all the little things nagging at me. She's pulling out all the stops with an autumnal feast, the scent of caramelized onions and garlic warming us from the inside. I'm ogling the miso sauce she's about to drizzle on her steamed sweet potatoes. Clem's made a spiced bourbon and apple toddy that we're all heartily drinking out of steaming mugs.

The scene is so convivial and toasty that I can start to feel my problems reduce to a simmer, existing only on the back burner.

But of course, that would assume I could get anything past my friends.

"Okay, spill," Rika says as she puts down all the food in front of us. "You're completely distracted, and I'm hoping Clem's cocktails are strong enough to get you to tell us what's going on, at *least* before the end of the evening,"

"Hey!" Clem gives her a look. "Don't bring my drinks into this."

"*I'm* grateful for the drinks right about now," I mumble as I pile copious quantities of food onto my plate, although I almost start laughing when I look up and see how pleased Clem is at the sliver of a compliment about her concoction.

"Is it Brigid? What's going on with her lately?" Rika asks.

Rika's really got that domestic goddess thing going right now, with her lilac apron and pixie cut slicked back. The crunch of crispy skin immediately distracts all of us as she expertly carves her roast chicken while barely looking at it. *Shoot, she's looking at me instead.*

"Can I have some of that skin?" I say, deflecting.

"Only if you answer the question."

I pout and signal with my hand for her to place the skin on my plate. If I'm going to be ambushed, at least I'm going to get golden crispiness wafting over me.

"Brigid is driving me nuts," I say with my mouth full.

"Have you made up your mind about the job?" Rika asks, finally sitting and making a plate for herself.

"No . . . ," I reply.

"Well then, she's probably just anxious to see what you do."

"Honestly, I feel overwhelmed when I think about it, so I'm . . . avoiding it," I say slowly.

"Which part?" Clem asks as she quietly refills my drink, liquid courage all but implied.

"I need to tell her what I want. I need to talk about keeping the job in New York. The company's always been based in New York, so it *should* stay in New York." I think of Jack and wince at how his advice has wormed its way into the leading position in my mind, even though a few weeks ago I practically yelled at him for giving me the advice. "But I'm having a hard time articulating it," I finally say.

"Well, you have a hard time generally saying what you want," Rika replies, so matter-of-factly it irks me a little bit.

"I do not. I'm forthright at work."

"Being forthright doesn't mean you're doing what *you* want."

"This isn't that simple," I argue. "I don't exactly *know* what I want here."

"You know what you want; it's just scary," Rika retorts.

"You sound like Jack," I mutter under my breath.

Rika puts her fork down and leans forward. "I'm sorry, let's talk about *that.*"

"What?" I say.

"What sounds like Jack?" she replies, looking gleeful.

I sigh. I've trapped myself, and Rika already knows it.

No use beating around the bush now or it'll make me look even more defensive. "He sort of said the same thing. He thinks I should take the job."

"I'm sorry, is there anyone who actually *doesn't* think you should take the job?" Clem interjects.

"No sidetracking," Rika says, tapping Clem on the shoulder. "Duh, you should take the job; yes, you should negotiate it. But when did *Jack* become the voice in your head?"

"He's not the—"

"Save it!" Rika says with a flourish. "You're all mopey tonight, and I thought it was about your job. But it's clearly not. This is about man problems."

Clem chuckles, and I shoot her a look. *Traitor.* She's usually the one on my side, but it's clear I'm not getting any backup tonight. I stuff a pile of sweet potatoes into my mouth as though I can save myself through an inability to speak.

But apparently that just gives Rika more leeway to keep talking. "Why is Jack's advice making you all angsty? Did you have . . . a fight?"

"No," I say a bit too quickly.

"Because you can't have a fight with someone who is completely *casual* and *doesn't mean anything.*"

"I can have a fight with anyone," I mumble.

"Can I ask a different and less taunty question?" Clem cuts in, tapping her fork to the side of her glass as though we need an auditory stir back to reality.

We both stare at her, basely acknowledging with our silence that whenever Clem wants to ask a question, we're clearly going to take her advice over pretty much anyone else's.

"What's bothering you so much that you're completely closed off to even the *idea* that the guy you're sleeping with might be allowed to have a worthwhile opinion on your life?"

Well, that shuts us up.

I take the silence as an opportunity to shove more roast chicken into my mouth, and I'm at least grateful that I can see Rika doing the same out of the corner of my eye. We all ruminate for a few moments, like cows chewing cud, and let my emotional brick walls have a moment for contemplation.

"Jack said . . ." I wait to see if everyone balks at me, but no one does. I breathe a small sigh of relief, even as I mentally chide myself for holding on to pathetic fears of judgment from my closest friends. "Jack said I allowed Lucas to take my confidence. Do you think that's true?"

"I think it only matters if *you* think that's true," Clem says quietly.

I consider it. Clem tops up my drink, another nudge of liquid courage, and I silently mouth *thank you* to her.

I sigh and look up at the ceiling. "I've been thinking lately that maybe I didn't give Lucas enough credit."

Rika practically spits out her drink. "Okay, *that* was not the direction I ever thought this conversation would go. Have you had a lobotomy, and we're now praising Lucas? After everything he did? After how much he put you through?"

I put my hand on hers to stop her before she can work herself up into the protective tizzy I know she's capable of.

"I don't mean it like that," I say, reassuringly. "I had this conversation with Jack a few weeks ago—not a fight," I insist, even though I can practically see the blinking lights above my head saying, *Okay, sure, if you want to pretend.* "And it sort of . . . illuminated something for me. I don't think I ever *really* told Lucas how I was feeling. I went along with what he wanted, and then it built up, and I got mad as a way to avoid being . . . sad?"

"He was still a dick," Rika retorts.

"I'm not saying he handled it well either"—*obviously*, Rika continues under her breath—"but I think my need to be in control also . . . kind of . . . emotionally closes me off sometimes. I never really allowed myself to let my guard down to him, ever."

"That's a good realization to have," Clem says supportively, while Rika immediately gets defensive on my behalf by saying, "Well, Lucas wasn't the right guy for you."

"Thank you, Clem. And Ri, I know. But that's all kind of part of the problem, right? It's why I said yes to a marriage that wasn't ever going to be right."

Everyone is silent again for a minute. Maybe they know that admitting just that basic emotional stuntedness is hard for me to say. It's the thing that's been swirling around in my mind for the last few weeks, needling at me. I worry it's affecting everything I do. *Can I really take this job? Can I even handle it if I do? Do I always shrink from the big things? Do I ask for help when I need it?*

"You know, therapy is a *delightful* option that I *highly* recommend," Rika says, breaking the silence and stabbing her fork into the last sweet potato.

"Because I have so much free time for that," I counter.

"You can make time. If you want to."

"Your cooking is my therapy," I reply, swiping another piece of the sweet potato that Rika's already cut. She rolls her eyes at me.

"Nice try. But that makes me your therapist, so I can ask you the inappropriate questions. Such as, When are you admitting to yourself that you're actually dating Jack Sander?"

My fork hangs in midair like a cartoon character. "We're not . . . dating."

I can see both of them eyeing each other like I'm a poor, foolish child, and I set my fork down so I can regain some control from this conversation, which has gone decidedly off the rails.

"Speaking of letting your guard down . . . ," Rika says.

Clem elbows her and cuts in. "I think what Rika's asking, very rudely—"

"She said I'm her therapist!"

"Food therapy does not count," Clem interjects. "So what we're all wondering is, Why haven't you even considered dating him?"

"He doesn't want that," I say assuredly.

"Have you asked him?"

"Of course not," I reply incredulously.

But seeing my friends' faces at that response makes me think perhaps that wasn't the right answer.

"Why not?" Clem asks.

"Because he has said quite clearly, to anyone who asks, that he likes being alone."

"But would you want to date him if he wanted to date you?"

"I'm a single mother trying to decide if I can become CEO of my company. I don't have time to date anyone," I say, brushing it off. I'm beating a drum I know they've already heard me beat before.

"Well, if you did?" Clem continues, ignoring my dismissal. "Would you want to?"

Clem's earnestness has always been kryptonite for me. It's like her sincerity is impervious to my bullshit and contains the keys to every tiny hidden corner I've ever locked myself in.

"I . . ." I pause, because the true answer smacking me in the face is sort of embarrassing, now that I think about it. "I honestly haven't ever even considered it."

"So you got to the realization that you protectively, emotionally wall yourself off," Rika probes, "but you haven't *quite* gotten to the part where you realize you've been sleeping with a guy for more than half a year, and it's a problem that it never occurred to you that dating him is even in the realm of possibility?"

It's so silent I imagine crickets should be chirping. I know my friends are waiting on me to say something, but I think I'm just as surprised by the query as they are.

"It never seemed relevant," I finally say, weakly. "We both decided, at the beginning, neither of us had the bandwidth for anything beyond being friends with occasional benefits. I mean, it's not just *me* being emotionally stunted here."

"Yes, yes, I'm sure he's stunted, too, you win," Rika says, laughing, and I narrow my eyes at her.

"He really hurt me the last time I tried to take him seriously," I point out.

"*Twenty. Years. Ago,*" Rika says slowly, like I'm missing the entire point.

"No, I'm going back to the question you keep avoiding," Clem says, ignoring Rika completely. "You're saying he's genuinely become your friend. And you have great sex. And he respects your busy schedule. Okay, fine, you hadn't considered it before this conversation, I buy that. But now we're talking about it. What's blocking you here?"

I take a deep breath, because the honest answer on the tip of my tongue is one I know my friends are going to argue with. But it's the truth.

"Get real, guys," I finally say. "No one my age is going to want to actually date me."

"I'm sorry. What?" Rika exclaims, and I fear that I've once again awakened the mama bear in her, so I quickly try to explain.

"This situation is good for right now, because he doesn't want anything serious. But if he changed his mind, he'd probably want someone who could, you know, have kids. Someday, when I have more time and energy, I'll date someone who already has kids and is also on a second marriage and doesn't care, and that'll be fine."

"That'll be . . . *fine?*" Rika says, incredulously.

"Well, yeah! When I do date for real again, it would have to be someone who doesn't care that my ovaries are duds."

"Nothing about you is a dud, Bea!"

Rika is now standing up, and I wince, genuinely concerned I'm about to get something thrown in my direction. Probably a chicken bone would be the closest blunt object, and that doesn't bode well for me.

"Come on, Ri," I say quietly, in the hopes a calming voice will make her view this rationally. "You have to admit that if I *was* going to date someone in any serious way someday, I'd have to be open about the fact that I can't have more kids."

"Your worth is not wrapped up in—" Rika starts.

But I can't help but interrupt her. "My marriage literally fell apart because my husband wanted more kids."

"Hold on, hold on," Clem says, pulling Rika down to sit and change the tone. "You're creating an unfair narrative for yourself. Your marriage fell apart because you married someone a little fast who turned out to not be the right fit. Yes, infertility pushed you both to face some harder truths earlier than you would have, but the relationship itself couldn't withstand a real trial. You got Bash and then you got separated, and *both of those things* were the right decisions. Don't let yourself believe your infertility is some barrier to a good relationship."

"I can't go through that again," I say quietly.

Even the memories of that time—the shots, the waiting, the hormones, the disappointment, the fatigue, the tears, the loneliness—make my stomach churn. It's like my body has a visceral reaction to even the thought of putting myself through it for one more minute. I may not be self-aware enough to know a lot of things about myself, but I know *that*.

"We know, sweetie," Clem says. "And yes, of course you shouldn't get in a relationship with someone who desperately wants more kids. I don't disagree with that."

"Thank you," I murmur.

"But can you please do something for me?" she asks.

I look up, unsure of what to say because I doubt I'm going to like it. When I don't say anything, she just continues on. "We can drop this conversation, because obviously your skin is crawling to get out of it. But since you're maybe considering a few things you haven't before, can you give yourself the mental space to consider what you actually would *want*, before writing it off? You have no idea what he wants. If being with him makes you happy, if you've found someone who genuinely is your friend and also lights you up in bed, then don't write off the chance of something more just because six months ago, you guys had an offhanded conversation about what you wanted then, and you have assumptions now about what he'd want in his future."

For a brief moment, I let myself imagine it. Two weirdo control freaks who belong to each other, even in their own overly independent way.

I think about Jack encouraging me (before I, admittedly, ruined it). *You can move forward.*

Maybe I *could* move forward.

Maybe. *Maybe.* It makes me feel lighter to give myself that permission to consider.

I see Clem smile, like she knows she's wormed her way into my mind the way she's already wormed her way into my heart. I give her a small smile and stand up to collect our dinner plates, getting us ready for whatever Rika's made us for dessert.

CHAPTER

TWENTY-NINE
MID-OCTOBER

Once Clem made me concede that I would consider what I actually might want, I'm now a little bit of an anthropologist trying to conduct a field study, but on myself. Is this how directors who act in their own movies feel? I'm not sure I have enough self-awareness to know something as basic as *what I want*.

Despite my earlier feeling that our fight had made Jack distant, he seems to be relatively back to his normal self. Maybe I'd read too much into it.

Jack and I are lying in bed, having made up for the lost time of our missing Ireland week. Made up for lost time more than once and in more than one place in the room. And that gooey, sated sensation means we've both crawled into his bed and collapsed on each other, with clearly no intention of moving again yet.

And admittedly, it's pretty great. My head is nuzzled right into that crook where his neck meets his chest. I love that if I tilt myself down, I get sturdy, salty sternum, and if I nuzzle all the way up, I get the feathery prickliness of his evening stubble. Straight on, it's the softness of being tucked into his neck. I can breathe him in from every angle, and my body is appeased and loose.

What I actually want right at this moment is for all that body heat and glow to stay snuggled up with me while the wind whips around outside. But do I want that because it's convenient? Because I'm a sucker for a sex haze? Because Clem's incepted me into thinking it? Or can it really be because Jack and I are good together, and the lack of melodrama has blinded me to that reality?

"Are you alive down there?" Jack asks, his voice rumbly and sleepy and sexy as all hell.

"Hmm?" I reply, trying to knock my brain back into reality.

"Just checking I didn't short-circuit you."

"You mean with your excessive enthusiasm this evening?" I chuckle as I smile into his chest, enjoying the memory of him immediately getting his hands in my hair and pushing me back onto the desk the moment I'd walked into the room.

"'Excessive' has implications," he teases.

"Not complaining. At all." I stretch, like a cat reminiscing about cream, as his hand slides slowly down my back. "Do you think . . ." I have a thought about sex, and in every previous iteration of myself I probably would have been too secretly prudish to say it out loud. But maybe because Clem's gotten in my head, or because I really have short-circuited, or maybe just because it's Jack, I find myself missing the normal need to self-censor. "Maybe the sex is so good because we don't see each other all the time, so it kind of builds up."

"And what?" He chuckles. "If we were around each other for a whole weekend, it would just be meh?"

"Probably! How could I miss you if you don't go away?"

He laughs. "I think some people have sex every day and do just fine."

"Okay, like who?" I challenge, a little goofiness also somehow sneaking out behind my normal merriment obscurer.

"Like *who*?" he snorts.

"Yeah, like, do we think Des goes home every night and bangs his wife in a haystack or something?" That gets a belly laugh, which makes me even more giddy. "Or boring Paul from the sales team sets an alarm for once a week on Sunday nights and informs his wife of the time?"

"You . . ." I love that being pressed up against him, I can feel every vibration of his laughter even as it dissipates. "You're putting too many images in my mind that I don't need. These are not sexual people in my life."

"You know that even the people who aren't sexual in the context of yourself are still sexual in their own lives, right?"

"I know that theoretically, yes."

"But you don't want to think about it?"

"I like to believe it's normal not to think about it," he retorts. I have no comeback to that level of maturity. I'm about to drop it when he adds, "But . . ."

"But?" I perk up.

"I mean, obviously the person on our team who low-key has the most sex is Lane."

"Lane?" I say incredulously, finding it hard to imagine our mild-mannered, bespectacled, exceptionally sweet CFO doing anything other than leading meetings and building Excel models.

"Yeah, freak in the sheets," he says.

I pull myself up to look him in the eyes to be doubly sure that he just did what I think he did. His attempt to hide his grin is all the confirmation I need.

"You did not just make an Excel spreadsheet sex joke to me."

"I did," he says solemnly, almost achieving his goal of not breaking.

"I didn't know you had that level of corniness in you," I deadpan.

"Buried about as deep as the need to think about my colleagues' sex lives," he counters pointedly.

"Touché," I say with a laugh. "But okay, sometimes you can't stop yourself. It's like when you're having a bad day and you remember that

underneath every serious-looking man in a suit is just a flabby penis."
Apparently my filter is fully set to off today.

"That's a strategy?"

"Yeah, a great one if you're nervous. Men's bodies are so comical."

He's smiling, and for a second I think he's going to kiss me again, but instead he softly tucks a curl of my messy bedhead hair behind my ear.

"This is certainly an informative day in the inner workings of your brain," he says quietly, pulling me back to him, and I nuzzle my way back into that warm crook I enjoy so much.

"Happy to amuse you," I say before realizing how true the sentiment is.

We sit in silence for a moment. He's still languidly playing with my hair while I let Clem's words make me overfocus on the ones I've just said. *Damn it, Clem.* It's impossible now to just enjoy a moment without analyzing.

But Jack mercifully changes the subject. "What's Bash dressing up as for Halloween?"

"Oh," I reply, not quite ready for the heart pang that accompanies that question this year. "He's really leaning into the rite of passage that is all boys apparently needing to be Spider-Man at some point."

"Not excited about superheroes?" he asks, clearly noting the hesitancy in my voice.

I sigh.

"No, it's not that. Halloween is over one of Lucas's weekends this year, so his parents asked if Lucas, Bash, and Mona could drive up and spend it with them. They thought it would be fun to have a whole spooky weekend, and I'm obviously not going to argue that Halloween is some meaningful holiday that I should be there for. Especially because Lucas and Mona's parents are so in love with Bash, and they'll all have a great time."

"But you're going to miss him." His voice is soft.

"Yeah," I reply simply.

I've been trying to not dwell so I can muster all my reserves of being the bigger person for Bash, but I'm unexpectedly relieved to be able to say that truth out loud. Jack stays quiet for a minute, and I'm glad he's the kind of person who doesn't try to find a silver lining in everything.

Lying there with him for a few minutes allows the sleepiness to start to take over. I look at the clock next to the bed and realize it's probably time for me to go back to my room and actually get some sleep before our early wake-up. I start to sit up, but Jack nudges me back down.

"It's cold in the hallway. Just stay here, and we'll set our alarm early, before anyone else is up."

His arm around me is warm, and I'm too tired now to let the part of my brain that wants to analyze take over. I nod and burrow myself in even deeper under the covers, a safe, cozy cocoon, happy to ignore the outside world.

"If you want some company next weekend with Mona and Bash gone, I could always come over," he says quietly.

The typical alarm bells start ringing, right on cue, as though it's the top of the hour. All the reasons that's a bad idea start floating through my mind, a bullet point list moving quickly like credits at the end of a film, starting with a ghosting twenty years ago and punctuated by every salient potential work-related issue of today.

But just as suddenly, I picture Clem as the conductor of the orchestra of all my negative thoughts. With a single flourish, she silences them all. *Can you give yourself the mental space to consider what you actually would* want, *before writing it off?*

Before I can stop myself, I mumble, "That actually sounds really nice."

"I watched this movie last night called *Yesterday*—have you seen it?" Brigid asks.

I'm in the living room in the morning, typing away email replies. I slept well and now am on a roll with getting work done, and I'm not really in the mood for another strange Brigid interaction. I'm still not used to this version of Brigid, who's pretending she even cares about small talk. I look up.

"I have. It's cute," I finally say, and I pointedly look back to my computer and start typing again.

"Yes, I liked it too," Brigid replies, clearly ignoring my overt signals that I'm not up for a chat. "Although I thought it was strange to have that redhead play the famous pop singer."

I look up again.

"You mean Ed Sheeran?"

"Is that the actor's name? I get that the main character was supposed to look like an everyman, but wouldn't they want the pop star who discovers him to be better looking?"

I take a deep breath. "Brigid. He's actually like one of the most famous singers in the world."

"Why?"

She's dead serious, and I find myself enjoying having a normal moment of Brigid being clueless about anything outside of work. It's the first time in weeks she's felt like her condescending self, and I'm a bit startled by how much I've missed it.

"I guess he writes great songs?" I reply.

"Well, who would've thought," she says, seemingly still befuddled by Ed Sheeran being an actual famous person. "I'm going to make more coffee; would you like me to bring you back some?"

Aaaand we're back to being weird and overly polite. I can't take it anymore. I shut my laptop.

"Brigid, this isn't normal," I say with as little intonation as I can muster.

"I know: Des refusing to make coffee instead of tea for everyone really should be a fireable offense."

I glare at her, but she just glares right back. At least that's typical.

"You know that isn't what I meant," I respond, and the look she gives me practically screams *No shit*. But even though she's clearly up for a chat about friggin' Ed Sheeran, we're not talking about her weird behavior yet.

"You still haven't told me why you're leaving, you know," I finally say, refusing to beat around the bush anymore and dangling the one piece I actually still really need clarity on.

She sighs. "I just feel done, Bea. I already told you that. It's time for new blood, and you're the right choice."

"I know we do the thing where we don't talk about our personal lives, but I'm going to need you to give me a bit more," I reply, in a tone I don't think I've ever used with Brigid. But something about last night has made me bolder.

Considering my actual wants and needs feels powerful. Maybe when I was younger, I needed to pay my dues—in relationships, at work, in my own mind—in order to develop into a fully formed person. But I've paid my dues. I've got literal C-section scars and the CEO job offer on the table to prove it. I need the context, and I'm not taking any job offer—no matter how good and no matter how much Brigid acts overly nice for a few weeks—without it.

I think Brigid can see it on my face because she sighs. "This isn't going to become a girl-talk session, Bea. *Jesus.*"

She rolls her eyes at me and picks at some nonexistent lint on her perfectly pressed clothes while I wait her out, the way Jack does when he's waiting me out. Finally the silence gets overbearing enough, and she relents in that ever-so-slight Brigid manner that, I know, feels like a major concession.

"My divorce has made me want a change of scene—that much has to already be obvious. The company is in a good place, and I want more time to think about what's next for me. So that's the honest answer. It's not that I'm suddenly messy. Everyone interesting is already a mess in their own little ways anyway. I know you're a mess too. I already know that. Strong women always are. We're just better at covering it. It doesn't mean you can't do this job, though. I know you're the best person for it, even if you clearly can't see it yourself."

"Yeah, but then maybe that means I'm not ready," I let spill out, the back-of-my-mind assessment coming to the forefront.

"That's such bullshit, and I imagine you know it," Brigid says forcefully, all the abnormal overfriendly facade now shed. "You have as much talent to lead as I have—probably more, since people like you better. That's really the only difference between me and you. I never shrink myself to make myself more likable. And maybe that's caused a lot of men to write me off or women to back away without a real consideration, but I've done what I wanted. I built my company from the ground up. And I didn't care what anyone else thought. I've found it to be an advantage, but not everyone wants to live like that, obviously. I think, though, for you there's a middle ground. You're capable of still being your slightly nicer self while also not shrinking away from it anymore. You're ready. I've been tired of this business for a long time, but recently, I've watched you get more capable and give less shits, and that's what you needed to be able to lead. I know you want this. Don't be too scared to say yes."

I'm staring at Brigid. Not because I'm upset by what she's saying or even surprised by her forcefulness—on the contrary, it feels more normal than any of her behavior in recent weeks—but because it's shocking how, deep underneath, what she's saying is eerily similar to what Clem said last week. I'm a foal on unsteady legs who everyone has noticed is suddenly ready to run. And apparently I just need to start taking first steps.

"It needs to be in New York for me to even consider it, Brigid," I blurt out. "*I* need to be in New York. My kid is there, and that's not negotiable."

"Well," she says, looking more pleased than I would have expected. "I'm glad you finally grew the balls to say something. I have no problem with that, if that's what it will take to get you to say yes. So just let me know when you're ready to say yes."

And at that, she walks away, coffee forgotten and imposter pleasantries abandoned, at least for a little bit.

Later that week, when I'm back in New York, I text Jack.

"How's Saturday to come over?"

Chapter Thirty

Halloween

I walk outside with two to-go cups of coffee. I'm only wearing a sweater over leggings, and while the unseasonable weather feels nice, I'm not sure we're supposed to get used to it being this balmy on Halloween.

Jack's leaning against a car he's parked outside my house. It's amazing how unaware he is that he's posing as a particularly hot stereotype, all windswept hair like he's on a magazine cover, his arms crossed over his chest while he waits for me to come down the stairs.

I wonder, if he'd had a car in high school, if he would've picked me up like this twenty years ago, all Jake Ryan in *Sixteen Candles*, and I'd have swooned because he was personifying a dreamboat from a teen rom-com.

The only reason I'm not swooning right now is because it's nine thirty in the morning, and I'm frankly a little confused as to why this is what he suggested. I'm nursing a bit of embarrassment from assuming that when Jack asked if I wanted company, I'd thought he'd meant sexy company. But no one picks up a woman this early in the morning in a rental car to do any remotely sexy activity. He's clearly just genuinely trying to distract me from my aloneness on Halloween. Like a friend. The friendly help of a friend.

I'm not sure why that thought suddenly sits like lead in my stomach in a way it never has before.

I hand him the coffee, and he takes it wordlessly, then opens the door for me. I shuffle into the seat, and he gets into his. He starts the car again, and Fleetwood Mac softly blares from the speakers. We drive in silence for a few minutes, and it's so like Jack to be completely unselfconscious about not explaining where we're going. Quiet always seems comfortable for him.

But after ten minutes, I can't take it anymore. "Okay, seriously, where are we going? I know you said to bring my passport, and I assumed that was a joke—"

"You didn't bring it?" His eyes flick over to me, and now I'm extra intrigued, because he seems concerned.

"I did," I say quickly, assuaging whatever needs to be assuaged. "I wasn't going to take any chances, in case you meant it."

"I did mean it," he says, distracted by merging onto the FDR Drive. He speeds up, and now I'm *really* wondering where we're going since, apparently, we aren't staying in the neighborhood. "You can't stop me once we get there, okay?" he continues, and now I'm practically ravenous to know. Jack is the most deliberate person I know, so something a little daring seems completely off the radar.

"I won't stop you," I assure him.

"Okay," he says, and the music sits between us again for a few minutes, the assurance that I'm not going to derail his plan allowing him to stay happily silent a little longer.

Until we go into the tunnel heading toward Brooklyn.

"Okay, *now* can I get a hint to where we're going?" I ask, adoring the way he immediately tries to conceal the impish grin that wants to spread across his face.

"You cannot," he says, in a tone that I know is intended to come across as firm but is falling short, and he turns up the music.

I pretend to be affronted, even though I'm kind of relishing this little burst of silliness from a person who so rarely lets any shine through.

We drive along the Belt Parkway, and it's beautiful watching the way the light dances along the water. We're driving farther and farther into Brooklyn, and I'm still totally stumped as to where we're going, but I'm not going to ask again. He's obviously looking forward to surprising me with something, even if he doesn't quite realize the surprise for me is in seeing this side of him—thoughtful, a little giddy, weekend casual. I like it.

Well, I like it until we round the corner into a nondescript parking lot of a building that looks like a strip mall with a locksmith, insurance broker, and pharmacy. I'm genuinely confused until I notice the largest sign of all declaring New York State Department of Motor Vehicles: Coney Island Branch.

My eyes go wide, and before I can even turn to Jack, he's already talking, in a clip much faster than his normal short, unhurried cadence. "Okay, so hear me out. First of all, if you hate this idea, we can absolutely bag it, and no harm done. Seriously. Sincerely."

He's watching me closely all of a sudden, and it's weird to see him a little nervous. I don't think I've ever seen Jack nervous—or rather, if I had, I didn't know it, since he's always been pretty good at concealing his thoughts and feelings from showing externally.

"Tell me the idea," I say cautiously, wanting to hear him out, wondering if we're doing what I think we're doing.

"I made you an appointment to take your driving test."

There it is. I'm torn between being touched and terrified, so I say nothing and let him continue.

"Apparently, if you let your license expire for too many years, you have to take the driving test again. And there's only a few locations where you can actually drive and not just renew. When I saw one was Coney Island, I thought it was the perfect plan for today, because we could rent a car, do the driving test, and then go on the Coney Island rides after, since that would be fun and distracting no matter what happened. And since it's Halloween, all the amusement parks have a lot of nutty Halloween stuff, so you'll get to enjoy the holiday, but it won't be too similar to what you'd do with Bash. It seemed like a good plan until . . ." He runs his hands through his messy hair and takes a much-needed breath. "Well, until we got to this parking lot, and suddenly I realized I was forcing you into a government activity."

I'm still not used to these Jack soliloquies he's started to occasionally hand me. Getting to hear the train of thought of a person who rarely uses a single extraneous word is rare and illuminating and, in this moment, exceptionally endearing.

I don't know what this day is exactly, but I feel a startling need to wipe that nervousness off his face, and my only reflex is to get him up against me. Without thinking, I pull on the lapels of his light jacket with both hands and kiss him. After a moment of surprise, he's kissing me right back, unbuckling his seat belt in a single flourish to move closer, one hand curling into my hair the way he always seems to need to. I'm suddenly wishing very much we were back at my apartment instead of in a car.

We sink into each other, ignoring that we're in a dingy parking lot at 10:00 a.m., with sunlight streaming in and people walking by. The slight pull of his hand in my hair is giving me goose bumps, and I'm wondering how bad it would really be to climb on top of him (*I don't know anyone in Coney Island, right?*).

But before I can make some truly terrible decisions, he's pulled back, enough to make me blink from the sunlight but still close enough that a single finger slips down to my collarbone.

"I'm going to take that as a yes?" he says, his eyes locked on mine in amusement.

"Sorry," I reply, embarrassed to be a little breathless. "I just . . . that was very thoughtful. I didn't mean to—"

"No, no. I didn't stop you for any reason other than I don't want you to be late."

"Oh." I look at the clock on the dashboard. "Right."

"Right," he says, and he gets out of the car. Before he closes the door, he ducks down and says, "Don't forget your passport—you do actually need it. For ID, I mean."

I nod as I fumble my way out of my seat, then follow him into the DMV.

The silver lining is that the surrealness of the moment numbs any nerves I might have otherwise felt before I get behind the wheel of a car legally for the first time in a long time.

CHAPTER THIRTY-ONE

"I can't believe I can actually drive now!" I exclaim, holding up my little paper temporary license for about the fifteenth time since we made our way to the Coney Island boardwalk.

Jack snorts, begrudgingly amused by my overt enthusiasm for the moment. "You always *could* drive. You'd just lost the legal ability to."

"Semantics," I say with a wave.

It's a touch colder here, with the wind coming in off the water, and I'm wishing I'd brought an extra layer. My arms are wrapped around my chest, and I want to believe it's mostly due to the cold, but also, a sliver of me is worried I might throw myself at Jack again.

He obviously didn't say no earlier, but he also hasn't touched me since, and I don't want to push on whatever is happening today. I'm grateful to have him as a friend, even if I also can't pretend like I don't find this version of him—the casually sexy, thoughtful-surprise-giving, still-quiet-but-punctuated-by-slightly-more-half-smiles week-end version—undeniably kissable.

"Are we going to the rides next?" I ask as we mosey in that direction.

I've always loved the boardwalk here, a long path of wood that separates the ocean and beach from a fantasyland stretch of amusement parks, an aquarium, and a baseball stadium.

The array of people today is like a New York City smorgasbord: amateur fishermen next to selfie-taking teens; elderly power walkers next to a unicyclist; kids in Halloween costumes running to the roller coasters with enthusiasm while tattooed men stand kibitzing and smoking outside the entrance.

"I've got a plan of where to start," he says as we walk through the archway of Deno's Amusement Park, ignoring the spooky carnival games and pumpkin-carving stations, and then go through the tunnel to the Wonder Wheel, moving determinedly deeper inside.

I follow after him until his destination is clear: the bumper cars. He raises an eyebrow at me and smirks.

"Thought you might be dying to ram a car into something at this point."

"I'm merely grateful that when I hit something with a car today, it will be on purpose," I reply, grinning and running to grab a bumper car with a sparkly green coat of paint and a yellow lightning bolt on the side. He walks more slowly to an understated black one and settles in. His legs are clearly cramped, and his knees come up a little high.

Laughter and the thrill of adrenaline take over once the cars start moving, since this is just about the silliest way to spend a day. You can't even go fast; it's like a herky-jerky twirl of gliding forward and then bouncing back from all the ramming. And he looks so ridiculous, his large frame unable to comfortably fit in his car, surrounded by small children in costumes, that I'm unable to strategize much and instead am getting continually bumped into. Which I guess is the point.

When the ride ends, I giddily move us onto the next and the next—spinning teacups, flying chairs, a seesawing Viking ship—one ridiculous attraction after the other until I'm a bit dizzy from the lights and sounds and screeches surrounding us.

"Hungry?" he finally says, and I nod, following as he snakes his way to the Nathan's hot dog stand.

He orders us two hot dogs each and some fries. We collapse onto the rubbery embedded tables and devour the first hot dogs instantly, woozy from the whimsy of the day.

I'm momentarily shaken from the bliss of a warm hot dog when a kid in a costume accidentally hits me with a light saber. Three little Jedis are attacking him back, and they're all screaming at the top of their lungs in gleeful abandon.

"I'm *so* sorry," a harried woman says as she tries to shoo them off. "My sons are a little hopped up on candy."

I give her a smile and try to wave it away. "No worries. My son is dressing as Spider-Man, and he's been shooting me with fake webs all week. So I totally get it."

"Been there," she says knowingly and grabs two of her brood by the collar, dragging them away, while the other two scamper off toward a ring toss game.

"I can't even fathom going back to that level of chaos on a daily basis," Jack says, breaking me away from watching the scene.

"Not a fan of kids?"

His eyes dart over to mine. "I like kids, that's not it," he says, a defensive edge to his tone. But with a sigh he softens. "I grew up in a big family, and I found it exhausting. I don't think I'd do well in it again, even in a different circumstance."

"Well, I'll use that as my excuse when I need to convince myself I never wanted a big family anyway."

I take a giant bite of a hot dog, embarrassed at letting that sentiment unearth itself.

"You could have a big family," he says softly, clearly recognizing the bruise in my voice. But even so, I cringe.

"With all my . . . stuff . . . I can't have more kids," I mumble, hoping I don't have to rehash this topic again. Usually one explanation about fertility woes tends to be more than enough, but maybe I assume too little of men.

"You could adopt—biology doesn't make someone your kid. You can do whatever you want."

He says it in such a breezy way, a casual wave of the hand and a dip of a fry into ketchup. Like it's no big deal. Like I'm not defective. Like this isn't the one deficiency that's kept me up at night for years—failing Lucas's needs, failing to give Bash the sibling he'd so desperately love, failing myself by feeling guilty over something I have no control over.

His nonchalance is like breathing in a gulp of air after thinking you're drowning. I know I shouldn't need to hear it from a man, and I don't *need* it, but his sentiment creaks open a small window that Lucas had bolted shut.

"Why are you looking at me like that?" he says, all my thoughts clearly plastered across my face.

"I just . . ." I'm not sure how to even word it. "I appreciate the confidence," I finally say, and he laughs.

"Family is always complex as all hell," he says with a shrug. "You're allowed to make your own choices."

"Living with my ex-sister-in-law is certainly proof of that," I say, a loopy grin curling up the side of my mouth at the thought of the strange little nest Mona, Bash, and I have made.

"Exactly," he says, stealing a fry from me and then dipping it in my ketchup with a flourish.

"I'm sorry I was rude to you a few weeks ago," I blurt out. I don't know where it comes from, but I can't stop myself from saying it. Something about his ease of acceptance for me makes me want him to *know* that I value him, that I value his opinion. He raises his eyebrows, so I try to explain. "You know, when I—"

"I know what you mean." He pauses and eats his last fry. "You already said you were sorry."

"I know." I push the rest of my fries toward him, another little sorry in the form of food. "But you didn't deserve to have me snap at you like that. You were right, and I did that thing you already knew I was doing, the 'getting angry instead of actually facing my shit' thing. And I need to get better at seeing that about myself. This thing with Brigid has really thrown me for a loop in a lot of ways. And you were right about that, too, by the way. I told her I needed to stay in New York, and she sort of seemingly agreed to it immediately. So this hesitation is my own stuff. You were just trying to help me push through it, and I was a jerk."

"That's great about Brigid," he says, ignoring everything else I've just spewed at him.

"Are you . . . did you hear what I said?" I retort, narrowing my eyes at him.

"Yeah, I heard you; I just didn't want to make you feel like I needed any of that."

"You don't want an apology when someone's being an asshole?"

"I take you at your word, Beatrice. You said you were sorry, and I knew you were, so it's fine."

I stare at him for a moment, stunned by the ease of what he's saying. It's one of the things I've never been able to figure out about him: how, when I'm expecting a grudge, he somehow never holds anything against me.

"How can you always let things go?" I finally ask.

"I don't let everything go, but with you . . . I knew you didn't mean it. I don't spend time with people anymore who are mean on purpose. I know your intentions are good, so it's easy to let things go with you."

I nod and sneak back one of the fries I already gave to him, and he clocks it and smirks a little. I want to delve into that last sentiment, but he's already standing up and moving me before I can pick at him (or his fries) anymore.

"Come on—we've gotta get ice cream after hot dogs."

He holds out his hand, and I let him pull me up. I can't pretend I'm not a little disappointed when he doesn't keep holding it.

"I wish you'd been this enlightened in high school," I joke as we walk back toward the boardwalk, wanting to go along with his attempt to lighten the mood. "Hot dogs, ice cream, and eternal forgiveness could melt a girl's heart."

He tries to stop a laugh, and I beam.

"I never said 'eternal forgiveness.'"

"I think you did, though," I needle with a chuckle, poking his arm as we get in line at the small corner ice cream shop on the boardwalk.

We're both still smiling as we order our ice cream, and we continue when I walk out with three scoops piled on top of my cone.

"On the note of saying sorry . . . I'm sorry if I hurt you back then," he says, and I'm so surprised by his uncharacteristic blurting that I accidentally press my ice cream onto my nose instead of into my mouth. His thumb wipes it off while I stare back at him, unsure of how to respond to that.

"We were kids, Jack," I finally say softly. "Me being rude to you as a grown adult and you being sort of moody and ghosty as a teenager aren't equivalent."

But he shakes his head. "No, I wasn't relating it to any of that. I was thinking that I never really took you out on a real date in high school, even for something as simple as hot dogs and ice cream, and that was sort of shitty."

He's doing that thing where he looms over me, and I have to look up at him, and I feel even more childlike because I'm licking an ice cream cone while we both watch each other. But his expression is so earnest that it does remind me of when both of us were younger.

"Seriously, it's okay," I say, wanting to remove whatever doubt this conversation is making him feel. As much as I *was* hurt by him then, and as much as I did hold a grudge against him for so many years, that version of us really does feel so far in the past now. "It's not your fault that a gawky teenage girl liked you more than you liked her," I say with a snicker. I turn to walk down the boardwalk again before realizing he hasn't followed.

I turn back around and see that he's standing still, looking confused.

"What?" I ask, wishing I could have this conversation without constantly needing to lick away the ice cream melting all over my hands.

"That's what you think?"

I nod yes, although, again, licking ice cream before it drips is probably not the cutest way to convey anything right now.

He scoffs. "It's so wild how different our perspectives are."

"Well, what was your perspective, then?" I ask, now genuinely curious despite my ice cream debacle.

"Hold on," he says, and for a moment I think he's fully leaving me here on this boardwalk. But then it becomes clear he's simply popped back into the ice cream shop for more napkins. "Sorry, I couldn't keep watching you fight against that while pretending nothing was happening."

I smile and take the napkins he's holding outstretched for me. He leads me over to a bench, and we sit down, staring out at the ocean and all the people in between on the sand, enjoying the sunshine on our faces amid the wind.

"I mean, I guess I can see how you thought that—I wasn't exactly forthcoming at that point in my life."

"As opposed to your constant monologues about your feelings now?" I rib jokingly, and he chuckles with acknowledgment.

"Hey, baby steps," he says, and I laugh. "I've gotten better, I think," he mumbles.

I nod. "You have."

I offer him a lick of my ice cream, and he takes a bite, a gleaming grin overtaking him when he sees the shocked look on my face.

"But of course I liked you," he says, licking the ice cream off his lips in a way that's more than mildly distracting. "You just scared me."

"*I* scared *you*?" I laugh out loud. Of all the things I thought he was going to say to placate me, that certainly wasn't it.

"Yeah! You were so fully formed. I was a mess and mostly focused on getting out from under my family. And you always seemed to know exactly what I was thinking, even when I said *nothing*, and that scared the shit out of me."

"That's . . ." I look up, letting this information wash over me, a recalibration of a twenty-year memory. "Illuminating."

"Why?"

"I always thought you lost interest, and then you graduated and left, so that was that."

"I didn't lose interest," he replies quickly before pausing, considering, trying to find the right words to explain. "At that stage in my life, I was relishing having everyone at arm's length. You seemed to worm your way in, even when I wasn't trying to let you, and I couldn't handle it."

"But what about . . ." I drift off, too embarrassed now to even be thinking what I'm thinking.

"Prom?" he asks, with that mischievous glint, clearly knowing that it's what I was thinking.

I roll my eyes, but now I really am curious. "Yeah," I say.

"I didn't realize how much that upset you," he says, now once again not looking at me. "I mean, I did a few months ago, when you said . . ." He pauses, and I can see he doesn't want to throw my words back in my face.

"When I said you ripped my heart out at an impressionable age?"

"Yes." He laughs and takes my hand. "When you decide to use your words, you really have a way with them."

He's silent for a bit, which allows a twenty-year-old memory to bubble to the surface. Where I accused him of hiding me because he didn't want to take me to prom with him, and he didn't deny anything. Where after I tried desperately and failed not to cry, he stood stoically, and I never spoke to him again. And he never reached out to me.

Finally he takes a deep breath. "My dad was really mad about me planning to go to a different college than where he went, and I was relishing not doing what he wanted. And separately . . . this is so petty, but he had all the prom photos of my brothers framed on the wall. It just . . . I wasn't ever going to go. It was the only other thing I could do for myself. But it would have sounded *ridiculous* to say that out loud. So I only said . . ."

"You couldn't," I finish for him.

"Yeah." He nods. "And I was so mixed up then that when you stopped reaching out to me, I figured it was better just to let it all lie and start over when I left for college. For so many years after, I always remembered you as being such a bright light in my life at a horrible time. I sort of blocked out how it ended. So I'm sorry that it wasn't the same for you."

"Well, thank you for telling me that," I say, squeezing his hand a little tighter. "I'm glad I know."

I smile at the memories, now with a lighter haze surrounding them, knowing now that all the angst and passion and yearning that enveloped me probably was doing the same thing to him, knowing now that we probably were two young dummies who weren't nearly old enough to delve into the complexities of a relationship.

He tries to take advantage of my daydream by sneaking another bite of my ice cream, but I pull it away in time. He gives me a sad puppy dog face, and I roll my eyes but move my ice cream toward him so he can take another taste.

We sit in silence for a few minutes, watching the castles being built in the sand and taking turns finishing my cone.

"Do you think we'd do better now?" he asks quietly.

I'm still looking out at the beach, and I don't face him, because the question is the same one that's been on the tip of my own tongue for weeks. But I haven't dared to say it out loud.

"What about your plan to die alone in Boca?" I say with a grin, deflecting, but I'm finally able to turn toward him because I've turned this actual important query into a joke, like always.

"Excuse me, Boca was so that I could remain independent while *not* dying alone."

"Okay, details, but I thought that plan of independence sounded very appealing. No one to disappoint you, no one to drive you nuts.

Seems ideal, really," I say, trying not to read too much into whatever he says next.

"I don't know, maybe we only think that because we've had bad examples," he murmurs, his fingers tracing mine in our entwined hands.

It's such a small statement, but with Jack it speaks volumes. We've both lived with relationships that have done more harm than good. We've fought hard for our independence. He grabbed his early and has never allowed himself to risk it. I handed mine over and have had to reclaim it piece by piece. The idea of handing some of those pieces back over to another person is *terrifying*. And as much as a part of me wants to push the conversation further—to push *everything* with Jack further—I'm not sure I'm ready for it yet.

I sometimes wonder if I'm like this vase that Bash has accidentally knocked over twice—the first time he did it, we were able to glue it back together, and it *almost* seemed normal. But when he knocked it over again a few months later, the cracks were just too embedded and warped to fix again. Am I really ready to risk the state I'd end up in if I was broken *again*?

And considering that neither of us can even get up the courage to actually have a straightforward conversation instead of this constant dancing around the topic of what we are to each other, I wonder if it's safer to keep our little bubble the way it is.

"In a perfect world, I'd like to believe we would," I say sincerely, finally answering his original question of whether we'd do better now. I squeeze his hand a little harder. "But I think we're doing better now anyway, because in this version we're genuinely friends."

"Oh, so everything we do together is what you normally do with your friends?" he says with an innuendo-laden smile.

"Mona calls it 'sex friends,'" I whisper.

He snorts, which warms my insides. "'Sex friends' is a nice way of saying 'fuck buddies.'"

"No, because we're *actually* friends," I reply with a nudge, hating his interpretation even if it was also mine only a few months ago.

"Do you tell this much to your other friends?" he teases.

"Yes," I say honestly, thinking of all the confessions my friends have pried out of me lately.

"Oh." The smile slips a little from his face.

"What?"

"I . . . don't," he says, and I immediately want to take the answer back.

But he's already let go of my hand, and he's standing up, and I have no idea how to rewind. Because hearing that from him makes me realize that I probably *do* tell him more at this point than anyone else in my life. And that thought is even more terrifying.

Although, even if I could somehow wrap my head around clarifying, he's clearly already barreling us away from this tentative moment. "Well then, you're right that I definitely need more friends. So I'm glad that that's what we're doing now."

His smile isn't reaching his eyes, and I bet he's looking at me thinking the same thing about mine. All I want to do is find some way to safer ground—somewhere where I won't have ruined whatever this moment is, and I've bought myself enough time to untangle everything spinning inside me.

"But sex friends is way better, right?" I ask, pushing my luck, trying to at least bring us back to joking territory.

He shakes his head, but I can see from the smidge of a smile I've gotten out of him that he's going along with it. "The phrase 'sex friends' is not becoming a thing."

"I don't know, that's what I said to Mona, but now you're using it, too, and I think we're stuck with it."

"You're just trying to confirm you're getting lucky tonight," he says, and he starts to walk down the boardwalk, back in the direction of the car. I almost trip because the thought of Jack in my apartment has suddenly made me all kinds of nervous.

But I need to play it off. "Well, obviously I am," I tease, walking a bit faster to catch up with him, letting myself career forward and not overthink it. "You wouldn't deny a girl who's just gotten her driver's license, would you?"

"Is sex a typical reward for driver's licenses?"

"Since they're usually the goal of teenagers trying to get away from their parents, I'm gonna assume that sex is quite often part of the equation, actually," I reply with a smirk.

"Okay, friend," he says with amused sarcasm. "I guess I can't argue with that."

CHAPTER THIRTY-TWO

He tries to insist that I drive us back, until I point out that I'm definitely not insured on this car and that that's probably not a great way to restart my driving career.

We head back to Manhattan late in the afternoon. We still have one more week of daylight saving time, so the sun is only now starting to lower, casting everything as golden. The sunshine on my skin and the water views as we speed along the Belt Parkway wrap the day in a clouded loveliness, the final backdrop to a driving triumph, carnival rides, and ice cream. We let music fill the scene, singing along to whatever seventies mix Jack has queued up.

By the time he pulls in front of my apartment, I'm so content that I almost forget we haven't decided what comes next today. But the nerves hit me instantly.

What's the expectation now? We've danced around it all day, but the suggestion is ultimately up to me—he's not going to automatically come in. If I want him to, I'll have to ask.

Even though the thought makes me feel squirmy and unsteady, it's hard to ignore that underneath all the hesitation is a deep want.

He puts the car in park and looks over at me, music still playing but somehow the silence between us echoing.

"Do you want to come in?" I rush out before I can stop myself.

"Do you want me to come in?" he asks.

I almost want to retort back, make it another joke like I always do: *Do you want me to want you to want to come in?*

But I don't. I'm not sure what threshold was crossed on Coney Island, but I can feel that something has been; he deserves my honesty rather than obfuscation.

Anyone else listening to our conversations for the last few hours would probably roll their eyes at two people who tiptoe around everything. But that meander on the boardwalk was unusual territory for both of us; I don't hand over my inner thoughts freely, and I know he doesn't either. Maybe it wouldn't be obvious to anyone else how much trust had to be earned to have those simplest of conversations about past impressions, fears, friendship, and apologies.

That would be another thing unsaid, of course. Just the thought is scary.

But I want more of it.

"Yeah, I'd like that," I finally say, and I get another one of his almost imperceptible small grins.

We get out of the car and head up the stairs to my apartment. I fumble my keys out of my purse and open the door with a flourish, beckoning him in.

He takes a moment to wander a bit around my living room, picking up and putting down small knickknacks along the way, observing the little pieces that make up my home. I stand against the door and watch him take everything in.

"I like this picture," he comments, pointing to a ceramic frame filled with a picture of Bash and me cackling at something outside the confines of the photo.

In a sea of furniture that Lucas chose and Mona's curated odds and ends, he's picked out the one thing I added. It's the one burst of me in the whole room.

It warms me from the inside that he's chosen it, as though little by little, over the last few months, he's found his way into my bloodstream.

I walk over to him, and he turns to me. I give him a careful kiss on the lips, so light that we barely touch, like I have to make sure he's real in this time and place, and not just a figment of my past or my Ireland imagination.

His fingers caress my jawline, like he's making the same calculations, calibrating himself to the obvious intentionality of being together here and not merely thrown together by work circumstance.

"Thank you for helping me get my driver's license back," I whisper.

He nods, his eyes on mine, but his hands move gently onto my hip, his thumb toying with the waistband of my leggings. It's a touch so gentle and yet so heated that my lungs involuntarily catch, and a small sound hisses out of me. My palms slide under his shirt because I'm desperate to feel him, hard planes against the softness of my fingers.

"Pleasure was all mine," he says, pulling me toward him, his hand still stroking my side while the other wraps all the way around my waist.

He leans in for a kiss, and I stand on my toes to meet him, suddenly hungry to close the gap between us. I don't know how we've gone from discussing home furnishings to practically jumping each other in the span of a few seconds, but I'm unable to stop myself from pressing against him. A low groan slips out of him, and my body arches closer.

"This wasn't why I wanted . . . ," he says, and I shake my head quickly.

"I know."

He deepens our kiss, his mouth sweet with the lingering taste of ice cream. It's frantic between us now. I pull his shirt over his head, and my sweater comes off over mine. I try to unbuckle his belt while he unhooks my bra, mouths still fused while we're clumsy and panting and trying not to fall over.

I push him back toward my bedroom, and we stumble our way in, layers shedding like a trail of breadcrumbs from the living room until we're both naked and on top of my bed. His hands graze inside my thighs, and my mouth is on his neck, his pulse beating on my tongue.

"Condom?" he asks, and I freeze.

"Damn it." I sit up. I'm so worked up I have to catch my breath for a moment while he stares up at me. "I don't . . . I haven't ever brought someone here."

I expect the implications of that to dull the moment, to scare him off, to shake us both back into reality instead of our usual boneheaded and frantic inability to consider the impact of our choices together.

But somehow the opposite is happening for me.

I was nervous to ask Jack here because I'm afraid of making things more confusing about whatever is happening between us. But I wasn't nervous to have him in my space—in my *home*. I've never wanted someone else to see beyond that threshold. I'm surprised to realize, belatedly, that Jack seeing that isn't scary at all. Even if what I'm starting to feel for him is.

But before that realization can freak me out, he's already pulling me back down onto the bed with him. He nuzzles into my neck. "There's plenty we can do without condoms." His voice vibrates against me while his hand dips lower. "You're going to have to let me lead your celebration for your driver's license victory."

I huff out a laugh before sharply drawing in a breath from the exquisite pressure of his fingers inside me. My nails bite into his skin as he moves against me, pulling me closer and making my mind go blank as everything else fades away except his skin and his breath and the sensation of our bodies on each other.

We spend the rest of the evening in a sea of that sensation—hands and mouths all over each other, relishing in taking time we usually never have, slowly undoing each other inch by inch, and then collapsing in between, tangling together in a mess of legs and limbs.

We come up for air after a few hours and scrounge in the fridge for sustenance, eventually settling on bringing boxes of leftover lo mein back into bed, as though we're only used to existing in a bedroom, and moving out to the kitchen would be a bridge too far.

I can hear the street filling up with the sounds of trick-or-treaters, kids squealing and parents chatting and the cacophony of people hopped up on candy. I've left the outside light off so that no one will ring our bell, but it's impossible to ignore how much is happening outside the window.

"The streets are all closed to cars around here, for trick-or-treating," I tell Jack, my fingers lazily snaking through his hair once we've put the food off to the side and he's pulled me close again.

"Does that mean I'm trapped here?" I can practically hear the smirk in his voice.

"I'm afraid so. I wouldn't want you to get attacked by a roving band of superheroes or dinosaurs or ninjas."

"Quite an array of treachery, it sounds like."

We're lying side by side, but he pulls back enough that our eyes lock, and we watch each other. I trace my hand along his jaw, and neither of us says anything as we examine each other, the streetlamps outside creating the only soft light in an otherwise dark night. I'm so drunk on his nearness that I think I could watch his face for hours.

He pulls me in for a kiss, but unlike the frantic mania of earlier, this one is slow. It's exploration and tenderness. His hands are delicate as they move down across every curve, each caress intentional, like he's cataloging me. It's calming, as though all the noise and mania outside is drowned out, and there's nothing in the world but Jack and me and our languid breathing in sync with one another.

It always feels good when we're alone together, but this feels different.

Something about this day has shed a layer between us, and suddenly my heartbeat thrums faster as an awareness creeps up on me.

I'm falling for Jack Sander—for the second time, yes, but oh so differently this time.

I'm not sure I could ever say it out loud, which comforts me in the delusion that maybe it still doesn't count. But even if it doesn't count, I'm not sure I could stop it if I wanted to.

CHAPTER THIRTY-THREE
NOVEMBER

November seems to speed by. With the help of my contract expert (I didn't mention to the board that "my expert" was also, more importantly, my ex-sister-in-law), we negotiated the particulars of my promotion. The job is slated to start in January if we can agree on the final terms.

My salary and equity will increase, but my travel will not. Mona made sure to get in writing that during the interim six-month ramp-up where Brigid will oversee my transition, we will only go to Ireland occasionally—whether to visit the team in Galway or if Brigid wants to hold an occasional board meeting there. By June, Brigid will officially step back and fully take over the role of board chairwoman, and I'll be on my own.

It doesn't quite feel real, which is why I'm happy that Mona is still nitpicking over the minor details and I don't have to give a definitive yes just yet. But it's coming; we're pretty much there. And between Thanksgiving coming soon and then Christmas next month, this will be our second-to-last trip to Brigid and Ireland before everything resets next year.

I should be ecstatic to get my time back, but a part of me already feels a little nostalgic for this biweekly forced break from my routine.

Because of all the end-of-year work, and my need to wrap some projects up before January, I haven't seen much of Jack outside of work the last few weeks. We haven't exactly been dodging each other, but it seems like we've both put a pin in whatever happened during Halloween weekend. When he left my house that morning—after we'd both lingered on a hug at my front door—we went back to normal work behavior from that day on at the office. I was still getting notifications from Scrabble, but I made myself not rush to answer them as quickly, and I wonder if he took a bit more time with his too.

But now, back here in Ireland, we've gently slipped back into our pattern, wordlessly finding each other late last night and making use of the excuse to be back in each other's orbit. We fell asleep together, but this morning he must have left my room early before I woke up. I don't know why I'd hoped he would still be here in the morning, since that's not something we ever do. But for some reason it felt wrong today—it's the only part of our routine that's suddenly felt out of place.

Though now, with my feet curled up in one of Brigid's velvet wing-back chairs in the library, a cup of tea piping hot on the brass coaster on the table next to me, there's a peaceful tone to the morning. It's drizzling outside, and the room has a palpable coziness. I need to soak it all up before my Ireland sojourns are gone.

"You're working early."

I look up and see Brigid. It's apparently not too early for her to look impeccable, lipstick and all, although her cuddly cream-colored sweater is as casual as she gets.

"I couldn't sleep," I reply, "and I have a lot to do before the holiday, so I figured I might as well hunker down in here before we get started on everything else today."

"Do you have big plans for Thanksgiving? Where are your parents again?"

I love how she says "again" as though she's ever even considered that I might have family outside of work.

She sits across from me and nestles into a chair of her own. Our conversations lately have mostly gone back to normal, but sometimes she still seems to not be able to shake her overly friendly negotiating persona. I'm hoping that, once I sign the damn contract, she'll go back to her regular blunt self.

But I don't want to be rude either. "Oh, my parents live in Florida now in the winter, and they don't come up for holidays. But instead, I'm actually getting the worst version of family Thanksgiving this year. I have to have it with my ex, since my son really wants us to all be together. Even though the following week, our lawyers are meeting again to hash out custody terms, since we still disagree, but both want to avoid court. So that's awkward. But my ex's sister (who I live with) will be there and two of our friends, so at least I'll have some buffers."

"Buffers or not, that sounds torturous."

"We both want to make our son happy, so I'm hoping that at least keeps things civil."

She narrows her eyes at me. "That's the bar?"

"That's the bar," I say, taking a long sip of my tea and warming myself up from this frigid topic. "And luckily, I'll have drinks on my bar as well."

At that Brigid smiles. "Well, that helps."

She's silent for a few moments. I don't say anything because she looks as though she has something she wants to mention but hasn't quite figured out how to. It's a little strange to see Brigid holding herself back.

I finally can't take it. "What?"

"I'm just wondering if you never loved your husband," she asks, as nonchalantly as if she'd mentioned the state of the weather.

"Excuse me?" I sputter out.

Of all the things I might've expected Brigid to say, that was certainly not one of them. Not because it's impolite—Brigid certainly never cares about that—but because it's so daringly personal and emotional.

"You just . . . you seem irritated and resigned to have to do this dinner. Normally when confronted with an ex, there's either atrocious pining or extreme anger over the love lost. I don't think I ever quite noticed your indifference."

"Oh, there's been a lot of anger," I correct, a false chuckle huffing out of me.

"Maybe I'm wrong." A sentence I never thought I'd hear Brigid utter. "I guess I always see your passion through a work context, and I desperately try not to think about my employees in a romantic context, so I hadn't really wondered about your divorce much."

"And now in your almost-retirement, you're suddenly interested in your employees' personal lives?" I say sarcastically, but she doesn't pick up on my tone.

"Oh god, no, that would be tedious. Everyone's well-being matters to me, of course. Although I don't need to hear about it." The genuine disturbance on her face from that thought almost makes me laugh. "But I am sorry if you had a husband who you felt indifferent about. I'm grateful for having had great loves, even if they've ended. It's altogether different to have someone you married for the sake of marriage."

It's an insight that hits me dead center. I certainly wouldn't have expected it to come from Brigid. But now that she's said it, it's hard to think of anything else. I don't hate Lucas with a passion that would normally be reserved for someone who has deeply hurt you. The *situation* hurt me. The futility of my pain hurt. The dissolution of my child's parents' relationship hurt me. But Lucas himself was more of a frustrating element that I couldn't get quite right, rather than a love who was lost to circumstance.

And weirdly, that's an oddly comforting way to look at it.

"Thank you for saying that, Brigid."

She snorts, likely assuming I'm being sarcastic, until she looks closer and realizes I'm not. "Why? I'm not known for saying things about people's personal lives that they appreciate hearing."

She's so ridiculous. I'm really going to miss having her strange perspective every day.

"I think . . . ," I say slowly, the structure of the thought coming to me as I articulate it, "maybe it would be freeing and give me some closure to see him as simply the wrong person for me, rather than as someone who hurt me. Things exploded in a lot of ways because I really didn't—or couldn't—express to him what I was feeling. We were on such different pages. But that's on both of us, really; it's not quite anyone's fault. He took something from me, but I gave it to him freely by silently trying to give him what he wanted, even though I resented it. We needed different things, and at the end of the day, I couldn't give him what he needed. It's okay for me to not want more kids, but . . . it was okay for him to need more. Our only strong connection *was* our kid, so if we couldn't meet that need for each other, it would never have worked anyway. I think I mourned the loss of what I wanted our relationship to be, not what it ever really had the potential of being. So I guess I can give him credit for the loss he suffered too. I don't usually do that. I usually just blame him for us disagreeing about so many things—but if we fundamentally didn't, then we'd still be together."

"You're going to need a lot of drinks for Thanksgiving," Brigid says after my long soliloquy.

I laugh. "Well, that was always going to be the case."

"I suppose," she says, perking up at that particular thought. "If I were you, I'd just let it all go."

"Oh okay," I say, although as soon as it comes out, I realize she's not joking. "It's not as easy as that."

"Why not? Closure is such a myth. He treated you like crap; you took it until you couldn't anymore. Move on."

Maybe I should've been coming to Brigid for tough love on my relationship all along. Is this what being her actual friend is like? Does she *have* any actual friends with this lack of tact?

But apparently she's not done with me yet. "Don't you want an actual great love?"

"Is that what *you're* after?" I ask, turning the tables back on her.

"Well, of course."

It's a challenge, as though she's daring me to not believe her. As hard as it is to imagine Brigid's friends, I find it even harder to imagine Brigid in love. But then again, I'd never bet against her.

"Even now?" I ask, my voice smaller.

"*Especially* now," she says. "Something doesn't work out, you move on. Men who start companies and fail don't wait to go after their next round of funding. It should be the same for love—especially when the original investment wasn't the right one. Dust yourself off, forgive the past, and move forward. We all grow up thinking when we become adults, we'll finally figure our true selves out, but that's such a boring way to think of it. We all have different chapters in our lives. We can find success but then change. We evolve. And thank goodness."

It's impossible not to think of Jack, not to wonder what could happen if I really *did* let go of all the hurt that's piled up on top of the ashes of my failed marriage. Could I be a real partner to someone? Would I want to? And perhaps even scarier—would Jack ever want that? He's been abundantly clear about the way he's set up his life to be quiet and uncomplicated. Just because I'm falling for him despite my protestations doesn't mean his outlook on his own needs has changed.

I wonder what Brigid would make of this whole situation if I actually shared it with her. Is it weird that I wish I could?

"You know," I finally say, testing the boundary, "once you're not my boss anymore, we could do this kind of thing over drinks."

"Oh, for chrissake, Bea, I'd really expected better from you than to get sappy over a little personal advice. But at least that's as good as a confirmation that you're definitely taking the job."

She stands up, her ramrod posture always intact, even in the most casual of settings. But as she walks out, she does briefly place a hand on my shoulder, and I'm going to take that as a win.

Chapter Thirty-Four

Thanksgiving

"Fuck, fuckity, fuuuuck!"

"*LANGUAGE, Mon!*" I shout from the bathroom, where I'm throwing on my clothes for the morning.

"You say that," Mona says, sticking her head in without a care as to whether I'm dressed or not, "but you'll feel differently once I share a lovely little piece of news with you."

Well, that has my attention.

"What?"

"The oven's broken."

I'm startled into place. "The oven is *broken*? On Thanksgiving?"

"Yuuuup," she says, her teasing smile confirming that she's at least getting some amusement from my bewilderment.

"Well . . . yeah. Fuckity fuck indeed," I reply, slipping past her and into the kitchen to see what's going on.

It's still early in the morning, but we don't have all day to resolve this; everyone is arriving around 1:00 p.m. Rika is bringing almost all the food, but my two jobs were turkey and a dessert. And considering

I bought the dessert (sue me), I really put all my eggs into the turkey basket. It's been sitting salted in the fridge overnight for a little dry brine (which Rika walked me through because, even though it made the most sense to have the turkey cooking in the apartment where Thanksgiving was happening, she still wasn't thrilled that I was in charge of the most important item). But obviously no amount of brining can counteract a broken oven.

I press the button on my electric wall unit, and it chirpily beeps back at me while displaying a message on the control panel: *F2 E1 error—Oven cannot turn on.*

I press the button a few more times, as though that might actually solve anything. But shockingly, mashing the same button over and over again doesn't fix the problem.

"Shit. What do we do?" I ask.

Mona is now standing behind me, silently waiting for me to come to the same conclusion she has.

"We could ask Lucas to use his oven—" she starts, but I immediately break in.

"Absolutely not. You know he'll never let me—"

"Of course he'd let you—"

"I'm trying to keep myself in my best spirits for Bash and rise above and all that, and if I start the day asking Lucas for a favor—"

"Oh, and you think a raw turkey is going to really make the day go smoothly?"

"Well . . ." I pause, not sure how to cut Mona off from that one. "No, obviously not," I admit.

"So . . ."

"So, there has to be a way I can solve this without pissing off Lucas."

"You can't fix everything on earth, Bea," she says, not unkindly but still with that trace of amusement lingering.

"Okay, but I *can* google it," I say. I pull my phone out with a flourish and type into the search bar, *How to fix F2 E1 error.*

I get a bunch of answers on websites with subtle names like Fixya and PartSelect. I scroll through them, scanning the complexity of what apparently is a wiring issue that can be solved with suggestions including pencil erasers, rubbing alcohol, toothbrushes, or (the real dark horse), turning everything off and turning it back on again.

I start there by opening the cabinet to flip the circuit breaker.

"Yeah, good luck with that," Mona says with a shake of her head. "Blowing on it is also probably not going to be the answer, so I'll save you that step."

"Oh, ha ha," I reply.

"Why don't you call an emergency oven repair service or something?"

"On Thanksgiving?" I ask, and she chuckles at the absurdity of that suggestion.

"Fine. But I'm giving you an hour, and then I'm calling Lucas. In the meantime, I'm gonna go take a shower and get ready. Enjoy your morning, MacGyver."

She walks off and shuts the bathroom door behind her, leaving me to the oven debacle I've now signed myself up for.

I know my stubbornness is probably not ideal in this moment, but I need to try to fix this myself.

It's not that I think Lucas will blame me for a broken oven. It's that everything Brigid said to me last week is still swirling in my head, and making a genuine effort today is already going to be hard enough.

I want to believe I can let go. I want to begin trying to forgive Lucas and myself and believe the past is in the past and no one is to blame. I'm going to try that mentality today, and I don't need to start on the wrong foot. And I don't need a damn raw turkey to laugh in my face while I'm over here trying to be a bigger person.

So that's how I find myself, Thanksgiving morning, preparing to repair an oven with a screwdriver, electrical tape, needle-nose pliers, and, yes, a pencil eraser (apparently it's great for cleaning tiny particles that might be junking up a system. Who knew?).

I look up my oven's warranty, and it's so far outside the zone that I'm okay with the consequences of trying to repair it myself. I carefully unscrew the oven's control panel and look for the offending wires.

Twenty minutes later, I'm sweating from the nervousness of it all. I did find a disconnected wire once I opened everything up, but trying to successfully fuse it back together felt as tenuous as tripping the wiring of a bomb that was about to explode. I cleaned the area without letting my hand shake, used the pliers to wrap everything back together, and gingerly secured it with electrical tape. I slowly put the panel back on the oven, careful not to jostle anything and detach any other wires. I finished by screwing the panel back in place.

And now it's time to say a little prayer and hope it all turns on.

But as I'm getting up the courage, Bash walks into the room, pajamas and hair rumpled from the night, and with a face so quizzical I almost laugh.

"Mommy, what are you doing to the oven?"

"It wasn't working, so I'm trying to fix it."

"Oh!" he says, now assessing things more carefully. "Good for you! I bet you'll do a great job."

He grabs a banana and goes back into his room.

It's a pep talk without even knowing it's a pep talk—the kind of thing a kid can say when they have no context to believe their parents won't always make everything okay. But it still bolsters me a bit.

I press the button, and the oven comes to life.

And I squeal with excitement.

I'm deliriously happy and in shock that it actually worked. It's such a stupid little problem, but it's as though the world is on my side. It's a victory on a morning when I could use one. I set the oven to 450 degrees and go tell Mona that our problems are solved.

By the time we sit down later that afternoon, it appears I might actually get my wish and Thanksgiving might run, inexplicably, smoothly.

Rika arrived with more food than I could comprehend for eight people (especially considering one was her baby, who barely eats). Although considering I spent the following hour stealing spoonfuls of her buttery mashed potatoes and hoarding fluffy biscuits, I guess I shouldn't blame her.

Mona decorated our dining room table to within an inch of its life, sharing more information about dried flower arrangements than I really needed to know. Bash is beaming with pride over the inclusion of his homemade place settings, for which he assigned us each a planet and then designed accordingly. (I'm Jupiter, and I really don't want to delve into whether he thinks I'm large, gaseous, and/or have distinguishing spots.)

And Lucas showed up on time, without overt complaint, and with bottles of the French pét-nat he knows Rika and I love. If there ever was a peace offering, beloved wine would be it.

Mostly, though, I'm marveling at the golden, perfect turkey sitting carved in the center of the table. To be fair, the majority of the credit for the turkey should go to Rika, since I followed her exact instructions. But between the oven debacle and the weight of the meal's centerpiece, the success of the turkey in front of me has filled me with a pride normally reserved for gushing over Bash.

I let Lucas carve it, which he initially seemed suspicious of. I guess I can't really blame him for being wary of my goodwill. We're so used to having our hackles up around each other, two opponents unable to move their fingers off the trigger.

But I don't want to live like that anymore, and I'm hoping the specificity of his wine choice means the same for him. He likes carving the turkey on Thanksgiving—he's the type of man who has special knives and takes them to a particular guy to sharpen them—so it seemed like as good a moment as any to start trying to get us to a less antagonistic place. Of course, like so many things with Lucas, I didn't communicate any of the sentiment behind the base statement of "Would you like to carve the turkey?" so he was left wondering if it was a trap of some kind.

But once he settled in and recognized that I didn't have any hidden agenda, it felt like some small truce was established, as though bestowing the job of carving the turkey was a token of peace, and the offering had been accepted.

Could Bash's attempt to have us all coexist peacefully over a meal actually work? Maybe we're like the oven—broken under the surface in places but perfectly capable of being taped back together to function for the greater goal of making a turkey. (I obviously can't explain this analogy to Bash, but I do crack a smile when I think of explaining to him a scenario where I'm an oven, and he gets to be a not raw, surprisingly pretty great turkey.)

But Bash wouldn't be listening anyway, because he's currently explaining to Randall how butterflies don't actually eat butter.

He's been happy all afternoon, clearly relishing having everyone together. His place settings have me on his left and Lucas on his right, and he's been bouncing back and forth between us in conversation, making the whole table hum as a unit. There's no avoiding anyone when Bash is at our center. He makes everything around him bright, illuminating every corner that could possibly be explored.

And it all flows. Lucas and Bash trade off telling the story of a football game they went to that turned into a series of unfortunate events—windy rain delays, a noisy seatmate, and getting stuck in traffic while trying to get home—but that they somehow turned humorous. Mona and Bash debate the usefulness of upcoming space missions to Mars. Randall gets particularly animated while recalling his own dramatic school bus trials once Bash goes off on a tangent about the badly behaved brethren he has to deal with.

We eat and we drink and we tuck in for seconds, even when we wonder aloud if we're feeling sleepy from the turkey or from the excessive carbs we've all partaken in. Then we dig into more carbs when I unveil my excellent cake (giving all the credit to Red Gate Bakery and not claiming it as my own), and Rika showcases a ginger goat cheese pumpkin pie that knocks all our socks off. So maybe we have seconds of that too.

It's perfect. And I'm lulled into hoping this version of our modern family isn't an anomaly of a day.

By the time it's getting dark, everyone has migrated to the living room to watch the game, and Bash is trying to point out everything that went wrong the last time he was in a stadium, even though everyone already heard the story just a couple of hours earlier.

Since sports isn't really anywhere near my vocabulary, I make my way over to the sink to do some dishes.

I feel someone sidle up next to me and am surprised when I turn to see Lucas.

"Need some help?"

"Sure," I reply.

We work together in silence for a few minutes, rinsing and handing over dishes to put in the dishwasher.

"I have to say," Lucas finally says, breaking the quiet, "I wasn't optimistic about this."

I let out a soft laugh. "No, me neither."

I hand him a rinsed wineglass to dry and grab for another. It's a moment before he speaks again.

"But we should do stuff like this for Bash more often. It was actually . . . nice."

"Yeah, I was genuinely just thinking that too," I agree.

I turn on the dishwasher and help him finish drying, but we've reached the point where pretty much everything is done. We've been sort of silently existing together as we go, which in itself feels like an accomplishment. I'm not sure if I want to press on it and potentially have the moment crumble.

"With your promotion, when you're done with traveling . . . ," he starts, but then he stops himself. Maybe he's thinking the same thing I just was. Logistics is often a trip wire for us.

Perhaps it's the excessive food or the holiday conviviality, or even Brigid's voice ringing in my ears, but I know I need to change the pattern here.

"You should keep your extra time with Bash," I say quietly, voicing the one piece of goodwill I know will be more permanent than an invitation to carve a turkey.

Even though I'm fairly sure that's the thing he was going to ask for, he looks completely surprised. "Why the sudden change in perspective?"

In the past I would've read the question as accusatory. But maybe that's been my biggest problem with moving forward. Even when I disagree with his perspective, I still should leave space for his to be valid for him.

"I'm just . . . Brigid said something to me the other day. And she related relationships to funding start-ups, so it's probably not the most valid way to look at the end of a marriage"—I get a laugh out of him, and I'm glad to see that maybe this isn't going to be a total land mine to say out loud—"but she pointed out that when you know things aren't going to work out, you should just forgive and let it go. And that actually seemed like a much better way to live. I know that's incredibly simplistic, but . . . yeah."

He's nodding, and I can't read the expression on his face. I guess I never quite could, really. We never got to that place—it was exciting in the beginning, the mystery and the newness. But that's not what sustains a partnership.

"I think that makes sense," he says quietly.

"Does it, though?" I'm not used to him agreeing with me.

"You can't force intimacy, and you can't want different things. We just . . . didn't have whatever that *it* is. You were probably right to call it when you did. Maybe it *is* like a company. You can start it and even have some success, but if it's not quite right, it won't expand."

"So you're . . . agreeing with Brigid?" I say with a smile.

"That woman is a dramatic pain, and I don't know what you see in her." He laughs, another small truth illuminating our differences, but this time with less of an edge. Not an accusation but a reality. "But I like the idea of that. Bash is our success, even if the rest of it wasn't. And we can be a team on that front."

"I'd really like that," I reply. It feels so strange to be expressing such a big truth through such small words. "I know the lawyers are meeting up next week, and maybe we can actually give them something to agree on finally."

"They'll be disappointed to not have more work."

"Let that be our biggest problem," I say with a chuckle. He nods, but I can tell something else is on the tip of his tongue. "What?"

"My lawyer said you wanted to buy out my portion of the house."

"I just figured . . ." Man, we've talked through lawyers for so long that the house has become merely an asset, a piece of money on paper, rather than our home.

"No, I get it," he says quickly. "I just wanted you to know I already told him that was fine."

"You did?"

Maybe Lucas has been having the same kind of softening I've had. Maybe Clem was right all those months ago: that for the temperature to be lower, we've really needed some time and space.

"Yeah, Bash is happy here, and I can find a place nearby so he can still come over easily. I think it's the right solution for everyone."

"I appreciate that," I reply, a little dumbfounded by the whole conversation but feeling lighter than I have in months.

"I'm sorry we've let it get like this," he says quietly.

"Me too."

I reach out for his hand, and he takes mine in his. He gives it a squeeze and then leaves to go sit next to Bash in the other room.

I can feel a tear rolling down my cheek, and I don't know whether it's from sadness or relief. There's a grief that comes with endings, but perhaps similarly with new beginnings. Hiding behind the grief and anger is sometimes easier than forgiveness and having to face a world with possibilities in front of you.

It's wild to me that this short conversation over dishes is almost the furthest either of us has let our guard down in front of the other, every admission small, all painful and difficult to uproot. And so few words spoken.

But I'm glad we've done this holiday together—glad that Bash *insisted* on creating the space where this type of interaction could exist.

I go and sit on Bash's other side on the couch, and he curls up into me automatically. When you're a kid, everything is so black and white—things are either insurmountable or they're completely fine. I love that today I got to allow him a fantasy where everything is perfect. And I hope someday, when he learns that adulthood is all about finding the beauty in the gray, that I've set the right example for him.

I give him a kiss on the head, feeling exceptionally grateful for everything that my little failed marriage experiment has given me.

CHAPTER
THIRTY-FIVE

The day after Thanksgiving, Mona and Lucas take Bash upstate to see their parents, and the apartment is quiet once again.

Maybe it's because I'm swathed in optimism after yesterday, but when my fingers itch to text Jack, I don't stop myself.

How was your Thanksgiving? I ask.

I can see the little dots pop up immediately, and I wait for his answer. But they stop and restart more times than I can count. Finally, after what seems like an inordinate amount of time to answer a simple question, his response finally comes through.

Fine

I wait, thinking there must be more to say, a little surprised by how curt he's being. But nothing else comes.

There's a part of me—that rejection-expecting, jaded, hardened part—that wants to throw my phone across the room and not text him back. But I'm too curious about what's underneath the nonanswer. Even when we've been sort of playing it cool over the last few weeks post–Coney Island, he's never brusque.

So I type a response. Wow, don't go into too much detail Jack, I really didn't need to know all those intricacies of your holiday.

I don't see any dots come up. Am I reading too much into this silence?

I get up and make myself a cup of coffee, willing myself not to look at my phone, even though I turned the ringer on for the express purpose of being able to pretend I'm not interested while still knowing when he texts back.

I probably make it ten minutes before I turn my phone over to stare at it. Maybe that last text was a little glib?

Sorry, if that was too sarcastic even for me, I finally type.

I'm shocked when the response to that is my phone actually ringing, the name *Jack Sander* floating across the screen.

"Hello?" I say tentatively.

"Sorry, I was . . . I'm sorry for the one-word answer," Jack mumbles, like he's distracted. Maybe I'm not used to hearing him over the phone, but there's something in his tone that makes me want to reach through and give him a hug.

"What's wrong, Jack?" I can't help but ask.

"Oh." It's as though he's suddenly realized he's called a person who can actually see him, even when I can't physically see him. "No, it's not anything. I didn't know what to say, but then I realized that that text probably came across as sort of rude."

I wait, doing to him what he so expertly does to me. I sit with the silence and give him the space to tell me or not tell me whatever is on his mind, without my incessant need to jump in and interpret for him.

And I guess that's the right instinct, because finally he speaks again. "I have to drive to Boston today to see my family, so I'm a little bit fidgety."

Ah. Okay. It's one sentence, but it speaks volumes. And I wish I could help make it better.

"That's understandable," I say.

"I guess," he scoffs, as though he's annoyed with himself for even verbalizing it. It makes me prickle on his behalf.

"Jack, don't minimize yourself. You're allowed to feel nervous about going into a toxic situation."

"I think 'toxic' is a little dramatic—"

"Don't do that either. You need a different word? Okay, Scrabble man: 'Difficult,' 'uncomfortable,' 'disagreeable'?"

"Okay, okay—"

"'Incommodious'?"

"Point made."

"Good."

We're both silent for a minute, and I'm not sure if I'm helping or making everything worse.

But finally he speaks again. "I just don't do well around loud people and tension. Their whole existence is like four on one, and since my mom is usually the one, when I'm around I feel like I take the brunt of it."

"That's a lot of extroverts for two introverts," I say quietly, and he scoffs again. It's as though every time he allows himself to admit a perfectly reasonable feeling, there's some Pavlovian part that has to discount it.

That overwhelming urge to give him a hug comes back. "Is there anything I could do to make it better for you?" I finally ask, verbalizing the one thing I really find myself wishing for.

He's quiet, and I wonder what he's thinking. I don't want to push him, but I get the sense that maybe there *is* something, and he doesn't want to ask. That while we've skirted close to being the kind of people who are there for each other, neither of us has ever actually requested anything from the other.

But maybe this is like the DMV, and it's okay for me to go out on a limb for him. I find myself *wanting* to go out on a limb for him.

"Do you want me to drive to Boston with you?" I ask quietly, as though if I say it faintly enough and I'm wrong, I can easily wave it off as a silly idea.

He lets a long breath out, weighty, considering. "I can't ask that of you," he finally says.

"Why not?"

I mean, I know the answer. We don't do that. We aren't that. We've agreed to not be that. And yet, we are.

"Because that's a lot," he says firmly.

"Being subjected to your musical taste for four hours *is* quite a burden," I tease, wanting to make him lighter, wanting him to expose that lightness that I sometimes wonder is only reserved for me.

He chuckles. "Well, it's really eight hours, because I drive up in the morning and then leave at night. I don't like staying over there."

"Oh man," I say, smiling now, even though I can't see him. "*Eight hours* of your musical taste is unfathomable."

"Exactly," he says, the smile in his voice evident too.

"Seriously, though," I press, not wanting to let it go, "I make a great buffer. I live to buffer."

"But we're not . . ." He pauses, the words dangling in the air.

"It doesn't matter," I answer, not knowing if that's the affirmation he needs or my own cowardly rebuke. I don't want to placate him or myself by saying *because we're friends!* because I'm not sure anymore if that's going to start sounding ridiculous.

But I do say the one thing that I know I can say. "Bash is upstate with Lucas and Mona this weekend. I'm not doing anything. Let me just . . . diffuse the brunt of it you normally take."

I wait, wondering if I'm reading him all wrong, or if he's actually considering it.

"Okay," he says softly, to my surprise. "Are you sure?"

"I'm sure," I say, and I really mean it.

An hour later, I throw my bag of snacks into the back seat of his rental car and slide in next to him. I wish I could pretend that brooding, contemplative Jack doesn't do it for me, but he looks all kinds of sexy.

And it doesn't hurt that he's dressed himself up like a model for clean-cut Americana, a soft fitted gray sweater pulled over a checkered shirt, with not a single hair out of place. I can't decide if the reason I love it is because I want to muss the whole look up.

But that's, obviously, not the point of my presence. I'm going to be the best buffer that's ever buffered. I've got my good dysfunctional family karma from yesterday going, so I'm going to smooth the path for Jack when he's faced with his own nonsense.

"First things first, though," I say. "Give me your phone, because my goal is definitely to mess up your musical algorithm and make you listen to something that's less than thirty years old."

"I don't have a musical algorithm," he says with a smirk toward me. He puts the car in drive and pulls away from my curb.

"Of course you do—that's how it all works," I say, rolling my eyes. For someone who learned coding as a nerdy high school passion, you'd think he'd understand how streaming works.

"No, I know that. But I play my own music. I don't have a music service."

"What do you mean you don't have a music service?"

"I just listen to the music on my phone."

"What music on your phone?"

"MP3s that I've downloaded and purchased over the years."

I do a double take. "I'm sorry—what century are we in?"

"I like to own my music. I want to know it's always there. For example, if we lose service on this drive, I'll have my music."

My head is slowly shaking back and forth, an involuntary reaction to being totally bewildered. "Yeah, but you can still download music to listen to offline in a streaming app."

"It's not the same."

I'm trying not to laugh at him, but it's too adorable and curmudgeonly. Luckily, I have *so* many questions to ask him.

"So, you can't possibly store that much music on your phone . . . ," I point out.

"No, I store it all on my desktop computer."

"And to get it from your . . . desktop computer . . . to your phone . . . do you have to use a physical cable?" I ask, trying to work out the mechanics in my head.

"Yup."

"So like, every time you want to listen to an album that isn't on your phone, you have to connect it to your computer, move some MP3s *off* to make space, and then add other ones on."

"Well, yeah."

He's so confident in his choices that I'm struggling to keep this facade of interest rather than incredulity.

"Isn't that a pain in the ass?"

"Yes," he admits.

"What happens when they sunset iTunes or whatever nonstreaming music app you're currently using that is obviously moving toward obsolescence?"

"Yeah, that'll be upsetting."

I'm still trying to grasp on to his entire mentality here. "But you listen to a lot of music—doesn't your process take up a lot of your time?"

"Yes, but it's a comprehensive organizational structure that I'm not willing to part with."

Now I'm pressing my lips together, desperately still trying not to laugh. But also kind of failing because it's so ridiculous and wholesome.

"You of all people know, there's a robot now that figures that structure out for you. *And* helps you find new things. Some might expect a person who loves coding and is the *chief technology officer* of a major company to, ya know, use technology."

"I love technology. But this is my music—I want to own it! It's tangible my way."

"No, records are tangible. This is a file on a computer."

"Records sound worse and play too short a time."

"Physical records are making a comeback," I point out.

"I know," he says, a small smile now brewing. "Maybe MP3s are next."

"You know they're not."

A little harrumph escapes him, which makes me giggle. "What if I got you a boom box?" I ask.

"Even I know that tapes and CDs are less efficient than digital music."

"Oh good, I'm glad we're drawing the line somewhere."

I love that I've finally brought out that lightness. I know that even this hint of a grin on him is worlds away from where he started this morning, unease radiating from him, replaced with amusement.

"Does Brigid know you hate technology?" I nudge.

"Well, it doesn't matter now, does it? I've got my future boss in the car with me, so I guess the secret's out. Your CTO likes some retro things, and apparently you're going to have to make peace with that."

I hadn't really thought about the fact that I'd be his boss until this moment. I knew things were already going to change without the trips to Ireland, but now I'm wondering if things are really going to have to end because, in that context, it would be inappropriate.

The thought makes my stomach tighten, and I try to brush it off.

"I guess so," I say with a reluctant smile. "So I'm stuck with your choices—is that what you're saying?"

"I guess that's what I'm saying," he says, and the smile he gives me makes it all worth it.

CHAPTER THIRTY-SIX

As morning turns to afternoon and we get closer to his parents' house, I nudge him to give me an overview of his family. And as with most things Jack doesn't want to talk about, it's the briefest of overviews.

His parents are Michael and Jean. Michael just retired from something to do with sales and health care, and it's clear Jack has no interest in even mildly understanding his dad's job. Jean is a homemaker who now spends most of her time helping out with her grandkids.

His three older brothers are Peter, Zack, and Simon, and I wonder if they're as generic in real life as Jack seems to make them out to be. All are married, all have kids (although Peter stopped at two, and Zack and Simon both have three). All work in something sales-y in Boston, and now they all live in the various suburbs around.

They always have their Thanksgiving meal on Friday, because on Thursday, Michael's brother hosts, but he doesn't invite all the grandkids. So Jean has just adapted to have her version on Friday.

"Does that . . . bother her?" I ask.

"I'm sure it does," he says without elaborating. "But I like not having to drive up when the traffic is heavy, and I get to volunteer at a soup kitchen on Thursday without worrying about getting anywhere for dinner, so I'm fine with it."

I'm not sure I'd describe anything related to Jack and his family as "fine with it," but I don't press further, so that's literally all I get before walking in: some names and some goodwill around traffic and volunteering. We delve more into our opinions about the differences between various suburban New England towns than we do about his entire family.

As we pull up to a house with a literal white picket fence outside, I feel the tension brewing in Jack. He's always quiet, but more often than not it's that comfortable quiet. It's a quiet that projects strength. This quiet is all nerves and a tightened jaw and palpable unease. I don't like it.

And without having a lot of details, I'm not really sure how I'm going to combat it. How can I diffuse this tension for him when I don't even know what I'm walking into?

But that thought is shunted to the side when he opens the door, because I'm instantly confronted with noise. Noise from every possible angle. Kids shrieking and giggling, two dogs barking at each other, men's voices loudly trying to talk over the din.

A small gray-haired woman comes into the hallway and wordlessly envelops Jack in a hug that I wouldn't have thought could be so encompassing for someone so tiny.

Then she turns to me. "You must be Beatrice. I'm Jean," she says, pulling me into a hug as well.

"It's really nice to meet you, Jean," I respond honestly.

She looks like a petite, feminized version of Jack, with the same striking eyes boring into me, only with a bit more initial warmth than I think Jack tends to allow.

"Do you need help with anything, Mom?" he asks, maybe to be helpful or maybe to get to hide in the kitchen instead of joining the bedlam of the loud living room.

"Oh no, I'm good," she says absentmindedly. "You should spend some time with your brothers and the kids."

I wonder if she doesn't pick up on the fact that Jack would probably rather be doing *anything* else. Or maybe she knows it and doesn't have the energy to make it any easier for him.

But she's already wandered off back toward the kitchen, while Jack and I silently take off and hang up our coats.

A thought suddenly occurs to me. "What exactly . . . what did you tell your family about why I was suddenly coming?" The unsaid words hang there too: *What did you tell your family I was to you?* How would we even answer that to each other?

"Oh, there's plenty of space; it doesn't matter," he says, avoiding delving into anything else. And I don't want to push, so I let him leave it at that.

We walk into the living room, and the cacophony is now at the forefront. Four men are sitting on two parallel couches speaking loudly over one another, beer bottles at the ready, snacks that previously were artfully arranged now dug into. Two women are sitting together watching over a pile of kids who are tearing apart pretty much everything else. Three of the children are burrowing in a fort of some kind made out of an array of pillows and furniture; two are building a tower out of Magna-Tiles; two more are hitting each other with sticks that I'm guessing are probably not supposed to be inside the house; and one girl is dangling her feet off a chair and reading a book, somehow ignoring every single other person in attendance.

The kids aren't fazed at all by our entrance, but the adults at least stand up, and if I didn't think Jack's jaw could get any tenser, I'm soon proven wrong.

"Jacky!" the one closest to us says, lumbering forward and clapping him on the back. "Glad you could deign to join us." He turns to me, seemingly oblivious to the linguistic jab he just threw. "And Mom said you're Beatrice, but we couldn't pry much more out of her."

He holds out a hand to me, and I shake it, not sure how to respond to that. But I imagine the best thing for Jack is to stay vague and smile a little brighter.

"Nice to meet you. Peter, Zack, or Simon?"

He laughs as though I've said something funny—as though it wouldn't occur to him that Jack hasn't described all of them in intricate detail. But he goes along. "I'm Simon. Peter is there"—he points to one of the similarly sandy-haired men in the trifecta of brothers and then points over to Zack, who's lost interest in our arrival and is now chatting to one of the women in the corner—"and that's Zack; his wife is Kira. Francesca is the one running after the kids, and my wife, Helen, is helping Mom out in the kitchen, but you'll meet her soon."

They all wave haphazardly, and I wave back, awkwardly, not really knowing what the protocol is here. I'm not loving the divide of all the women being on either food or kid duty, but no one else seems to care.

The older man standing with them, who must be Jack's dad, scoots around Simon, subtly blocking everyone else's path, to stand in front of me.

"I'm Michael. Nice of you to join us."

I shake his hand, and his grip is firm, like he's playing a one-sided game of showing who's boss that I'm not even clued in to. I try to see how Jack is doing out of the corner of my eye. He's still that subdued, stiff version of quiet, and I'm sort of desperate to grab his hand to give him something tactile to hang on to.

Luckily (unluckily?), Michael is clearly going to steer this ship, whether I have any plans or not. He beckons Jack and me over to two small chairs next to the couches and indicates we should sit. Everyone plops back down, and now they're all staring at us, no one talking, and with a frisson of awkwardness in the air.

"So Jean told me you're about to be Jack's boss," Michael finally says to me. I guess we're skipping pleasantries.

"Uh, yeah I guess so," I reply, not sure where this is going. "I mean . . . yes. It's not final yet, but I should be taking over in January."

"Why isn't it final?" he bounces back.

"Oh, I'm just negotiating the last terms of the contract. Nothing more than dotting the i's at this point."

"Is that normal at a start-up? To have a founder leave like that?"

"Oh well, we're not really a start-up anymore, at this stage—" I start to say, but Simon has already cut in.

"Everyone bounces around so much more now at these tech companies. Especially when they're backed by private equity money. It's not unusual," he says, while I'm sitting there wondering how someone in device sales for a health care company (*I think? Is that what Jack mumbled at me when he was avoiding talking about them?*) thinks he has a better grip on my industry than I do, or even his own brother.

"I always liked stability at the helm," Michael says, now speaking to Simon directly. "The team needs strong leadership and continuity to be able to go out and advance the product."

He continues on like this for, I swear, another twenty minutes. Zack has a few points he inserts about the restructuring going on at his company, and I watch silently as Michael, Zack, and Simon debate the merits of various company organizational structures, talking over each other without ever again asking for input from either Jack or me.

It's sort of fascinating to watch. It reminds me of that board game Hungry Hungry Hippos. Everyone is grasping madly to take hold of the center and get as many points as they possibly can, no matter how loud and erratic and slapdash. And it's clear that a meticulous Jack just never could even imagine joining in on such a game; he's all Scrabble.

I don't say anything after that, but I do press my ankle up to Jack's, and the moment I do, he's pressing right back and doesn't move again until his mother calls us all to the dining room.

There's a kid table set for the eight children, and they all scramble to their seats. Jean has set out simple place cards for everyone, so I don't have to wonder where to sit (and fortunately for this Thanksgiving, I'm not being subtly compared to a giant planet). I introduce myself properly to Kira, Francesca, and Helen, and then we all sit.

Michael talks the entire meal. It's the Michael show. He's boisterous and bombastic and occasionally funny, but it's all encompassing. It's politics; it's the neighbors' dog escaping; it's the new pharmacy and their terrible pricing; it's some friend's golf game; it's Simon's job that is somehow better than Zack's job. Jean says nothing. I wonder if she's actually listening or if she deals with him by merely tuning him out. I wonder if *I'm* allowed to tune him out.

Until, of course, he finally turns his diatribe to Jack.

"So, Jacky, if your girlfriend's getting a promotion, does that mean you will too?"

I'm fairly certain Jack wouldn't have described me to his parents as his "girlfriend," but clearly the point of this remark wasn't to be welcoming. Now Jean is paying attention. She's not going to butt in—Jack is clearly on his own on this one—but she's waiting.

And Jack seems almost resigned. As though this is what he expected at some point anyway. "Well, I'm the chief technology officer, so I already have exactly the role I want."

He's not going to rise to the bait of talking about me, and I'm glad. If we're both uncomfortable talking to *each other* about what exactly our relationship is, he sure as hell isn't going to be put on the spot by this agitator.

His father chuckles. "You techies and your made-up titles."

Okay, well maybe *he* isn't going to take the bait, but I sure as hell don't have the ability not to.

"I'm sorry, I'm not sure what you mean, Michael?" I say, irritated after being subjected to a droning, hour-long, one-sided conversation and not quite able to make my question sound as blandly inquisitive as I intended.

"Oh, you'll have to excuse my ignorance, dear," he says, probably not intending to be as patronizing as he is. "I never really had to deal with the IT department."

I force myself to take a deep breath. I can't even look at Jack. "The CTO of a company doesn't handle *the IT department*," I say, trying not to grit my teeth. "Our company manages and organizes complex data and then sells it to other companies to streamline their products. The CTO manages the product, the code, the innovation, an entire team.

Sales and marketing wouldn't have jobs without the complexity of the technology underpinning everything we do. It's—"

I feel Jack's hand on my knee and look over at him. He's shaking his head ever so slightly. It's clear that he doesn't want me to keep going, even though I desperately *want* these people to understand even the tiniest fraction of what Jack oversees every single day.

But I can see on his face that he doesn't need that from me right now. He doesn't want me to force him into the light—he just wants me to stand next to him in the darkness. And so I go quiet, making myself stand with him like he needs me to, even though I'm otherwise raring to go.

"The turkey is really great, Mom," Jack says, deftly moving the subject.

"Thank you, dear," she responds with a small smile.

"Anyway, Kira," Jack says, shifting the conversation even more and pulling Zack's wife into the mix, "tell me about the baseball season. I'm sure it's hard managing two kids' game schedules now."

Kira looks surprised at being asked anything, but she nimbly takes the topic and starts explaining the mechanics of juggling the games of a second grader and a fourth grader. Of course, within a minute, Michael has cut in again, extolling the virtue of one grandkid's baseball skills while ignoring the other one. Everyone falls in line again, with Simon occasionally adding his two cents.

But Michael apparently isn't ready to let go of whatever curiosity he's latched onto. "So. Probably not appropriate to be dating your boss, though," he says to Jack, as though this is a simple observation and not a gross invasion of privacy.

"We're not—" I start, but I don't really know how to finish. It *is* kind of the same thought I had in the car. I don't even know how I feel about it, and I certainly don't know how Jack feels about where we are on this precipice of a moment. But it's *definitely* not any of Michael's goddamn business.

I'm so frustrated on Jack's behalf that I don't stop the next words that fly out of my mouth. "Probably not appropriate to make your son deliberately uncomfortable, either, but here we are."

I hear Kira choke a little bit on the water she was drinking, and I notice that all four of the women at the table are avoiding looking at me directly while trying to hide their amusement. Peter's eyes have gone wide, and Simon and Zack are staring at Michael to see what he'll do next. I can't bring myself to look at Jack.

But Michael carries on as if he hasn't even heard me. "Well, I'm glad everyone's careers are doing so well. Chips off the old block. And Peter's bound to get promoted soon, too, as well. I bet, son, if you were just a little more assertive . . ."

It goes on like this through dessert: Michael sharing his hot takes on everyone else, and Simon, Peter, and Zack chiming in and talking over each other, and they all build on their own little world without noticing the other people around them.

And it's amazing how all four of these men never really address anything to Jack. It's Diana Ross and the Supremes over here, with one lead singer and three backup singers, and everyone else is like an insignificant roadie. It hurts my heart to think of Jack off to the side during his whole childhood, not relating to the main acts living in the spotlight.

They're not bad people. They just really, truly, clearly do not get Jack. It's like they're observing the world on a completely different frequency—they see green, while he sees polka dots. And maybe that's what makes this so hard. There's no real villain or hero. They're sort of annoying, but they're not bad people. Jack isn't being *deliberately* misunderstood. But he is misunderstood.

I wonder if being an observer to this train wreck is what it's like to watch Lucas and me try to communicate. That different frequency applies to us too. In recent weeks, now that I've started seeing Lucas through a new lens, I can't unsee it. It's as though instead of being the desired two peas in a pod, we're one pea and one carrot in a banana peel.

It's sad to watch. In theory, everyone wants to get along. But maybe it's okay to accept that some things don't go together.

And man, Jack does not go with his family.

When the evening ends, I thank everyone, and Jean pushes leftover pie onto me, hugging me with perhaps a bit more force than I would have expected after my probably inappropriate outburst.

When the door closes, I look over at Jack. I worry that I've embarrassed him. That instead of being a buffer, I put a big old target on his back.

But he grabs my hand, kisses me softly on the lips, and says quietly, "Thank you, Beatrice."

Then he walks over to the car and leaves it at that.

CHAPTER THIRTY-SEVEN

It's already dark when we pull away, and we let Jack's music fill the car as we get on the road. After all that noise, it's soothing to get swept up in melody.

It seems like only moments have passed when I'm stirred awake by Jack, but I quickly realize it must be hours later, since we're back in the city. And by some absurd parking magic, he's managed to pull into an open spot just half a block from my apartment.

"You let me sleep the whole way back?" I ask incredulously, while simultaneously wiping my face to ensure I haven't been drooling by accident.

"It's late," he says with a shrug.

"Well . . . thank you."

But he just huffs. "You're thanking me for letting you sleep after subjecting you to hours of droning?"

I nod. "I'm glad I went."

Jack doesn't respond, with so many things about the day not needing to be unearthed again. We don't need to discuss it ever again if he doesn't want to.

He looks tired, and all I want is to run my hands through that perfect hair of his. I always want him; I always feel so physically attracted to him that it's sometimes hard to look at him. It's how I've justified whatever is happening between us, because the physical need to get near him can always override whatever else happens after.

But right now, all I really want is to soothe him. The thought jolts me, even in my just-woken-up haze, but I don't care enough to let it stop me.

"Do you want to sleep over?" I let myself ask.

"I'm exhausted, Beatrice," he says gingerly, affection contained in those extra syllables of my name. But I can see that truth written all over his face.

"I know." And this time I don't stop myself from leaning over and delicately tangling my fingers in his hair, the way he always does with me. He leans into the touch. "I really meant sleep. I thought maybe you'd want to not sleep alone tonight."

He nods and gets out of the car. I open my door and come around onto the sidewalk. We move silently toward my apartment, nothing else needing to be said. He hasn't been back since the night of Halloween, but it's automatic once we're inside. We wordlessly stumble into my room, strip down, and curl up next to each other. I can tell he's asleep almost immediately, and even though I had a few hours in the car, I find that with his arms around me, I drift off almost as quickly as he did.

I wake up the next morning and reach over, but he isn't there. The waft of the scent of coffee indicates where he might be, though.

I throw on a T-shirt and wander into the kitchen. Jack is sitting at the table in his boxers, cup of coffee in hand, while he reads a book he must have pulled off my shelf. I take a moment to watch him, because I never get to see him like this, morning mussed and stubbly. It's delectably cute.

"Good morning," I finally say, and he looks up.

"I made coffee—I hope that's okay."

I roll my eyes and wander over to the pot to pour myself a cup.

"Never apologize for coffee."

I sit down across from him. He's reading again, and I'm enjoying the vantage point. But I can't get one thing from yesterday out of my mind.

"I hadn't really thought about the fact that I'm going to be your boss."

"I'm glad to see we're fully admitting you're taking the job now, even if Brigid is practically clawing at you to get you to sign the contract."

"I just like driving her nuts," I say with a mischievous grin.

He puts his book down and looks up.

"Do you want to stop?" he asks.

"Driving Brigid nuts? Or are you asking if I want to stop staring at you—am I that obvious?"

That gets a tiny smirk. "Pervert. But no, I meant . . . we won't be going back to Ireland after next week. You're going to be my boss. I'm wondering what you want to happen now."

I'm frozen to my seat because, while he's always direct, other than Clem mentioning it a few weeks ago, no one else in my life has ever asked me what it is that I *want*.

I know this is probably the moment where I could admit everything that's been churning through me over the last few weeks and months. Everything I've been scared to say; everything I find myself wanting; everything he makes me feel.

But sitting in this apartment, where my marriage fell apart and where every day I'm struggling to keep it all together, it feels heavy. In Ireland, it's a different world, untethered from reality. But here, in this home, I've already been broken down and had to rebuild myself. The idea of handing over the sledgehammer to someone else and trusting them not to use it is terrifying.

"I don't really know," I say honestly.

"Okay." He has no expression, and I hate that I can't read him.

"I only mean . . . I'm scared, Jack," I admit.

"Do you want to talk about it?"

"I do. But I don't know how."

That gets a small laugh. "I wish I could pretend like I know how to, but I think I'm just as inept at this as you."

"In a perfect world—" I begin, but he puts his hand on mine.

"You don't ever have to explain anything to me. Last night you got a front-row seat to why I've been happy as a clam on my own. I understand wanting that."

My heart sinks at the resignation in his voice. I hate that that's what he thinks. That I'm hesitating because of what I want and not out of sheer terror and fear of wrecking everything. He's always clocked me for walking so fast, but I don't think he realizes that it's probably been so I don't have to actually consider what might be in front of me if I slow down.

And, all stunted emotions aside, I really *do* worry about whether it's appropriate to even consider dating someone I know I'm about to manage at work. I know this didn't start out that way, and I could probably explain it or disclose it or whatever, but is that really how I want to present myself right at the start as a leader of this company?

And I don't know if that fear is a real fear or a justification to ignore everything else.

I allow myself to wonder the one thing I haven't really let myself consider: I wonder if maybe what *he* wants has changed as much as it has for me.

We've miscommunicated before; we spent twenty years assuming the other felt a certain way about how events had unfolded and how we'd felt about each other. Is it possible, even with every bad example we've both had, that maybe now we both just want each other?

But maybe I should also take him at his word and recognize that he is happier on his own. Yesterday I saw why he's doggedly chased his own quiet and independence. So it's clear that that's what he needs.

But maybe not.

Maybe . . .

I can get the courage to ask him.

But he starts talking again, and I see that whatever window was open, my silence and uncertainty have forced him to close it. "It's been a long weekend. And besides, you haven't even signed your contract yet." He's smiling, but once again it's not reaching his eyes. He grabs a box from the seat next to him. "Luckily, I found where you keep your Scrabble, so even if you're going to be my boss, I can still kick your ass at this."

I know we're going to have to face whatever is coming next. I'm probably going to have to end this whole thing in order to start this new job fresh.

But for today, I can play a game of Scrabble.

CHAPTER THIRTY-EIGHT
CHRISTMAS EVE EVE

Luckily or unluckily, the next few weeks leading up to Christmas don't leave me a lot of time to consider my personal life. With Mona and the board finally reaching an agreement on my contract, I have to actually prepare to shift my role. I hand over most of what I've been doing to a few of my direct reports; I have one more trip to Ireland; Bash insists I chaperone a field trip to the American Museum of Natural History, which honestly takes more mental energy than any of the other stuff combined. (Have *you* ever had to watch twenty-five seven-year-olds in a public place? Sheesh.)

Brigid has been in New York all week to attend Christmas parties, because "It's an opportunity to wear my favorite dresses and watch drunk imbeciles reminisce."

I'm the opposite—all I want is to rot on the couch with a good book. But since I signed my contract today and Brigid is leaving tomorrow on Christmas Eve, she's *insisting* on taking me out to dinner tonight. So instead of heading home, I'm meeting her at some overpriced Midtown steak house for whatever Brigid's version of a celebration is.

She's already there when I walk in, her royal purple tailored jacket upgraded with a broach since the afternoon. A bottle of red wine is already open, and glasses have been poured. She beckons the waiter over the minute I sit down.

"What would you like, Bea?"

"Uh . . ." I quickly scan the menu, trying to move at the speed Brigid clearly wants me to. "I'll have the rib eye, rare, and the creamed spinach, please."

The waiter jots it down and turns to Brigid.

"I'll have one of each of the sides, please," she says before closing her menu with a flourish and handing it back to him.

"Why are we at a steak house if you don't want a steak? We can go somewhere else," I point out.

"Oh god, no. I love all the sides at a steak house. That's the best part."

I stifle a laugh. Only Brigid could have that kind of logic.

"Well, I appreciate you taking me out tonight," I say, shifting gears. "I'm excited to get started in January. Thank you for your faith in me."

Brigid looks a little uncomfortable at all that sincerity, but even she must recognize she can't brush it aside. She pats my hand awkwardly.

"Well, you've earned it. Congratulations, Bea. You're going to do a wonderful job."

I don't stop myself from beaming. For all her idiosyncrasies, I admire Brigid. And I'm really grateful that she didn't give me any choice in grabbing this opportunity for myself.

But apparently, the goodwill is going to be short lived, because then she asks, "So what's going to happen with you and Jack?"

I almost spit out my drink. That was *not* what I was expecting. I'm so caught off guard that defensiveness is really my only option. "What do you mean?"

She levels me with a stare that could probably murder kittens. "We're not really going to play coy, are we?"

"I—"

"Especially not when you've used my house as a glorified sex den for the better part of a year."

"Brigid!"

"What? That's not an insult."

"'Glorified sex den' isn't an insult?" I say, unable to hide the touch of amusement even in this deeply embarrassing conversation.

"Well, I hoped the house would help me in my next chapter, and to find my next great love. But I'm happy it was doing that for somebody. Why shouldn't people get frisky in a beautiful castle?"

I put my head in my hands. "This conversation is mortifying."

But Brigid just tsks. "Stop being such a prude."

"I'm not being a prude," I say, feeling like a sulky teenager being forced to talk about the birds and the bees with her mother. "But besides, I can't date Jack. I'm about to be his boss. And he doesn't want that anyway."

She snorts, and I'm guessing I should feel insulted by whatever is coming next. "Okay, first of all, men have been doing that forever. This isn't a public company, and it's not like you're exploiting him for something. Please get off your damn high horse. You tell the board (a.k.a. now me), you move on, big deal." She takes another sip of wine and stares at me for a moment before continuing. "But as to the second part of your ridiculous statement. That man is crazy about you. Are you kidding?"

"No?" I say, not really sure how to answer that.

"I don't know who you two morons think you're fooling. But please don't blame *my* company on your pathetic inability to handle your own love life."

Well, *that* gives me a little courage (or maybe it's the wine). "Excuse me, but I think after what we signed today, it's my company too."

That gets the biggest grin of all. "Damn straight, Bea. And don't you forget it."

Our meals come, and Brigid and I eventually get back to our comfort zone of work chat, thank goodness. It's invigorating to bounce ideas off each other like this. The next six months of working side by side are going to be fun. I sort of can't wait for a period where I get to learn again, and with someone I admire so much. It makes every other difficult part of my life seem more doable.

After Brigid pays the check, she hands over an envelope. "I have a little something for you," she says.

I open it up and see a printout of two business class plane tickets to Ireland next week, on December 30. I give her a quizzical look, unsure of what the game is here.

"I want you to bring your son for New Year's. Not for work, just as my guest. I think he'd really enjoy the castle. And Des has already planned a bunch of kid-friendly things for him, since obviously that's not something I'm capable of. And anyway, I thought it would be nice for us to ring in this new year together, since it's a new chapter for us both."

I stare back at her. I can feel tears forming, and I try to wipe them away before Brigid notices, but she's already stood up.

"I'm going to leave before you start snotting all over yourself, Bea. I'm going to take this hideous display of emotions as a yes. See you next week."

And with that she walks out of the restaurant.

I head across town to meet Rika for a drink. I slip in next to her at the bar at one of our favorite restaurants, Shukette. She already has glasses of wine for both of us and an array of their signature dips with steaming pitas. She slides my favorite, their creamy labneh, over to me. I thought I was too full after dinner, but clearly not.

"Nice celebration?" she says, and all I can do is huff out a breath.

"Well, considering Brigid decided to drop one bombshell after another, I'd say I'm a little shell shocked by my celebration more than anything."

Rika smiles and pats me on the back. Nothing surprises her anymore about my dynamic with Brigid. "What happened?"

"Well, it ended with me crying because she invited me to bring Bash to Ireland for New Year's, which obviously was very touching, and then, of course, once I even hinted at crying, she left."

Rika laughs so hard she has to put down her drink. "That's the most adorable and disturbingly Brigid story ever."

"Oh, it gets better," I reply, taking a long swig of my wine. "Apparently, she's quite aware about me and Jack and not only has no problem with it but was mortifyingly encouraging. Can you imagine?"

I'm trying to keep my tone light, but the look Rika gives me makes it clear that nothing's getting past her.

"Well, good," she finally says.

"Good?"

"Yeah. *Good.*" She's watching me now like she's trying to smoke me out. And I'm a little surprised that maybe this time, I want her to.

"Tell me why it's good," I ask quietly.

"Remember when I was being dense about Randall years ago, and you told me to stop being so scared and take a chance?"

"I think if anyone said you were dense, it was probably Mona—"

"Save it," she says, cutting me off. "I'm the pot, you're the kettle. Or maybe the other way around. Whatever. Either way, it's my turn to save you from yourself."

"Oh, from myself, huh?"

"Yes!" she says emphatically. "I know you're scared. But this year you've gotten stronger and stronger. You've *let* yourself get stronger for the first time in a long time. And maybe some of that was Jack, but mostly it's *you.* You're an amazing mother to Bash, and you've figured out how to coparent. The way you handled Thanksgiving was a complete turnaround from what would've happened a year ago. You've gained control of your career and dragged yourself kicking and screaming into feeling worthy, and now you've said yes to an opportunity that you're going to do an incredible job with."

"Thank you," I mumble.

"But I think the hardest thing of all for you has been that you've let someone new in. You let him in, even though you've been drop-kicked and let down by love, and you're allowing yourself to love and be loved. That's incredibly brave."

My stomach churns a bit, but before I can even react, Rika's back in my face. "And don't even give me whatever crap you're about to say about it not being love. I know you. You like to help people, but you would *never* spend an entire day in a car to suffer through someone's horrible family dinner if you didn't love them."

I can't tell whether I'm laughing or crying at this point. Maybe Brigid cracked me open, and Rika's simply coming in for the kill. But either way, I'm finally open to hearing what I've known for a while now.

"Okay, but what do I do with that?" My voice cracks, and the one thought that terrifies me more than any other comes to the forefront. "What if he doesn't want me the way I want him?"

"I highly doubt that."

I let out a long breath. "You're morally obligated to say that as my best friend."

"What did Brigid say?"

I smile as I think about it. "Oh, she said I was ridiculous."

"There ya go."

"Oh yeah, because Brigid is really the person whose judgment I trust most on relationships."

Rika swipes a giant piece of pita through some hummus and shoves it into her mouth. "Yeah, but that's not what this is," she says. "First of all, Brigid is the sharpest tack around, and she's apparently been watching you two be dum-dums for the better part of a year. But I think even if that weren't the case, you'd owe it to yourself to find out. He's found his own ways of being there for you. And you for him. People don't just do that. You can't hide behind the label of 'friends'—"

"Sex friends," I mumble with a smirk, and Rika rolls her eyes at my attempts to make light of what she's saying.

"You need to tell him how you feel. The worst outcome is still one where you've grown enough to be honest about your feelings and face them head on. And that's pretty great in and of itself."

"You're pretty great," I say honestly, leaning over to kiss her head.

"Well, that we already knew," she jokes, but she gives me a kiss right back. "Now come on—I'm out without my kids. Let's get drunk and strategize your love life."

CHAPTER THIRTY-NINE
NEW YEAR'S EVE

It's a little surreal to be pulling up to Callaghan Castle with Bash, especially when I'm so tired. He's been talking nonstop ever since we landed, a little fountain of knowledge about Irish history after he inhaled the Irish edition of his favorite history book series, Horrible Histories, once he found out we were going to Ireland.

"Did you know Celtic warriors fought with no clothes on? And the Romans were so jealous of them that a lot of the barbaric things we know about them are actually just Roman rumors? Did you know Irish people tell jokes at funerals because the Druids used to think of it as happy occasions since your soul was reborn?"

But Des is ready for him the minute we pull up, and they're quickly attached at the hip. Somehow we get from Irish history to botany to falconry within ten minutes of our arrival, and Bash has already scarfed down the sandwiches that were waiting for us in the drawing room.

"We can put on a glove, and then they fly right to your arm," Des is saying to a wide-eyed Bash. "Falcons've got incredible eyesight, so their accuracy is pinpoint. We have two that live here—Samhradh and Saoirse."

"Ask them how they spell those names," I butt in, knowing that Bash will love the linguistic specificity of Irish names.

Des writes them down, and I grin at Bash's delight when Des makes him repeat the names about fifteen times. Bash is joyously shocked that they aren't spelled *Sow-ruh* or *Ser-sha*.

"Well, now that you know how to properly pronounce some Gaelic, I think yer definitely ready to meet the falcons."

"Can I go see, Mommy?" Bash asks, whipping his face toward mine with his most pleading expression.

"Well, I'm sure Des has other stuff to do—"

"Oh no, not at all, Bea. It would be my absolute pleasure to escort Mr. Richardson here down to the falcons."

"I don't want to put you out."

"Not in the slightest! It's New Year's Eve, after all, and you should rest up before the festivities later."

"Well . . . but it's a holiday for you too!" I say, incredulously. "Shouldn't you be off with your family or doing something relaxing?"

"Nah, my only necessity is drinkin' a tipple at midnight. And Brigid's out for the day, so you go lie down for a few hours, and I'll take him all around."

"You sure?" I ask, not really able to keep pretending like having a few hours to rest after a long flight, while Bash gets to have fun, isn't the best-possible scenario for me.

"Sure as anyting," he says, grabbing Bash by the hand.

I watch Bash bounce off happily with Des, and when it's clear neither of them is spending even one second thinking about me anymore, I grab our bags and head up to my room.

But being alone as I walk down this hallway, the wood flooring squeaking underneath the ancient carpets, inevitably makes me think of Jack.

After Rika and I had our drinks, she primed me like a windup toy, and I was bursting to talk to Jack. But when I didn't see him in the office after Christmas, I let my apprehension give me all the excuses to wait. (Of course I was the only fool who came to work between Christmas and New Year's.)

I'm great at delaying difficult conversations. Maybe Rika's right and I've grown, but come on, no one expects a miracle, right? I texted him Merry Christmas a few days ago; isn't that something? He didn't exactly reply with an indication that he wanted to see me, so it's not like I'm avoiding him.

I'll deal with it when I get home. I know I have to talk to him. I know I do. But my inevitable rejection can come later. For now, I want to enjoy this time with my son.

Yet walking these halls in Ireland is apparently motivation of a different kind too. I miss him here. I want to be able to open my door, find him inside, and exist in that little bubble of honesty and understanding that somehow seems to happen every time we're alone together.

Which is why, when I open my door and see Jack sitting on my bed reading a book, I do a double take. I know I'm pining a little, but jeez, I wouldn't have chalked myself up to being delusional.

Only . . . I'm not delusional, because he's really sitting in front of me.

"What are you doing here?" I ask, dumbfounded.

"Well, you know I always take that earlier flight," he says with that small grin of his that I find so goddamn adorable.

I want to laugh, but I'm still completely shocked by his presence. I drop my bag and stare at him. "You know what I mean."

"I do," he says, nodding.

He's quiet, now looking so uncomfortable I'm almost wondering if I've walked into the wrong room. But then he seems to shake it off and instead stands up in front of me.

"Okay, you know how you were telling me about the way caterpillars liquefy first before turning into butterflies?" he says, in what is the most surprisingly random thing that could possibly come out of his mouth.

"Uh . . . yeah? . . . Bash has been obsessed with it," I reply, and he nods.

"Right. Exactly. Okay. Well. I think I'm like . . . I think you and I, we're both just sort of . . . well, we're the caterpillars. Or we were. And I'm wondering if maybe together we could be like . . ."

"Jack . . . ," I say, stepping toward him while starting to wonder (or hope) that he's trying to say the kind of thing I've been wanting to say to him, but it's coming out in the exact kind of verbal blackout I would have expected from myself. "Are we butterflies in this metaphor?"

"It's not . . ." He pauses and takes a deep breath. And I wait him out while he gathers whatever he needs in order to get his words together. "Okay, now that you say that out loud, I'm realizing that the 'butterfly' part is extremely cringey and cheesy, and also it's terrible to compare a person to a liquefied caterpillar."

At that I can't stop myself from laughing. I'm laughing so hard that I lean forward, and when I do, he wraps me up in his arms like I'm a small child having a fit. His familiar scent fills me, and my entire body edges into him, like all my subconscious wants is to get closer. But after a minute, he pushes me back by my shoulders so he can look me in the eye.

"I need to start over with something different."

"No, I really want to hear where you're going with that one," I say honestly.

"But I'm incredibly embarrassed at this point."

"Jack, no matter what you're going to say . . ." I'm realizing, standing here, that whatever it is, I'm in. Whatever he wants from me, whatever version of us this is going to be, I'll take it. Maybe someone else would look at us—bumbling around, two people too messed up to actually be able to speak honestly—and say we're hopeless. But I know how hard this is for him, showing up here, because I've been fearfully avoiding this exact thing. And I need him to know how grateful I am that he's wriggled his way inside me, so much that I'm willing to face the scariest possibilities in order to simply stand here with him.

"I think I love you, Jack, okay?" I finally blurt out, apparently as inarticulate as he is right now. "Or rather . . . I know I love you. So, that's all my cards on the table, and now, whatever else is embarrassing about the butterflies, you can just say it, because I've said the more embarrassing thing."

He's looking at me in a way that doesn't look quite as pleased as I would have hoped. And—shit—maybe I've *completely* misread this entire situation. Maybe Brigid simply invited him here, too, and he wanted to say hi. Or be sex friends. Or anything other than a woman professing her love to him before they've even actually decided to date.

"You kind of just stole my thunder, you know that?" he asks with that perfect single eyebrow arch.

"'Stole your thunder'?"

"Yes, I flew all the way here and had a whole plan, and . . . you know, the caterpillar thing was stupid. It made sense in my head, because I think I, sort of, self-preservation-cocooned myself off from everyone for a long time. But you make me want more than that. I was lonely, and I didn't even *realize* I was lonely because I had no idea what it felt like to not be—to have someone who actually sees you. And that makes me feel like a completely different version of myself. But a better version, and the version I was always supposed to be."

"Okay . . . ," I say, my heart now pounding, still not even over the shock of him being here, let alone hearing everything he's saying. Yet there's one part I still don't get. "But how did I steal your thunder?"

He sighs and brushes his hand so softly across my jaw. "I love you, Beatrice. Of course I love you."

"You do?"

I know I just said the same thing to him, but it's still a shock to hear it. My breath catches, and I can feel my eyes start to water.

"Yes, but it took a lot for me to admit that to myself, and by the time I did, I wanted to tell you, and now you're going to think I said it to you because you said it to me, and I—"

But I don't hear whatever he's about to say because I'm already on him, kissing him, needy and filled so far to the brim with joy that I'm genuinely afraid I might burst.

I think about that first time we kissed, so many years ago, and realize that we're right back in that moment in so many ways, finally allowing ourselves to have what we've always wanted.

And even with all our jumbled nervous words, I'm certain we'll do better this time.

His hand brushes down my neck, and he pulls back to look at me.

"I brought you something," he says, and when he steps back to grab it, I feel the absence of his touch immediately, like he's sunlight, and I'm cold being even mildly in the shade.

I look at what's in his hands and smile. It's a small painting, a simple piece of paper that I've seen before, but now it has a small modern black frame around it. It's his artwork from that day at the Whitney, with the central blue triangles. But he's added to it. He's intertwined the triangles with marigold circles.

I guess to him I'm a little bit like sunlight too.

He comes to stand behind me, and we both look down at the painting. "I have to admit, I'm still probably on an island. I don't think I'm capable of not being that way. But I'd like it if I could be on that island with you. And Bash. I mean, Bash needs to be on the island, too, if you're there. I know that."

I turn around and loop my arms around his neck, stretching onto my toes to reach. He picks me up, and I squeal with delight as he moves us toward the bed so he can place me down and I can keep holding on to him while he towers over me.

"So what does this mean for now?" I ask.

"I don't know—I was hoping I could take you on a date that isn't hot dogs on Coney Island or somewhere inside these four walls."

"I'm pretty fond of being with you in these four walls," I say. I lightly kiss him on the mouth because I can't stop myself.

"Yeah, but I'm ready to take you outside, okay?"

"Okay, Jack," I say, grinning, enjoying how much my sixteen-year-old self would've *loved* those words. "I think I'd like that."

"Good."

His fingertips graze my ear and then go back down to my jaw. Mine are tracing along his chest, a physical exploration that's leading to nowhere and everywhere. We're watching each other, both stunned into fizzy happiness that we can be together in this quiet again, but without any secrets or unsaid words between us.

"I do have one really important question," I finally say.

"You? Only one question?" He grins, and I lightly tap him on the shoulder.

"Well, for now anyway. But seriously—how are you here? What did you say to Brigid?"

He laughs, and I know instantly that it must have been the other way around. "Yeah, Brigid told me, and I quote, 'If I have to drag you back to Ireland and lock the two of you in a room until you actually tell each other how you feel, I'm firing you both.' I tried to point out that you probably can't get away with firing someone over emotional blackmail, but she didn't agree with me."

"But then, why here? And now?"

"Oh, come on. You know Brigid's actually a softy. She told me you and Bash were coming for New Year's and then stared at me until I cracked and asked if I could join."

I chuckle. "That sounds right."

"I didn't want to crash your weekend with Bash. But I just thought . . . it's going to be a new year. And I'd like to start it differently this time."

"And here I was thinking you wanted to kiss me at midnight."

He presses me down onto the bed and kisses me so hard it takes my breath away. "Maybe that too."

"But wait—" I sit up, realizing something else. "What if I'd walked in here with Bash?" He smiles sheepishly, and it hits me. "You told Des too? You got Des to play wingman with my son?"

He's kissing my neck and trying to distract me, but I'm not budging. "Listen," he finally says. "I don't think we were exactly keeping a grand secret from anyone." I think back to Des's commentary after our day by the lake and have to acknowledge that he's right. "By the time I arrived, Des was practically jumping up and down trying to find some way to be useful to my grand gesture. So since I figured you wouldn't want to have this conversation in front of your son, I took him up on the offer."

As his hand drifts down my side, I have one last question for him. "So does that mean he plans to take Bash for a few hours?"

And without any more words, I get my answer to that.

CHAPTER FORTY

This might be the most wholesome New Year's party I've ever attended. Des and his wife are dancing in a corner like they're in their own little world. Brigid has a gaggle of friends gathered together (apparently this answers the question of whether she has friends, and frankly, they all seem just as badass as she is), but they've all kicked off their shoes and are pouring their red wine a little too liberally into glasses held right over the velvety upholstered couches and antique rugs. A group that I was introduced to as Brigid's cousins are crowded around the makeshift bar, trying to one-up each other into laughing more uproariously.

And at a coffee table, Jack and Bash have been playing Scrabble for over an hour. Jack is clearly assisting Bash and making purposeful errors (something he'd *never* do with me, although I'm trying to not be envious of a seven-year-old's advantage).

I've been watching the whole scene, content to soak it all in, relishing how full I feel, as though I'm competing with Brigid's friends' wineglasses for practically sloshing over the brim. I want to squeeze myself in between Jack and Bash and get high on the anticipation of a new year bursting with both possibility and serenity.

When Bash jumps up to get some snacks, Jack turns and looks at me like he wants to devour me but is stopping short.

"What's going on?" I ask, still a bit giddy from our afternoon alone.

"I just . . ." He glances over at Bash. "I don't know what you want here."

I narrow my eyes at him. "Was the 'I love you' speech not enough to convince you, or do we need to go back upstairs and talk about butterflies some more?"

He snorts, and I beam at my ability to see through him so easily.

"No, I got that, thank you." He takes my hand under the table. "I meant I want to be respectful of whatever you want to say or not say to Bash, but I'd also really like to hold your hand. And, as you said, preferably kiss you at midnight."

"Like an after-school special?" I smirk.

"You're a pretty bad influence for being a mom," he teases.

"All moms are bad influences in their own ways."

"Be-a-trice . . ." He stretches the syllables, coaxing me into being serious. I love that he's the only one who uses my full name, as though to him I'm worth the extra effort.

"I want to tell Bash," I say sincerely. "I want to hold your hand. And kiss you at midnight. And be able to kiss you an apology when I kick your ass in Scrabble."

"I'm totally on board with everything, except I'm not going to acknowledge that last one."

I'm grinning when Bash comes back to the table with a plate piled high with snacks and a glass of sparkling apple cider that Brigid insisted on him drinking out of a champagne flute.

He sits down and looks at both of us expectantly. I guess this is now or never.

"Hey, Bash," I say slowly. "How would you feel about me going out with Jack?" I'm holding my breath, nervous for the blessing of a small child, apparently.

"Like he's your boyfriend?" he asks guilelessly, and I hate how quickly I look over at Jack to see what he thinks of this label.

But he's already a step ahead of me. "I'd like to be your mom's boyfriend," he says. "But I want to make sure it's okay with you first. You're the main man in her life, so it's really up to you if there's another one."

Okay, for a guy who pretends to be indifferent to children, that was all kinds of swoon.

But Bash doesn't even hesitate. "Sure. As long as you guys don't have any other kids. I don't think I'd like that."

I gracefully have some combination of both choking on my drink and spitting it out at the same time. Jack hits me on the back while trying to hold in the chuckle he clearly wants to let out.

"Why is *that* your main response to that?" I ask.

"Well, I was reading in *The Guinness Book of World Records* that this one woman had sixty-nine children. So I really don't want that many siblings."

"Bash . . . ," I say, bewildered about how to possibly respond to that.

"Really? How would that even be physically possible?" Jack says, now clearly interested in this little nugget of a fact and not at all fazed by his new girlfriend's (!) kid (!) asking about babies (!) on their first night of agreeing to date. "I mean, she'd have to have had a lot of twins or triplets."

"That was actually my thought too!" Bash says, now completely ignoring me and clearly blowing past whatever thoughts he's had about Jack and me dating. "So I looked it up, and it turns out she had sixteen pairs of twins, seven sets of triplets, and four sets of quadruplets."

"That's nuts," Jack responds, fully engrossed. "But yeah, that's sort of the only way it would have made sense, especially since women only have so long a window anyway."

"What do you mean?" Bash asks. I shoot him a look that says *ABORT*, because you do not want to go down any road with Bash where he can keep asking more and more awkward questions, but apparently Jack is unaware of what he's stepped into.

"Well, sixty-nine kids in like a thirty- to forty-year span seemed impossible. If you were optimizing for time, you couldn't start until you got your period at like, twelve? Thirteen? And then they can't anymore with menopause at like . . . fifty?" He looks over at me, and I shake my head.

"Oh no, I think you get to finish this one," I say, taking a large swig of my drink and smugly waiting to see at what point he's going to realize the error of his honesty.

"Oh my *god*, so that means when I'm in middle school, kids could start having *babies*?" Bash asks, wide eyed, and now I'm starting to see it click for Jack.

"Well, no, I mean, just because biologically you could, doesn't mean people are . . . you know . . . doing anything that could . . ."

He's trapped, and now I'm leaning on my elbows to get the closest look at this shit show in the making.

"How do babies get made, anyway?" Bash asks, completely sincere and totally unaware of the bomb he's now dropped.

"Kind of like . . . ," Jack starts, looking at me but clearly not getting whatever he's hoping for. "Well, a man and a woman make them together. Or, I mean, some people make them with science. You know, like if two women or two men . . ." Oh boy, he's drowning now.

"Yeah, I know you need an egg and a sperm, Jack," Bash says matter-of-factly, scrunching his nose, and now Jack is the wide-eyed one.

"Oh. Okay then," he says, mistakenly thinking he's in the clear and not yet knowing Bash well enough to realize this is only the start.

"But like . . . can you accidentally make a baby? Like if I bump into one of the girls in my school, could we have a baby?"

Jack looks over at me, and I wave him on. There's no chance I'm saving him because this is the best entertainment I'll be getting all night. "Uh, no, that's not . . . well, to start, you'd have to be naked, and you wouldn't be naked in school . . ."

I burst out laughing, and he shoots me daggers from his eyes. "Anytime you want to take over, Beatrice—"

"Oh no, you're doing *great*, Jack," I say, grabbing some popcorn out of a bowl and settling in.

"Could we bump butts? Do the sperm and egg just fall out? Why don't men have periods? Do people *plan* to have quadruplets and triplets, or do you think it just happens?"

"Ya know, Bash, I think on second thought, your mom really is the person who has these kinds of answers for you, and I'm just going to go get a drink for a minute . . ."

He stands up, and I can't stop myself from staring up at him and beaming.

"Coward," I whisper quietly with a grin.

"Totally true. But you love me anyway," he says in my ear.

He gives me a peck on the cheek, and as he walks away, I mumble, "Yeah, I really do."

The night continues on a sea of bubbles, apple cider, Scrabble, and increasingly loud Irish folk music. Both Brigid and Des take their turns coming over and saying "Told you so" (her) and pinching our cheeks (him).

The jet lag goes in the right direction for us, so when it's almost midnight, Bash is still wide awake and enjoying himself. He and Jack are now playing gin rummy. I've bowed out, since I have no desire to learn a new card game, and instead have been learning all about Brigid's cousins' murder mystery book club, where the only rule is that the person murdered has to be "a shitty man we don't feel bad about getting knocked off anyway."

But I'm distracted by seeing Jack whisper something into Bash's ear. I then watch as they shake hands. Des pulls Bash away to dance, and I saunter back over to Jack.

"What was that about?" I ask, and Jack turns, looking a little startled to see me.

"Oh, nothing," he says, pushing his hair back in a way that makes it clear he's avoiding. I fix him with another stare, and I know he's going to cave instantly. "I wanted to ask Bash a few things."

"What kind of things?"

He's looking at the ground, but I can still hear him. "Well, I wanted to let him know I wasn't trying to take any of your time away from him and that if he ever feels like I am, he should tell me immediately."

My breath catches. It shouldn't be such a large thing, that open-ness, but it feels so hard won for both of us. Allowing another person the space to begrudge you, but letting them know you want to hear it anyway, isn't something I think either of us could've imagined. It's the opposite of lonely. It's expansive in its permission; it's trust and will-ingness to listen.

"That's not the only thing, though," he says, looking up with a teasing grin waiting beneath the surface.

"Oh no?" I say, and he stands up and pulls me into his arms. I start to hear the countdown to midnight behind us, but all I can see is him.

"I asked him if he would be okay if I kissed you at midnight. I told him I needed to start the year off right."

"And what did he say?" I ask.

"'Gross! But sure,'" he responds, in a pitch-perfect imitation of Bash's voice. I laugh, but it's caught in the countdown. As everyone else makes it to one, I'm pulled into a kiss that feels like the promise of a new year ahead.

EPILOGUE
A YEAR AND A HALF LATER

"Shit, shit, shit, you cannot give birth on the sidewalk. Your husband is going to *kill us*," Rika shouts.

It's hot, in a way June shouldn't be hot when it's this late at night, mugginess lingering in the air and making me wonder if I'm sweating from the temperature or from the absurdity of the situation. We're pacing outside my house, panicking in a completely unhelpful way.

"I tried to get a cab, but it's Saturday night, and nothing is available!" I shout back.

I turn around when I hear Clem laughing at both of us.

"What's so funny?" I demand.

"Guys, I've done this twice. It's going to be a few hours. Just because I need to get to the hospital doesn't mean I'm giving birth on the sidewalk."

Rika and I both stare at her, struck dumb by her rationality in a moment where we are otherwise chickens without heads.

Thankfully the window above us opens, and Jack peers out. He's shirtless, and I'm not going to complain. "I know I'm not supposed to interrupt girls' night," he calls, and I realize I should probably focus on more than his chest in this moment, "but this seemed like extenuating circumstances. I called an ambulance, and they said it would only be three or four minutes. Oh, and I texted Andrew. He'll meet you at the hospital."

That . . . yeah . . . an ambulance and an update for Clem's husband is probably the better response.

"Thank you!" I call up, letting Jack's grip on the situation calm me down.

Clem tries to sit on my stoop to wait, and Rika and I instantly grab her arms to help her down, as though she's going to keel over any minute.

"I'm not sure either of us are great in a crisis," Rika whispers to me.

"That's usually Clem's job, though," I whisper back.

"Jack's a good backup," Rika says, and a smile blooms out from under all my panic.

"You're both doing great," Clem says as she pats both of us on the hands, a reassuring gesture, even though she's the one having contractions every few minutes.

"Hey, Beatrice," I hear, and I turn back to see Jack again. "Heads up—"

A bag falls out the window, and I move (not particularly gracefully) to catch it.

I quickly untie the unceremonious knot on top to get it open, and when I see what's in it, my insides practically melt. Three burger buns with chocolate bars stuffed in the middle have been lovingly wrapped up, ready to serve as late-night snacks whenever we need them.

I look back up at the window, certain that Jack will still be watching me, waiting to see the effect his simple gesture has had.

"Have I told you lately I love you?" I call out to him.

"Actually yeah," he says with a grin.

It's amazing how easy it is these days to know what I want. I *have* what I want, even if it doesn't look like what everyone else might imagine for themselves, and it certainly isn't perfect. But I have the best kid. I have friends who would literally jump into ambulances for each other. I've got a company with revenue up 22 percent over last year and a board chairwoman who isn't afraid to give me real advice about my personal life (that's really the one I never could have anticipated). And I've got Jack. Jack, who wraps sandwiches up while simultaneously wrapping me up in our own cocoon of a safe space, together.

The ambulance pulls up, and we help Clem stand. They thankfully let Rika and me ride along with Clem, and soon we're on our way east, ready to spring into whatever useless action we definitely won't be needed for.

The evening is a blur of momentum and monotony. We get to the hospital, and they check Clem in. Andrew arrives looking disheveled and thrilled about an hour later, once he's settled their kids with his parents and is able to duck out. We make Clem play cards; we breathe with her through contractions; we distract her as much as we possibly can. And when it's time for us to leave the room in the middle of the night, we collapse and sleep under the harsh fluorescent lighting of the waiting room, leaning against each other to counterbalance the bony plastic chairs.

I'm woken up with a kiss pressed to my forehead. I groggily look up and see Jack.

"Hiii," I say, his figure towering above me like something out of a dream. The way my neck feels after a night leaning against Rika is definitely *not* a dreamy experience. But none of that matters when Jack sits next to me and takes my hand.

"At the bus stop this morning, Bash and Ella made me promise to tell you that they think school buses should have a dual evening use of picking up women in labor. Something about efficiencies and buses not getting enough use or something."

"Did they have a cohesive plan?" I ask, my face cozy with the contented smile of waking up to my favorite view.

He looks good this morning, even in typically unflattering hospital lighting. I'd think it was unfair except I get to be the one who looks at him.

"Nope. It devolved into an argument about whose idea was more workable."

I grin as I think of the two of them arguing all the way to school. The more things change, the more they stay the same.

"Thank you for taking over for me this morning," I say.

"Perk of living together now," Jack replies, absentmindedly brushing back the hair from my eyes with a smile. "He didn't even ask where you were."

I gape. "You shouldn't tell a mother that! I still want to believe he needs me to take him to the bus every morning!"

"You should just be grateful he hasn't decreed that he's walking to the bus alone, making you stay ten feet behind him for fear of embarrassment."

"But embarrassing him now is my favorite thing," I counter, smiling at the memory of last weekend, when we stopped at a band playing in Tompkins Square Park, and as Jack twirled me around, Bash declared it "extremely sus and mortifying."

"Well, tomorrow's another day," Jack says, taking my hand and squeezing it. "How's Clem?"

The question makes my smile grow in tandem with the size of my heart. "She had another girl," I whisper. "Everyone's napping now, but Rika insisted on walking like ten blocks to get decent pastries, and we'll bring them to Clem once she wakes up. Definitely not subjecting her to hospital food, and Andrew already went home early to check in on the kids before they go to school."

"Yeah, he sent me a picture a few hours ago."

He holds up his phone to show me, as though I haven't also been drooling over the pictures of the newborn Clem texted the minute she got her phone back. I love that my little friend family has pulled Jack in and embraced him as another member of our New York tribe. I love how he shows up for me and takes things off my plate, but I've added to his plate and made his world fuller.

My contrarian island keeps getting more and more boats moored onto his dock.

"Do you need to head into the office now?" I ask, leaning my head on him and squeezing his hand. He waits and doesn't immediately answer, knowing that I'm not saying everything. "Okay, let me rephrase that. Do you need to go to the office now, or do you mind staying here with me for a little bit? I'd really like it if you stayed here."

"Aww," he says, in what I can already tell is his most condescending but endearing tone, "you used your words instead of hoping I'd intuit what you were thinking."

I roll my eyes, but he's already pulled me into a kiss, negating any attempts I might've had to regain the upper hand in the conversation.

"I *do* use my words now," I say, trying to be pouty but knowing I'll never succeed when he's staring at me with such unabashed fervor.

"I know. And thank goodness, because I always want to hear everything you have to say."

"Everything?" I tease.

"Yup," he says with a challenge.

"What if I want to spend an hour going over the merits and detriments of a chocolate burger?"

"I could for sure do that."

"What if I insist on showing you all my friends' baby pictures?"

"Sounds delightful."

I lean in and whisper in his ear, playful now and fully awake. "What if what I want is to play hooky from work after being up all night, and I'm planning to drag you down with me?"

"Whatever you want, Beatrice. We can do whatever we want."

ALTERNATE ENDINGS–
INSPIRED RECIPES

Sometimes I visit a place that makes me fall in love so hard that I can't stop from letting it take over a little piece of my heart. Ireland immediately did that for me—its Technicolor greens, its kind people, its commitment to humor everywhere. But I was also surprised at how much I loved the food. From dairy to baked goods, I fell in love with Irish cuisine as much as I did the people and the place.

I wanted to include recipes, because recipes can connect you to a place even when you aren't there, and these are based on some of the foods in the book.

If you want to not just cook at home but actually go to Ireland and be in a place like Callaghan Castle—there *are* as many castles as Des mentions, but I need to point out that Brigid's is really based on one that you can actually visit—Ashford Castle is a hotel that blew my socks off (and really does have falcons! And all the amazing food!), so the spirit of Callaghan Castle is based on that. If you want your own Irish adventure, I couldn't recommend a place more.

But in the meantime, I'm assuming recipes will suffice for most people to get our Ireland kicks! Hope you enjoy them!

Irish Cheddar GOUGÈRES

This is an appetizer that no one can argue with: it's cheese and bread—
come on! Gougères are technically French, but we're making them Irish
here with one of the best exports you can get from the Emerald Isle—
assuming you can get Irish cheddar, of course.

Makes 30–35 small gougères.

Ingredients

1 cup water
8 tablespoons (1 stick) unsalted butter
1/2 teaspoon salt
1 cup all-purpose flour
5 large eggs
2 cups grated cheddar cheese (Irish cheddar preferred)

Preheat the oven to 450°F. Line 2 baking sheets with parchment paper.
Combine the water, butter, and salt in a saucepan and bring to a boil
over high heat. Turn the heat to low and immediately add the flour,
whisking it into the liquid. You want to stir quickly and long enough
for the dough to get drier and much smoother—a bit of starch on the

bottom is totally fine. Transfer to the bowl of a mixer and allow to cool for a few minutes. Then add the eggs slowly as the dough mixes (if you don't have a stand mixer, you can use a hand mixer, but put it on a low setting). The eggs should be fully mixed in and incorporated. Then add the cheese and fully incorporate that—the dough should be sticky but manageable.

Scoop out the dough into approximately 1-tablespoon balls and place them on the parchment paper.

Put the gougères in the oven and immediately turn it down to 350°F. Bake for 25 to 30 minutes, rotating the pan once halfway through. They should be golden and puffy when cooked.

Note: you can also freeze the uncooked balls and then cook them for just a few minutes longer, and they should turn out almost completely the same.

Irish-ish Stew

What makes a stew an Irish stew? As with anything related to food culture, there's probably a pub gathering that has debated this topic for hours. But for me it's a hearty stew that uses lamb instead of beef and potentially adds a bit of savory beer like Guinness to the proceedings. Either way, it's perfect for those cold nights when you want something hearty to eat while curled up with a book.

Serves 4 to 6.

Ingredients

Dash of olive oil
2 pounds boneless lamb shoulder, cubed into 1-inch pieces
Dash of salt and pepper
1 large yellow onion, diced
8 garlic cloves, diced
1/2 pound carrots, diced
1 pound small roasting potatoes
6 large radishes, diced
1 cup dark beer (whatever your preference, but Guinness is ideal)
4 cups (1 quart) beef or chicken stock (to your preference)
1/4 cup heavy cream

Chopped parsley and mint to garnish

In a large Dutch oven on medium-high heat, heat up some olive oil and add the lamb, along with the salt and pepper. Cook the lamb until browned, around 8 to 10 minutes, stirring occasionally. Remove the lamb and add the onions, garlic, carrots, potatoes, and radishes, along with more salt. Cook for about 5 minutes, or until the vegetables start to brown a bit. Add the beer and scrape the brown bits off the bottom. Add the lamb back in, along with the stock and heavy cream. Bring everything to a simmer and then cover and lower the heat. Cook for around 1 hour or until the lamb is tender. Add more salt and pepper as needed and top with parsley and mint.

APPLE TURNOVERS

I think almost anything is better with puff pastry. And while I can't guarantee that a search for these will lead to a fantastic night with the future love of your life (sorry), I will at least promise that they'll be an easy, delicious breakfast or dessert whenever you need them.

Makes 8 turnovers.

Ingredients

1 tablespoon unsalted butter
3 medium Granny Smith apples, peeled, cored, and diced
2 tablespoons brown sugar
1 teaspoon cinnamon
1/4 teaspoon salt
1 pound (2 sheets) thawed puff pastry
1 egg, beaten

Preheat the oven to 400°F. In a medium pot, melt the butter on medium-low heat. Add in the apples, brown sugar, cinnamon, and salt. Cook until softened, stirring every few minutes, for about 10 minutes. Remove from the heat to cool.

Cut the puff pastry into 8 equal pieces (4 per sheet). Place the cooled apple mixture on one side of each square, leaving a bit of room at the edges. Brush the edges of the puff pastry with the egg, then bring the edges together and crimp with a fork. If they're too soft to crimp, you can put them in the fridge or freezer for a minute to firm up.

Place the turnovers on a parchment-lined baking sheet, and cut 3 small slits in the top of each turnover. Brush the top with the egg. Place the turnovers in the freezer (or fridge if you don't have space) for 5 minutes.

Put the turnovers in the oven and bake for 20 to 25 minutes or until they're golden.

CURRANT SCONES

I lived in Scotland for four years, and we had "Scone Time" every after-noon. So when I was imagining what Des would make to ply everyone with baked goods, I couldn't imagine anything better than scones. These are made with currants, but you can substitute whatever speaks to you!

Makes 16 mini scones.

Ingredients

1 1/2 cups all-purpose flour, plus additional
1 cup oats
1 tablespoon baking powder
1/2 teaspoon salt
1/2 cup sugar
1 cup heavy cream
1 egg
1 teaspoon vanilla
6 tablespoons unsalted cold butter
1 cup currants

Preheat the oven to 400°F. Combine the flour, oats, baking powder, salt, and sugar in a bowl. In another bowl combine the cream, egg, and vanilla. Grate the butter into the flour mixture and combine—you can use your hands to really get in there, but try to be light so the butter doesn't all melt. Carefully toss the currants into the flour mixture and then gently add the liquid. Mix until the dough just comes together.

Sprinkle flour on a surface. Take half the dough and form it into a ball, then flatten it out. Cut the circle in half, then quarters, then eighths. You should have 8 small scones. Repeat with the remaining dough.

Line a baking sheet with parchment and cook for 15 minutes.

Note: you can freeze the unbaked scones and then cook from frozen at 400°F for 16–18 minutes when you want to have them.

CHOCOLATE SANDWICH

Come on, you knew I'd have to include this one, right? While I think Jack had the best of intentions, I want to believe there's an even better version of a chocolate sandwich to be had. And it barely takes much more work than shoving two bars between hamburger buns! I like to think of this as the sweet version of a grilled cheese.

Makes 1 sandwich (but can be doubled, tripled, etc.).

Ingredients

1 teaspoon unsalted butter
2 slices bread (the better the bread, the better the sandwich)
1–2 ounces dark chocolate, broken into small pieces
Sea salt

In a frying pan on medium heat, melt the butter. Add one slice of bread to the pan and top it with the chocolate. Sprinkle the sea salt on top. Add the remaining slice on top and flip the bread. Make sure the chocolate has softened and both sides of bread are golden brown. Serve hot.

ACKNOWLEDGMENTS

Thank you mostly to my mom.

I'm starting with my mom because in my last book, she didn't find herself fast enough in the acknowledgments, and I wanted to rectify that here, even if I laughed all the way through her and my brother's ridiculous search for themselves. Mom: you deserve to always see yourself first because you put us first, and I'm ever so grateful.

Thank you to Wendy Sherman, the best agent a person could dream of, but more importantly one of the best people to go to for any and all advice. I'm so damn lucky to be guided and believed in by you. Lauren Plude: I know I don't even have to say it because our mind meld is that strong, but thank you for being my champion, my mercenary plotter, and my friend. Lindsey Faber: you promised me that a second book with less time to gestate wouldn't need eight hundred rounds of revision, and that was *only* true because your insights are so perfect. Thank you. Bill Siever, I'm sorry to tell you this, but after your masterful work on two books, you're on the hook to copyedit every book I ever write— you save me from every nonsensical, grammatical, tensetastic mistake (and yes, I know "tensetastic" isn't a word). Anna Barnes, I so appreciate you getting into the details here and making the book that much better. Thank you! Kyra Wojdyla, thank you so much for overseeing this book's journey, and Lauren Grange for taking the reins. Thank you to my cold reader, Angela Vimuttinan. Thank you so much, Sarah Horgan, for your gorgeous covers for both of my books. Katrina Escudero, thanks for being such a champion for my stories.

It's strange to write acknowledgments for a book so long before it comes out, because so many people shepherd its release and also deserve thanks. So to the people who supported *Recipe for Second Chances*, this is my belated thank-you. Jessica Brock and Kristin Dwyer: I am shocked I didn't scare you both off, but I'm incredibly grateful to you both for making my debut shine. I could talk about romance books all day with you two. Allyson Cullinan and Courtney Greenhalgh, thank you for taking every loony request and making it reality. And a massive thank-you to all the Bookstagrammers, BookTokkers, and other people in the book community who have posted about my book. It really means the world to authors when you share their stories. Thank you as well to the authors who embraced a newbie and shared words and/or posted about my book for their communities: Abby Jimenez, Adriana Herrera, Alexis Daria, Christina Lauren, Elizabeth Bard, Jen Comfort, Jenny Mollen, Lynn Painter, Maya Rodale, Priscilla Oliveras, Susan Lee, Tarah Dewitt, Tia Williams, and Zibby Owens (and anyone else it seems like I'm forgetting but actually just was supportive after these acknowledgments were due!).

Alana, it's all in the dedication, but extra thanks for supporting this book through reads, rereads, brainstorms, and all Ireland-related perfect discourse. Thank you, Nicole, for reading a very early draft and giving impeccable feedback—you next! Matt, I love your insights and support, but most of all your writing. McKee, forever my Kiki, thank you for reading when I couldn't look at it again and being my one-woman hype machine for over twenty years. Chris Magnani—thank you for allowing me to utilize your bonkers music setup as a character point. And to my Kid Pics and Better Jobs crew, thanks for letting me steal our texting dynamic. I'm very lucky to, as Bea says, "have that kind of chemistry you can only get with people who watched your awkward ascent into adulthood."

While Bea's story isn't mine, one big piece of it was: I dealt with secondary infertility after my son was born. Unlike Bea, I desperately wanted a larger family, so it's really important to me to thank the three people who made that dream a reality: Dr. Jeffrey Braverman (truly missed), Dr. Andrea Vidali, and Stephenie Kammeyer. You gave me my girls, and no amount of words on a page will ever encompass how much that has changed my life. But in sharing some of the emotions of that part of my tale with others, I at least wanted to put that gratitude on the page as well. And I couldn't bring up that time in my life without thanking Alexis Adlouni—you were the friend who stood with me and helped me exist outside of the light. I'm so grateful we both got our happy ending to this particular part of our stories. For anyone dealing with fertility issues, I hope you know there's always a community waiting for you, even if it's not the one you usually rely on.

To my family: Thanks to my dad, not just for being my dad (a role at which he excels), but also for being my divorce-lawyer consultant on this book! Noodling over New York State custody scenarios was as amusing as it was endearing. Thanks for supporting me always. Will (I'll put you first this time, since you always get the shaft) and Annie (seester)—I'm the luckiest to have siblings like you two, and extra lucky that you gifted me Skye and Jon as bonus siblings. Yehuda, Natalie, Aaron (and always missing Rachel)—love you all, my Gourbralters.

I don't ever take for granted the gift of my three kids—Guy, Rae, and Joy, I love you so much. And extra-special thanks in this book to Guy, for letting me recount so many of our conversations practically verbatim. And "Just the Two of Us" still belongs to us, even if I let Bea and Bash borrow it.

And lastly, always, to Daniel. Our love story will forever be my favorite.

About the Author

Photo © 2022 Melanie Dunea

Ali Rosen is the author of *Recipe for Second Chances*, a novel for which *New York Times* bestselling author Fern Michaels said she "couldn't turn the pages fast enough." Her second novel is *Alternate Endings*.

Aside from loving escaping into fictional worlds, Rosen is also the Emmy Award– and James Beard Award–nominated host of *Potluck with Ali Rosen* on NYC Life, as well as the author of cookbooks including the bestselling Amazon Editor's pick *Modern Freezer Meals*, *15 Minute Meals*, and *Bring It*. She has been featured everywhere from the *TODAY* show to the *New York Times* and has written for *Bon Appetit*, the *Washington Post*, and *New York Magazine*.

Rosen is originally from Charleston, South Carolina, but now lives in New York City with her husband and three kids and can usually be found wandering the Union Square Greenmarket or curled up in a chair reading a romance novel.

Connect with her online at www.ali-rosen.com or via Instagram and Twitter @Ali_Rosen.